A man walks into a bar.

Sure, I know, but stay with me now. A man walks into a bar.

In old Chicago you wanted to pay attention to that kind of thing. You didn't want to go wandering through the wrong door. Ourselves were known to take the ears off Poles who came into our pubs, and if a Donegal lad fresh off the boat chanced to stumble into a Polish or, God help him, a German beer hall, well, you could safely say he was after writing his last letter home to mother.

Anyway, this man coming in doesn't look Irish to me. He's duded up like a Yankee in a morning coat and beaver hat, all starched and buttoned in the sweltering heat. But his skin is dark as an Injun's, and the brim of his hat lies low so I can't get a good look at him. Well, I don't like it and neither does Mike the barkeep nor anyone else. Still, we let him take a corner chair, and out he comes with a watch on a chain and lays it open on the table, like he's expecting company any moment. We like that even less, of course. Old Flaherty, he picks up a jar of pig's feet from the bar and makes as though to throw it, but the stranger doesn't so much as look up. So Flaherty puts it back down again. 'Twas all very queer. There was just something about the hot air and the quiet that sat on the nerves in a funny way, and all the stout in the world couldn't soothe it. Why that evening even Flaherty went home to the missus, sober as a priest at Mass. But I'm racing ahead of myself.

Well now, not a minute later, a second stranger bursts through the doors—a Swede, I think, his nose running blood—and another man chasing after him waving one of those big slaughterhouse pig-stickers. Up I get shouting and so does everyone else, except our Injun. But before we can get between the two of them, the Swede is falling to the floor with an extra hole in his throat. Men die quieter than hogs, I'll say that much for them. A lot of blood hit that floor in the years I had its acquaintance. Still, you must understand, hard as we all were then, it was rare for one man to murder another in broad daylight in such a way. Now, of course, they take these tommy guns and bang-bang—anyway, there we all stand gawping as this poor creature coughs his life out. And what does the Injun in the coat do? Closes up his bastard watch and lays it on the bar, touches his brim to Mike, and strolls out as cool as you please.

An odd tale, wouldn't you say? But I haven't told the oddest part. That was October the 7th of 1871. Sure, it was two firemen who carried the dead man out, having come to raise a brotherly pint to their victory over the big fire the day before. That fire was after burning up four blocks over on Canal, and a long hard fight they had to put it out. So the city gave the lads their pay and told 'em to take a well-earned holiday, and that's exactly what they did: holidayed to the horizontal.

And that very night, a certain cow kicked over a certain lamp....

ISBN 1-58846-870-4

First Edition: March 2006

Printed in Canada

White Wolf Publishing
1554 Litton Drive
Stone Mountain, GA 30083
www.white-wolf.com/fiction

THREE SHADES OF NIGHT

By Janet Trautvetter, Sarah Roark, and Myranda Sarro
Vampire created by Mark Rein•Hagen

The World of Darkness

The Murder of Crows

by Janet Trautvetter

janet trautvetter

Another dead crow.

Loki picked up the black-feathered corpse gingerly by one stiff little leg and dropped it off the edge of the balcony, watched it fall into the darkness of the alley three floors below. Let the city clean that shit up. He had other things to worry about. He did wish the damned things would pick someone else's balcony to croak on. That was the third one this week. Fucking birds.

He hopped up to the wooden railing and crouched there, balancing on the balls of his feet, one hand lightly curled around the support post for the balcony above. It was a thirty-five-foot drop. Dangerous, had he been mortal—but he was not. Loki was a vampire, an undead predator of the night—and he relished the little thrill of risk he felt up there on his precarious perch. It was almost like being alive again.

Now, the real test. Eyes closed, he reached out with his other senses, hearing, smell, and touch. Those senses were particularly keen, courtesy of his Mekhet clan heritage, and the unlamented bastard who had made Loki what he was. *Practice makes perfect, they always say…*.

It had been a warm day. As he let his awareness drift outward, he could feel the last vestiges of heat radiating up from the bricks and concrete of the street, from the wooden structure of the balcony tier and the building behind him. He could pick out the hum of traffic from Lake Shore Drive, and snatches of conversation from the alley below and from the open windows of the next building over. The breeze from Lake Michigan carried the scent of fresh-cut grass, car exhaust, garbage, and the faint, almost nauseating echoes of cooking odors from a dozen different households, coming from up and down the street. Just another summer night on the North Shore.

Then he smelled the blood.

Immediately, his entire body tensed, every nerve alert, his hand suddenly gripping the support strut to maintain his precarious perch. *Blood.* It had been two nights since he had last fed. Now the hunger was suddenly an aching chasm somewhere deep in his belly, an emptiness that demanded to be filled.

His eyes snapped open, only to wince painfully shut again from the unexpected brilliance of the opposite streetlamp. *Dammit!* Reflexively, he damped his enhanced Mekhet senses until he could bear the light.

Blood—where? Where was it coming from? The alley? One of the adjacent apartments? It was so strong—so fresh, so compelling. *Inviting.* Blinking furiously, wiping blood tears out of his eyes with the heel of his free hand, he took a quick look up and down the street. Nothing. But the blood-scent was still there, tantalizingly near. Just down below.

He judged the distance down to the pavement of the alley with his eyes. Nobody in sight in the alley, no one at a nearby window. No one watching—and no one would see him if he didn't want them to. And the stairs would take too long.

He gathered the darkness around himself, and jumped.

His landing was absolutely silent, but less than graceful; the force of the impact sent shooting pains up both ankles and shins. Loki staggered to his feet, but his first few steps toward the alley were decidedly uneven and wobbly. *Shit. That hurt.*

Somehow, he stumbled into the cover of the alley, and sank down against the brick wall, willing blood to his ankles until the pain began to fade. "Resolution," he muttered under his breath. "Don't expect to sprint away from a three-story drop without a fucking parachute." Then, once again, he inhaled, seeking the blood-scent. Where—

Nothing.

What the hell? Warily, he extended his senses again, carefully shielding his eyes from the streetlights. It had been so strong, just a moment ago. So *fresh*.

But now, nothing. Only the limp, pathetic corpse of the dead crow, sprawled against the gritty pavement. Only the smell of rotting trash and some neighbor's spaghetti sauce. Nothing more.

Nothing.

Now, that was just fucking weird. Loki poked around the alley for a few minutes more, just to make sure, but found no trace of anything even remotely plausible as the source of the blood-smell. Nothing—which made no sense at all.

Then he heard his cell phone ringing upstairs. Of course, by the time he'd run up three flights of stairs to get to it, Norris had hung up, leaving only a terse text message: *10 pm TONIGHT. USUAL PLACE. YOUR PUNCTUALITY IS APPRECIATED.*

So much for his evening of sinful leisure, music and dancing with warm-blooded chicks in black leather corsets and Victorian lace. Why did Norris always call these things on a Friday night?

Loki poked around in the room-sized closet that served both as his wardrobe and sleeping chamber for a clean T-shirt—punctuality wasn't the only detail his boss insisted upon—and a decent pair of black jeans. The long, black leather coat, with its straps and buckles, went on over that.

He ran his fingers through his hair, sending it up in black, spiky tufts—the Prince's spymaster might still favor white shirts and bow ties, but Loki preferred to face the night with a bit more of a contemporary style. And, with any luck, the meeting wouldn't take all night, and he could still make it to the Skullery before the sweetest items on the buffet went home to sleep it off.

He put the mystery of the blood-smell in the alley aside for puzzling over later. Time to go to work.

There was a new scent on the wind tonight. The bear rose up on its hind legs and inhaled, nostrils flaring to catch every nuance. Blood—old blood and new blood. Smoke, the acrid taint of burning wood, tar, and flesh. The scent of fear, of putrid flesh and stinking, decaying offal choking fresh water, of disease, of death, of open latrines, and too many poor people living too close together. The scent was strong, biting, burning—but elusive. When the bear turned its head to better determine the direction from which the scent came, the death-scent dissipated like the very mist, and all that was left was the woods, the freshness of rain-drenched leaves, the crisscrossing trails of foxes, raccoons, rabbits, and deer, the warm decay of fallen leaves and dead wood. No—wait. There. There was a death-smell, though not quite the same. The bear dropped down to all fours and padded in that direction, until its questing nose found a small, black-feathered corpse, sprawled awkwardly against the forest loam.

The bear was hungry, but it did not feed on carrion. It left the crow for the scavengers.

A sound reached the bear's ears—the flapping of many wings, the raucous calls of the dead crow's kin, high overhead. But there was something wrong in what the bear heard.

janet trauvetter

Troubled by the wrongness, but unable to define it, the bear lumbered out into a clear space, a patch of prairie amid the trees, and rose again to its hind legs. Its eyesight, however, was not the equal of its other senses. It emitted a small growl of frustration at that limitation, and then its form rippled and shrunk, fur fading away to denim and leather, a weathered brown face and long black hair, adorned with bone and feathers. Like the bear's, her black eyes glinted with keen intelligence; like the bear, she did not breathe, save when necessary to read the scents on the breeze.

Rowen's keener eyes picked out the last stragglers of the passing flock, black wings blotting out the stars in the indigo canopy overhead. But crows were not usually nocturnal flyers. And so many now were dead, like the one she'd found in the brush. A new sickness had arisen this summer, and the local roosts that had once held thousands were often forsaken by the survivors, as if shunning cursed places.

Rowen stalked silently back under the trees and dropped to her haunches beside the stiff little corpse of the fallen crow. She pricked one finger with a knife, and let a drop of her own dark blood fall on the black beak, murmuring soft words to soothe its spirit. Then she plucked three pinions from the outstretched wings, dropped them into a plastic baggie, and slipped that into a pouch at her hip.

There was only one reason she could think of for crows to fly at night. But Rowen was not inclined to gossip, or to easily panic. She would wait until she was certain—for nothing happened without reason. If the Crow Woman had indeed returned, Rowen would know the truth of it soon enough.

Another midnight shift at the hospital morgue. The rest of the staff avoided working midnights alone, but Gwyn—his hospital employee's ID said *Dr. Jason Hyndes, Resident Intern, Forensic Pathology*—preferred it that way. Truth be told, he found his patients to be better company than some of his fellow interns—and his patients were already dead.

The first new arrival of the night, lying silent and still on the gurney, already awaited him in the morgue receiving area. Might as well get the worst part over with, he reasoned, and laid his hand on the sheet that covered the dead girl's head.

—*Pain like a vise gripping her skull, like needles behind the eyes, stabbing up and down her spine and every limb. Burning burning burning… so sorry Mommy I couldn't hold on, it hurts so much, the darkness feels so good… I want it to stop hurting, please, God, make it stop… I'm so tired, just let me sleep….*

Gwyn blinked several times, forced the vision of the patient's last coherent moments from his mind's eye, and took the file from the front of the gurney. He already knew what it would say: *Cause of death, viral meningoencephalitis.* She was only sixteen.

He pushed the gurney up to the massive refrigerator unit, got a body bag from the shelf, and started to open it up.

"You're not really going to put me in that, are you?" The voice was petulant and thin, coming out of thin air—or a place invisible to Sleeper eyes.

Gwyn touched the necklace of bone charms that hung under his working scrubs with one hand, and traced two quick glyphs on the sheeted corpse before him. That brought her into clear view—not lying on the gurney, but standing on the other side.

But this was not Kimberly McLaren, the girl on the gurney—this ghostly child was ten years younger, and wore a red velvet dress with flounces and lace and a row of bright gold buttons down the front, in a style that had been out of fashion for nearly a century.

What the fuck? He knew the name of every deceased patient currently in storage, and none of them were children. And, judging from her dress, this little girl had died a long, long time ago—but he couldn't see the nature of her death in her face, which for him was odd. "Where the hell did you come from?" he demanded.

"I had to give you a message." The spectral child reached across, and laid something on the sheet: a black crow feather. *"Because you can see."*

There was something subtly different, something wrong about the body on the gurney. He wasn't sure how it had happened, but he knew something had changed. He also knew he had to look.

Warily, Gwyn raised the sheet. There, instead of Kimberly, lay this same little girl—a gruesome, bloody, and blackened figure reeking of smoke and burnt flesh, her limbs reduced to charred stumps, the ashen gray of her skull showing through where skin and hair had burned away down to the bone. He could recognize her only because there were still remnants of the lace visible around the neckline of her dress and the row of buttons, no longer bright, down the front.

"Shit!" Gwyn yelped, and dropped the sheet again. "What the fuck is going on—" he started, and then stopped abruptly, as the growing chill in the room settled down into his very bones.

The morgue was no longer empty. A half-dozen or so other gurneys, each with a sheet-wrapped occupant, were lined up one side of the room; along the others, covered bodies lay in ordered rows, both adult-sized and much smaller. So many bodies. How could he be expected to handle so many, working this shift all by himself? Did they even have room enough in the units to store them all? Where did they all come from?

"How did they—" he started to ask, then stopped.

"Go and see," the little girl said.

All he had to do was touch each one of the covered corpses to know how the poor unfortunate met his or her tragic fate; he could all but see the moments of their deaths unfolding before his eyes. Children trapped in a burning theater, choking on smoke, trampled by panicking adults. Women dying in childbirth. The poor and weak, succumbing to typhoid, cholera, or diphtheria. Men in a prison camp hundreds of miles from home, overcome by starvation and exposure to Chicago's harsh winter. Those condemned for murder and conspiracy, real or imagined, still wearing the hangman's noose around their necks. Victims of the river, bodies bloated with trapped gases, their clothes still dripping with water and sludge from the river's bottom.

This isn't real, Gwyn reminded himself desperately. This was a vision, a spirit journey of some kind—and he would wake up, eventually. He hoped he would, anyway.

"Too late for that," the little girl told him. *"Too late to stop seeing. What are you going to do?"*

But then he noticed that the last victims were wearing modern clothing, and he felt a cold sweat forming on his forehead, his back, and under his arms. He laid his hand on a woman's sheet-covered head, not daring to look beneath, and heard the grinding of powerful steel girders, saw a bridge opening when it should not, and the sensation of falling, the impact of other cars hitting hers even under the dark water, the muffled screaming of a child.

With an icy shock, he realized this tragedy hadn't happened yet. But it would, probably very soon. He was never able to stop these things from happening—

He did wake up then, because someone was shaking him. "Dr. Hyndes! Dr. Hyndes, are you all right?"

"Jesus—" he blurted, then lurched to his feet, pushing aside the confused orderly so that he could see the rest of the morgue.

Empty. No little girls, no rows of corpses—just the gurney with its one sheet-covered occupant. But there on the sheet, he could still see the black feather resting exactly where the little burned girl's ghost had placed it.

Blood is the only true sacrifice, or so the Crone's Liturgy went. Fortunately, the blood did not have to be one's own.

The masked priest finished making his offerings to the four Quarters, murmuring the invocations to the gods he honored. The source of the blood offering, now deeply under the influence of the doctored drink he had consumed, lay supine on the floor nearby. For safety's sake—the priest's, not the mortal's—he was also manacled to the adjacent wall. His true contribution to the ritual would come later, for only at the end of the ritual could the priest's own hunger be satisfied.

It was near dawn; the priest could feel the leaden weight of torpor beginning to pull at his limbs, erode his consciousness. This was as planned, for only in the dream-state of torpor could he see what was hidden, rediscover what he had lost. Had his quest been less personal, less vital to his own survival, there were better rituals to invoke the dreaming visions, more effective for obtaining the answers he sought, than this. But to even disclose his need for such enlightenment would be to reveal too much, and so the priest invoked his gods alone.

Murmuring words in an ancient tongue, he lifted the black serpent out of the basket, dedicating the snake to his purpose. Then he snapped its spine, right behind the head, and held the body until it grew still. He arranged its body in as perfect a circle as he could, forcing the mouth open to slide the tip of the tail within. "Great serpent Ouroboros, beginning without end, eternal guardian, truth-seer, who returns to the beginning, in whom all things are contained and nothing hidden or lost. Let me see clearly, let the truth shine as the stars in the heavens."

In the center of the serpent's circle, he placed a great silver bowl, and poured into it consecrated water, gathered directly from the heavens and blessed by light of the waning moon. From the rune-bag, he drew three of the marked wooden tiles without looking at them, and slipped them into a silk bag, which he hung around his neck. They would guide his dreaming and help him recall the meanings tomorrow when he woke.

The last step—and this blood could not be shed by another. He lifted the curved, claw-shaped blade of his ritual knife, and sliced his own wrists open, from mid-forearm to the heel of his hand, first one and then the other. Blood flowed down his arms and over his hands, and he let it drain, into the water and the silver bowl. The Beast, already restless and irritable from a week of fasting, growled in its hunger and annoyance at the pain and new loss of blood, but the priest held firm, and let the blood flow.

Blood dripped into the water, forming odd swirls of color against the silver. Shapes coalesced, shifted, re-formed, moved into one another, and the priest watched them, letting his mind drift freely, letting himself sink into those shifting shapes as the shadows seeped upward into his mind.

"Let me remember, let it all return, let me see—"

Somewhere, as if from a great distance, he heard a roaring—a thunder like a hundred steam locomotives, the screams of women and children and clanging bells, neighing horses. He remembered a sky stained red, billowing with a heavy, choking smoke, ash and soot, and the wind—the deadly wind that drove the swirling sparks that sent the fire ever onward.

"You damned fool, do you think this is some petty game of praxis and politics? Do you not see the flames, smell the death all around us—do you not hear the city screaming? That which rises now cannot be so easily put down—It will return, it always returns. And it will never forget the blood that it is owed."

He remembered the taste of fear, his name spelled out on a disk of bone, drawn from a cauldron of blood… the price that was demanded. Blood was the only true sacrifice. But the blood of mortals was too weak to sustain him—the sacrifice had to be something more.

In the distance, he heard a man's voice, words in an unknown tongue, and the crisp ticking of a gold watch. "Oathbreaker, cursed are you once; murderer and drinker of souls, cursed are you twice; false priest and deceiver, cursed are you three times and forever, until the blood you have stolen is repaid—"

The mage's blood burned him even as he swallowed, spreading ice and fire through his veins. Even when he dropped the body, it continued to burn inside, as though he had swallowed some vile poison that made his limbs weak and the blood that animated his undead flesh as thin as water.

And the ticking of the watch continued, despite all his attempts to find it and smash it into fragments, to break the curse before it took effect. He looked in every pocket in the corpse's fine suit, every corner of the book chest; the watch was nowhere to be found. It just kept ticking, ticking, ticking, relentless and unforgiving.…

"It will return, it always returns. And it will never forget the blood that it is owed.… "

Beneath the gothic spires of the Tribune Building, below the pavement of North Michigan Avenue, there was an equally gothic but far less romantic and picturesque catacomb of subterranean corridors, sealed-off storerooms for archaic office equipment and broken chairs, forgotten photo archives and dead-letter files, boiler rooms, telephone closets, a veritable labyrinth of water pipes and electrical wiring, and the cramped offices, lockers, and break rooms for the maintenance staff.

The Prince's Hounds met in one of those dingy rooms, accessed by a emergency stairwell near the loading docks. Their number varied, depending on the Prince's needs and Norris' whim. Loki had been on Norris' call list for nearly a decade now, and he was never sure if his longevity in the spymaster's good graces was an indication of his competency or his expendability.

There were three of them tonight: himself; Baines, the hulking blond Iowa homeboy called "the Earth" because he was big as a mountain and immoveable once he set his feet down; and Marek Kaminski, a fellow Mekhet with far too much education and an ego to match. Loki would have given up his fangs for a week to know what hold Norris had

janet trautvetter

over Marek. Loki couldn't imagine the Ordo Dracul's golden boy playing Hound for an Invictus Prince and mixing with the hoi polloi like himself and the Earth unless it was punishment for something.

"Thought you couldn't die from the Muskegon virus," Loki said. "That's what they're saying on the news, anyway. Said it wasn't a big deal, most people who get it don't even know they're sick."

"Well, you can't," the Earth pointed out affably. "You're already dead." The Daeva laughed at his own joke, slapping his massive thigh, sending the chains of bling round his thick neck jingling.

Loki chuckled, too—it never hurt to humor the big guy, who wasn't exactly the sharpest knife in the drawer but was damned good to have at your back in a fight. And besides, the levity had the effect of causing Norris' already thin lips to purse even tighter in disapproval. Norris did not have much of a sense of humor.

The spymaster did, however, have the ability to chill even the Earth's guffaws into subdued silence with little more than an icy glare. "If you are quite done with the juvenile display, I shall endeavor to explain—so that even your minds can comprehend the serious nature of the problem we are currently facing."

Norris dropped three plain brown envelopes on the conference table in front of them. "As you will see from the information provided, these mortals did not die of the so-called Muskegon virus—at least not in its more prevalent common form."

Loki, being closest, pushed an envelope across to Marek, and one down to Earth, and then opened his own. Six photographs, six personal dossiers, including medical and coroner's reports. "A new virus?" That hadn't been in the news.

"What you have before you are the unedited laboratory reports," Norris said. "Naturally, the records at the hospital have been appropriately purged of any data that would appear to contradict the official, public diagnosis."

Loki skipped past the hospital lab reports, which were in medicalese anyway, and skimmed over the personal information. Young, teens or twenty-somethings, otherwise healthy. Students or young working types. Four chicks, two guys. Three from the North Shore, that wasn't good news. One from the University of Chicago. One from Cicero—hmm. And the last one… "This last guy, he's not even from Chicago. He's from Gary."

"An astute observation, Mr. Fischer," Norris said coolly.

"What's en-encepha—something. What it says here." The Earth's dark-gold brows beetled over the medical terminology. "Under cause of death."

"Encephalitis," Marek put in, "is an inflammation of the brain. Meningitis is an inflammation—a swelling, if you prefer—of the membrane surrounding the brain and spinal cord. And before you even attempt to mangle it, meningoencephalitis is a combination of the two, and can result in high fever, convulsions, coma, paralysis—and, if you're lucky, death. Or permanent brain damage. Fortunately, not something either of you needs to worry about."

"Yeah, yeah," Loki muttered. Fucking college boy, showing off with four-dollar words. Loki flipped through the names and the photographs. *John Nathan Duncan. Jillian Sheridan. Kimberly Jean McLaren.* Damn, she was a babe. Young, too, only sixteen. Too bad…. Something clicked in his mind just then, and he scanned the personal information again. Yes… yes, possibly… and yes. A bit young, but—possible, if they went to the right kinds of parties, or looked old enough to lie their way past the bouncers. He saw dozens of mortals just like these every night; so did any Kindred who hunted the club scene. *Prey.*

"They died sequentially." Marek clearly had picked up the same details. "Three days, maybe four at most, apart. And died within three days of their first symptoms of being sick. Jesus. Three days?"

"A blister," Loki said it aloud, partly to ease the almost painful look of concentration on the Earth's face, and partly just to beat Marek to the punch line. "It's *not* the same virus. You think there's some Kindred out there spreading this nasty little bug around."

"The evidence seems to indicate an unusually selective vector," Norris replied coolly. "Most mortals affected by the so-called Muskegon virus have been elderly, or already in frail health. These are young and healthy. They succumbed, as Mr. Kaminski points out, extremely swiftly, and four of them were hospitalized at the time and undergoing treatment. Their deaths form a regular, almost predictable pattern, that has continued over a period of the past two weeks. We cannot be certain their susceptibility was not simply a coincidence, or represents a new strain of a naturally evolving viral organism, or is the result of some supernatural vector. But we can't yet rule it out. That is, naturally, where you come in."

Naturally. This was what the Hounds did, find things out—though Loki was not naïve enough to assume the three of them were the only ones Norris or Maxwell had put on the trail. Someone had clearly compiled the dossiers, after all, and Loki wasn't even betting they'd been given the complete files, either. Norris was very much of the 'need to know' school, and he was the one who decided what you needed to know.

"Could be a nomad, passing through," Marek mused, looking through the files. "Though if it is, he's poaching rather upscale."

"Indeed," Norris agreed. "I'm sure you can see the delicacy of the situation. It's one thing if virus fatalities are relatively uncommon and affect only the old and infirm. But what appears to be more of a serious epidemic might lead mortals to discover what else these victims have in common—and could have disastrous consequences for this city."

"If we find it's a blister doin' this," Earth rumbled, "what d'ya want us to do with the fucker?"

"If a Kindred vector is involved, of course, the Prince will require uncontestable evidence of his guilt—which, I will point out, Mr. Baines, cannot be gained from ashes. It would also be most regrettable and inconvenient should the Prince find himself having to deal with this matter publicly in Elysium. We therefore have every confidence that you will proceed with the utmost discretion."

So, by 'utmost discretion,' Norris really meant 'total secrecy.' That wasn't going to make their job any easier. "I got a question," Loki said. "What, exactly, is uncontestable evidence? Does this new virus show up in blood tests or what? I mean from one of us, not them."

"Obviously, if we knew the answer to that, Mr. Fischer, we would not need your diligent powers of observation," Norris replied coolly. "As for the nature of the evidence—well. We will leave that up to your ingenuity. The ultimate proof, of course, would be the cessation of reports like those you hold in your hands. Death is many things, gentlemen: commonplace, pervasive, inevitable—sometimes even tragic. But when it is also mysterious and creates a traceable pattern, it can also lead to unfortunate publicity. I trust I have made myself clear?"

The Skullery wasn't the biggest club in the city—far from it. Crobar had bigger crowds, especially on weekends, and Metro pulled in bigger names to grace its stage. But size wasn't everything—style counted, too, and Moyra had a sense of style that a Daeva might envy. She also had a keen sense of how to please a target audience, and keep them coming back—which benefited both her bottom line and those Kindred she counted as clients and permitted to feed at her pseudo-medieval gothic crypt of a nightclub. Loki considered himself lucky to be counted among those fortunate few.

Tonight, the Skullery was packed, with a line of black-clad hopefuls standing on the sidewalk outside the club's deceptively mundane brick warehouse exterior. The bouncer at the door recognized him and waved him through, much to the petulant annoyance of the nearest line-standers. Loki grinned and blew them a kiss, and then slipped inside the door.

He could feel the throbbing beat of bass and percussion through the soles of his boots, reverberating in the concrete and steel of the steps, the fake stone blocks along the walls. A live band—sounded like Icarus Falling. Yes, it was. Damien always brought in a good crowd. Moyra would be in a good mood, and feeding would be easier.

The dance floor was crammed with black-clad bodies, moving in rhythm to the electronic pulse of the music. Up on the stage, Damien hit a riff, fingers sliding down the neck of the guitar, evoking an aching wail from the strings, which was echoed by Rina's synthesizer, reverberating and fading into empty silence. The band members froze in position. The lights went out for a second, then the beat kicked back in, the lights came back on, and the guitar and synthesizer picked the underlying rhythm again.

Loki made his way around the club's raised perimeter, between the tables set between the massive columns of the aisle and the candlelit alcoves along the outer wall. Some of the alcoves had bones and skulls embedded in their walls, some had glass-fronted crypts in which skeletal figures dressed in rotting rags could be seen resting within. Leering gargoyles and skulls of various human and inhuman creatures were carved into corners and archways. The pillars reached upward two stories high and supported gothic arches overhead.

The stairs to the balcony above were roped off, with a little sign in medieval calligraphy MEMBERS ONLY. The bouncer unhooked it for him and stood aside. Loki flipped him a salute and went on upstairs.

Loki strode down the length of the balcony overlooking the dance floor to the back of the club. Moyra came down the stairs on the far end to meet him, the long, trailing hem of her gown rippling along behind her, almost invisible against the black of the carpet.

Damien once said that half of Moyra's haven was full of costumes, and Loki could well believe it. Moyra claimed that she got bored wearing the same old thing—in fact, Loki couldn't remember her ever wearing the same thing twice, or at least not twice in a given year. Tonight it was a strapless black sequined gown, fishnet opera gloves, and a red feather boa; her hair up in a sleek blonde chignon with a black hat with a little black veil that hung down over her eyes. Very chic, very vintage—even her lipstick was 1940s red.

"Ah, good evening," she said, and gracefully extended a hand for him. "You're supposed to kiss it," she added, when he failed to get the hint.

"I knew that," Loki said, and did so, with his best continental flair.

"That's better," she said, and lightly brushed his cheek with one gloved palm. "We have guests tonight, by the way. Do try not to be rude."

"Oh? Who?"

Moyra didn't answer. She turned instead and opened the door behind her to the dimly lit room beyond. Loki followed her. Here, hidden behind faux stone arches, heavy red velvet drapes, and strategically placed sound baffles, was the more exclusive and lavishly furnished Loft, a private lounge where Moyra and other Kindred she so favored could indulge themselves and their mortal guests.

Or in this case, Kindred guests. Loki recognized them immediately, and understood Moyra's injunction. Although to be fair, Jed Holyoak wasn't a bad sort, if a bit too smooth and eager to please. Jed had the dubious honor of playing Summer King in the Circle's ritual cycle this year—a temporary reign destined for a ceremonial duel and sacrificial defeat when the Horned King avatar was chosen in a few weeks, so Loki didn't blame him for enjoying the limelight while he could.

But as for Bella Dravnzie—well, he hoped Moyra wasn't expecting any miracles tonight.

"Loki!" Bella smiled and rose to her feet to come greet him, as if they were old friends. "It's been so long since we had a nice chat."

He felt it still, the pull of her goddamned blood, even from six years back. Or maybe it was just that Daeva charisma trick—he could never be sure, really.

Moyra laid her hand on his shoulder. Not quite possessive, but a quiet reminder to Bella, who had recruited him, of just whose coven he had finally chosen to associate himself with. Her action gave him the excuse to look away, look up at the ivory features behind the little black veil. It helped.

Bella returned to what was likely the original topic of conversation. "Birch is on one of his psychotic rampages again."

"So what else is new?" Loki shrugged. "What is it this time? Someone he ate disagree with him?"

"Apparently more than one someone, if the rumors are true," Bella said. "It seems that the Bishop's past victims are less than forgiving. And they converged on the Sanctified cathedral *en masse* last week to tell him so. During the middle of Mass, no less. And apparently a number of the congregation were quite disturbed to find their former victims sitting beside them in the pews, wounds gaping open, nails still in their hands—smelling rather ripe, too, as I understand it."

Bullshit. Loki managed to not laugh out loud. "Is that what Birch said? I'd have paid to see that."

"Don't tell me the Sanctified are afraid of a few ghosts," Moyra said, amused.

"No, not Birch, of course not," Bella huffed, and leaned forward, her voice dropping to a conspiratorial whisper. "What I heard, of course, was told to me in strictest confidence—as you know, I do have my sources inside the Palmer House."

Persephone. Loki wondered if Persephone knew that telling Bella anything of interest 'in strictest confidence' only insured its getting spread as quickly as possible. Probably she did. Persephone certainly wasn't dumb, and she'd been burned by Bella before.

"What Birch is saying is what happened at his little Sanctified circus was witchcraft. Heathen Circle witchcraft, to be precise, intended to disrupt and make mockery of the Sanctified's holy rites."

janet trautvetter

This time Loki did laugh, and even Moyra's lips curved slightly under her veil. "Cute," Moyra said, "but I doubt even Rowen knows how to pull that off—or would bother if she did."

"You and I may know that, of course," Bella agreed. "But whether it's true or not doesn't matter, if he persuades the Prince to ban our rites next week in retaliation. Which is exactly what Birch is demanding, of course. And the next Elysium isn't for two weeks—which will be far too late to get it settled. He knows our rites are tied to the lunar calendar."

"That's if Maxwell even listens to that bullshit," Loki pointed out. "He's not stupid. He knows what Birch is like."

"We all know what Birch is like," Jed added. "But the Prince has favored him over us before. And Bella is right, it's a perfect excuse for them. Blame it on pagan witch-craft—because who else could have done such a thing, the Carthians?"

"You have to talk to him, Loki," Bella said, earnestly. "You have to explain—"

"Explain what?" Moyra asked, coolly, and Loki was grateful for her interruption. "What explanation do we owe to Solomon Birch? If he cannot manage his ghosts, he should not create so many of them. What answer do we owe the Prince, when he has not even asked a question? Why play into Sanctified hands by defending ourselves before an accusation is even made?"

"And who is there for him to ask, even if he wanted to?" Bella countered. "Who is there to counter Birch's ridiculous accusations? Who speaks for us outside of Elysium? Rowen? She doesn't even have a cell phone! I'll do what I can, of course, but there's a limit to how much I can ask of Persephone—she's far too young to be taken seriously, and she's not one of us in any case."

"Well, technically speaking," Jed reminded her, right on cue, "Loki's not fully one of us either."

Ah, I knew it. Here it comes. Loki reminded himself he'd promised Moyra not to be rude.

"Not yet?" Bella feigned surprise. "You're not still in the Chorus after all this time, are you? Loki, darling, what are you waiting for? I would have initiated you years ago!"

It was jealousy, or so Loki told himself. The Chorus were the beginners, new to the covenant, still learning its philosophies, history, and rituals. It was true, of course, that some never advanced beyond that point. But Moyra was known to have higher standards of her students. And Bella knew perfectly well why he'd chosen Moyra's guidance over her own, and it was Bella's own damned fault.

"Loki will face initiation when he is ready, Bella," Moyra said quietly. "It is not for me or anyone else to choose that time for him."

"But you believe he's ready, don't you?" Bella asked.

"I have nothing more to teach him at this time," Moyra replied. "What remains, he must learn on his own—for some things cannot be taught, only experienced."

"Indeed, that is so true," Bella agreed, nodding wisely. "Experience is always the best teacher, if the harshest. It is in our tribulations that we find true enlightenment."

"And learning from our mistakes means not repeating 'em." Loki could keep quiet no longer. "Experience is useful that way, don'tcha think?"

"Is that all you've learned from your mistakes, Loki?" Bella purred. "Then perhaps Moyra is mistaken—you're not ready for initiation after all. A pity, after all these years."

A flood of feelings he wasn't used to experiencing welled up inside him: shame, guilt, and resentment. She was trying her nasty little Daeva tricks on him again, trying to yank his chain. Loki clamped down hard on his anger, struggled to keep his fangs from coming out. He didn't dare respond. To show how badly she'd rattled him would only make it worse, and yet the insult demanded a response of some kind, if he could do so without losing what remained of his temper.

Surprisingly, though, it was Jed who intervened. "Bella, darling, you're not helping, you know. And we did want to get to talk to Justine this evening—"

"Oh, yes, of course," Bella said, and the feelings—well, most of them, some of the anger still remained—dropped away like a discarded shirt.

He hated it when she did that. *Bitch.*

Somehow Loki managed to hold on to civility for the few more minutes it took for Jed and Bella to say their goodbyes, and depart the loft. Moyra walked out with them, as befitted her role as hostess.

He didn't have to listen in—in fact, he knew it was rude, and likely would only piss him off even further. But the band was on a break, and it was good practice, or so he told himself, to pick out one conversation out of the hundred-odd going on down below. Norris had told him to practice whenever he could.

—*"You know people are wondering—not that I'm suggesting he has anything to hide, of course not—just where his loyalties truly lie. We all know how Norris runs his little operation…"*

"Bitch," Loki muttered, and forced himself to tune them out again, refusing to let Bella ruin his night. He'd promised himself a sexy chick in black leather, and there were several dozen down there to choose from.

He was just coming down out of the Loft to the balcony when he heard voices in the shadow of an archway just ahead, and spotted a tall, distinctive profile.

"About an hour ago, you remember. Sharee said she wasn't feeling well. A really nasty headache, one of the migraines she gets sometimes. You remember hearing her tell you about it. But she didn't want to spoil your evening. She said she'd just take a cab home, take her meds, get some sleep. She said you should have a good time and call her later this weekend…. "

Damien, doing his Ventrue mind-fuck thing on a tall girl, in the hallway. He wasn't aware of Loki yet—he was focused on his subject, making sure she remembered only what she was supposed to remember. And the girl wouldn't see him either. Damien commanded all her attention. Problem was, they were blocking the way out, so Loki slipped through the side door, into one of the private rooms.

Ah, here was where Damien had stashed the girl with the headache, sprawled across the bed, one arm over her eyes to shield them from the light, even though it was only a dim table lamp on the other side. Maybe she really did have a headache, though that would be odd of Damien to hide her in here and send her apparently healthy friend away.

But then Loki smelled sweat, and sickness. She wasn't breathing. He couldn't hear her heartbeat. *Oh, shit.*

"What the fuck are you doing?" Damien demanded, from the doorway. "Don't you even—"

Loki stepped back quickly, raising his hands. "Didn't touch her, I swear. Fuck, she's dead, what the hell happened?"

janet trautvetter

"Nothing! Nothing happened!" Damien sat on the bed, slid fingers up under the girl's jaw, looking for a pulse. "She said she had a headache, so I got her some aspirin and let her come up here to lie down. She was fine when I left her!"

"I thought you said she had a headache."

"She did! I thought it was just a touch of the flu or something—"

A touch of the flu. In September? "Then why did you send her friend away like that?" Loki shook his head. "Come on, Damien. Don't fuck with me here. Don't give me this bullshit about a headache if you just got carried away—"

"Goddammit, Loki, I am not shitting you. That's what she said! I hadn't even touched her yet!"

"All right, all right—chill out, dude. I believe you, okay?" Loki assured him. *Fuck.* He remembered the dossiers on the table, those young, smiling faces. "Okay, then. Who's been doing her, besides you? I mean, in the last week. Anybody? You give anybody freebies?"

Damien scowled. "No, she's one of mine—why? I mean, I did—shit, I don't remember when! Maybe a week or two ago. I don't keep a fucking appointment book!"

Well, that much was probably true, Loki had to admit. But this looked bad. Worse than bad. *Not Damien, for chrissakes. Please God, don't make it be Damien. Somebody's poaching on him, gotta be.* That was possible, he had to admit. Damien's groupies were pretty easy, on all counts. They were one of the reasons he liked coming here himself—Damien was also pretty generous about sharing when he had a good crowd.

Damien rubbed the heel of his palm against his forehead. "Shit. This is that fucking virus everyone's talking about, isn't it? Moyra is gonna fucking kill me, man, if the cops come. Or worse, if the health inspectors come snooping around here again—"

"Well, I'm not gonna call the cops." Loki thought for a second. "Lemme see her wallet. Where's her place?"

Damien dug around in the purse until he found it. "Here," he said, flipping it open. "What, you think we should just take her home and dump her?"

"Sure, why not?" Loki tried to project a confidence he didn't entirely feel. "Let someone else find her and deal with it. Her friends think she got a headache and went home early, they're not gonna call her until sometime tomorrow at the earliest."

Damien looked at the address again. "Shit. Lake Shore Drive? This is one of those high-rises. No way we can do this without being seen."

"I think I can manage it." He'd never tried to conceal anything as large as a human body before, but what the hell. "And if that doesn't work, you can make 'em remember her being alive, just sick or something. We're just helping her get home. You still got the keys to Moyra's car?"

"Yeah, I got 'em. I've got one more set coming up in about fifteen, after that's fine. So long as Moyra doesn't find out."

"She won't. I'll handle that."

"Thanks, man. I owe ya one, Loki."

Loki figured Moyra would want to talk to him anyway, once Bella and Jed were safely gone, and he was right. Fortunately, she waited until after he'd had a chance to sequester one of the unattached dancers in a dark corner for a while. A full belly improved his disposition immensely.

"You could pass the initiation at any time, you know that," she told him. "You know the Litany, and you have the strength of spirit. What are you afraid of?"

"I'm not afraid," Loki retorted, stung. "I'll do it, I promise, but only when I'm ready."

"But not at next week's rites, is that what you're saying?"

"I wouldn't want Solomon Birch to give up hope of luring me to the dark side."

"Solomon Birch knows nothing about the dark side," she said. "We represent what they most fear—the darkness within their souls. They seek to chain the Beast Within, appease it with hollow rituals, buy its complacency with the blood of nameless sinners whose sacrifices are empty and meaningless to those who shed their blood. We know the Beast is part of ourselves, and do not deny its nature or the blood it is due. Solomon Birch fears his ghosts. We sing their names and welcome them to dance around the Samhain fire. Fear only makes us stronger."

"I thought it was 'that which does not kill us makes us stronger.'"

"Indeed, but remember that fear can also kill. Those who face fear and survive it become strong."

"I just knew you were going to say something like that."

"Hey. Loki." Damien stuck his head in the door of the Loft. "You coming or what? *Carpe noctem*, get your ass in gear, man."

"Coming—"

Damien could move surprisingly quietly for someone his size, and a Ventrue at that. Loki felt a pang of guilt, or something like it, just leaving poor Sharee sprawled across her bed, with her parents snoring just down the hall, unaware of the tragedy awaiting them when they woke. But there was nothing else he could do for her now, except carry out his mission from Norris as best he could.

"So, who else has been in the club lately?" he asked, as Damien was merging back on to the Drive. "I mean, Kindred other than the usual. Anybody new?"

Damien thought about that. "Well, Jed's been by a couple times. Toby Rieff came trolling for trouble last week, you know how he is. Rafael dropped in the other night. That was a treat. You shoulda been here."

"I can just imagine," Loki said dryly.

"Oh, and Jed brought by a couple of nomads one night, showing them around. Don't remember the biker's name. The chick was Beth. Both Daeva, I think."

"Circle?"

"Yeah, I think so. She had a crescent moon pendant, anyway. Silver."

"Did Moyra let them hunt?"

Damien frowned. "I don't know. I had a gig, so I didn't stick around. Maybe, if Jed had asked. Why?"

"I was thinking of bringing a guest sometime," Loki said, trying to sound casual. Maybe it was the nomads after all. That would make more sense, and make his job easier. Nomads came and went; nobody paid much attention. "Just wondering what the score was."

"Well, you got a freebie on me, after tonight," Damien said. "Like I said, I owe you one. You want to go back and pick one out now?"

janet trautvetter

It was tempting, but somehow he resisted. "No, thanks, I'm good. But I'll take a rain check."

"You got it," Damien agreed.

Kimberly McLaren had seemed such a nice, average girl, based on the dossier. A good, if not perfect, student, who played the piano, attended football games, parties, and dances, and obsessed over the usual movie stars. Judging from the stacks of paperbacks on the bookshelf in her room, she was a voracious reader. And, of course, she had a computer.

Breaking in had been easier than Loki had expected—they hadn't put alarms on the second-floor windows. Getting up there had taken some effort, however. In the end, he'd jimmied the lock on the toolshed out back and found himself a ladder. Knowing he could recover from a two-story fall didn't mean he enjoyed it. He punched the middle pane out with a heavy chunk of rock, then reached in and unlatched the window.

It was late; there were hardly any lights on the whole street. The family wasn't home. There had been no cars in the garage or the driveway, and there wasn't a single whimper or bark from the dog, so Loki guessed they were probably out of town, but kept his senses alert just the same.

Kim's room was easy to recognize. It seemed undisturbed, the door closed. Probably her parents hadn't been able to face it yet. Which was just lucky for him. He wasn't sure what he was looking for, pawing over a dead girl's things, checking under her mattress, in the bottoms of drawers and the back of her closet. He figured he'd know if he found it, whatever that was.

His search was not in vain. There was a locked overnight bag in the back of her closet (which he broke into easily), containing a dark green robe, ritual knife, assorted herbs and oddities in neatly labeled plastic baggies, bowls, candles, and incense, and a tiny, wax-sealed vial containing a quantity of dark red fluid that Loki did not even have to sniff to identify. He also discovered a couple of crow feathers under her pillow—a bit weird, but you never knew what some people believed.

The computer, however, proved to be a gold mine. She'd left all her passwords on auto-fill, too, so it was a piece of cake to access her email. It was amazing how trusting some people were. Especially if they actually had secrets to keep, like a boyfriend Loki was quite certain her parents would not have approved of, and a clear interest in the occult. Apparently, she'd started going out with this guy who called himself Raven—jeez, how unoriginal—and he'd been teaching her some interesting things.

Actually, some of it looked suspiciously familiar. There were a number of Kindred in the Circle of the Crone who maintained their own mortal covens, primarily for feeding, but also to teach a much-diluted version of the covenant's doctrine. Rituals needed blood, and a pool of willing donors who believed there was a valuable, mystical purpose in their sacrifice of a pint now and then made an Acolyte's task much easier.

It was also interesting that when Kim had asked this Raven fellow for a photo ("*I promise I won't show it to anyone, I'll keep it under my pillow, I just want to have something of you with me when we're apart…*"), his vague-sounding excuse had something to do with secret FBI files, the Witness Protection Program, and the safety of his mystical identity, all of which smelled of utter Kindred bullshit. Loki didn't have to look at the mirror over the bureau to know his own reflected visage was blurred and indistinct. Kindred didn't show up clearly in mirrors or in photographs without great effort. Loki was willing to bet Kim had never seen Raven by daylight either, though she failed to ask about that.

He wished, briefly, that this didn't have to be a Circle problem. That was the last thing they needed. If Solomon Birch and his holier-than-everybody Sanctified Gestapo found out, there'd be political hell to pay. The Circle of the Crone had enough PR problems, dammit, as Bella's story the night before had demonstrated. Why couldn't this dickhead have been Invictus or Carthian instead?

Utmost discretion, Norris had said. No shit.

So who the fuck was Raven? The Circle was the least organized covenant of Kindred in Chicago—there were at least a half-dozen covens he knew of, plus some loner types who never attended the group rites. And that probably wasn't the name he used among Kindred, either.

Of course, Loki did have Raven's email address, right here.

He took great care in composing the email. Several times he cut-and-pasted whole sentences or phrases from previous emails she'd written, either to Raven or her best friend KoolJoolie17, so it would sound as if it came from Kim herself.

I guess you heard I was sick, but a lot has changed since then, and I'm feeling ever so much better now. I've missed you so very much and I can't wait to see you again! You always make me feel so safe so special. Please come see me again soon, I feel so empty inside without you. Love is eternal after all. –K.

He read it over one more time, added a few smiley-faces at the end, then with a little smile of his own, pressed SEND. "Come and see me, Raven," he murmured, "if you dare."

Remembering Norris' comment about evidence, Loki rooted around on her desk for a blank CD, slid it into the drive, and started copying the last three months' worth of emails. Moyra and Damien were a lot more involved in the Circle's loose social networks than he was. It was always possible one of them might know who this guy was, or who might be running a coven for yuppie high school girls up in the North Shore. It wouldn't hurt to ask a few leading questions, at any rate.

In the back of his mind, he had been aware the room was getting cooler, but he'd just assumed it was the AC kicking in. But just then it got *really* cold, *really* fast—and he couldn't hear anything like an AC unit running anywhere.

There was a loud *pop* from somewhere else in the house, and both the desk lamp and the computer screen went dark. At that same moment, a real, honest to fucking goodness chill touched his spine, right through the T-shirt and leather of his coat, like an icy hand against his skin.

"Fucking shit!" Loki shot up out of the chair, sending it skidding backwards. He was over closer to the window in a single leap, fangs bared in a fearsome snarl as he turned around. His gaze caught the mirror.

He could see himself.

He could see himself, as clearly as if he was still alive, still breathing, with a heart that beat in double-time and a pasty-faced grimace that showed no fangs at all, though he could feel them with his tongue. He could hear a heart beating somewhere—double-time—but it wasn't his.

And he could see her, in the mirror. Sitting up in her bed, as if he'd just awoken her from a sound sleep, staring at his reflection in the mirror, eyes open and blood streaming down the front of her nightgown, from a wound in her neck. She reached out to him.

He stepped backward, glanced sideways; the bed was neatly made and empty. No one was there. Kimberly McLaren was never going to sleep there again.

But in the mirror, the girl who looked just like Kimberly McLaren got out of bed and walked toward him, hand outstretched. There were crow feathers on her pillow.

"Fuck." Loki almost cracked another window pane, he jerked the window open so fast. He missed the ladder entirely on the way out, and landed painfully in the bushes below, jabbed by a hundred tiny twigs and branches, but spared impact with the less forgiving patio.

He scrambled to his feet and away from the house, then dared look up at the open window.

The flutter of white he saw emerging could have just been the curtain, caught in a draft—but Loki didn't stay to make sure. He raced across the backyard, vaulted over the privacy fence, and headed down the alleyway to the El, as fast as he could run.

It wasn't until he'd gone a good six or ten blocks that he remembered he'd left the CD in the fucking drive.

Shit.

Loki stopped, took a deep, deliberate breath, then let it out with a hiss. He couldn't afford to be sloppy like that, dammit. Norris had said *discreet,* and he didn't take excuses. And Loki was not about to admit (at least not to anyone else) that he'd run away from a dead girl's image in a mirror, no matter how cold her hands were. *I'm already dead, what can a ghost do to me? And I sure as hell didn't kill her—I'm trying to find out who did. So even if she is haunting her bedroom, it's not like she's got cause to be pissed at me personally.*

Still, he'd heard stories. Sometimes ghosts were nothing but a bit of ectoplasmic videotape, left running on a perpetual loop. Sometimes they were able to throw furniture around, slam doors and windows, chill the blood even in undead veins. And then there were those other times—the real horror stories that even the undead told only in whispers, when what had appeared to be just a ghost turned out to be something far worse. Loki liked listening to those stories, but he wasn't at all keen on actually being in one.

The Red Line train clacked and clattered by on the elevated tracks a block away. A couple left the bar down the street, the woman giggling and hanging on her date's shoulder while he had his hand on her ass. The traffic light changed.

Loki stepped back into the darker shadows of the alley, out of the painfully bright headlights of the oncoming traffic. Damned SUVs, their beams were always too high—but the sudden shiver of warning that touched him then was not due to the light. Instinctively, he pressed himself against the brick wall, willed the shadows to deepen and himself to blend into them. Yes, there. The black Jeep, that was slowing a little as it passed his hiding place. Loki caught a glimpse of two people in the front seat, the driver glancing around as though he, too, had sensed another predator close by.

Shit. Loki forced his muscles to relax, and quashed the hunter's instinct that saw the passing driver as a rival invading his turf. This wasn't his turf. He had nothing to defend, and he was well-hidden. If he stayed still, the other would just drive on. *Nothing to see here, nobody here, move along, move along.*

The driver of the car behind the Jeep, impatient to get moving, hit his horn. With an obscene gesture, the other Kindred hit the gas and the Jeep roared away.

Moving carefully, Loki took the chance of easing out a little so he could watch it drive away. Indiana plates, interesting—and even more interesting, that it turned right two blocks down, onto the same street where Kimberly McLaren had lived.

Well, shit. Like they say, be careful what you wish for. So, Raven had taken the bait. Given the speed of his response, he probably had a haven in the neighborhood. And out-of-state plates—maybe a nomad, maybe an immigrant, but it didn't matter. If he was the blister, his visa was about to run out.

Loki hefted the backpack onto his shoulder again, drew the shadows around himself as best he could—no point in attracting any more attention than absolutely necessary—and took off at a jog back the way he had come.

He slowed his pace once he got within a block of the house, and cut back around to the alley back behind the row of houses. There was the Jeep, parked in front of the garage door, but empty. The backyard gate Loki had simply climbed up over was swinging open.

"Doesn't look like anyone's home. Where the fuck's the key? You said you knew where it was."

"I'm getting it, I'm getting it, just had to remember which rock it was." A girl's voice, breathy and nervous. "Here it is. I really don't like this, I mean, if they're not home—"

"Shut up. The window's open up there. Looks like someone broke in."

"That's her room. Maybe someone just stole her computer."

Loki crouched down low next to the fence. They were trying to be quiet—but the girl's heart was going like a hammer, and her companion was wearing heavy boots that grated against the brick of the patio. There was the soft click of the key in the lock, the muffled creaking of the back door. They were inside.

Before going in the gate after them, Loki took a better look at the car, committing the tag number to memory. A couple of black garbage bags in the back, and what looked like the shiny metallic corner of a space blanket poking out from under one of them. He could smell stale cigarette smoke, menthol, and the stale, sour reek of sex. Well, that explained why the back seat was clear.

Keeping close to the shadows, and keeping a wary eye out for anything even vaguely spooky or weird, Loki slipped through the gate and crept up to the house.

"Shit. Somebody was here. That email came from here, look."

"Let me see—" There was the clickity-click of keys.

"I'm going to have a look around. You stay here."

"Don't leave me alone! Suppose whoever it was comes back?"

"Will you calm down! Jesus, girl. No one is coming back—and I'll be right down the hall. Just sit tight. See if there's any other emails going out, maybe we can figure out who the fuck's trying to jerk us around here."

"Okay. Just hurry. It's creepy, being in here… it's like they expected her to come back, y'know, leaving everything just like it was."

Loki was expecting the same thing.

There was silence for a while, just the clicking of the keys. And then, a hissed obscenity. "What—why you dirty, two-timing cheat—Raven!" The girl's voice slowly rose in volume; Loki could hear the heavy tread of the boots coming back at a swift pace.

janet trautvetter

"Keep your voice down, are you crazy? You want the neighbors to call the cops?"

"You were sleeping with her! You lying little fuck! You told me she was nothing, but that's not what you told her—you bastard—"

Loki heard the slap, as sharp as a gunshot, and the growl that followed, and the scuffle and the girl's whimpering. His own Beast snarled in response, and it was all he could do for a moment to keep quiet, keep the Beast down and hidden.

"Now you listen to me," Raven hissed. "I had to keep her happy, you know how she was. She would have spilled the whole story to them. I tried to explain, but she didn't want to hear it. She was always jealous of you, baby. She knew you were special. She knew you had the real talent, and she was so jealous. She knew it was you, and she just couldn't stand it…. I was just playing with her, baby, you know that. It wasn't anything… she wasn't even that good a fuck, not like you, you're the hot one, you're the sexy doll…. "

The girl's heart rate had increased, her breathing had gone shallow. "I—I am? You really mean that—"

"You know I do, baby. I would never lie to you, you'd see right through it anyway…."

Daeva. Had to be. No other clan could lay on bullshit that thick and get away with it every damned time. Raven was kissing her now, probably had his hand up inside her shirt from the way she was moaning. Loki heard the chair get pushed aside, heard the creaking of the mattress.

"Raven—this is her bed—"

"So what?" Raven's voice was muffled. "What's she gonna do about it, baby?"

Loki was thinking the same thing. *Hey, Kim, look who's doing it in your bed, whatcha gonna do about it?*

But then the girl gave a little cry of pain, that turned into a whimper. Loki could tell the instant Raven's fangs pierced her skin, and when he began to suckle. The irritation his Beast had felt earlier at Raven's mere passing was nothing compared to the sudden rise of jealous rage and hunger that stabbed at him now, listening to the interloper feed. Loki's fangs extended, his entire body tensed, muscles coiled to spring; it was all he could do to hold his position, fight the red haze that threatened to overwhelm his vision, and shatter his self-control. *No way, not gonna lose it, not now. Breathe in, breathe out. Easy, take it easy, chill out, Loki, not your fucking problem. Breathe, nice and slow and easy. One. Two. Three. Four….*

He continued to force himself to take deep, slow breaths, talking the Beast down, promising it a real hunt later, satisfaction delayed rather than denied. He reminded himself why he was there, crouched on the roof outside a dead girl's window—that his real hunt was for information, not sustenance. And if his suspicions were correct, the last thing he wanted was to get into a direct fight with a nomad plague-rat.

And where was that damned ghost? It would hardly be fair if the ghost, if that's what it was, gave him the goosing but let her two-timing boyfriend get off scot-free. Irritated, Loki rose slightly so he could see inside, steeling himself for what the mirror might show, half-expecting the unseen lovers to leap shrieking from the bed any moment.

There she was, pale and translucent, just staring… assuming she could see what was going on in the real world. As he watched, the pale figure brought her cupped hands up to her face, and blew, releasing a cloud of fluttering black feathers that drifted down toward the bed. Then she smiled. It wasn't a particularly nice smile, either. For a moment there, her face was too pale, haggard, and cruel—she didn't look like the girl in the photos at all.

A chill touched him then, a breeze far too cold to be natural for late summer, coming from the open window. The curtains billowed, and three or four black feathers came swirling outward, in his direction.

What the— Shit! Loki jumped back, spun around on the ball of his foot, took two long steps, and leapt outward and down to the back yard. The landing was nowhere near as jarring as the one from his third-floor balcony; he was able to get up and keep moving out the back gate, which he pulled shut behind him.

In the alley, he could no longer feel the same chilling breeze, and he didn't see anything wafting over the high fence to pursue him. Now that he was out here, he felt a little stupid. *Feathers, you idiot, you're running away from feathers!*

But he didn't feel particularly inclined to prove what a badass he was by going back inside.

Instead, he went back to the Jeep. It was unlocked, and she'd left her purse on the floor. He opened the door, fumbled around inside the purse—why was it girls needed to carry so much shit with them all the time?—until he found her wallet, and her name. *Julie Marie Wooster.* And her address—not far, just one El stop away.

So. If Raven was the blister, then Julie would get sick. And then Loki'd know for sure. Part of him was appalled at his own reasoning—some nagging echo that maybe he should care more about this girl's fate than see her as a test case to be checked off as positive or negative. He ignored it.

Sometimes life just sucked, and there wasn't a damned thing he could do about it.

The El was usually quiet this late at night. There were the typical homeless drunks and ne'er-do-wells, a smattering of working stiffs with graveyard hours, and the occasional gang of troublemakers looking for excuses for mayhem. And then, of course, there were the nocturnal predators, like himself.

Sometimes Loki hunted on the train. This was the hour to do it, when mortal riders were tired or stoned out of their minds, and the chance of witnesses was practically zero. Find a mortal alone in a car, strike as soon as the train started moving, and be prepared to disembark or change cars at the next stop.

Tonight, however, he was not hunting. He was just going home.

"Next station, Addison. Doors open on the left side."

As the train pulled into the station, a shifting mass of swiftly moving shadows fluttered by the train window to his right. Something hit the glass with a clatter, and Loki jumped, startled, staring out across to the streets and alleys below the elevated tracks. *What the—*

There was something down there. A figure on a motorcycle, riding without lights, barely visible in the shadows. The rider dismounted, stepped out of the darkness into the dim yellow glow of the streetlamp. A slim figure in a cowboy hat instead of a helmet, with a fringed jacket, tight jeans, and a tangled mass of dark hair, stepped slowly and deliberately out into the open, and looked up, directly at the train.

Directly at him.

Loki had felt "the vibe" when meeting other Kindred before. He knew that little twinge of fear, the sudden desire to back away rather than challenge someone older or stronger.

But what he felt now wasn't just a twinge—it was the icy clutch of sheer terror, bordering on mindless panic. His muscles went suddenly weak on him, and he sank back into the seat, fighting the intense urge to hide under it instead. His fangs extended, pressing painfully against his lower lip. If his heart still beat, it would have been going like a jackhammer. He wanted to scream at the driver to close the doors, get the train moving, get the hell out of here before it was too late.

Before *she* took it into her head to come aboard.

He couldn't see her face, shadowed beneath the brim of her hat, the veil of her hair. But he did not have to see her eyes to feel the power of her gaze. To a hunter like this, he was nothing, or worse, he was prey. He realized he was trembling, and fought down the urge to give in to the panic bubbling up from his Beast, and flee like a scared rabbit.

If he ran, she would pursue him. It was a predator's natural reaction, and in showing herself, she was daring him to do just that.

Instead, he froze, unable to move, unable to look away, pinned by her gaze. He'd heard the stories, of course. He knew who she was, who she had to be, even though he'd never seen her before, and even though he hadn't believed that those stories were true until this instant. The Unholy was a hoary urban legend among Kindred, the oldest and baddest of all the nomad drifters, who hunted when and where she liked and bowed to neither Prince nor Traditions. He'd liked the stories a lot better, however, when they had been happening to someone else. Part of him didn't want to believe them even now, though from the silhouette, the hat, and the flurry of crows settling in nearby trees—and the gut-chilling fear the mere sight of her aroused in him—she was quite real, she was in Chicago, and she had wanted him to see her.

Wanted to see if he would break and run, and give her the excuse to hunt him down.

It felt like forever before Loki heard the familiar chime and the doors closing, before the train lurched forward. The movement broke his paralysis, and, in that moment, she was gone.

But the aftermath of that numbing terror stayed with him all the way back to his haven, and he stared intently into every murky shadow, listening furtively for the sound of crows flying in his wake. Only when he saw the first sign of the sky lightening in the east did he begin to feel safe again.

Despite the lateness of hour, Maxwell took Loki's call. It was a privilege to have the number, and Loki had always been careful, in the years he'd been in the Prince's service, not to abuse it. Maxwell listened gravely to Loki's report of what he had seen. "I'm afraid you're right," the Prince agreed somberly. "You're not the first person to report seeing her, or her crows."

"I think she wanted me to see her, in fact," Loki said. "Maybe that's her way of announcing she's in town, warning the competition to stay out of her way."

"Perhaps," Maxwell replied. "There's not much to be done about it, in any case. My experience has been that the best thing to do is leave her alone, and attempt to minimize the damage. I appreciate your report, Loki. Do keep your eyes open, and let Norris or me know if you spot her again, but don't go looking for her, and don't mention this to anyone. The fewer who know about her presence in the city, the better. Good day's rest to you, Loki."

"Yes, sir. You, too, sir."

It wasn't until he was getting comfortable on his futon, safe in the darkness of the deep closet that was his bedroom, that a worse thought occurred to him. Of course, it seemed most likely that it was Raven who was the blister—all the evidence pointed to him, and he'd certainly had contact with at least one, possibly two, of the virus' young victims. He hoped it really was Raven now, even if that did mean turning a fellow Acolyte over to the Prince's judgment. Raven, at least, could be dealt with.

But if it was the Unholy carrying this nasty little plague around, they were all well and truly fucked.

The fluorescent lights in the hospital men's room were brighter than Loki liked, but he couldn't wear his shades indoors without attracting unwelcome attention. And besides, what he needed to do required seeing clearly, as mortals saw.

He stared at the image in the mirror. It was not translucent, just indistinct, blurry, as if seen through a foggy glass. Loki dug into his wallet, slid a dog-eared photograph out of a back pocket. The picture was small, a decade old, and no longer perfectly accurate, but it helped him with the details. He studied it a moment, and then concentrated on the mirror.

Start with the easy part: clothing. Black, sleeveless T-shirt with a gargoyle spreading its wings across his chest. Black cargo pants riding low on his hips, loops of dull silver chains dangling down from his belt, tucked into heavy, steel-toed boots. Bare arms, wiry-muscled and pale-skinned, save for the intricate barbed-wire pattern of the tribal tattoo that twisted around his left bicep. Heavy studded leather cuff on his right wrist, skull ring on his index finger….

The blurred figure in the mirror slowly sharpened, came into focus. Short hair, dyed jet black and twisted into irregular spiky tufts. A long, youthful face, with sharply defined cheekbones, boyishly smooth. Ears that sported a series of silver rings on one side and a dangling ankh on the other. Eyes, blue-gray and half in shadow under straight brows, a straight nose, full, expressive lips, and the wary, guarded expression that his father had called his 'sullen rebel look.'

It took some effort to bring that face out again, human features sharp and clear, so that no chance reflection would betray him, no security camera would show cause for questions or alarm. The final touches didn't really require the mirror's aid, but he kept his focus on it nonetheless. Reaching inward, he brought blood out toward his skin, infusing his skin with color and human warmth. Breathe, yes. Remember to breathe, remember to fidget a little, the small, seemingly innocuous movements that mortals never thought about, but felt a subtle unease when they were missing. Remember what it felt like to be *alive*.

Loki leaned forward until his nose was almost touching the mirror's surface, and exhaled. A mortal's breath would have fogged the mirror—but the air in his lungs was cool and dry, and the mirror remained clear. There were limits to his illusions—but illusion was all he had, so it would have to do.

"I'm sorry," the receptionist repeated, a bit more sternly this time, "but this hospital has rules, and federal law requires we protect patient privacy. I can release information on a patient's status only to his or her immediate family. They'll probably be coming out when visiting hours end, in about fifteen minutes—why don't you wait and talk to them?"

"Her father doesn't like me," Loki explained, looking as crestfallen and desperate as he could. "He says I'm a bad influence, whatever that means. He wouldn't tell me shi—anything, he's more likely to call the cops and have me arrested or something. Please, ma'am, she really means a lot to me—she's my best friend in the whole world, and I'm really worried about her."

"Look, honey," the receptionist said wearily. "I'm sorry. But I can't help you, and I can't listen to your sob stories all night either. Now you can sit down, wait, and talk to the family—or I'm going to have to ask you to leave. And don't even think about trying to sneak by me, or I'll have security on your butt so fast you'll wish you had taken your chances with your girlfriend's father."

Like you'd catch me, you bitch. Loki scowled—which ruined his look of boyish sincerity, but since that wasn't working anyway, he no longer gave a shit. In fact, it was all he could do to keep his fangs from sliding down, he was that pissed. The temptation to grab the woman and haul her bodily across the top of her counter was very strong. But the waiting room was not empty. There would be witnesses, and then there would be trouble—serious trouble, too, if Norris heard about it. So he bit down his anger, shoved his hands in his pockets, and stalked away, out of the waiting room and down the corridor.

Then he ducked back into the men's room, which was fortunately otherwise empty. Well, so much for doing it the easy way. Fortunately, he was Mekhet, and there was more than one way to find out what he had come to learn. It wasn't easy to go from full visibility to none, but it beat having to tangle with the hospital bureaucracy.

The lights hurt his eyes far less with his shades on, and the receptionist didn't even look up as he sauntered past her station. He gave her the finger as he went by.

He had to wait only a minute or two before someone came out of the swinging doors to the intensive care unit beyond. Stepping aside to avoid a collision, he then ducked quickly inside before the door swung closed.

Once inside the IC unit, it took him only a few minutes to learn Julie's status, by overhearing a conversation between one of the doctors and a man Loki assumed to be her father. Diagnosis: as expected, Julie was seriously ill with the so-called Muskegon virus. Prognosis: critical. Loki had to slip as close as he dared to hear some of their words. The doctor's voice was low, modulated, concerned. Her father's voice was strained, desperately worried for his little girl, perhaps more worried than he wanted his little girl's mother to realize.

The door to Julie's room was ajar. Loki slipped inside, silent and unseen, to stand beside her bed.

She was surrounded by machines, tubes, and diagnostic displays, an IV in her arm, and some plastic mask over her lower face to help her breathe. Loki could hear her heartbeat, slow and labored, even without the monitor. He could smell the perspiration on her skin, feel the heat of her fever. Her face was pale, eyes closed, tendrils of hair sticking to her cheeks.

You could have stopped it, you know. His conscience always kicked in at the worst possible times, and this was one of them. *You could have interrupted them, given him something*

else to focus on. You could have told Norris your suspicions when you learned his name. She didn't need to suffer to prove your case.

But I needed proof, he argued. This is proof. I can stop him now. She'll be the last one.

Will she? Are you sure?

He wasn't sure, not yet. But he'd make sure. For her sake, and Kimberly's, and Jillian's, and the rest. "I'm sorry, sweetheart," he whispered, touching her hand. Her skin was hot and clammy. "I'll get him. He won't hurt anyone else."

Her hand moved slightly under his. He looked down.

Where her hand had lain, against the white hospital sheet, was a black crow feather.

Shit.

Loki left her room, dodging a nurse on the way. At first he headed for the exit, and then he stopped, turned, and looked down the corridor, the doors on either side. While he was here, might as well indulge himself with a few more questions.

A half-hour later, he had his answers. This ward contained forty-eight patients suffering from some version of the Muskegon encephalitis virus. Forty-eight confirmed cases, only a quarter of whom qualified as elderly, who might logically be the most vulnerable. The rest were younger, otherwise healthier. And over half of the forty-eight were classified as critical. Julie was one of them.

It was theoretically possible, of course, that Raven could have been responsible for infecting all of them. Possible, but unlikely. Somehow, he just couldn't picture Raven traveling all over the city, biting a dozen or more random people a night.

It was far more likely, however, that at least some of them had been infected by someone else. That meant that Raven wasn't the only blister out there, and Loki's hunt had only just begun.

It also meant that either a lot more patients had been admitted to the hospital in just the past couple of days, or the real number of possible Kindred-spread virus cases represented one of those little tidbits of information that Norris had decided the Hounds didn't need to know.

Fuck.

Loki headed out, slipping past the receptionist in the waiting area without a second glance. Damn Norris and his stick-up-the-ass secrecy! There were times that trusting your own fucking people might actually help them get the fucking job done—

"But if the virus isn't natural in origin, that is, if it's supernatural—"

Loki stopped abruptly, his attention refocusing, trying to identify the speakers. There, in the coffee shop—three twenty-something mortals, sitting close together, huddled conspiratorially over coffee mugs and the remains of sandwiches. The speaker was a petite pixie of a girl with a heart-shaped face and a stylishly unruly mop of red curls.

"There's no if, Glorianna," her companion, a lanky, earnest young Asian with curly dark hair and wire-framed glasses, assured her. "I know it's supernatural. Trust me on that."

"All right," the girl agreed. "I'm willing to accept your expertise, at least for the moment. So I suppose the real question is where did the virus come from, and how is it getting around?"

janet trautvetter

Loki moved silently closer, checking the gift shop window as he passed, making sure he could see nothing of his own reflection in it—then they shouldn't be able to see him either. Just the same, he didn't try to get too close. The third member of their little group, a black-clad goth with hair so blond it was nearly white, seemed more alert and wary of possible eavesdroppers than his companions. Fortunately, if Loki extended his senses in their direction, he could hear them just fine from here.

The Asian seemed indifferent to their surroundings, intent on his topic. "Exactly. And I can't even begin to determine that without much more real information than I've got right now. I'd need to run some tests on the blood and spinal fluid extracts from some of the victims, for starters."

"Well, then, fine," the girl said. "Could you test it here, or would you need to take it back to a lab or something? Are you equipped for that kind of analysis?"

"We have everything we need back at the Lotus," the Asian assured her. "Thing is, we may be dealing with more than one strain. We should really test the whole ward if we can, and, for that many, we'll need to bring the samples back to the shop."

Shit. Just what the doctor hadn't ordered—exactly the kind of investigation that Norris didn't want. Did the virus show up in regular blood analysis? Loki had no idea. And who were these guys? Not hospital staff, that's for damned sure. It was possible they worked for Norris, or maybe even Marek, who was certainly able to afford mortal operatives and equally likely to not tell his fellow Hounds about them. But they hadn't mentioned an employer or superior yet, and Loki knew from experience that Kindred operatives didn't tend to take the initiative on dangerous, potentially illegal activities without prior authorization.

The girl cocked one eyebrow. "You're talking about stealing medical samples from a hospital."

"It's not stealing," the goth put in. "All right, technically it is, but for a good cause. If Bai can get enough samples to analyze, we might be able to pin down where the virus is coming from."

"Well, then," the girl said. "What's the plan? What do you need me to do?"

The two young men exchanged a glance across the table. "Honestly, you don't have to do anything," the Asian said. "I appreciate the offer, but you're under no obligation—"

"Nonsense," she said, briskly. She drew something out of her fanny pack—some kind of fancy combination cell phone/PDA. "My father helped your grandmother, I can help you. And then maybe you'll be able to help me as well. Just let me know what the plan is—you do have a plan, don't you?"

"Actually, I was planning to improvise," drawled the goth, leaning back in his chair. "You got a better idea, I'm all ears."

"Then I suggest you use them and listen. Now. The first things we need are the patient names and numbers from the hospital's database, so you know which samples to actually take, but that's the easy part. Second, we need to locate where the samples are actually stored before they're sent out to the lab."

"I work in a fucking hospital, sweetcakes. I know where they keep the lab samples—"

She ignored him. "Third—it would be a very good idea if we could make sure you won't get caught—"

Loki disagreed. Making sure they got caught seemed like a very good idea, and the most efficient way of thwarting their plan he could imagine.

The three would-be blood thieves broke up after their initial discussion. Loki followed the two young men, whose primary topics of whispered conversation (once their female co-conspirator was out of earshot) varied between the Asian's worry over his sick grandmother, and the goth's dislike of the way the red-haired girl had just, in his words, "barged in and fucking taken over" where she wasn't wanted. The incipient argument ceased, however, when the two got down to business of infiltrating the lower levels of the hospital. They proved themselves very adept at acquiring orderly uniforms and ID badges, and walking blithely right by hospital staff who never challenged them. The goth seemed to know where they were going. The Asian had a tiny earpiece receiver with which he could communicate with their distant partner, who somehow made it possible for them to know when the testing lab was empty of other hospital employees, have their stolen ID badges programmed to allow them access, and the names of patients whose test samples would be of primary interest.

It occurred to Loki, much later, of course, that that should have tipped him off about them right away, but no—he wasn't thinking they were anything more than they appeared.

Once the two miscreants were inside the lab, looking for their samples, Loki made a convincing call to hospital security on his cell phone, and when he saw the security officers actually coming down the corridor, he pulled the fire alarm for good measure. *Let's see you talk your way out of that.* He slipped back upstairs again, chuckling to himself, imagining their expressions of dismay when faced with all the scrutiny the Chicago Police Department could provide upon their naughty little nocturnal activities.

Calling it a good night's work, Loki sauntered out of the hospital's main doors, and headed for the El, and home.

The feeling started as a tickle in the back of his mind, an uneasiness hard to identify and without any obvious reason. There wasn't much in the way of pedestrian traffic at this hour. The stores for which the Magnificent Mile was best known had long since closed.

Loki paused on the corner of Michigan Avenue, taking advantage of the intermittent but swiftly moving traffic to glance casually around him. Nothing obvious, not so much as a cruising cop, within sight. A homeless woman, head pillowed on the sack of her odd belongings, slept on a bus stop bench. Passing cars, heading home for the condos of the North Shore, whizzed by, blind to all but the next traffic light. And yet the feeling persisted, the sense of not being alone, of someone watching him.

Cautiously, using his hand to shade his eyes from the streetlamps, he sharpened his senses, wary for anything out of the ordinary. He could hear the homeless sleeper's snoring, and the slow, even beat of her heart. He could spot rats scurrying along the gutter and pick out the last embers of a discarded cigarette butt winking out against the pavement. But no sign of crows—a fact he noted with a considerable degree of relief—and no sign of Kindred, or anything else worthy of concern.

Yeah, like the Unholy is really gonna be lurking around Neiman-Marcus, just waiting for the midnight specials. Get a grip.

He kept going another block, taking one last look around before he skipped down the stairs to the Red Line station below.

Still, the feeling refused to fade. Loki pulled the shadows close around him, passing unseen through the station, down the stairs to the platform. Only three other late-night travelers waited there. None of them noticed him.

The train pulled in a few minutes later. Loki scanned each car as it passed, looking for other Kindred, but this train, at least, had no other hunters aboard. He got on the last car, sat near the back, ignoring the handful of mortal passengers. Once again, he let his vision shift, this time even further, until the three mortals at the other end of the car were warmly pulsing centers of heat, and the car's interior was lit by their living auras. As the train began to pull out, he glanced back along the way he had come.

There were faintly glowing footprints on the platform that marked a path from the stairs to the edge, right where this very car had stopped. A sudden knot twisted in his belly. He spun around and checked the floor of the car behind him, and found his wildest and most unpleasant thought confirmed. Those were his own tracks, his own footsteps marked in a luminescent silvery blue.

Fuck!

He sat down and all but wrenched his feet out of the boots he wore. First he examined the soles of the boots themselves—nothing unusual there. Then, leaving the boots where they were, he cautiously walked down the center of the car in his socks, only to turn and see the faintly glowing imprint of his feet on the floor. Bare feet produced the same result. So it wasn't the boots—it was him.

Don't panic, he told himself, dodging out of the way as the train came to a stop at the next station, settling himself back in his back corner and pulling his boots back on again. *Think, dammit. What's the deal here? What the fuck's going on?*

The doors closed, and the train moved on into darkness. Loki stared out the window, and then froze. His reflection stared back at him, blurred and indistinct, except for the gargoyle image on his T-shirt, which was sharp and clear, and limned with the palest of silvery blue light.

Even when he concentrated on pulling the shadows around him, and saw his reflected image fade into obscurity, his extended senses could still pick out the faintly illuminated shape of the gargoyle.

Shit. Loki peeled out of the shirt, dropped it on the seat beside him, and was relieved to now see nothing in the darkness of the window, even when he reached out and touched the glass. He had to find an unmarked section of floor to test his footprints on, but those, too, seemed clear—at least, he wasn't leaving any visible traces that he could see.

So, someone had bugged his T-shirt. How fucking cute. Now what?

Someone's following me. Loki felt his fangs pressing downwards in response to the growing irritation. *Well, fuck that.* He could just abandon the shirt, of course, but that meant running away without any answers, and that didn't appeal to him. He wanted a piece of whoever was behind this, and he wanted to make sure they weren't going to be able to follow him any further.

The train began its braking for the next station, the recording rasping out of the aging speakers. "This is Belmont."

Belmont. Loki grinned. *You wanna follow me on my own turf, asshole? Be my guest. Let's go play hide and go seek.*

He pulled the T-shirt back on, and left the train, heading for the streets below.

Belmont would have been a lively, interesting place earlier in the evening—coffee shops, music stores, tattoo parlors, and alternative clothing shops, a long row of two- and three-story storefronts and once-stylish apartments not yet yuppified. Now, even the gay bars over on Halsted had closed, and only a few lights showed in upstairs windows. There were still occasional cars going by—traffic on Chicago's streets might sometimes slow to a trickle, but it never actually stopped—but the sidewalks were pretty much deserted, with only the infrequent late-night straggler, heading to or from the El into the wee hours.

Loki put his shades on again to protect his eyes from the glare of the streetlamps, glancing back to make sure he was still leaving a trail for whoever it was to follow. No one else had gotten off the train, at least that he could see. The possibility that he wouldn't be able to see whoever it was following the trail also occurred to him, but he dismissed it. The bugged T-shirt implied tracking, not tailing. And the next train wouldn't come through for at least ten minutes. He had time to lay his trap.

He ambled up the sidewalk, even stopping to look in store windows. *Just passing through. Not thinking about anyone following my ass, no, not a care in the world.*

Halfway to Clark, there was a narrow alley that split off to the right. He took it. Down between two buildings, past the parking lots in the back, to where the alley met the main alley that paralleled the street, where all the backyards and parking lots met. Loki turned right, heading back toward the tracks. Nice and dark back here. The only real light came from the south end of the station platform above. A lot more shadows. He walked up to where the alley dead-ended, under the overpass of the tracks. And then he took off his T-shirt, and tossed it back deep into the darkness.

He carefully walked backward, treading in his own faintly glowing footprints, then jumped as far to the side as he could, before checking to make sure he wasn't leaving any trail behind. He wasn't. Good.

Now it was just a matter of time and patience. Pulling the shadows around him, moving as silently as he could, he found himself a good vantage point on a second-floor fire escape where he could watch the alleyway, and hunkered down to wait.

As it turned out, she was only one train behind him. He recognized her immediately: the red-haired girl from the hospital, walking cautiously down the alleyway, following his trail. She held her electronic gizmo in her hand—it seemed to have some kind of tiny glowing screen, though Loki couldn't see what the screen displayed.

She was also clearly on her guard, looking all around her, taking cover behind a parked car and carefully surveying the back alley before continuing on, keeping a row of cars between herself and the open length of the alley and the trail she followed.

Loki let her get through the entire parking lot before silently descending from his vantage point and falling in behind her. His fangs slid down, almost instinctively. Although he had fed earlier that evening, he could feel the hunger rising up from somewhere deep in his belly. He could smell her blood, hear the pounding of her heart, imagine the taste of her blood, spiced with adrenaline. It was not his usual style of hunting, to stalk and pounce from behind. Not with chicks, anyway—and yet the temptation to do so now was almost unbearable. It would be so easy. The Beast all but trembled with eagerness for fresh blood, taken in the sudden violence of the hunt, rather than the slow dance of seduction.

Her aura flickered with deep blues, edged with orange, as she stepped closer to the dark shadows of the underpass. A tiny light flickered in her hand, her PDA emitting a pale, weak beam that combed through the trash and storm debris under the steel and concrete pylons, picking up the faintly reflective shape of the gargoyle from the crumpled black fabric of his discarded shirt.

"Shit," she muttered.

Loki bent, scooped up a bit of broken concrete from a weed-choked break in the pavement, then flung it across the alley. It made a sharp *crack* when it hit the fence on the opposite side.

She jumped, turning sharply to face the noise, sending the beam of her little flashlight in that direction. He heard her heart rate speed up, and a brighter wave of orange shimmered through her aura, followed by a myriad scattering of sparkles, almost like tiny stars. So close—only a few steps away, and she was looking away from him now. So easy....

Above them, a rumbling grew—a train pulling into the station. *No one will even hear her scream*, the Beast whispered.

No. Loki forced himself to take a deep, slow breath. *Not like this. Not like a fucking mugger, jumpin' from behind—*

A gust of displaced air from the incoming train sent a fall of debris wafting down into the alley. No, not just debris—feathers. A swirling, fluttering rain of black feathers.

"*Fuck!*" Loki jumped backward, so as to avoid any touch of the unnatural rain.

At the same time, his quarry spun around herself, and saw him. The look of sudden panic on her face was very satisfying.

Loki smiled, which exposed the tips his fangs. "Looking for someone, sweetheart?"

The narrow beam of her light—coming from the same device she'd been carrying in her hand—blossomed into the painful white intensity of a spotlight, searing his dark-sensitive vision. With a hoarse cry, he covered his eyes with one hand, and lunged toward her, or where he'd seen her last, seeking to tackle her bodily and knock the source of the light out of her hands.

He almost succeeded. His grip on her wrist sent the light-source gadget flying off into the darkness, the light winking out as it left her hand. But before he could follow up on his advantage, she twisted out of his grasp, kicking his feet out from under him and sending him sprawling, to land hard on his backside on the unforgiving pavement.

Why, you little bitch—Loki rolled away and lurched to his feet again, blinking furiously to clear the huge dancing white splotches out of his vision. Fangs down, he snarled, answering her physical challenge with his own. Niceties no longer mattered—all that mattered was the hunger and the blood.

Her face was pale, and she was breathing hard, but she didn't run. Instead she raised her hands, spoke words in a language he didn't recognize. The PDA flew out of the darkness into her hand, while with the other she reached up and made a gesture toward the tracks above their heads. Something sparkled between her fingers.

Idiot, you fucking IDIOT—It was all he had time for, one brief second of self-recrimination for not seeing the obvious, when it had been right in front of his nose the entire time. *She's a MAGE, they're all*—

There was a loud *crackle-pop* from above, and then a flare of blinding white light as the lightning struck him, arcing down from the third rail above. All Loki's muscles went suddenly rigid. A jolt of incredible heat seared through every nerve in his body, burning him from the inside out. His vision went totally white, his mouth filled with blood as his jaw clamped down, fangs piercing his own tongue. He dimly remembered falling, his skull impacting the pavement, the stabbing of a thousand needles as his muscles twitched and convulsed with the aftershocks.

Then a new pain—stabbing through muscle and between his ribs, splinters embedding themselves in his flesh as she leaned all her weight down on the shard of wood she held, forcing it through to his heart. The numbness that spread outward through his body then seemed almost a relief. He barely had time to panic, to realize what was happening to him, before the darkness rose up and swept him away.

He had witnessed the lottery before, but not like this. In the rituals he had seen (though he was not yet eligible to participate), all candidates stained small, wooden markers with their own blood, whispering their prayers and desires to the Crone. The markers were gathered in a single vessel, and a mortal woman (in theory, a virgin sacrifice, though Loki had never asked how she was chosen) would choose one from the bowl and offer it to the priestess. The priestess then would seek the chosen out of the crowd, and draw him forward . . .

He did not recognize her. Too short to be Rowen or Moyra, too old to be Bella or any of the other priestesses he knew by name. She wore a black-feathered mask with a sharp black beak, and behind the mask she had yellow eyes. Her robes were shapeless, black and feathered, and adorned with thousands of tiny bones. She walked by the others gathered there without seeing them, came right to him, and held out her closed hand, slowly opening her gnarled talons to show his own blood pooling in her hand.

It was like watching television without a remote, unable to change the channel, change what he was watching, or even kill the sound. He bent—he could not stop himself—and tasted the blood in her hand. It was not entirely his own, he knew that as soon as he tasted it, but there was nothing he could do.

The mortal girl came to him. "Blood is the only true sacrifice," she whispered, and kissed him. Hunger already rising in him, he kissed her back. She was warm, sweet, eager, her pale skin adorned with writing, thousands of names carved into her flesh. He drank deeply of her, and still hungry, drank even more, and more, and yet her veins did not run dry, though her flesh grew cool and then cold beneath his hands. Her form crumbled in his arms, until all he held were feathers that slipped between his fingers.

All around them the city burned. Loki could feel the heat of the approaching fire, hear the roaring just outside the windows, the screams of people fleeing for the safety of the lake. He couldn't remember how they had gotten to this house, what he was doing here. The lottery chip lay on the polished surface of the table, but it was not his name inscribed on the disk.

"There must be some mistake—" He turned around, to face the mysterious priestess again. "It's not my name. It's not me!"

There was chanting from somewhere, low and unintelligible under the tumult outside the windows. Already he could smell smoke; perhaps the roof was already ablaze.

The priestess stepped forward. Behind her stood the Horned King, clad in a cloak of bloody furs, his mask a skull with great black pits where his eyes should be, and crowned by a pair of branching antlers. In his hands, he held a bloodstained scythe.

"Those who look will see," the priestess intoned. "Those who see, must act. Blood is the only true sacrifice."

"What the fuck are you talking about? Don't you smell it, the fucking house is on fire! We gotta get out, call nine-one-one—"

But he could not run. He could not move. Cold hands took him, laid him on the table, as though on an altar. Overhead, the ceiling was even painted like the night sky, with stars sparkling in the light of the chandelier.

"Blood is the only true sacrifice," the Horned King whispered. But there were eyes behind the skull mask now, blue-gray eyes hard and cold as stone.

"Blood is the only true sacrifice," the Chorus echoed, drawing closer. They were not wearing masks, but Loki didn't recognize a single face. And they looked wrong—some pale and bloated as if from drowning, some with faces pinched and drawn from pain, some charred and still smoking, barely recognizable as having once been human, and some sporting the bloody wounds that had caused their deaths. They all looked hungry.

And all around them, the crows gathered, flying in through open windows, perching on the chandelier, on furniture, on heads and shoulders of the ghastly Chorus, all watching him with glowing red eyes.

"Wait—" Loki wanted to say, but he couldn't speak; his lips and tongue were sluggish and wouldn't obey him anymore. "Wait—it's not me, look again, it's not supposed to be me—"

"What is given freely is accepted and blessed; what is due and withheld shall be taken without mercy," the priestess said, as the Horned King stepped up beside her, raising the scythe. "So let it be done."

The scythe came down, and Loki's chest exploded in agonizing pain.

Pain woke him, suddenly and abruptly. Loki's first instinct was to curl up into a fetal ball around the source of the pain, the gaping wound in the center of his chest, but that was impossible. He lay on his back, hanging spread-eagled across some kind of frame, with manacles on wrists and ankles. There were figures standing around him. His second instinct was to break free and get the hell out of there. Pain and panic lent strength to his limbs. He screamed in fury, fangs bared, yanking hard against his bonds.

He was vaguely aware of the figures to his left flinching slightly; he could hear wood creaking somewhere around him. But he lacked decent leverage, and even after his chest muscles had healed somewhat, he could not break himself free.

His captors simply watched as he spent precious energy trying to fight the bonds they'd placed on him, as the unforgiving metal of the handcuffs cut deeply into his wrists. For some reason, their silence irritated him even further, as if his attempts to escape amused them.

Get a grip. Stay calm. One hand free, see if you can get one hand free. Think. Focus. Distract them.

He focused all his ire on the nearest of his captors—who happened to be the Asian geek. *Of course. Her accomplices.* "Fuck you!" he snarled, letting himself hang limp in the bonds for the moment. "Is this how you get your fucking jollies, dickhead?"

Asian geek and the red-haired girl exchanged glances. Loki could see their colors—he'd rattled them. *Good.* "You want a ride, bitch?" he snarled at the girl. "Let me go, and I'll show you—"

"That's enough, Mr. Fischer." The voice was stern, commanding, and familiar—very familiar, though he hadn't heard it in ten years. "I don't know where you got that mouth," she continued, "but you'll keep a civil tongue in your head. In case you haven't noticed, you are not in control of this situation."

Loki's head snapped around, staring up in disbelief at the black woman in the gray business suit standing over him on the other side, too solid to be a ghost, her glare still capable of putting a check on his tongue. As if he were still a seventeen-year-old truant and almost-juvenile delinquent, caught out after curfew, by the only adult who still gave a damn when he broke the rules.

The black-clad blond goth stood beside her, looking extremely self-satisfied.

"Shit," Loki whispered, because it just had to come out. *This has got to be a fucking torpor nightmare. I hope I wake up soon. Please, God, let me wake up soon.*

"Yeah, that pretty much sums it up," the goth agreed, and shot a look across at the Asian geek. "See, I told you it'd hold."

Loki was sorely tempted to put all his strength and some extra blood into one left-handed lunge—but with Gretchen McBride standing over him like that, a lot of his ability to focus had just gotten shot to hell. And then the next connection was even more disturbing. *Mages. They're all mages. Even McBride.*

I am so fucked.

"I see you comprehend what's going on, Mr. Fischer," McBride continued sternly. "Now. Are we going to have a civilized conversation, or are you going to stay tied down there?"

Well, if they were going to offer him a choice.… Loki took a ragged breath—ragged because there was still damage to his chest muscles, though the act of actually breathing, even just enough to speak, tended to help calm him down.

"Civilized means what, exactly?" he asked, focusing now on regaining his cool. "Cut me loose, and I don't rip anyone's face off? And you don't turn me into a toad?"

McBride didn't even crack a smile. "You don't rip anyone's face off. We don't turn you into charcoal." She glanced around at her younger colleagues, none of whom seemed inclined to interrupt. "We sit down in chairs and sofas, and we talk about this little situation that we've all found ourselves in."

Loki tried not to think about charcoal, and took one more deep breath. "Okay, deal," he agreed. "No face-ripping, no charcoal."

She nodded. "Let him up, Gwyn." The black-clad blond dug a ring of keys out of a pocket and began to unfasten Loki's bonds. "Baihu, if you don't mind, I think we could all use some tea."

It hurt like hell to pull himself up to a sitting position, and then to his feet, but apart from the bloody mess of his chest, which was partially healed now, and what fighting the handcuffs had done to his wrists, he was apparently not too much the worse for wear.

They were in someone's apartment—Asian geek's, he guessed, from the Chinese calligraphy scrolls on the walls and the fact that he was the one now putting the kettle on. Spartan and neatly kept, the apartment was furnished in an eclectic collection of family hand-me-downs, including the futon couch on which Loki had been restrained, and which Gwyn and the red-haired girl were now putting back to its usual configuration when not being used as a Kindred torture device.

The windows were only a few feet away, but he could tell they weren't at street level. Third or fourth floor, at least, so jumping would be a bad idea, and the fire escape would be slow, assuming he could even get to it. No, if he was going to make a break for it, he'd have to time it just right.

"The bathroom's in there, if you'd like to… uh, clean up a bit," the Asian said, a bit awkwardly. "I could get you a T-shirt, if you'd like…."

Loki found his hand going almost self-consciously to the bloody mess of his still-healing bare chest. "Yeah, okay," he agreed, aware of all their eyes on him. What the hell, might as well go along for now. And then, a bit belatedly, "Thanks."

"No problem."

What the fuck have you gotten yourself into?

Loki was grateful for a few minutes of privacy, in which he was able to ascertain that none of his extremities were scorched, despite the extreme voltage they'd sustained. The chest wound seemed to be the worst remaining injury, and that was nearly healed, as were the places on his wrists where the metal of the handcuffs had bit into his flesh. It was just a matter of cleaning up what remained of the drying blood from his skin. Healing had been costly, though. He'd definitely have to hunt later, or take Damien up on his offer. Meanwhile, he was just relieved to still be in one piece, and not be stretched out like a trussed chicken.

Gretchen McBride. It had been years since he'd even thought of her. There had been a time, back when he still breathed, when she had been the only adult who'd still given him shit when he skipped school or got into trouble. The only one who had faith in him, the only one who had cared. But that had been years ago, too, and there wasn't anything he owed her any more.

If the bathroom had offered an easy exit, however, he might have been tempted by it.

What are you afraid of, Loki?

Well, until a few minutes ago, he would have put being held staked and helpless by a coven of mages pretty high on the list. But so far, so good—and he wasn't helpless anymore.

And besides, if by chance they knew anything more than Norris did about this damned virus—well, it was Loki's job to find that out, wasn't it? Maybe Norris had access to this kind of information. Maybe not. But, in any case, it was to Loki's advantage to learn all he could.

The Asian geek had left him a T-shirt proclaiming some nerd-chic slogan on the doorknob, but at least it was black. Well, it wasn't as though he was ever going to wear it to Elysium. Loki pulled it on over his head, and went to join the party.

"You've looked better, Mr. Fischer," was McBride's stern observation as he reclaimed his seat.

He shrugged. "I've looked worse."

Her mouth twitched slightly. "If you say so. Let's start with introductions. Trey Fischer. Baihu, our host for this evening. Gwyn. And Glorianna. And contrary to what you might recall, *my* name is Tiaret. Now, why don't you tell us how you came to lock my colleagues in the hospital testing lab?"

For some reason, the inherent accusation in her question irritated him. "I came from behind," he quipped. "Very quietly. The rest was easy."

"Mr. Fischer. Might I remind you—"

"Contrary to what you might recall, my name is Loki," he corrected her, flatly. "Trey Fischer is dead."

He regretted it the moment the words left his lips. There was a brief flicker of unguarded emotion across his former social worker's face, that rippled through the colors of her aura before she clamped down with her usual iron control. Anger. Regret. And guilt. *Guilt? For what?*

"Loki. A Norse god." The red-haired girl, Glorianna, had her little gadget out again, balanced on the arm of the chair she had perched herself in. "The trickster who's supposed to start Ragnarok. How apropos."

"Very well… Loki." Tiaret's nails tapped on the arm of her chair. "What *were* you doing in the hospital, then?"

"Visiting a sick friend."

"Tiaret—please." Asian geek—Baihu—interrupted. "Look. Uh, Loki. You must have overheard some of our discussion, right? You didn't just shut us in there for a lark. You knew why we were in there."

"Yeah," Loki admitted, warily. "I heard all that."

"So that implies you must have had a reason to do that, even as we had a reason to be in there. You didn't want us to succeed—you didn't want us to get those samples. Why not?"

"Look, I'm sorry about your grandmother, okay?" Loki said, trying to sound sincere. He'd seen a little, old Chinese lady in the ward. She had been one of the critical ones, too. "But it's one thing, you know, to try to help her—she probably wouldn't mind, even if she didn't understand what you were up to. But all those other people—well, it's an invasion of privacy and all. And you could fuck up the tests for everyone else—"

"Bullshit," Gwyn interjected. "What the fuck do you care about anyone else's privacy? You're a fucking vampire, you take samples without permission all the fucking time! Don't you?"

"It's not the same thing," Loki retorted, though he wasn't entirely sure he even convinced himself.

"But wait a minute. If the virus is usually spread by mosquitoes—" Glorianna said suddenly, looking up from the miniature screen of her gadget.

"Yeah, exactly. Mosquitoes aren't the only bloodsuckers in town, though, are they?" Gwyn pointed out. "That's it, isn't it, Fangs? That's the connection. That's what you didn't want us to find out."

Loki's fangs were already itching to come out, and that did it. "You don't have a fucking clue what you're talking about—"

"Enough!" Tiaret's sharp command was coupled with a single clap of her hands that resonated throughout the room like a sudden crack of thunder. "Enough. Gwyn, that civil tongue admonition applies to you as well. All of you. Do I make myself clear?"

Silence. Even Gwyn shut up. Loki forced his fangs to retract—anyone who could manage a thunderclap indoors could probably manage the lightning, too, and he didn't want a repeat experience of that.

janet trautvetter

"However," Tiaret continued, calmly, "Gwyn does have a valid point. The virus—at least one variant of it—does appear to be supernatural in origin. And, therefore, the possibility of a supernatural vector as well is a plausible conjecture."

"Oh, it's definitely supernatural," Baihu said. "The ritual proved that. At least the eight instances we were able to test, plus Granny's. It appears to be some kind of arcane mutation, I suppose would be the best description for it, of the original virus. Much more virulent, though, and faster-acting. And powerful—" He hesitated for a second, and then added, "My grandmother is a maga also—and she hasn't been sick a day in more than fifty years. We didn't think it was even possible for her to get sick anymore. And yet—this is strong enough to…" His voice grew strained, and trailed off.

"Forty-eight instances," Loki said. "In the ward," he added, when they all looked at him blankly. "I counted, how many were marked as having encephalitis. About half of them were considered critical. I saw your grandmother, I think."

"Forty-eight? Jesus," muttered Gwyn, who rubbed his forehead with one hand, as though something pained him. "I really didn't need to know that…. "

That was an odd reaction. "What?" Loki asked.

"Never mind him," Baihu said. "For what it's worth, I don't think a vampire could have created this thing. And it is created, by someone—a powerful magus, most likely, though I can't imagine why."

"Because you're not a sick, twisted little fuck, that's why," Gwyn pointed out. "But a vampire could spread it, couldn't he?"

"It's possible there's a Kindred—a vampire—that's spreading it, yeah," Loki admitted. "So we're looking into it. Believe it or not, we really don't want to draw that kind of attention to ourselves. That's what I was doing at the hospital. Trying to find out who it was, so he can be… dealt with."

"How would you know—how many vampires are there in Chicago, anyway?" Baihu asked.

"Process of elimination. Wait and see who gets sick. But I think I know who it is now. So he'll be taken care of." Loki ignored the second question. He didn't know the answer anyway.

"A lot of people could die during your process of elimination," Tiaret pointed out. "And what if there's more than one?"

"That's just the—" He hesitated, realizing that Norris most likely would not approve of his spilling the beans here. Then again, what Norris didn't know—assuming there was anything Norris didn't already know—wouldn't bite him in the ass later.

"Is there more than one?" Tiaret asked. "Is that what you're saying?"

"I don't know yet," he admitted. "But there's just too many of them for one source, considering how fast it works. Even if he was fucked up enough to be doing it on purpose, he'd have to be running his ass ragged, those people were from all over the city. And—no offense," he added to Baihu, "but he'd have to be batshit crazy to go after someone like your grandma. So either there's more than one, which is bad, or there's more than one way to catch this thing, which could be worse."

"What if it is the mosquitoes?" Glorianna added. "You know, if this mutated virus gets into the natural ecosystem, the usual vector cycle between the mosquitoes and the crows? Would it spread like the natural virus does? Across the country?"

"Wouldn't that require a mosquito to bite a vampire? Do vampires even worry about other bloodsuckers, anyway?" Gwyn frowned.

"Mosquitoes?" Shit. Loki hadn't even thought of that. "No, they never bother us. They don't like the way we smell, or something. I don't know. The crows are dying right and left, but I thought even the regular virus could do that."

"Yes, crows are the natural barometer," Glorianna said. "Big die-offs among the crow population indicate how far the virus has spread."

"Maybe we can help with the process of elimination," Baihu suggested. "I'm not familiar with the properties of vampire blood, but if I can isolate the virus traces in human blood and spinal fluid, I should be able to do it in vampires, too. Then we'd know if a particular vampire was a carrier or not."

"I didn't think it showed up on blood tests," Loki said, doubtfully. "Or else they'd have it in the lab reports on the victims. Which it's not, far as I know." At least, it hadn't been in the lab reports Norris had shown them.

"But we're talking about magic here," Baihu pointed out, pushing his glasses back up his nose with one finger. "Not biochemistry. The laws of reality are subject to change."

That was a good point, Loki had to admit. "I could look into it," he agreed. "Have to ask the right people, though—the powers-that-be get rather prickly about shit like that. But I'll pass the message on, at least."

"It would help," Baihu went on, "if I had a sample of your blood to start with."

A dozen alarms went off in Loki's head. He remembered reading a story once—or maybe it was in a movie or something, he wasn't sure—about how people used to be careful to burn their hair trimmings and nail parings to keep witches from casting spells on them. As Baihu had said, the laws of reality were subject to change. "Uh, no, if it's all the same to you," Loki said. "Nothing personal—but we just met, okay?" *And I haven't got any to spare just now, anyway.*

Baihu actually chuckled. "I guess I can understand that," he said. "Okay, how about a phone number?"

"Where to?" Tiaret asked. "I'm guessing you don't live with your old man anymore."

Loki grimaced and shook his head. "No." He still wasn't sure why he had accepted the offer of a ride anyway. Not like there wasn't an El station in Chinatown, once he got his bearings on where the hell he was. "Any El station on the North Side's fine. I like my privacy. No offense."

"None taken." She pulled out of the parking space.

It took him back, riding in her car. Not the same car, or at least he didn't think it was. In ten years, even a social worker could get a new car. But it was like before, when she drove him home from the police station. She'd made them take the handcuffs off, too, and bought him lunch. And then she'd done exactly what she was doing now—raked him over with that stern Look of hers, and said absolutely nothing until the weight of the silence forced him to fill it up himself. Maybe it was a spell or something—he had no way of knowing. But that silence got him talking every fucking time.

"It wasn't your fault, you know," he said, finally. "What happened to me."

"What exactly did happen to you?"

janet trautvetter

"Well, you know how it is. Wrong place, wrong time," he temporized. "There was a girl. Sometimes bad shit just happens. Wasn't my idea, for whatever that's worth."

"Yes, there's entirely too much bad shit happening in this city." There was a new bitterness in her voice he didn't remember hearing before. "I see it every day. I saw something even back then—a shadow on your future I couldn't identify. I'm sorry I couldn't prevent it from overtaking you."

That caught his attention. "You knew something like this was gonna happen to me? Why didn't you say something about it then?"

"Would you have believed me?"

She had a point there. "Probably not," he had to admit. "Do you see things like that often?"

"Often enough, especially in my line of work. I do what I can. Sometimes it isn't enough." She made a turn on to Clark, heading north. "I'm afraid I don't know very much about vampires. Other than what I see in the movies."

Loki snorted. "Well, most of what's in the movies is bullshit. You know, the coffins, crosses, garlic, all that crap. I knew one guy who slept in a coffin, but he was crazy."

She gave him a measured look. "And the blood?"

He looked away. "That part… the movies got mostly right."

"I see."

Now that he'd mentioned it, the smell of her blood was getting to him, in the enclosed space of the car. Hunger gnawed at him, and he reminded himself of Damien's promise. The Skullery wasn't far, just another half-mile up the road. He could hold out until then.

"I don't go around killing people, if that's what you mean," he said. "I don't need that much, anyway."

"I never saw you as a murderer, Loki," she replied evenly. "Though I'm sure the same can't be said of many of your associates. How do you get along—with the others, I mean? Rumor has it that what passes for vampire society is pretty nasty."

"I do okay. I know some people. I do what I have to; they mostly leave me alone."

"Is that how you came to play virus investigator? So they'd leave you alone?"

"Something like that." Ah, getting close now. "You can let me off anywhere here, that'd be great."

"All right," she said, and clicked her turn signal on. "You have the phone numbers, right?"

"Yeah, I got 'em. Don't expect me to answer during the day, though."

"I suppose not." She pulled over to the curb, flipped her hazard lights on.

"Thanks for the lift," he said, and reached for the door handle. Only a few blocks to the Skullery from here, fantastic.

"Loki—" She reached out, caught his wrist, and he jumped, forcing his fangs to retract, trying not to snarl in her face. She let go almost immediately. "I should tell you," she continued. "That shadow… it's still there. Or it's back, I'm not sure which."

It took a second to sink in, what she was saying. "You mean, like you saw before? What does it mean?"

"I don't know, unfortunately. It's never that clear. Be careful."

Well, at least he believed her now. "Right. Thanks."

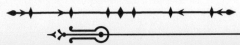

The Skullery's dance floor was black and silver, patches of light reflecting brightly off silver buckles, studs, or glitter, surrounded by murky shadows, deep blacks of velvet and leather, the gleam of high-gloss vinyl. Loki avoided the direct touch of the light, preferring to study his prey from the cooler, more comfortable shadows.

Prey. Something in him still sometimes balked at describing them so, at least when he wasn't hungry. Tonight, the label sharpened his appetite, his perceptions—as his gaze slid from one bobbing, swaying dancer to another, looking for a likely mark. A single girl, dancing alone, but open for some interaction—he wasn't in the mood to deal with a jealous date. The younger, the better—there. His gaze settled on her, watched where her eyes traveled, where she focused her attentions.

He liked the way she moved, the way she closed her eyes, the soft roundness to her face that belied the makeup and way the black velveteen clung to her form. Her hair was twisted up on top of her head with a spray of black feathers, baring her throat. Nice. Young, pretty, and alone. Almost too young, but it wasn't his job to keep the under-aged urchins out. Perfect.

Loki slipped out of the shadows and up onto the floor. He swayed to the rhythm without thinking, feeling the pulse up through the floor, reverberating off the ceiling and walls, resonating through undead flesh and bone. Throbbing bass, sharp repetitive beat from the percussion pulsed through his ribcage, the pounding of the music substituting for the throbbing of a silent heart.

Eye contact first. An exchange of smiles, interest and acceptance communicated without words. He moved closer, dancing with her now, within arms' reach, though not yet touching. Her movements were sinuous, seductive, hips swaying, pert little breasts stuck out. She danced closer, meeting his gaze with a smile of invitation. Thus encouraged, Loki let his hands rest on her hips. Her arms slid up and around his neck. She had eyes of two different colors, one blue and one brown, and she wasn't wearing contacts, as far as he could tell. She also wore an ornate jet brooch that caused the neckline to sag forward a bit from its weight, allowing him an occasional tantalizing glimpse down between her breasts. *Nice.* Loki breathed in her scent, savored the mix of feminine sweat, makeup, and body lotion, listened to the rapid patter of her heart. *Oh, yeah. Very nice.*

When the song ended, he drew her gently from the floor toward the stairs, trying hard to restrain his eagerness. "Come on," he said, offering his most earnest smile. "I've got member privileges upstairs."

"Cool," she said, and followed, holding his hand.

One of Damien's girls, had to be, though he couldn't recall seeing her before. Well, Damien had promised him a freebie, and tonight he could certainly use it. "Yeah, I know what you mean," he agreed, and led her past the bouncer and up the stairs.

She stopped on the landing, pulling him back. "This is good," she said, and ran her fingers across his collar bone suggestively. "I know what you want."

"Do you?" Loki asked. He stepped closer, let his hands slide up her arms to her shoulders, then caressed her cheek gently with the backs of his fingers. She smiled, so he bent down and kissed her, savoring the sweetness of warm lips against his own, a warm and pliant body in his arms. As she responded, he slid his hands down her backbone, pulled her hips against his. One of her hands rested on his shoulder. *Very nice . . .*

There was a sharp, sudden scent of blood. "What—?" Loki broke the kiss, his eyes drawn to the tiny red beads now appearing in a line at the base of her throat. She held the jet brooch, pin outward, in her free hand.

"It's what you want, isn't it?" Softly, intently. Her heart was going like a jackhammer. "Isn't it?"

"Oh, baby," Loki murmured, and bent to capture those tiny drops with his tongue. His fangs were already extending; with that tiny taste, his hunger opened up like a vast empty well, almost painful in its intensity, and he abandoned any attempt at resisting it. Arms wrapping around her, he sank his fangs into the side of her throat. *Oh, baby, you know it.*

The Circle of the Crone had a number of gathering places scattered around the city. But for the major seasonal rites, for Solstice and Equinox and multi-coven rituals similar to this one, the Circle preferred to meet in the woodlands of the forest preserves, under the open sky.

There were no lights in the parking lot. Even the nearby streetlamps had been extinguished, and everyone drove without headlights. There were over a dozen cars parked there already by the time Loki and Damien arrived.

They could hear the drums as they approached, a low, deep, throbbing heartbeat in the night, one great heartbeat for all the ones that were now silent. *Dum-DUM. Dum-DUM. Dum-DUM. Dum-DUM. Dum-DUM.* Without thinking, Loki's feet found the rhythm of it. The drumbeat drew him in.

The path they followed wound through the trees and into a clearing where a great bonfire blazed on a hillside, beside an open picnic pavilion. That was what it would be in daytime, anyway. Tonight, the play of firelight and shadows, and the throb of the drums made it something else, something darker and more primitive. A medicine lodge perhaps, or ancient Celtic feast hall. The firelight was painfully bright to Loki's enhanced senses to look at directly, but if he squinted, he could make out dark figures dancing around it, daring a Kindred's natural terror of open flame to answer the challenge of the drums. He thought he recognized Moyra's slender form among them.

Most Acolytes had dressed for the occasion. Large group rites were rare, and offered opportunity for demonstrating one's particular beliefs and recruiting any newcomers to their own coven's practices. Moyra favored minimal clothing, body paint, and an owl-feathered mask. Damien preferred leather and multiple strands of beads, with amulets of carved stone, bone, teeth (some of them human), and fossilized amber, either woven into braids in his hair or around his neck. His bare arms sported spiraling bands of tattoos, mystical symbols and animal shapes intertwined.

Loki had gone for basic unadorned black: a well-worn pair of cargo pants with useful pockets, T-shirt, and a plain black hoodie that he left unzipped just enough to reveal the tattooed crescent below his collarbone. Even his black high-tops had black rubber soles. It was a combination designed to fade into shadows rather than stand out—the garb of a hunter, or a spy. He wasn't sure if that made him feel better about his real mission here tonight or not. The stake felt horribly conspicuous in the deep pocket along his thigh.

The altar, a huge, flat-topped boulder, sat on a rise of hill a little apart from the firelight. The altar already reeked of blood, both Kindred and mortal. The cracked and pitted surface was slick with it, and gleamed wetly in the flickering light of the torches. A tall, imposing figure stood beside the altar, clad in leather and fur, made even taller by the bear's head she wore as headdress and mask. Bear claws and amulets hung around her neck. In one hand, she held a staff with a brass snake twining around it, and topped by an ankh, with a number of brass rings suspended from the ankh's looped arms. In her other hand, she held a bone-handled bowie knife with a bloodstained blade.

Loki recognized her, felt the shiver of fear chill his blood from coming under the unblinking stare of a vampire decades older and more powerful in the Blood, even though he had seen her any number of times before. Rowen was the Hierophant, the highest-ranking priestess of the Crone in the city, and she had that effect on almost everyone. Even Maxwell treated her with respectful deference when she deigned to show up at court events.

Now the Gangrel priestess stared at him, then raised her hand—also stained with the blood of earlier offerings—and beckoned him forward.

Loki obeyed, pushing up the sleeves of his hoodie to bare his wrists and forearms. He stopped before her, and bowed his head, raising his two wrists together in front of him, palms up, in a gesture of submission and supplication.

Fortunately, Moyra had drilled him enough on the Liturgy so that he did not need to be thinking clearly to remember it. "In the service of the Crone, in the name of the Morrígan, Goddess of Battles, and Arawn the Horned King and Lord of the Underworld, I pledge my blood and my sustenance: the first blood of the hunt, the first fruit of the field, firstborn among all herds and chattel. Let my blood spilled now stand in promise of the offering yet to come."

"And if more is required?" Her voice was low, a bit rough, as though she didn't use it very often. What's more, her question was not in any section of the Liturgy Loki knew.

He raised his head, puzzled, uncertain of the correct response. Her eyes were shadowed behind the bear mask, her features hidden and impossible to read. He did not dare try to see the colors of her nimbus just then. "What?"

"Those who look will see. Those who see must act. What will your answer be?"

A trick question—what did it mean? If more what was required? Blood? Or something else? He hadn't a clue. None of this was in the rituals Moyra had taught him. "I don't know," he said finally.

The bowie knife came down, slashing deeply across his raised wrists. It hurt like hell, but somehow he managed not to cry out. He didn't know if this meant his answer had been acceptable or not.

Rowen raised the blade and drew a sign in the air, returning to the familiar lines of the Liturgy. "What is given freely is accepted and blessed; what is owed and withheld shall be taken without mercy. Slake first the thirst of the altar, and then you may slake your own."

Loki knelt, turned his bleeding wrists over, and laid the open wounds against the altar, adding several new dark glistening trails among those already staining the surface of the stone. When he could feel the wounds healing, he rose and stepped back again.

"The promise is made and witnessed," Rowen intoned. "So let it be done."

"So let it be done," Loki echoed, bowed slightly, and then made as dignified a retreat as possible, before she took it into her head to ask him anything else.

The throbbing heartbeat of the great drum had picked up in tempo, while other lighter drums added in a syncopated pattern around its steady pulse. Damien, long hair falling over tattooed shoulders, nodded in time while his fingers beat out a rapid rhythm on his dumbek. Beside him, a ivory-skinned goth in a black leather corset played an Irish bodhran. Someone had a violin, sending a eerie melody wailing out over the percussion.

Across the glade was the gate of fire—a pair of closely set torches—that guarded a path to the higher altar, for Kindred alone. Later, the Acolytes would pass through that gate to go participate in the higher rites, including the initiation of any who had passed the gate for the first time. He'd heard enough stories of what went on beyond the gate of fire, most of it likely bullshit intended to scare away the timid or gullible. Loki did not consider himself either, but the gate marked a passage of no return—a dedication of one's Requiem to the path of the Crone. It was the path Moyra had been gently pressuring him to take for more than two years now. Some night, he probably would. *But not tonight.*

He stepped into the shadows behind a stand of trees and let himself fade into the darkness. He was a shadow, moving silently and unseen among both his fellow Acolytes and their mortal kine. Aware that there might be some who could pierce his cloak of shadows, he kept to the edges of the light, extending his senses rather than attempting to get too close to any conversations of interest.

There was his quarry. Tall, black-clad, wearing a raven's mask, black feathers that flowed into his hair. Talking to Jed Holyoak—of course. That fit. The nomad Jed had brought to the Skullery. That had to be him. Loki sharpened his senses, focusing on their conversation.

"The Circle has a long history in Chicago, of course," Jed was saying. "We've always been here. Rowen has held the serpent's staff for nearly a century."

"It's the crossroads," Raven said. "All energies flow through here."

Loki glided closer. It was a hunt, though not of the usual kind. His prey was not mortal tonight, and it was not blood he was after.

A sleepy *cawk* came from somewhere above him. A crow startled in its roost. Crows again. Loki looked up, warily.

There was a sudden flurry of black across his vision, the beating of wings almost in his face, sharp little talons scratching at his cheek. Loki swung wildly at it, and let himself fall backward into a roll, bringing his arms up to shield his face from their attack.

The crows came after him in a swarm, pecking and clawing at him. Loki scrambled up to his feet again and dodged sideways, looking desperately for some kind of cover, or something to use to defend himself. He spotted a fallen branch on the ground, wrenched it free from the debris of the forest floor and swung it wildly at his attackers, ready to beat the damned things to the ground.

The branch passed through the diving crows as though their black-winged shadows were as insubstantial as smoke. And still their claws and beating wings scored hits, on his hands, outstretched arms, and unprotected face.

In the firelit clearing, the rest of the Acolytes and mortals continued their dancing and chanting without missing a beat. Raven and Jed continued their conversation. They didn't hear—perhaps they couldn't. Loki didn't know, and he had no time to find out.

He threw the branch aside and ran, shielding his face, especially his eyes, as best he could with his arms. Running bent over, he looked for some bit of brush or undergrowth too thick and close for the crows to follow—and also to avoid running headlong into the unforgiving trunk of some poplar or oak. The crows came at him from the right, and he swung left; if they wheeled around and came from the right, he headed left.

Then the ground suddenly opened up, the pit appearing without warning under his feet, and he fell. He landed hard, and painfully, on some large and unforgiving wooden object below that cracked and splintered upon impact. One outstretched hand broke right through it, right up past his elbow, as the rest of his body bounced and slid off the edge. His head took a hard knock as well. A sparkle of white stars edged with the red of almost-frenzy flashed across his vision. He felt a bone in his trapped arm snap.

Somehow he managed to push himself up to his knees, using his other hand for support, and ease his broken arm out of the splintered hole it was stuck in. Gritting his teeth against the pain, he pulled it straight again, until the ends of the bone met. Then he could let his blood mend the break, while he took stock of his surroundings.

There was no sign of the crows—they had apparently vanished into thin air. The pit was at least six feet deep, and perhaps five feet wide, and seemed to be freshly dug. What he'd landed on was some kind of old chest or trunk, the base and one end of which was still partially buried in the earth. His hand had broken right through the wooden lid. And where he knelt…

Bones. Human bones, he recognized, though some were broken now due to his landing, or perhaps the action of the digger, whoever that was. He could just make out the skull, only partially unearthed, off to the side. There had been a body buried here in addition to the chest. That implied all kinds of trouble—murder, at the very least—and he'd stumbled on it entirely by accident. How long did it take a body to decompose into just bones? He had no idea.

But the digging was recent—had to be. Someone knew this was here, had known where to dig. Possibly the person didn't expect anyone to find it, deep in the woods, and thought it was safe to leave it overnight, and come back in the morning to finish.

What was so important that someone once committed murder to protect it? Loki looked at the chest again, sharpening his vision to make full use of the limited light filtering down from the crescent moon above the trees. Gingerly, he slid his hand inside the broken hole, felt around within. His hand fell on something flat and square, covered in some kind of dusty wrapping and tied with twine. Carefully, he closed his fingers around it and drew it out.

The flapping of wings, somewhere above. Loki ducked down, almost instinctively, and looked up. Was that something moving, against the shadows of the tree branches up there? A few leaves swirling in the breeze? No, that wasn't it, either. Warily, Loki shoved the mysterious package, wrappings and all, into a deep pocket for safekeeping.

Then the wind shifted, bringing with it a cloud of black feathers that came swirling down out of the darkness and into the pit right on top of where he crouched, driven by a blast of bone-chilling cold air.

Fuck! Loki scrabbled for the top, using the chest to boost himself up and out of the pit. Thankfully, the chest's wooden top didn't crack under his weight. Once out, he ran, back through the woods toward what he vaguely remembered was the Circle's bonfire. Yes, there it was—he could just see the light of it through the trees.

This was all just too fucking weird. He wiped his hands on his pants, and looked back, half-afraid to see the bones rising from the pit in pursuit, or something. What was happening—why was he suddenly the target of freaky shit all of a sudden? Ghostly crows with real claws, and he had felt the scratches (now thankfully healed) to prove it. Ghosts, period, dammit. What had he done to deserve this shit?

Better get back to civilization. He stopped long enough to wipe the dried blood from his face and hands with his sleeve—for ghosts, those crows had damned sharp claws—and started walking back toward the firelight.

janet trauvetter

"Come on, baby, you know better than that. They're just jealous, that's all. You know you've always been my best student—"

Loki turned his head, listened. Raven's voice, and the same old lines, too, off to the left. He willed the shadows to hide him, and crept in that direction.

"You've got such potential, baby. I knew it the moment I met you. You're a natural, you must have been one hell of a priestess in some former life—"

Raven had her up against a tree, hands kneading her breasts as she stared enraptured into his eyes.

Loki drew the stake out of his deep pocket, and gritted his teeth against the sudden rise of his own hunger and the nagging of his conscience. *If you let him bite her, she'll die.*

But he didn't know how fast Raven was, or how dangerous. Loki'd only get one chance with the stake, and he didn't dare miss. Thankfully, Raven was distracted, but he couldn't afford the girl being a witness either.

Raven moved in, nuzzling her throat. Her arms wrapped around his back, and she gave a little moan as his fangs pierced her skin.

Loki gripped the stake and moved silently closer, careful where he put his feet, until he stood only ten feet away. The scent of her blood was almost overwhelming. It took all he had to keep the Beast quiet and still.

The girl's arms relaxed and fell away. Raven raised his head from the girl's throat, licked the wound closed, and let go, leaving her to slide down the trunk of the tree, apparently unconscious. "That's my good girl," he murmured. "Stupid slut."

Loki drew on all his blood-enhanced speed, and took three quick steps forward, wrapping his right arm around Raven's throat from behind and pulling him back and off-balance. Then he jabbed upward with the stake in his left, forcing it through the Daeva's ribcage, aiming for the heart.

He missed. Raven threw himself backward, knocking both of them down to the ground. Loki almost lost his grip on the stake, as the impact drove it even further through Raven's twisting body. Fortunately, Raven seemed more interested in getting away from Loki's hold than ridding himself of the stake. His thrashing loosened it enough so that Loki could change the angle of the stake's thrust. The next time Raven rolled in the right direction, Loki set the stake's butt against the ground, and Raven's own weight drove it home. With a strangled gasp, the Daeva went limp.

Loki pushed the inert body over on its belly, and made sure the stake pierced the Daeva's heart all the way. Then he checked on the girl. She was still breathing, and her heartbeat steady, but her temperature was already rising. *Shit.* Well, there was nothing else he could do for her now.

Pulling his cell phone out of his pocket, he made a quick call. Then he grabbed Raven's arm and leg, maneuvered the Daeva's limp body up on to his shoulders, and carried him away through the woods toward the appointed rendezvous.

It wasn't until late the following night that he was able to investigate the package he'd found in the pit. The wrapping was cloth of some kind, old and faded from its years buried in the ground. He snapped the twine and unwrapped it.

There were two items inside. One was a gold pocket watch, probably an antique, with a strange design etched into its case. On the back, there was the shape of a book with a lock on it, and, on the front, there was a skull. Around the circumference of both sides was a running design that almost looked like writing, though it was no alphabet Loki had ever seen before. When he pressed the catch, it opened easily, the miniature hinge moving as if it were new. There were more funny letters on the face where the numbers should be, and three hands of equal length. The inside of the lid had an inscription in the same weird lettering, but with a row of numbers clearly readable: *27 juillet, 1817–14 octobre, 1871*

It wasn't English, but it looked like dates. For what? Someone's birth and death? And what were these other letters, if that's what they were? He'd never seen anything like them.

The other item was a small, slender book, with an embossed leather cover. The design had a snake twining around a staff topped with an Egyptian ankh and a crescent moon, within an oblong frame, and odd letters around the edges, though not the same as on the watch. These looked like more like the hieroglyphs from the Egyptian tombs. The staff, though—he knew that symbol. Rowen carried it, the serpent staff of the Hierophant.

Curious, he opened the book up to a random page. It seemed to be a personal journal of some kind, handwritten in an elegant, slanty cursive hand he'd seen only in museums. It took some effort to read.

Many dangers press us on all sides. The weather remains hot, and the city dry as tinder—there were three fires last night alone, if the ringing of the bells can be of any judge. The air in the poorer shantytowns west of the stockyards is thick and close, and appears to incite men to even greater violence than is in their original natures. Delilah reports there were no fewer than five brawls in the Irish quarter last night, in which two men died. Three more of her working girls have been beaten by their customers, and one has disappeared.

Nothing more has been heard of Maynard himself; rumor has it that he has left the city, and only his followers remain. In particular, the Reverend Talley has not given up his crusade, and since he has been denied a proper pulpit, he has taken to preaching his message by grandstanding wherever mortal men are gathered. He is clever, and now restricts his preaching to daylight hours only, and has taken to passing broadsheets in the taverns and factories. So far, neither the Prince's servants nor my own have been sufficient to stop him, for broadsheets are far harder to stop than a man, and disseminate much more quickly. It is fortunate that his knowledge of our kind is yet limited, and that the remedies he recommends to ward off the 'devils of the night' are based on deceptive folklore rather than hard experience.

It does not help our cause that too many of us have grown careless. Phinneas has on several occasions taken young Invictus whelps to task for snatching hotel maids or laundrywomen without a thought to the consequences, and yet their sires defend them in Elysium, as if those women did not sometimes have fathers or brothers who might seek some kind of vengeance upon the murderers of their blood.

A Kindred journal. Had to be. A journal written by a Crone follower, maybe even Hierophant. But not Rowen—how long had she been Hierophant, anyway? A long time, but was even she this old? Somehow, she didn't seem to be the journal-writing type. He flipped to the beginning.

There was a note inside the front cover, in a different hand: *For Nicholas: Memories fade, but what is written endures forever. –A.*

He turned the page to the first entry.

September 5, 1871—I write this at the urging of my long-time associate Aristede, whose arcane foresight has led him to insist I make a record of our doings here. And I suppose he has

a good point, for the weight of years can be heavy, and memories crumble into fragments in the long sleep, though I did not speak of that to him. And yet I trust his instincts in this, as they have served us well in the past, and will, I trust, into whatever future awaits.

He kept reading. It took a while to get used to the handwriting, though it was quite neat and consistent. The writer occasionally used odd abbreviations, and referenced things that didn't make any sense to him. The name Maynard sounded familiar, however. Where had he heard that before?

And then the significance of the date hit him.

Fires. A city dry as tinder. October 1871.

The Fire. *The* Fire, the Great Chicago Fire that had lasted for more than two days and burned down half the city, all because of some cow kicking over a lantern or something. An old wives' tale, good enough for the mortals. Blame it on the cow.

But that was where he'd heard of Maynard before. Solomon Birch had said it, something about Maynard being inflicted on Kindred for their sins, or some shit like that. And Maxwell had disagreed. *We were careless, back then,* he'd said. *Too numerous, and too arrogant, taking men for fools. Maynard was just a man, but a man who had seen too much, and that made him dangerous, a man with a mission from God.*

Which was pretty much what this Nicholas guy was saying, too. And this journal was the real thing, Loki was willing to bet his fangs on it. It even smelled old. How old was Maxwell, anyway? Old enough to remember the Fire? Old enough to remember who this Nicholas was? Might be worth asking Maxwell, if he could do so without sounding too obvious about it.

Loki bent to reading again. Apparently, Nicholas had known someone named Delilah who was prone to having visions. Probably Kindred, the way he talked about her. Her visions were all the doom and disaster kind.

…the theme of all her visions remains consistent. Something is dreadfully wrong, setting the balance of natural forces quite askew. Like a festering boil, it swells with angry pus, ever growing, the poison spreading, until it either be lanced or until it bursts, and the gods alone know what will become of our city then. Her visions speak of unnatural death and suffering: the massacre of the first settlers of Fort Dearborn, the countless victims in the plagues of cholera and smallpox that have decimated this great city in its past, the haggard, hollow faces of wretched Rebel prisoners from Camp Douglas, the family killed when their hovel in the Patch burned down last week.

And in all that is revealed to us, we see the crows gathering—but are they a warning to be heeded, or do they represent that which awaits to gorge itself on the spoils when at last our doom comes?

Crows. A figure of speech? Or literally crows? Here was another reference: *The crows are ever more numerous and bold.*

…it was most peculiar, that what the wind sent swirling around us where we stood was not the leaves of early autumn but a veritable rain of black feathers…

Black feathers. Loki felt a chill pass down his spine, for no apparent reason. He looked up, sharply, stared around at the four corners of his little apartment.

There was something in his pocket, slim and soft. He drew it out, and then jumped back with a curse, flinging it away. A black feather drifted down to the floor in a graceful zigzag path.

Where the fuck had that come from? How had it gotten in his pocket—maybe when he was climbing out of the pit? Maybe. He bent and picked the feather up again, gingerly, took it to the window, raised the screen, and flicked it out into the alley. The feather disappeared down into the darkness below.

He took both the book and the gold watch into his closet-bedroom, then flicked on the light to continue reading.

For it is a great doom we face, of that I am now certain, and yet there may yet be some way to avert it, if we act quickly and with courage. The rites of Mabon approach, and with the greater Sacrifice under the Hunter's moon, to which my esteemed colleague Mr. Hill has pledged himself, perhaps we shall find a means by which this doom may yet be averted.

Those who look will see. Those who see, must act. Blood is the only true sacrifice.

The same thing Rowen had said. Maybe it was part of the Litany after all, just a part Moyra hadn't taught him. Maybe.

He stretched out on the futon with the book, and continued reading until the rising sun forced him to sleep.

Loki had not been a particularly diligent student when he was still in school, but he still remembered how to use a library. It was even easier now that so much was online. Unfortunately, that was an amenity he lacked in his current apartment, and so he was dependent on the public library. The library had resources that weren't online as well, such as century-old issues of the *Chicago Tribune* on microfilm. And once the librarians and the cleaning staff left for the night, he had the run of the place, and he didn't even need a library card.

What he found, especially in the *Trib* archives, matched what the journal said. There had been fires on the dates that Nicholas had reported them, and the weather, as he remembered it from school, had been unseasonably hot and dry.

Through the library computer network, he could tap into the Chicago Historical Society archives as well, which included a lot of personal letters that discussed things no newspaper would bother to print, such as reports of a large flock of crows appearing near the scene of several unsolved murders. Or the riot at the stockyards one afternoon, when some witnesses insisted that the carcasses of slaughtered pigs and cattle rose to the stumps of their legs and attempted to hobble toward the river. Or the black feathers that blew on the wind in swirls like miniature tornadoes, the wind appearing at random and then dissipating, leaving the feathers to flutter to the ground. There were also stories of two-headed calves being born, people seeing long-dead relatives turning up for supper, and a Confederate regiment marching down the street to a local graveyard, playing taps, and then disappearing.

The story about the flock of crows caught his interest. The Crow Murders, the broadsheet called them. Seven adults and one child found dead and pecked to death by crows, the story claimed, mostly in the outlying farms. All the murders had taken place at night, and the victims were alone—either they'd gone out to piss, or to get something from the barn, or call in the dog. The last murders had been three men all at one time—they'd gone out hunting for the crows, armed with shotguns, and been found the next morning. One man had his throat ripped out; another had his chest caved in, as though he'd been hit with a sledgehammer. The third had not a mark on him; it was speculated he'd died of fright. Crow feathers were found at the scene, but very little blood.

The story all but shouted Kindred, and one Kindred in particular. Had the Unholy visited Chicago back before the Fire?

"Well, if you really want to hear stories about the Unholy, you'd need to ask that guy Masterson out in Cicero," Damien said, gesturing with a lit cigarette. "You remember, he said the Unholy sired him, and the whole room went dead silent, if you'll pardon the expression. It was great. The look on Birch's face, especially."

"Oh, yeah, I remember," Loki said. "Wonder if she's dropped in on him lately? She hunts Kindred, too, doesn't she?"

"I guess if she's that old, yeah. Mortals must taste like weak dishwater to her now."

"Haven't heard of anyone going missing, though," Loki mused. "I mean, I probably wouldn't have heard it personally, but you'd think stories would get around eventually."

"Well, she probably goes after the stragglers. I would, if I were her. The unaligned loners, the nomads, the ones already under a blood hunt somewhere. The ones who aren't going to be missed."

"Yeah, that would make sense."

"I also heard that she doesn't always kill. If you surrender to her, instead of giving her a fight or running, then she just takes what she needs and leaves you with nothing but the memories."

"Or the nightmares." Loki grimaced. "Where'd you hear that? Masterson?"

"No, not from him. Think it was some Carthian punk, come to think of it. So I don't know how much stock I'd put in it. Oh, there's Sybil—I promised her a ride home."

Loki spotted her, too, a nicely decked-out goth with an artful white streak through her dyed-black hair and a long burgundy velvet cloak, lurking near the front of the stage, but clearly too shy to interrupt. "Yeah, 'cause you're such a nice guy. She got a friend?"

"Don't get greedy." Damien dropped the cigarette butt in the ashtray and stood up. "See you later. Don't wait up."

So, maybe it had been the Unholy. She did seem to be at least that old, by all reports. She was known to keep company with crows. He'd seen that himself. And she did kill, with apparently very little care for the consequences.

Had the Unholy been responsible for some of the Kindred disappearances Nicholas' journal reported? And just who was Nicholas anyway, and his Society of the Crow?

Well, there was another Kindred Loki could possibly ask, who might actually remember something from back then. But he'd have to be careful. Sometimes Kindred didn't remember things all that well if it happened long ago. Especially if they'd spent any of that time in torpor. A long sleep played tricks with the mind, mixing dreams and memories up until sometimes it was hard to tell them apart, or so he'd heard. That was, in fact, exactly why Kindred might keep a journal like this one—to help them remember things properly when they woke up decades later. Sometimes Kindred came out of torpor more than a little crazy, until they had a chance to get re-acclimated to whatever had happened while they were asleep and work out most of the hash between what was real and what was nightmare.

He'd had some pretty freaky dreams when he was in torpor himself, and that was just for a day or two's sleep. He didn't even want to think what it might be like, trapped in those dreams for years at a time.

This wasn't a conversation for over the phone, though. He wanted to see the Prince's face, hear his voice undistorted by telephone circuitry, get a sense of whether he was even asking the right questions to get to the answer he needed. And it would have to be a private meeting, so Maxwell wouldn't feel obligated to lie to save face in front of witnesses. And, to arrange that, he'd need to call in a favor.

Bella wasn't the only one with contacts at the Palmer House.

"This is how it is," Persephone said. She was dressed to go out somewhere, in a little black dress with spaghetti straps and a fancy red-and-black fringed scarf that sparkled with beads and sequins. Loki wondered idly if she was hurrying off to meet Bella, but he didn't ask. "Maxwell had a meeting with this zoning board guy, that started ten, no, eleven minutes ago. Watch your timing. In about five minutes, no more than six or seven, because that's all I promised him, you dial this number, which is his cell phone. He knows that means his time's up, and he'll make some excuse and he'll leave. That should take him one minute, tops. You be waiting outside the humidor room. As soon as you see him leave, count to ten, then you go in. You should have him all to yourself for at least a half-hour after that, maybe longer if he lit up a big one and no one else thinks to look for him in there."

"Got it," Loki said, taking the card she handed him. "Thanks, Persephone. I owe you one."

"Yes, you do," she agreed. "But don't worry, I'll let you run up a tab for a while. What's so important you want to talk to him about, anyway?"

"Nothing that interesting," Loki assured her. He was sure she didn't buy a word of it, but that didn't matter. She knew he wasn't going to tell her. "Really, this is on behalf of a anonymous third party, and they wanted it kept hush-hush."

"Tell your anonymous third party they're full of shit. I'll find out eventually anyway."

"Let me know when you do."

"You'll be the last to find out." She flung the long end of the scarf around her shoulders. "All right, you now have four minutes. See you, Loki."

Maxwell rubbed at his beard thoughtfully with his free hand. "The Fire? Oh, yes. I do remember that. I was there. It was a night of chaos. Those of us who escaped the flames the first night had no idea, when we lay down to rest, whether whatever safe place we'd chosen would indeed prove safe enough. There were some that we never saw again, I remember that as well."

Loki nodded. "I remember you talking about the dangers from Maynard beforehand, too."

"Yes." Maxwell had a strange faraway look, coupled with a slight frown. Loki couldn't tell if that meant he was remembering something in particular, or was working on remembering anything at all.

"Do you remember someone named Nicholas? Or Delilah? Kindred, I mean, from back then," Loki asked, after a while. "I think they were both in the Circle of the Crone, if that helps."

janet trautvetter

janet trautvetter

"Nicholas or Delilah," Maxwell mused. "Delilah… In the Circle, you said. I didn't have many dealings with them, that I recall."

"There was someone called the Colonel, too. I think his first name was Phinneas."

"Oh. Colonel Redding, that would be, Colonel Phinneas Redding." Maxwell nodded. "Yes, I remember he was one of the Old Settlers, the high society." His voice took on a darker, deeper tone. "They had their own little Invictus aristocracy, back then. Colonel Redding was a bit of an eccentric, but he was still one of their kind. They had their fingers in everything, If you weren't one of them, you might as well have been Carthian for all the good it did. They never noticed you."

Maxwell paused, and Loki waited. If the Prince really was remembering something, he didn't want to interrupt.

"Nicholas," Maxwell said at last. "Dr. Nicholas Crain. Mekhet, I think. He had a cane with a brass serpent twisted around it. Wouldn't let anyone else touch it. He'd been to Egypt, had quite a collection of antiquities. One of them—he had to have been one of them, too. Dr. Crain. Always had to show them proper respect."

"Them?" Loki echoed, confused. *Dr. Nicholas Crain.* That sounded right. And the initials matched, he hadn't even thought of that, and the description of the cane, and the hieroglyphs. But what Maxwell was saying after that didn't make sense.

"Their gentleman's society, that's what the Invictus was back then," Maxwell continued. Whatever he was remembering, it sure as hell wasn't pleasant, given the bitterness in his voice. "Old Settlers club for old white men, either living or undead, no one else need apply."

"But Dr. Crain wasn't Invictus," Loki said. "He was an Acolyte—"

"I was there," Maxwell repeated, his voice rising just a little. "I remember. The only Acolytes back then were the Irish. Or the Indians. But they never mixed."

"Rowen? Was she around back then?" Clearly whatever memories Maxwell had of about Dr. Crain weren't very pleasant, so maybe it was time to move on to something else.

Maxwell took several slow puffs of his cigar. "Rowen." He shook his head. "Can't recall one way or the other. And what's the source of this sudden interest in Kindred history?"

Loki shrugged, and tried to sound nonchalant. He'd expected the question, but he couldn't answer it too fast. "I was just thinking about what you told Solomon Birch that time. When he was saying Maynard was inflicted on us for our sins. But I read something in the paper, about all the weird shi—stuff happening back then, that folks said was a warning of something bad coming. Lots of disease, fires breaking out all the time, the river full of blood and entrails from the stockyards. And spooky things, dogs all howling at noon, ghosts walking into bars, dead animals trying to escape the stockyards. And crows acting weird."

"You've been reading too much *Weird Chicago*, I think," Maxwell said. "I wouldn't go talking about ghosts too much just now. Solomon Birch still insists that it was one of the Circle witches that cursed his Mass last week."

"It wasn't," Loki said. "Honestly, they wouldn't bother." He stuck his hands in his pockets. His fingers touched something long and thin and soft—*What the fuck?* He jerked his hand out; a few black feathers came out as well and fluttered down toward the floor. *Shit!*

Maxwell stared at the drifting feathers, holding out one hand to catch one on his palm. "The crows were acting very strangely," he murmured. "And the feathers swirling everywhere. The black feather rain—oddest thing I ever saw."

"You saw it rain feathers?" Loki asked. That had been in the journal too—had Maxwell seen the same thing? Loki tried not to think about the feathers, or where they had come from. This was getting too weird. "When—before the Fire? Or—"

Maxwell suddenly dropped the feather, his entire stance shifting from casual to stiffly formal, just as the door to the humidor lounge opened.

Loki felt it then, too, the approach of other Kindred, the Beast recognizing others of its kind and stiffening its spine in response. Even though these Kindred were individuals he knew, their unwelcome interruption still put him on edge.

"Good evening, sir," Norris greeted Maxwell politely. Trailing in his wake, in a smartly tailored business suit, Marek Kaminski offered his own polite and deferential greeting. Neither of them acknowledged Loki's presence. The Prince was the only one apparently worthy of their attention here.

Dammit. Loki took a step back, forcing down the moment of not-quite-guilt for being caught out of place. The pointed suspicion in Norris' stare alone sent a chill through his veins. Loki wondered if his conversation with Maxwell had been overheard. He was keenly aware of the black feathers lying on the carpet at his feet, but unwilling to risk drawing notice to them by attempting to get them out of sight.

"We didn't mean to interrupt, sir," Norris said. "But you had asked to be kept informed as to our progress, and Mr. Kaminski had discovered some additional data of interest."

"Of course," Maxwell said. He was fully back in his role now, brisk, professional and commanding…. "Thank you, Loki." It was a dismissal, and Loki wasn't about to argue.

"Loki should hear this, actually," Marek said. "If that's quite all right, sir. I think he'll find it very interesting."

"Then by all means, Loki, stay." Maxwell agreed. "Go ahead."

This was trouble, Loki knew it already. Marek didn't owe him any favors, and this obviously wasn't intended as one.

"I've been investigating the second blister," Marek continued. "As we discussed, the next critical case of the virus that occurred after Raven's capture could have been infected prior to that night, so I discounted it. But there have been two other cases since then, that had to have been infected afterward, if the pattern remains consistent. One who died earlier today, and one who just made the critical list at Northwestern. Looking at all three, which I've done, we find a common thread. They're all from the North Shore. They're all in their late teens or early twenties. They all seem to have a fondness for wearing black. They all seem to have the same taste in music. And they have all been seen here." Marek laid a card down on the table, black and gray with a familiar design.

Moyra's card. The Skullery. *Fuck.*

"Do you mean they've been seen there in the past week?" Loki asked, keeping his face a mask of casual indifference. "Or did they just happen to have the card in a desk drawer? You're stretching, Marek."

janet trautvetter

"Here are the photos we've been able to obtain," Marek said, opening a leather attaché case and withdrawing out a manila envelope. "Perhaps you can answer your own question. Have you seen either of these two young ladies there?"

"A couple hundred mortals any given night at the club, and I'm supposed to remember two in particular?" Loki took the envelope, slid the two photos out.

He'd already been mentally preparing himself, just in case, and it was a good thing. He managed to control his facial expression, letting it shift to thoughtful pondering, as if he was really trying to remember. Fortunately, his heart could not race, and he would never break into an involuntary sweat. He throttled down his emotional response as best he could and hoped the chilling realization settling in the pit of his stomach didn't actually show in his aura.

He did remember them, intimately. *No, it can't be true,* and then he banished even the thought, lest either Maxwell or Norris be watching too closely.

"I think I've seen this one," he began, laying the photos down on the table to get them out of his hands. "Trying to remember when, though. Is she the one who's at Northwestern?"

"She's dead," Marek said. "Try again. Think real hard."

"I told you," Loki said, letting some of his stress escape as irritation, "there's a lot of chicks at the club, especially on weekends. And they don't exactly dress like their yearbook picture when they come, either. Maybe I saw her, but I don't remember when, or if it's even really her—do you remember every mortal you brush by in a crowded room?"

"Perhaps another approach would be more efficient," Norris said, silencing whatever sharp retort Marek had been about to make with a single glance. "I'm sure Kindred are more memorable than mortals. What Kindred do you remember seeing at the Skullery the nights you were there? Let's narrow this down, say, in the past two weeks?"

Thin ice. Loki could feel it cracking beneath him. He had no way of knowing if Norris already knew who Moyra's regulars were. Or who had visited. "Well, there's Moyra, of course. And Damien. Jed Holyoak and Bella. Raven, he visited once or twice, I remember hearing that. Rafael from Cicero. Toby Rieff. There might be some others, maybe."

"And you." Marek pointed out.

"Yeah, well, obviously," Loki said. His eyes strayed again to the dead girl's smiling face. He tried to ignore the chilling dread beginning to spread like poison in his veins. Tried not to think about how carelessly predictable his feeding had become. Tried not to remember Raven's staked body being shoved into the back of the SUV, or wonder what had become of him since.

"Loki?" Maxwell's voice was always so calm, so rational. "You know how important this is. If you have any idea who might be responsible—"

"Damien," Loki said, and hated himself bitterly for it, even as he could see Marek and Norris nodding in agreement, clearly pleased that he had verified the one who had been their chief suspect all along. "There was one girl, about two weeks ago—died almost in his arms. I thought it was Raven who'd infected her then. It was possible, he'd been in the club once or twice. I helped Damien get her body back to her place. He swore to me he hadn't touched her."

"And of course you believed him." Marek's inflection turned the very idea of trust in a fellow Acolyte's word into an accusation of pathetic naiveté.

"He never lied to me before," Loki retorted. He had no idea what his aura was showing now; he could only hope that any guilty colors would be attributed to the act of betrayal, and not something far worse. "Maybe he doesn't know. I mean, you'd think he'd be more careful if he did. He's not stupid, after all."

"After the first incident, you'd think he would have paid more attention to the fate of his vessels," Norris said coolly. "I presume this means that we should not rely upon you to deliver him as you did Raven. We don't want to cause any unnecessary awkwardness in your position among the Circle of the Crone."

"It's not like we don't know where to find him, after all," Marek added, and smiled.

Loki had always hated the smugness in that smile. But at that moment he was too numb inside to even pay much attention to it. The only good thing was that Marek was enjoying his gloating so much, that it apparently hadn't occurred to him that he might have been lied to.

Once Loki'd gotten a safe distance away from the hotel, and was certain that no one had followed him, he pulled the cell phone out, and held it for a moment in his hand.

He could warn Damien. He owed him that much, didn't he? Damien had always been decent to him. It wasn't Damien who was guilty of anything.

It wasn't Damien who'd killed those girls.

It was him.

What the fuck happened? Did I get it from Raven, when I staked him? But Marek was close to him, too, and he's not infected. At least, I don't think he is.

When had it happened? How? As he'd told the mages, mosquitoes didn't bother Kindred. And he didn't feed on crows. Was it the crows in the woods? They had scratched him, drawn blood. Could that have been it?

How was he going to feed, if every time he did it became a death sentence for the mortal he drank from? How long would it be before Marek or Norris figured out who the real blister had to be?

Loki slid the cell phone back into his jacket pocket. He was already getting hungry, just thinking about it.

What the fuck am I gonna do now?

It was less than an hour before dawn by the time Loki returned to his haven, no more sure of what his next step should be than he'd been when he left the Palmer House. Worse still, he was starting to feel the hunger again, which would only grow stronger when he arose the following evening.

The first thing he noticed upon entering his apartment was that the kitchen window was open. The second thing was Damien's recognizable silhouette standing in front of the windows on the other side of the room.

The Beast, however, only recognized a trespasser in its very den. Loki snarled, baring his fangs in sudden fury. How dare another Kindred invade his haven uninvited? He could sense Damien's own guilt at being there as well, his uncertainty about which of them would prevail. The Ventrue dropped his gaze first, acknowledging submission. Loki almost began to relax.

Then Moyra stepped out of the concealing shadows to the left. Bella was with her.

The Beast's anger spiked again, but it was now tinged with fear, poised between challenging the invaders and escape. Both of them were older, more powerful in the Blood. No doubt sensing this, Bella smiled. "Good evening, Loki. What a pleasant surprise."

The smug arrogance, the mockery in her voice, was just too much. "*Bitch—*" he growled, barely resisting the red starting to seep across his vision. He started forward, preparing to either fight or run with all the speed his blood could muster.

Ambush. Invasion. My haven, goddammit, MY HAVEN, get the fuck out of here, get out get out get OUT!

Behind him, the front door slammed shut.

Loki spotted only the shadow of a tall figure behind him out of the corner of his eye, but that was enough. Fear won over fury. He turned and dashed toward the back door, thinking only of the fire escape down to the alley. But even his fastest was not fast enough.

Something hard slammed into the middle of his back with bone-crunching force, sending him crashing into the unforgiving bulk of the stove. His legs turned to jelly beneath him, and he fell. Panic drove him to pull himself around the stove, crawling toward the door on his forearms and belly.

Damien and Jed dragged him away from the door, snarling and cursing. Lazar Soto laid the baseball bat aside to help them hold him down and still while Moyra drove the stake through his heart. His last memory of that instant was of Moyra's eyes—cold blue and unblinking, her pale cheeks stained by the darker threads of her tears.

They knew.

No, no, you don't understand, I'm so sorry, I didn't mean it, I didn't want it to come out this way. But he could not speak, could not shape the words to apologize, or defend himself.

And a moment later, the cold darkness enveloped him, and he couldn't do anything at all.

The city lay in ruins, whole blocks collapsed to ashes, the occasional ragged brick wall that still remained nothing but a broken shell of its former self. The reek of the smoke was everywhere, a bitter and pungent aftertaste of the destruction the fire had wrought.

Even here in the woodlands, the reek of the smoke still lingered. Wood smoke, the remains of a meal, makeshift shelters of canvas and lashed trees for a handful of refugees who could claim shelter here by right. There had been one who had wandered away from the security of the herd, despite the host's warnings. All her meager belongings in a two-wheeled shopping cart, bundled up against the October chill, she had gone looking for a sewer grate, or perhaps another shelter. She begged him for a couple of dollars, but he didn't come to give, only to take.

He left her lying in the underbrush and returned to the wagon. (Where were the bricks? He thought there ought to be bricks, a wall, concrete, but that was silly. There were no buildings out here on the prairie.) It wasn't enough to satisfy him. It never was anymore. But it would have to do for now.

He hadn't been able to rescue as much as he wanted. The fire had moved too fast, and the sacrificial ritual had taken too long. But the crow spirit had accepted the substitution. He felt the burden lift, even as his body absorbed the power of the old priest's blood. Now he needed to find a safe place to store it when he slept, and he knew exactly where that would be.

Somehow he wasn't surprised to see the tall man in the long coat waiting for him there.

"I know why you've come," the magus said. "And I know what you've done. You cannot keep a secret when his ashes themselves cry out the truth."

"This is Kindred business," he snapped back. "He had no right to tell you what he did. It was a violation of our traditions, and he has now paid the price for it. He deserved what he got."

"It was your price he paid, Jedidiah Hill," the magus said. "You broke your oath, and betrayed your brother. I'm here to tell you that you won't get away with it, not in all eternity."

He bared his fangs. "I'll only kill you, too, if you interfere."

The magus smiled. "Indeed. But not soon enough." The magus then started chanting in some unknown language.

He was aware of a clock ticking, somewhere close by. For some reason, the sharp, repetitive rhythm cut into him like pellets of birdshot. He realized it was counting down, and when it reached the end, the magus' spell would be complete.

He drew the pistol, aimed, and fired. (He wasn't sure why he was shooting right-handed. He could never hit anything worth a damn with his right hand.) He threw the gun aside, and leapt down from the wagon.

The magus raised his hand, pointing directly at him. "Oathbreaker, cursed are you once; murderer and drinker of souls, cursed are you twice; false priest and deceiver, cursed are you three times and forever, until the blood you have stolen is repaid—"

The mage's blood burned him even as he swallowed, spreading ice and fire through his veins. Even when he dropped the body, it continued to burn inside, as though he had swallowed some vile poison that made his limbs weak and the blood that animated his undead flesh as thin as water. All the rush of power he'd gained in the first sacrificial death drained way in an instant upon the second, until he felt as helpless as a newly Embraced fledgling.

And the ticking of the watch continued, despite all his attempts to find it and smash it into fragments. He looked in every pocket in the corpse's fine suit, every corner of the book chest, but the watch was nowhere to be found. It just kept ticking, ticking, ticking, relentless and unforgiving....

"It will return, it always returns. And it will never forget the blood that it is owed...."

Once again, Loki woke to the agony of a stake being yanked out of his chest, leaving him gritting his teeth against the pain as he forced his body to pull itself back together, to rebuild his shattered spinal column, and to fill in the gaping wound in his chest. It cost him blood, but the alternative, to be wounded as well as captive, was unthinkable.

He lay on his side, curled in an almost fetal position on hard concrete, his hands cuffed behind his back, something thick and heavy tied over his face. Unable to see, he was forced to rely on other senses. He wasn't alone, obviously. Kindred didn't make much noise unless they moved, so he could only guess at how many others were nearby.

janet trautvetter

But he could assume that most of the welcoming party were still around, at least. He could also hear the rustling of leaves, the singing of crickets, the plink-plink of water dripping into a puddle. And he could smell the forest, and the distinctive acrid bite of smoke from patio torches.

"On your feet." Lazar's gruff order was accompanied by a sharp tap of the baseball bat against his shins.

"Be a lot easier if my hands were free," he said, looking in the direction he thought the others might be. "Not like I can actually get away from all of you, is it?"

Whack. The bat smacked the side of his knee. "Fuck," he hissed, gritting teeth against the pain.

"It would be a lot harder if both your legs were broken," Lazar told him. "And you would still be required to stand and face our judgment."

Judgment? *Fuck.* He rolled and pushed himself up to his knees, and then up to his feet. Thankfully, his spine seemed to be back in working order, and his legs didn't wobble too badly.

"Do I get to at least see who's judging me?" he demanded.

"If you like." Moyra's voice, cool and remote, right at his elbow. She untied the blindfold and took it away.

Loki blinked and forced his eyes to adjust. The forest preserves. He'd expected that. He stood by himself in the center of the picnic pavilion. Around him, spread out in a rough circle, were about a dozen Kindred, all Acolytes he knew. Bella and Jed. Moyra and Damien. Lazar, Miriam, Richard Tabor, and a few others, all with grim faces. And right across from him, seated on a picnic table in full priestess regalia, was Rowen herself, aloof and regal, the Hierophant's staff across her lap.

"Well, here you are," Bella said, stepping forward. "The question is, do you have even the slightest notion why?"

"No idea," Loki said. He refused to look at her. Refused to let her get to him, not here, in front of everyone else. "But I'm sure you're just dying to tell me."

Lazar growled, slapping the baseball bat against the palm of his other hand. "Watch your tongue, whelp."

"No, Lazar," Bella said. She started to circle around him, just two steps away. "I think Loki deserves to know. Don't you all agree? He probably thinks we have no idea what he's up to when he visits the Tribune Building. Or the Palmer House. Or that no one notices when he and a fellow Acolyte go into the woods, and he's the only one who comes back."

"You don't have any idea what you're talking about," Loki retorted. He glanced around at the others, trying to pick up on their colors without appearing to actually be looking. What little he could see wasn't encouraging. He could only hope his own aura didn't betray him. In a circle of predators, the weak and fearful could easily become prey. "I do some work for the Prince sometimes, everybody knows that. It's not a secret, and it isn't news."

"Really?" Bella asked. "Pardon me, but the last I looked, Norris Kleinspiegel wasn't the Prince in this city. We know who pulls your strings, and it's not Maxwell Clarke. And now we're beginning to see where your true loyalty lies. Not with your coven, obviously. And not with the Circle of the Crone."

"That's not true," he protested. Somehow he managed to still avoid meeting her eyes, though seeing Moyra standing there, cool as a marble statue, or the way Damien was avoiding Loki's gaze in turn, was beginning to chip away at his resolve. "Yeah, I work for Norris, he's the one who gives the orders, that's all. It's still the Prince's business. Doesn't have anything to do with the covenant's business."

Jed Holyoak stood up, took a step forward. "Doesn't it? In that case, you can tell us what happened when you and Raven walked into the woods. And you can perhaps tell us where he is tonight, because no one has seen him since."

"He's a nomad," Loki started, then thought better of it. "Look, I don't fucking know—"

The next thing he knew, Lazar's baseball bat had come in low behind him, striking him on the backs of his knees and knocking his legs totally out from under him. Loki landed on his back and shoulder on the concrete, the steel of the handcuffs biting into his wrists.

Then Lazar kicked him, hard, where he lay on the ground. Loki let out an involuntary gasp, fangs coming down, as he doubled up, pulling his legs up to shield himself better. Loki not being mortal, it wasn't really damage—but it still hurt like a motherfucker.

Rowen spoke for the first time, her voice low and smooth. "Let that be a lesson in the perils of falsehood and the virtues of truth."

"On your feet, whelp," Lazar growled.

Fucking maniacs. Loki gritted his teeth and struggled up to his feet again. It hurt, and he let it continue hurting. The pain helped him focus.

"Answer the question," Bella prompted, and smiled. "Try the truth this time. It'll hurt less."

Fuck Norris and his policy of utmost discretion, anyway. "Raven was a blister," Loki said. It hurt to draw breath enough to talk—he'd forgotten that was what his diaphragm was for. "That's the truth, the whole nasty truth. You know that virus that's going around, the one that even healthy young people are dying of? He was carrying it. Everybody he fed on, they got sick and fucking died a few days later. I followed him. I kept track of who he took, what happened to them all."

"What did you do to him?" Jed demanded.

"It's against the Prince's own edict to destroy another Kindred," Bella said. "I imagine that even applies to blisters, doesn't it?"

"He's not dead. Just in custody," Loki admitted. He hoped that was true. "So he won't infect anyone else. I don't know what they're going to do with him. I just had to… make sure he got taken out of circulation."

"And what about Damien?" Moyra asked coolly.

Something cold and slimy settled in the pit of Loki's bruised innards. Not so soon. How could they have heard so soon? How could they know? Then he saw Bella's mocking little smile.

I do have my contacts in the Palmer House, you know.

Not Persephone, surely. She hadn't even been there this evening, at least not for that. It had to be someone else. Someone who had known entirely too much already.

"How low you've sunk, Bella," he said. "Sucking up to the Dragons. Or was it just sucking cock? And you want to lecture me about loyalty?"

janet trautvetter

Bella could be beautiful, when she put her mind to it, but that faded fast when her temper snapped. Her hand moved fast, too, faster than he could see, sending his head snapping around and knocking him off his feet again.

"You pathetic little whiner," she hissed. The weight of her fury and disdain was a heavy, bitter fog, holding him in place on the ground, in submission whether he willed it or not. "You skulk in the shadows, spying for your masters, blowing with the wind, standing for nothing, committed to nothing, believing in nothing. The Requiem is not a game, Loki, and you cannot play us for fools, now that we see—"

Rowen stood up in one fluid movement, and rapped the butt of her staff on the concrete floor, setting the brass rings suspended from the ankh's loops jangling harshly. "Silence!"

Even Bella shut up. The guilt and shame didn't go away entirely when she released him, but he could at least attempt to get up again. And he had to get up, he realized that now. It didn't matter how many times someone knocked him down, he had to keep getting up. To do otherwise was to surrender, and then the predators would close in.

He got up to his feet again.

Moyra came forward. "What about Damien?" she asked again.

It had been easier to endure Bella's ire, even the crushing weight of her blood-driven scorn, than to face Moyra at that moment. Moyra, who had always been gracious and patient with him. And behind her, Damien, who had trusted him to keep his secrets.

"I'm sorry," Loki said. God, this was worse than he'd ever thought. Worse than the act of betrayal itself. "I really am, you gotta believe me. I didn't have a choice. I had to tell them. Damien's a carrier, too."

"Fuck, no," Damien blurted out. "No, that's not true. It can't be true. Loki, you gotta be shitting me, man. Don't do that to me."

"It's true," Loki said. "Marek tracked you, I didn't. I didn't want to know. But there's been two more deaths, since Raven was taken down. They both hung out at the Skullery. And they had all your music, man. Autographed and everything."

"What did they do with Raven?" Damien demanded. "What did they do, Loki? What are they gonna do with me?"

"They're not going to do anything, Damien," Moyra said, laying a hand on his shoulder. "Calm down. We will not let them do anything." She turned to Rowen. "There must be another answer. We cannot allow them to dictate to us like this."

"It is said the Lancea Sanctum priests have a way of burning poisons and disease from Kindred blood," Rowen said. There was nothing of panic or concern in her voice, though there was little comfort in it either.

"Hell, no," Damien muttered. "I'll go nomad first. I don't trust those Sanctified fuckers farther than even I can throw 'em."

"Neither would I, were I in your place," Rowen agreed. "But we do not even know for certain if this accusation is true. The tongues of dragons are twisted and full of deceit. But it is something that can be proven, one way or the other, if you will submit yourself to the test."

Damien hesitated, and then nodded. "I will. Just so long as it's not them doin' it."

Rowen tapped the Hierophant's staff once sharply on the floor. The rings jingled against each other. "So be it," she said.

Then she turned to Loki. "Questions have been raised about where your loyalties lie," she said. "The questions are valid, and deserving of an answer. But this answer must be more than words alone. Because of you, one of our Acolytes is imprisoned, at the mercy of outsiders, and his fate uncertain. Because of you, Damien is now under suspicion, and we must take risk upon ourselves to learn the truth, and, if necessary, protect him from a similar fate. Because of you, this has happened. Because you put your duty to outsiders first, and kept silent among the children of the Crone."

"I—" The guilt and shame wallowing in his gut threatened to rise up and choke off his very voice. "I didn't mean for it to come out like this."

"That is not an answer."

Shit. "I'm not sure I understand the question. I mean, really. What do you want me to say? I'm sorry. I wish I could do it differently now, but—"

"The question is simple. Whom do you truly serve? If it is the Prince, then you would serve him better among the Invictus. Or another covenant, if they will have you, but you will have no place among us here."

Casting him out. It surprised him how much that hurt, how it made the very pavement beneath his feet feel uncertain. "No! I mean—"

"If it is the Crone you serve, then you must serve her in truth. But that path is no longer as easy as it was. We must know if you are strong enough to walk it." She beckoned to Lazar. "Release him."

Loki had a feeling she wasn't freeing his hands out of kindness or mercy. Those were not qualities the Crone tended to honor. Still, it did feel good to be unbound.

Rowen strode a few paces away before turning to face him again. "This is your judgment and your choice. There are two ways to leave this place, and by that choice your path is set. One way has no direction, save that it leads away from here and from our Circle. Take that path, and go serve the Prince or his spymaster as you choose. Seek your fellowship among the Invictus, or whoever else will have you, for if you take that path, you have turned your back on us, and your place in our Circle is forfeit."

She raised her arm and pointed off to the left, where two torches were set into the ground, the twin flames burning about four feet off the ground, only an arm's length apart.

"The other way leads there, through the Gate of Fire. On that path, you will be tested and purified, your true nature revealed, and your transgressions forgiven. But such revelation does not come without cost, or without pain. It is the trial by ordeal, the purification by fire, from which you will emerge stronger than before, or you will not emerge at all.

"Think hard and well on this decision, for there is no returning, only going forward on whichever path you choose."

Rowen turned away, and left the pavilion, walking between the pair of torches. One at a time, the others followed, and formed another circle on the other side, leaving an opening facing the torches. In invitation—or perhaps in challenge.

Loki stood in the center of the empty pavilion, staring at those two burning torches and thinking of what it meant to walk between them.

Where do your loyalties lie? Whom do you serve?

Trial by ordeal. Purification by fire. Was that description intended to be figurative or literal? Either way, it was going to be hell, he was sure of that. But what choice did he

janet trautvetter

have? He could walk away, sure. But where would he go? The Invictus? Yeah, right. Like he'd fit in there, where the only way to get ahead was to polish your nose on someone else's ass. The Carthians were full of talk but short on action, their infighting all the more bitter because what they had to squabble over was so petty and meaningless. The Ordo Dracul—no, not like they'd ever even given *him* the time of night, fucking snobs. And as for the Lancea Sanctum, even the thought of facing Solomon Birch turned Loki's stomach.

Of course, facing Bella didn't exactly thrill him, either. But the Circle was greater than any single Kindred in it, its disparate covens free to follow their beliefs as they saw fit, to associate with whomever they wanted. The most disorganized and least dogmatic of all the covenants, the Circle would never be united enough to pose a political threat to any of the others. And yet, the Circle in its chronic disunity offered him something that none of the others could match.

Offered it, but not without cost. *Blood is the only true sacrifice.*

It would be blood, then. *Let my blood spilled now stand in promise of the offering yet to come.* He'd already promised it, in fact. It was owed. *What is given freely is accepted and blessed; what is owed and withheld shall be taken without mercy.*

Those who face their fear and survive it become strong.

There was only one path he could take and still stay true to himself. Loki walked out of the pavilion, and through the Gate of Fire, trying not to think of how close those flames were on either side.

As he approached the opening in their circle, however, Rowen came forward to meet him and bar his way with her staff. "Will you enter and face the Horned King's judgment, and pay the price he demands?"

The Horned King? That sent a chill down his spine, especially since he could see someone on the far side of the circle had already donned the Horned King's mask, with stag's antlers, and the long cloak of fur. Lazar, perhaps, or Jed, but in truth it didn't matter. The Horned King was not known for being merciful. None of the Three were.

"Yes." It was the only answer he could give.

Rowen raised the staff. "Enter, then, and face judgment."

Loki walked forward, into the center of the circle. The Beast in his soul hissed and arched its back. It wanted to fight, to run, to do something in the focus of so many unblinking predator stares. Every instinct for survival cried out for him to flee, but somehow he held himself in place even as the circle closed in around him.

The masked figure of the Horned King stood before him, holding a long spear. "You who have been the hunter are now the hunted," he said. "As the rabbit runs from the fox, the fox in turn runs from the hounds. As the fox and the rabbit, you will run, and as hounds we will pursue you. Wherever you run, wherever you try to hide, we will be close behind. Do not seek refuge or assistance from outsiders, or we will count you as one of them. This hunt shall last from now until sunrise on the third night. Stay clear of the hunters until then, and you will have passed the ordeal."

Loki thought it might be Lazar's voice, but he wasn't sure, and didn't dare look around the circle to figure out who was missing. "What happens if you catch me?" he asked. "The Prince's Tranquility, that still holds, doesn't it?"

"There are far worse things than Final Death," the masked figure continued. "Once you break free of this circle, you will have thirteen minutes to begin your run before we follow.

Your ordeal lasts until dawn on the third night. Whether that time is spent in freedom or enduring whatever ordeal your captors believe you deserve is in your hands."

Those in the circle surrounding him had knives in their hands now, and they were standing much closer together. *Once I break free? Fuck!* A quick look around saw no friendly gaps. He was almost shaking with the effort that it took to keep the Beast contained. It wanted to bolt like a rabbit, run anywhere, not choose its route through the weakest point.

"Run." Bella began a chant from somewhere behind him, and the others picked it up. "Run, Loki, run. Run, Loki, run."

They came closer.

Loki made a quick decision, before drawing deeply on what blood-enhanced speed and strength he could muster. He made a feint in one direction, then an even faster turn and dive to the right, aiming for the slight gap between Bella and Jed.

They blocked him, of course, but neither Jed nor Bella was big enough or strong enough to hold him back for long. He felt the bite of at least three knife-blades stabbing through his clothing into his flesh. Pain and the smell of his own blood gave him a desperate new strength, however, and he wriggled through, suffering more trauma in the process.

Once he was free of them, he let the Beast's instincts take the lead, and he ran.

Thirteen minutes. Not very fucking long, when every moment counted. He hadn't even checked the time when he started running, so he had no idea if the grace period was up yet or not. It didn't matter. He kept running.

It helped a lot to not have to breathe, to not have to worry about his muscles getting sore, or even tired. He could run pretty damned fast for a pretty long time. Of course, so could his pursuers, and chances were some of them could run faster, and follow his scent, too. First thing he had to do was hide his trail, lose his scent in the belching of diesel exhaust and carbon monoxide fumes. A bus. Any bus, going anywhere.

He caught one about fifteen minutes later, managed to slip aboard unseen through the back door when someone else was getting out. He went to the back and slunk down in the seats to do some fast thinking. Returning to his haven was right out. Obviously, they knew where that was, had known it all along. That probably meant most of his usual refuges were known. Certainly any he'd ever mentioned to Damien or Moyra were. And appealing to any of his casual allies and acquaintances outside the Circle would be seen as seeking refuge with outsiders. Not something he'd totally ruled out, but not on the top of his list of things to do just yet, either. It was too early in the game for desperate measures, and, besides, there really wasn't another covenant he felt right about being part of. They wouldn't destroy him. He was pretty certain of that, as certain as he could be of anything where other Kindred were concerned. Rowen would honor the Tranquility, and she'd probably have a pretty dim view of anyone else who didn't.

On the other hand, getting his ass beaten into a bloody, boneless pulp—which was entirely within the realm both of legality and possibility—wasn't something he wanted to experience either. So he had to stay out of their reach, as far ahead as possible, for three nights.

janet trautvetter

So what did that leave him? Where could he go? Cicero? Maybe, if he could keep the locals from noticing him lurking about. Stickney, though that wasn't guaranteed to be neutral turf. Old Mike had his own agenda, and Loki had enough trouble balancing his own at the moment. The South Side, if he got desperate enough. There were neighborhoods here and there that weren't as bad as others. But they often had Kindred in the neighborhoods, too, and he wasn't on good terms with any of them down there. There had to be places where there weren't many Kindred. Problem was, when Kindred avoided a neighborhood, it was usually because something else claimed it, something that made Kindred back away. Lupines, for instance. Hostile mages. Or other things not so easily defined.

His cell phone chimed. Growling a curse for not silencing the damned thing, he dragged it out. A black crow feather came out with it. He jumped, flicked the thing away. *Goddammit!* He didn't recognize the number on the phone, either. *Fuck.*

"Yeah?"

"You could make this a lot easier, you know." Jed's voice, smug and honey smooth. *"We could come to an accommodation. I'm nowhere near as brutal as—"*

"Fuck you," Loki snarled into the receiver, and hit the button to cut the connection. Then he turned the phone off. *Nobody I really want to talk to, anyway.*

He got off at the next stop, ran two blocks, and climbed the stairs up to the El platform. There was a train coming in, going south. One about to leave, heading north. He jumped inside the north-bound train, just as the doors closed. If he was going to be skulking in shadows and hiding from everyone, he'd feel a hell of a lot safer doing it in the part of the city he knew.

Loki spent his first night on the run doing two things: avoiding his pursuers, who were apparently cruising every likely hunting spot in all the North Side Rack hoping to flush him out, and methodically investigating a number of possible but hopefully not terribly obvious places where he might take shelter during the day with some degree of safety.

An hour before dawn began to lighten the sky over Lake Michigan, Loki returned to the most promising of those, an old apartment building with a basement storage area that was not as well secured as it could have been. The cheap chicken wire enclosures did not go all the way to the ceiling, and so it was possible to climb up there, filch a tarp and sleeping bag from someone's camping supplies, and slide down into an enclosure mostly full of empty boxes, thick with dust. He made himself a niche there behind them, wrapped himself up in the sleeping bag and tarp, prayed no one would need either the camping supplies or the boxes for the next sixteen hours, and allowed himself to sink into sleep.

The keen edge of hunger was not something any Kindred could ignore.

Only two nights into his ordeal, Loki was acutely aware of the mortals around him, both those across the street and thus out of immediate range, and those passing within a few quick steps of his grasp. He could smell them, the heady scent of blood overpowering the reek of too-sweet perfumes, stale cigarette smoke, booze, or human sweat. He could hear their breathing, the scrape and slap of their shoes on concrete, the pattering cacophony of their beating hearts. His eyes automatically sorted them solely by risk factor and level of vulnerability, skimming over those in groups, looking for individuals, not totally aware of what was around them, who might be careless enough to turn down a poorly lit street alone. The ones who wouldn't be able to run, who wouldn't be likely to fight back.

The Beast was a predator, and mortals were its prey. The Beast did not care about viruses. It did not care what happened to its prey after its own needs were satisfied. Only the hunger mattered, and the hunt. The longer he put it off, the stronger the Beast would grow, and the less control he would have over himself when he finally did sink his fangs into warm, living flesh.

Even thinking about it made it worse. His fangs lengthened in his jaw, and his entire body felt like a tightly-wound spring, like a cat crouching in the bushes watching the birds in the garden. The hunger was a physical ache that was centered somewhere in his belly but extended through every nerve, bone, and muscle. Without blood, he could not survive, and the Beast demanded survival, no matter what the cost.

Loki knew from bitter experience what would happen if he waited too long, if he let the hunger get too deep.

But his bite was poison. If he fed now, he would kill.

Then again, if he waited too long—he would kill anyway. He knew that. He'd done it. Not intentionally, of course. He'd been too new to his Requiem then, and he hadn't fully absorbed the bitter truth of what had been done to him. It had been the Beast that had killed that girl, the terrified street kid whom his sire had thrown into his arms. He hadn't known when to stop, that he needed to stop, and then she had gone limp in his arms, her heart faltering, and then going silent forever.

It had been the Beast. Not him. That was the only thought that had kept the horror at bay that night. *It wasn't me. It was the Beast.*

I didn't kill those girls. The virus did. I didn't know. It wasn't my fault.

But this time it would be different. This time he knew.

And he would kill, regardless. Whether the mortal victim died in the hospital, feverish and in pain, or under his fangs in a dark alley made no difference in the end. The only choice that remained to him was to pick who his prey would be, and how quickly she would die.

It is given to Man to eat of the fruit of the field and the flesh of the beasts, the Litany ran. *As the rabbit to the fox, and the deer to the wolf, so is man to the Crone's children and the huntsmen of the Horned King. Deny not the hunter his prey, nor the Beast its just satisfaction, nor the Crone the sacrifice that is due.*

And in that moment, when he accepted the inevitable, the physical discomfort from the hunger lessened, and the Beast quieted its strident complaints. It seemed his perceptions were clearer, his senses sharper. He'd called what he did on the dance floor at the Skullery hunting, the careful, earnest courting of a youthful mortal met in deceptively casual contact, the small talk and tentative caresses, luring with alcohol or narcotics or the promise of sex. It was not.

This was hunting, moving unseen from shadow to shadow, watching the mortal herds splinter and divide along the urban game trails, waiting for a straggler to peel away from the rest and take the more dangerous, solitary path.

janet trautvetter

It was slow and tedious. The first mortal he was following turned the wrong way, climbing the stairs to the El station above rather than continuing on her solo way into less traveled streets. Once a passing car had thwarted his timing, and the mortal then had time to reach her own car in safety.

And then he'd heard the motorcycles. To his enhanced and alerted senses, the particular fluttering roar of one was familiar, and that awoke the Beast again, not to hunt, but to retreat, climbing over a narrow bit of fence between two closely packed buildings to reach the alleyway behind.

Then he ran, leaping fences, cutting through alleys, putting as many physical barriers between himself and the hunters as he could. Now he was glad he'd opted to stay in familiar territory. He didn't know every last street, but he had a good sense of where he was in relation to the places he did know, and that meant he at least knew which direction to run.

He spotted a likely set of back stairs and balconies, with access to the adjacent roof, and went up to higher ground. Lying flat on his belly on the roof, he had a decent view of the alley, the intersecting street, and the raised tracks of the El. Invisible, unmoving and totally silent, he waited, soothing the Beast with promises of resuming the hunt as soon as the coast was clear.

Scents and sounds reached him there, the faint music and gunshots from someone watching a video, someone else snoring loudly enough to cause his neighbor to pound on the wall. There was the bitter scent of someone's cigarette smoke, garbage that needed taking out, old laundry, tar from the roof, stale cooking odors, burnt popcorn.

Across the alley, in the next apartment building over, an elderly woman struggled to raise her window and let in a little breeze. From his vantage point, he could see inside her bedroom, the knickknacks and family photos, the chair and the television, the mahogany bedstead with only one side turned down, and the cluster of pill bottles on the side table. He could see her making her way slowly back across the room to her bed, using a walker to steady her steps.

Alone.

The Beast's interest immediately sharpened. *No,* Loki told himself firmly. But he couldn't look away from that window, either. No one would question it, after all. The old were more vulnerable to the virus, everyone knew that. Not even Marek would think twice about it.

No, he told himself again. There had to be someone else.

But to find someone else would require going back to the Rack. Back to where the bars and the drunks could be found. Where the Circle's hunters would be looking for him, knowing he had to feed, and expecting him to try for his usual stalking grounds.

So many pills. Maybe she was sick. Maybe she was going to die anyway, in a year or two. Maybe she was lonely, sleeping in that big bed all alone.

With one last look up and down the alley to make sure no one was watching, Loki swung down from the roof to the fire escape, went down the stairs, and then up the other side, to the old woman's back door.

The door was locked, but the window next to it was not. He opened the window slowly, to minimize any noise, and then slipped inside. The apartment was small and cramped, packed with furnishings that had once graced far larger rooms. The walls and every horizontal surface contained the accumulated photos and knickknacks of a lifetime.

Only the most accessible photos were free of dust, showing a middle-aged couple and two children. Stacks of mail were piled on the dining room table, most unopened.

Loki moved silently through to the bedroom, and up to the bed. Lots of medication bottles, but someone had taken the time to lay them out for her in a plastic tray, labeled with when she was supposed to take them. They were untouched.

"Ricky?" A hand touched his.

Loki jumped, fangs sliding down without him willing them, and turned to look at her. "I—shhh," he said, trying to sound reassuring. "Shhh, you should be sleeping."

"You haven't changed a bit," she said, "I knew you'd come. I knew they couldn't keep you away."

Shit. Loki knew he should leave. He couldn't do this. It wasn't right. But when she caught his hand, he didn't pull away.

"I knew you'd come back for me," she mumbled, raising her arms to him. "Here, now. Don't be shy. Give us a hug."

Loki sat on the edge of the bed and let her gather him into her arms. For a minute or so, it almost felt good—it had been so long since anyone had held him like this, as if she actually cared about him.

But then there was the scent of her blood, just below the soft, drooping skin of her throat, the rasp of her breathing, the rapid pattering of her heart. His fangs slid down, his lips parted, his hunger deepening swiftly into a physical ache that could only be soothed by one thing. She gave a little moan when his fangs pierced her flesh, her blood thin and delicately sweet on his tongue. Her fingers clutched at his coat as he gently laid her back against the pillows, suckling slowly, letting that sweetness fill the void within.

He stopped when her heart fluttered and skipped, licked the wounds closed. There were tears on her cheeks. "I think… I should rest a bit now," she mumbled. Her eyes drooped closed.

Now you've done it, you bastard, he told himself angrily. *What, can't you finish the job? Let the virus do your dirty work, 'cause you can't finish what you fucking started?* Something cold and wet ran down his own cheek as well, he wiped it away with the back of his sleeve, not wanting to see if it was clear or reddish-tinged. He remembered the patients in the ICU, the needles and machines, wracked with fever, dying alone and in pain.

It would be mercy to continue, wouldn't it? To spare her the pain and the fever, to spare someone else the necessity of dying for his thirst. It was too late to spare her life. All he could do was spare her any further suffering. He bent down over her again, and kissed the slack cheek. Then he drank until her heart slowed, and then finally stopped.

I never saw you as a murderer, Loki.

Well, maybe Gretchen McBride hadn't seen him so clearly after all.

Of all the Acolytes who were pursuing him in obedience to Rowen's imposed ordeal, Jed and Damien proved to be the most persistent and difficult to avoid. It didn't help, of course, that he and Damien had hunted the same streets of the Rack, and hung out at so many of the same clubs. Damien knew Lakeview, Lincoln Park, and Wrigleyville as well as Loki did himself, and, with Jed's assistance, seemed to have an uncanny sense of where he was going to be at certain times of the night.

janet trautvetter

There had been several close calls, when Loki had managed to duck down an alley or crouch down between parked cars just in time to avoid their notice. He knew he could use the shadows to cloak himself, and Damien would walk right by and not see him there. But Jed was Mekhet, and his perceptions might be keen enough to see through the concealing shadows.

On the third night, Loki was passing the huge curving hulk of Wrigley Field, having just barely escaped his pursuers again, when he noticed two things of immediate interest. The first was that the Cubs were obviously out of town tonight, because the stadium was silent, the interior mostly dark. The second was that there was a delivery truck parked at the loading dock. Whatever delivery it had been, it seemed to be done unloading, and the receiving guy was signing off on the delivery slip, but the gate behind him was still open.

Silent and unseen, Loki slipped past the mortals and inside the stadium. A few minutes later, he heard the gate clang shut, and the bolts of the locks shoot home.

Until dawn of the third night, Rowen had said. All he had to do was hang out in here until almost morning, and then he'd be home free. Assuming, of course, they didn't know where he'd gone.

No such luck.

Barely fifteen minutes later, Loki found himself crouched on the sloping ramp up to the terrace, as the two motorcycles pulled up on the sidewalk below.

Damien studied the stadium's wall. "Lots of places to hide in there," he observed. "No food source, though, not tonight."

"Is there a way in?" Jed asked.

"Over the fence behind the bleachers, maybe. Think he might be in there?"

Behind them, Loki caught a fluttering of movement. A trio of crows, settling on the edge of a sidewalk trash can, out of the direct streetlamp illumination and barely visible. They didn't seem interested in its contents, however. They just perched there, watching.

Jed reached inside his jacket and brought out his ritual knife, which he balanced on the palm of his hand and rotated around until it was pointing directly at the stadium where Loki crouched. "Oh, yes," Jed murmured. "He's in there. How well would he know the inside?"

Shit. Jed clearly knew more of the Circle's blood magic tricks than Loki had realized. Had Jed's knife been one of those to mark him during his escape? Possibly. *No wonder the motherfuckers keep finding me.*

Damien shrugged. "No idea. We never talked about baseball."

A half-dozen or so more crows flew down to street level and landed on the back of a bench, thirty feet or so from the two vampires.

Jed noticed, turning slightly to stare at the birds, which stared right back, shifting only slightly on their perch. "Look," he said, his voice dropping so that Loki could barely hear him.

Damien turned, then glanced up as several more landed on the crossbar of the traffic light. "Crows don't fly at night," he said.

Jed put the knife back inside his jacket, got back on his bike, and kicked the stand up. "Hers do."

"*Shit.*" Damien looked around, more urgently. "You think they're with—"

"Don't even say it," Jed snapped, then roared off, leaving Damien to follow a few seconds later.

The birds didn't even startle, much less fly away. They just stayed right where they were, waiting. A couple more flew in, and jockeyed for perch positions on the steeply slanted flagpoles.

Loki strained his vision to pierce into every possible shadow, scour every square foot of sidewalk and street. A growing dread sent a cold shiver through his veins. Because Jed and Damien were absolutely correct. Crows didn't fly at night.

Except hers. The Unholy.

Even as he thought her name, he saw her, standing on the curb across the street. He hadn't seen how she got there, she was just there, a tall woman with a shaggy black mane of—hair?—under a black cowboy hat. She looked up, studying the stadium's exterior as if she knew he was there, could see him huddled in the shadows, pretending he could hide behind a wall that was nothing more than a chain-link fence.

The fear clawed at him, a panic urge to run, run as fast as he could, any direction at all, just to get away from her. Suddenly, being staked and beaten into a bloody pulp by Damien and Jed looked pretty damned good, compared to being caught by an inhuman monster like the Unholy, who belonged to no covenant and followed no rules. Not even Maxwell's Tranquility.

She started walking across the street. His gaze was fixated at the odd way her arms bent as they swung at her sides. He could hear the steady *thock, thock, thock* of her boot heels on the asphalt. She didn't even look for traffic, just kept walking slowly and deliberately, eyes facing forward. Somehow the passing cars missed her, crossing behind or in front of her, but never intersecting her path. Maybe they didn't even see her, for all he knew.

As she passed the birds' perches on the sidewalk below, the crows took flight, spiraling upward, past his hiding place and out of sight above. Loki glanced up, listening, trying to determine if they'd flown in over the stadium's high walls, or—

There was a sudden blur of motion, and a loud metallic clang, as the steel-tipped, pointed toe of a boot jammed itself into the chain-link barrier a foot from his nose. Loki let out an involuntary yelp, and scooted backward twenty feet on his ass, slamming into the railing behind him.

She clung there, on the other side of the chain-link fencing, a good thirty or forty feet up from the pavement below. He caught a glimpse of gnarled claws ending in wickedly curved black talons, the glint of yellow eyes under the shadowing brim of her hat, and her teeth, white fangs curving down behind slightly parted lips.

Then he let the Beast have its way, and he ran, actually scrambling on all fours for a few feet before he was fully upright, legs pumping hard as he tore up the ramp to the upper deck. Behind him, he could hear the rattling and high-pitched grinding of metal on metal, as the Unholy began to methodically rip the chain-link barrier away from its support posts.

He made it around the bend of the ramp and dashed through the gate out into the seats of the upper deck, then forced himself to stop, gripping the railing to hold himself still. *Wait. Think, you idiot. Think, don't panic. THINK.*

He couldn't outrun her. He knew this instinctively. He was too young, not strong enough in the gifts of the blood to dare match his speed or strength against hers. He didn't know what she was capable of, but it had to be pretty fucking impressive.

But she was Gangrel, not Mekhet. Gangrel were known for being tough and savage, for their affinity with the Beast. She had that, all right. What did he have?

Shadows. The stadium was mostly dark, with only emergency lighting. *Check.* Lots of places to hide, Damien had said, which was true. *Check…* Loki was good at hiding—but could he hide from her?

He didn't have much of a choice but to try. Unfortunately, the upper deck offered damned few hiding places.

Loki drew the shadows around him again like a concealing blanket, and opened up his senses, sharpening his sight and hearing as far as he could. Looking up and around, he spotted the crows coming in to roost on the backs of seats, on the railings, or up on the high steel frames supporting the lights. There were a lot of them, many more than he'd ever noticed before. Maybe all the crows that were left in Chicago now. *Shit.*

Moving as quickly as he dared, Loki jogged around the curving center aisle, then ducked back through the next available gate, running back down the length of its ramp to the terrace. It was all too open up here, too exposed, the stands sweeping down in a shallow slope to the field, the open ramps going up, the chain-link fencing of the outer wall. But if he could get down to the lower levels of the stands, make it over to the bleachers—Damien was right, the wall wasn't all that high along there. If he could get that far, he might be able to get out.

Then he heard the hollow *thock, thock, thock* of her boot heels on the ramp just over his head.

Quickly, he ducked under the ramp itself and froze in place, willing himself to be without substance, scent, or sound. Silent and invisible, a shadow on the concrete and nothing more. If she just kept going in the same direction she was now, he might still have a chance.

Instead, she turned at the bottom of the ramp, and walked right past him. In the light coming in from the street, he could see her clearly, a tall woman in well-worn denim and cowboy boots, with a long, shaggy mass of hair that flowed over her shoulders and sported glossy black feathers among the strands. Her arms did bend oddly, the elbow joint disproportionately high, her forearm unnaturally long and ending in a scaly avian talon and sharp claws. And the way she moved her head was odd as well, tilting it to one side and then the other in quick, abrupt jerks as she looked around and sniffed the air. Her face seemed human enough, though, what he could see of it under the shadow of her hat.

Until she turned and looked right at him, and then he remembered the yellow eyes and the fangs, and felt every nerve in his body tighten in utter terror from the unblinking force of her stare.

The Beast wanted to run in a panic. Loki held it in, though it felt like every muscle was literally trembling with the effort. She turned her gaze away and the immediate pressure of the panic lessoned slightly, and then, as she walked on past him, he realized she hadn't seen him.

She couldn't see him.

The wave of pure relief arising from that thought was so great he had to clamp down on it, before he got careless and blew it all by moving too soon. He waited, watching until she was a quarter of the way around the curve, until the sound of her boot heels on the concrete had all but faded away.

Then he walked as quickly as he dared in the opposite direction, and took the first ramp down to the concourse below. He broke into a run, trying desperately to calculate which gate would give him the best chance at reaching the bleachers and its relatively low outside wall.

But as he emerged up into the stands, a half-dozen or so crows that had been roosting on the railing overhead suddenly startled and took flight, squawking indignantly at being disturbed. *Fuck!* What was it about those birds—he hadn't made a sound, and yet they'd somehow known he was there.

Worse, she now knew he was there. He spotted her in the stands, only two sections up and three over, a lot closer than he thought she'd be.

Loki ducked back inside, cursing his luck, and the unerring instincts of crows. She might not be able to see him, but the birds would gave him away every fucking time. In fact, three of them had just followed him inside, finding perches up on the support beams, where they could see exactly which way he chose to run.

Wait a minute. The crows.

There had been something in Nicholas Crain's journal, one of the numerous mentions of crows doing odd shit. He'd described the crows following him, even after dark, when he passed unseen before all mortal eyes. And then later that night, he'd written of meeting someone he referred to as the Crow Woman, a manifestation, or so he'd claimed in his journal, of the Morrígan, the Battle-Goddess aspect of the Crone.

He'd described the encounter almost as a vision, and Loki had thought it was just that. But it could have been literal, now that he thought about it. The whole part about surrendering to her, which was straight out of the Litany—the way mortal coven members surrendered to the fangs of their Acolyte priestess. *She demanded one thing of me,* he'd written. *And I knew she could take it whether I willed or no.*

Had Nicholas Crain met the Unholy? Damien said that he'd heard she didn't always kill when she fed. That if you surrendered to her, she would drink but not destroy. It was a rumor, as almost everything about the Unholy was a rumor, second-, third-, or even fourth-hand. But if Crain's journal was accurate, his account would be firsthand. And everything else he'd written, at least as far as Loki could verify it, had been absolutely true.

Don't be an idiot, he told himself. *The journal's over a hundred years old. Maybe it was a dream he wrote about. You've certainly had some wacko ones lately.*

But the description matched. Okay, he didn't mention the claws, or the yellow eyes, or the network of black veins that pulsed in her soul's aura. But still, it matched. The wanderer known as the Crow Woman, the legend without a name, only an appellation: Unholy.

A holy rite, Crain had called his experience, offering himself as sacrifice. An act of faith to the dark gods he worshipped, to the Crone herself.

And if more is required?

Thock. Thock. Thock. Thock. Coming down the aisle in the stands overhead, a slightly brisker pace than she'd used before. Maybe she was getting impatient. And she knew how to find him now. Not much time to decide.

He didn't have Nicholas Crain's faith in the Circle's ancient gods, and he was currently all but throttling the Beast to just stand here long enough to think. But he did have Nicholas Crain's word, which had proved pretty reliable so far. If nothing else, maybe he could have a bit of faith in that.

Loki found a good place to wait, let the shadows drift and fade away, and promised himself that if Nicholas Crain turned out to be lying, he'd hunt the old bastard down in whatever corner of hell he was hiding in and kick his fucking ass.

But when she stepped around the corner onto the concourse, he was very glad he had a cinderblock wall to his back to lean against. It helped keep him from succumbing to the Beast's frantic demands to flee.

She stopped, hesitated, as if seeing him there had caught her off guard, and studied him for a moment. He met her gaze, but only for a moment. It took no effort at all to acknowledge her power and drop his eyes first.

"Got tired of running, did you?" Her voice was low, surprisingly smooth, with the faint hint of a drawl. Somehow he'd expected her to croak.

"Yeah." His voice came out squeaky, barely audible. *No.* He would not let that be the last word, no fucking way. "Seemed kinda pointless after a while, y'know?"

She came a few steps closer, moving both forward and slightly sideways. Stalking him. The talons protruding from the sleeves of her denim jacket opened and closed. Limbering up, perhaps. Her thumb didn't move right, it wasn't connected to the other... fingers... anymore, but totally opposable, like the talons of a bird.

He tried not to think about that. "I heard, from—from a reputable source," he began, hoping his voice wasn't shaking, "that if someone, a—a Kindred someone that is, just surrendered and let you drink—" Every instinct he had screamed at him to run or perish, and yet somehow he managed to keep his feet still, though he had to shove his hands deep in his coat pockets to keep them from drumming against the wall. "Then you would let that Kindred survive afterward."

Closer. Still partly forward, partly sideways. Almost circling, except that the wall prevented that. She was limited to a zigzag approach. She couldn't come at him from behind. "And you're wonderin' if that's true." She sounded almost amused. "'Course, you ain't in a real good position if it's not, are you?"

"Well, I'm really kind of relying on it being true," he said. It was smart-ass bravado, but it helped him keep his wits together, keep the fear at bay. "It was Nicholas Crain who said it. He met you once, long time ago. Do you remember?"

He thought she actually tried, for a moment. She stopped, tilted her head slightly, and the hint of a frown passed over her face, what he could see of it under the brim of the hat. Then she shook her head slowly once. "Can't say as I do."

Shit. Well, even Maxwell hadn't remembered the journal's author all that well, and he'd actually put some effort into it. "I'm surrendering," he said.

"Good," she murmured. He could see the fangs sliding down behind her lips. Only about ten feet between them now, and she stopped, held herself absolutely still for three whole seconds.

Her attack was so fast he could only register the results. One moment he was standing there, arms at his sides, and ten feet between them. The next, he was spread-eagled against the wall, her talons around his arms holding them apart, the claws digging into his flesh through the leather of his jacket.

Then there was pain—sharp, intense pain—that started at the base of his throat and penetrated inwards, racing along veins and nerves down through his torso to his groin.

There something changed, some misfiring of the nerve endings that suddenly shifted frequencies over from intense pain to equally intense pleasure, going from agony to incredible ecstasy in an instant. Where the pain had moved inward, the pleasure started somewhere deep within and moved outward, running through his veins to where she suckled at his throat. Every movement of her mouth against his skin sent a new shiver of delight rippling through him. He was sexually aroused as well, but that seemed almost beside the point. This was an orgasm that reached every cell of his body.

This was what surrender meant, to not only be held helpless and rocked by waves of sensual bliss, but to know that even though each wave drained away a little more of his existence, he still wanted it to go on and on, even if it ultimately destroyed him. This was what the mortals felt under the Kiss, this was why they willingly prostrated themselves at the priestess' feet and offered themselves at the altar. This was why Nicholas Crain had considered his encounter a act of worship, a religious experience. He could almost see the Crone, waiting for him—beside the dark gateway that was getting steadily closer.

No, not the Crone, exactly. The priestess he'd dreamed about before, the strange, old woman with the black-feathered mask and cloak. *Those who look will see*, she said, *and you see. Those who see must act.* She held out her hand, and he could see the token in it. But she closed her fingers over it before he could read the name. She tightened her grip, and blood began to seep out between her fingers and drip down on the ground. *It is not the blood that brings enlightenment*, she told him sternly.

That was true. It was difficult to think, floating down the dark river as he was, the water rocking him gently, washing over and through him so sweetly. No, he remembered the Litany now. Enlightenment came from—

But then he was torn away from it all, the waves of pleasure that had sustained him suddenly draining away. Light burned his eyes, he felt cold cement at his back, as he lay sprawled on the floor, bereft and alone—

Well, not entirely alone. A cool tongue laved his throat, easing the pain but not the sense of loss.

"Good," the Unholy murmured again, and then she was gone.

After a few minutes, he got up, half-expecting to feel woozy or dizzy, though he did not. Kindred physiology did not react to blood loss that way. He was simply hungry, and incredibly amazed to have survived. Nicholas Crain had been right after all.

He was aware then of the crows squawking, a veritable chorus of them, out in the ball field. Curious, he walked through the nearest gate out to the stands to see what was going on.

The crows were circling, a constantly moving, black-winged pillar around the pitcher's mound in the center infield. They were flying in such close formation near the base that it took a minute before he spotted the Unholy sitting cross-legged on the mound, clad only in her cowboy hat, her discarded clothing on the turf beside her. The crows innermost in the pillar were landing on her shoulders, her outstretched, misshapen arms, on her legs, until it seemed she was covered in a moving cloak of black-feathered bodies.

The breeze wafting across the field from the lake brought him the scent of Kindred blood, and he realized what she was doing.

janet trautvetter

The blood. Her blood. *His* blood. And the crows. The natural virus was carried in the blood, that was how it passed between the crows and the mosquitoes, and then from mosquitoes to mortals. The crows would probably die—their bodies were so small, even the natural virus killed them.

But it wouldn't kill the Unholy, and she was a nomad. Anywhere she went, she would infect crows and Kindred alike. And sooner or later, the mosquitoes would pick it up as well, and pass the virus along into the natural ecosystem. It would become a real epidemic, spreading across the whole country.

And it would all be his fault.

There were worse places to spend the day than a mausoleum, but that didn't make Loki feel any better to wake up in one. Or to owe a favor to its proprietor, who had an very exacting memory for such things. He was, however, greatly relieved to see not a single crow anywhere in evidence when he at last emerged into the night and closed the iron gate of the mausoleum behind him.

His cell phone chimed. He reached for it out of habit, glanced at the screen. The caller's name was listed as Private Number. What the hell. He tapped the answer button.

"Hi, Loki, it's Baihu."

"Hey," Loki started to say, but the voice on the other end continued without waiting for a response, and he realized he was listening to a recording.

"*I guess you must be sleeping, I just realized what time it is. Sorry. Anyway. Something's come up, some new information on the virus and where it's coming from. We think what's going on is a lot bigger than just the virus, actually, but we're still trying to figure out exactly what that is, and, more importantly, what we can do about it. We're hosting a meeting of interested parties to discuss what we know, in hopes that we can put a few more pieces of this puzzle together, and maybe find some answers. I think you may be able to contribute something to that, and find it of interest to your own situation as well. I'd like it very much if you would attend.*

"*Circumstances being what they are, I can understand if you're feeling a bit leery of our hospitality, or coming to a meeting where you don't already know all the participants. In that regard, I can promise—no, I swear it by my name—that if you come, you have my personal vow of safe conduct, to enter our sanctum, participate in our discussion, and leave as freely as you came. Oh. I suppose I should tell you the particulars, too. We're meeting on Thursday night, starting at around nine—that should give you time to get there after sundown from wherever you are, I hope. And here's the address—*"

Today was Thursday, and it was already eight-thirty. Shit. No time to go home and change, assuming he didn't want to be too late. Assuming he wanted to go in the first place.

"*I hope you can make it. Give me a call and let me know if you're coming, or if you need a ride, or if you have any questions. Thanks. Bye.*"

According to his cell phone, Baihu, whatever his name was—had called Tuesday afternoon. Of course, since his phone had been turned off, he'd gotten the answering service, and Loki hadn't checked his messages in the past three nights.

Well, maybe he could call and at least find out who else was coming. Loki touched the keypad again, looking for the menu option for returning a call.

Nothing happened. The cell phone screen was dark. Loki pressed the power button, but the screen only displayed the words *LOW BATTERY. RECHARGE NOW!*

"Well, shit," he muttered, and stuck the phone back in his pocket. Should he go? It wasn't that far from where he was now. On the other hand, the Unholy had drunk deeply, and he badly needed to replenish himself. He doubted Baihu and his associates would be serving suitable refreshments.

But he would still infect anyone he fed upon, and that person would get sick and die. That hadn't changed, and Loki was not at all keen on finding out the hard way just what Norris had done with Raven. And if this virus was magical in nature, as Baihu insisted it was, that meant it could be cured only by magic as well. And he was no magician.

So he really had no choice at all.

The address Baihu had given turned out to be a huge Victorian mansion in Wicker Park, with ornate gables, bay windows, and a wide porch. The house sat back from the street, next to one of Chicago's sprawling cemeteries on one side, with a small private cemetery within a stone-and-iron fence on the other. A large sign sat out in the front that said POOLE & UPDIKE FUNERAL HOME. A driveway led to a parking lot on the other side, and what Loki assumed was the delivery entrance and morgue—there was an ambulance parked back there with its lights on.

There were lights on within the massive house, too, and as Loki got closer, he recognized Baihu standing on the porch.

Loki walked up the flagstone walkway, though he paused before he set a foot on the step. "Sorry I'm late," he said. "Didn't get your message until just a while ago."

"I'm glad you came," Baihu said, and sounded as though he even meant it. "Come on inside. Everyone else is here already. We were just about to get started."

Loki still had a few questions about who "everybody else" was, but he'd find that out soon enough, so he followed the magus inside.

Baihu led the way up a magnificent oak staircase to the second floor. "We're meeting in the chapel," he explained. "That won't be a problem for you, will it?"

"A little late to be asking, isn't it?" Loki said. "But no, I'm agnostic."

"Oh, one more thing," Baihu said, and paused in front of a pair of closed double doors. "I should explain something. No violence is permitted within these walls, for any reason. If something happens—which it shouldn't, but just in case—it's for the master of this house, who has been kind enough to allow us to meet here, to deal with. And he's more than capable of doing so. Will you promise that?"

"That's for everybody, right?" Loki asked. "Okay, then," he said, when Baihu nodded. "I promise."

Baihu opened the door, and Loki followed him down the center aisle. Tiaret and Glorianna sat on the left, and Gwyn was standing near the front. There were a bunch of scruffy-looking folks he didn't know seated together on the right side.

"What the hell happened?" Gwyn asked, looking him over suspiciously. "Trouble on the way here?"

"Nah, I just got the message late," Loki started, suddenly reminded of the rips in his pants and shirt, the grime smeared on his jacket, things that hadn't exactly been his top priority over the past three nights. "I had to—I, uh, had my cell phone off. Sorry."

janet trautvetter

He stuck his hands in his coat pockets, ignoring the feathers that had once again managed to sprout there, suddenly uneasy about these strangers, who were all watching him very intently. He edged around the front of the pews to the left, preferring to take his chances with Tiaret and Glorianna, who were at least familiar. He caught a glimpse of the framed portrait on the easel up front, a smiling young woman, whose face was also familiar. *Fuck.* Raven's victim, the one from the woods.

"Well, just don't get dirt anywhere," Gwyn continued, "I won't be responsible for the results, safe conduct or no. Folks, this is Loki. He's a, a representative as I understand it, of the, er—"

"Kindred," Loki prompted him, now standing where the portrait of the girl was not easily visible to him. Marek had said there was one death he wasn't counting, because of the timing. *Shit.*

"Right. The Kindred of Chicago."

"You look like you been rode hard and put up wet." The speaker was the nearest of the strangers, a lean guy with red hair and gingery stubble, who spoke with a distinct Southern twang. "You quite sure everythin's all right?"

"You're sure as hell not local," Loki observed, warily. None of the strangers had been introduced yet.

"No, Heartsblood's from out East," one of the others said, a dark-haired woman. "But he's with a pack of… well, they've got a good reputation back home. And he's come specifically to help with this."

Heartsblood? What the hell kind of name was that?

"Yeah," the red-haired man said. "And these are the Haunts, a pack with a good reputation here." He gestured around. "Mercedes, Erik, Little Blue. And this here's Anna."

"Pack?" The Beast was suddenly alert, on guard. Loki felt his muscles grow tense, picking up its warning without knowing what it was. "Interesting way to put it." He could see it then, as he dimmed his perceptions of the visible world and let what was unseen sharpen. The rippling colors in their auras were too bold, too primal, to be merely human. And there were five of them, and he was alone. "Fuck. Fucking shit."

Loki snapped his vision back to normal and was across the width of half the chapel in an eye blink, as the Beast snarled, a mixture of fury and terror. "You didn't say that!" he shouted at Baihu in a fury. "You didn't fucking mention! You set me up, you motherfuckers!"

"Loki," Gwyn interrupted, "if you're gonna tell us werewolves are the freakiest or the scariest thing you've ever met, especially this week, I'm going to let Glory here stick another stake in you for pure mercy's sake. Stop being a pussy."

"Pussy, hell." Loki turned his anger on Gwyn, who likely deserved it more anyway. "You left out a relevant fucking detail!"

"Gentlemen, please—" Tiaret rose to her feet. Loki could almost hear the thunder rumbling in the background.

"I left out a relevant detail," corrected Baihu, stepping forward so as to stand between them, but facing Loki. "Yes. I'm sorry. But, frankly, we were already worried enough that you might decline, and we do need your help."

"Just hold on, son," Heartsblood interjected, holding up his hands in what might be intended as a calming gesture. "Nobody's here to do anything but talk."

"Exactly," Tiaret agreed. "This is a situation that affects all of us, Loki. We've all got a piece of this problem, and I personally believe our best hope lies in putting the pieces together."

Loki felt the Beast's fury fade a bit, felt the tension easing in his muscles, his eyes on Tiaret.

She crossed her arms, turned to face her associates. "Besides," she added, "the non-aggression pledge binds all of us while we're under this roof, and our host is not a magus to be trifled with. Therefore, there will not be so much as a whisper of the word 'stake' or anything else even slightly similarly discomfiting. Is that clear, Gwyn?"

Gwyn shrugged. "Just trying to calm him down," he protested, apparently not the least bit repentant.

"Well, it was a pretty spectacular failure, even for your social skills," she said, and Loki was gratified to see Gwyn flinch. "Let's proceed."

That was apparently Gwyn's cue, as he walked back to the doors and closed them, then put his hands up on the dried wreaths that decorated the upper panel of each door. They wriggled and sent out ghostly tendrils of shadowy vines that spread fast and wide, encircling the entire room and completing their circuit in a huge knot in front of the stained-glass window. Loki felt a shiver across his perceptions as his peripheral awareness of anything outside the room went suddenly blank and silent.

"There. Protections are up." Gwyn sat down near the back of the room, as if invoking the sorcerous vines had taken something out of him. "Who's going to do the honors?"

Glorianna stood up, a stack of papers in her hands. "Let's distribute the handouts first. This is a comprehensive analysis of the Muskegon virus. As you'll see, it's pretty apparent that the new strain circulating is not a normal mutation—"

Loki accepted his handout and was soon totally lost amid the confusing diagrams, graphs, and textual explanations that didn't explain a damned thing in a language regular people might actually understand.

Fortunately for his self-esteem, he wasn't the only one. The Lupines looked equally confused. "What the hell is all this about?" Heartsblood asked. "Don't make a lick of sense."

Gwyn's explanation that followed didn't make much sense either. Something about the virus being totally unnatural, as it both fed back on itself and generated itself in a wholly impossible loop, so it had to be an artificial magical construct, which Loki knew already.

"Then this falls on your doorstep," said one of the other Lupines, a thin, angry-looking young woman in a hoodie. Anna, if Loki remembered right.

"It might," Glorianna admitted, after glancing at Tiaret, perhaps to get permission to say it so plainly. "We're not aware of any other way such a thing could be done, though we're obviously open to suggestions. But it was done with purpose. Specifically altered not only to be more deadly, but to spread more easily through more vectors—including supernatural ones. That's on top of the old vectors of mosquitoes and crows."

"Yeah, the crows, that's the key," Heartsblood blurted out, excitedly. "The Murder of Crows."

That caught Loki's attention, and he jumped on it. "What do you know about the crows?" he asked.

"You noticed 'em, too?"

janet trauvetter

"I know there's some spooky-ass crows around lately, and they love dropping dead on my balcony," Loki answered, wondering what kind of crow activity the werewolf had seen. "You got an explanation?"

If there was a straight answer, however, Heartsblood seemed incapable of providing it. "They're the ones trying to warn us," he explained. "I mean it is, the Murder is. I guess it ain't so much warn as—well, it's what they are. They can't even help it."

"Okay, that was persuasive," said Anna, shaking her head.

"Shit. It's like a rash, all right?" Heartsblood continued. "You scratch at it and scratch at it and all you're doin' is spreadin' it around, but the rash can't help it. It's immunological, y'know what I mean?"

"The rash is just the symptom," Baihu translated. "The real problem is underneath."

Having someone understand his babbling, however, only encouraged the werewolf to babble further. "See, they came to me last night. I finally understood. It ain't like a regular spirit. I don't even know what it is, but it's always been here. This is its home. And anytime somethin' happens, somethin' bad I mean, why the crows take it up. They try to take up all the carrion, but there's too much. They been takin' it up and takin' it up till they're full to the gullet and can't hold any more. For Chrissake, you were there, you know what I'm talking about."

That was to Baihu, who apparently did understand, but given the blank looks exchanged around the room, he might have been the only one. "Yes," the Asian mage said, finally. "It's really hard to explain, especially in a way that doesn't make you sound crazy. But there's a… force of some kind. And the crows are its way of manifesting, expressing. And it's in pain."

"And it's supposed to be here," Heartsblood added. He seemed to think that was an important distinction.

"Wait. I thought we were supposed to stop it." That came from one of the other werewolves, a big, blond guy whose name Loki didn't remember.

"It is supposed to be here," Baihu said thoughtfully. "But it's not supposed to be this way. Something went wrong. Now it's trying to right things as best it can, but, uh, let me see if I can put it into words. It is kind of like an immune response, in that it can go overboard. It can kill the host trying to cure it."

Those who look will see. Those who see, must act. Something in what they were saying reminded Loki of the priestess in the black feather mask from his dream, and the black feathers that showed up everywhere, even when it didn't make any sense, like reappearing in his pockets all the time.

"Like the encephalitis," Heartsblood continued, pointing to the handout. "It's the inflammation that squeezes their brains to death. We got to bring the inflammation down."

Crain's journal had also described the local natural balances being off-kilter, like a festering wound that had to be either lanced or it would swell up and burst. And the crows, always there. *Ready to take it up*, as Heartsblood said.

It made sense after all, in a strange way. Loki hoped that didn't mean he was crazy, too.

"So the crows aren't the enemy, but they might kill us anyway, so we have to figure out what's bothering them and stop it?" Gwyn threw up his hands in frustration. "Anybody else awed at the sense of progress?"

"Well." Loki hesitated, though seeing Gwyn as confused as he'd been earlier was perversely satisfying. "Actually, we might be getting somewhere now. If we can figure out what set it off the last time."

"Last time?" Glorianna echoed. She fumbled in her bag after her electronic gadget.

"Yeah." Loki stepped forward. "This has happened before. You guys don't know anything about it?"

Baffled looks all around, but he certainly had their attention, so he straightened up to his full height and continued. "Eighteen seventy-one. The Great Fire. Weird shit went on back then, too, and a lot of it had to do with crows."

"Care to expand on the phrase 'weird shit'?" Gwyn prompted.

"Well, lots of fires, a couple a day, 'cause of the drought." Loki shifted through the details he remembered, which incidents would sound sufficiently unusual to be tied into the whole, and which were too Kindred or Circle-specific to share. "Lots of violence. I guess that's not too weird by itself, but then the crows were acting up as well, and some really bizarre rumors floating around. Slaughtered livestock standing back up. More hauntings than usual. Black feathers appearing out of nowhere, and I know that's happening again—"

"The black feather rain," Heartsblood interrupted.

Shit. Loki froze for a second, and then realized he wasn't the only one who was reacting to that one.

"That's right." Baihu seemed a bit taken aback. Perhaps he thought he was the only one who'd seen it. "Black feather rain on a dead city."

"And the Maynard party," Loki finished.

"Maynard?" Baihu echoed, but without obvious comprehension.

"Maynard, Maynard. That rings a bell," Mercedes broke in. "I think Sarah's mentioned it. But it was back before any of us were born. Something to do with somebody finding out too much. The People almost being discovered."

"Everything almost being discovered," Loki corrected her, though he was a bit surprised at the blank looks he was getting from the mages. Didn't they keep a history of some kind, as bookish as they were? "Us, you, you guys, everything that goes bump in the night. Maynard knew, and he tried to expose us. Most people didn't believe him, of course, but he did wind up with followers. According to the journal they kept on even after he left, headed up by some witch-hunter named Talley."

"But what's that got to do with anything?" Anna asked.

"Well, that's the thing," Loki explained. "You know how everybody says it was Mrs. O'Leary's cow that started the fire?"

Of course, since he mentioned the Fire and the fucking O'Leary cow in the same sentence, someone had to answer with the damned song, and all the rest of 'em joined in. *Hot time in the old town tonight,* yeah, yeah, though only the youngest werewolf, the punk kid with the blue patch in his hair and the excessively decorated jacket, got all the way to the end with the "Fire! Fire! Fire!"

"Okay, I was born here, I know the fucking song!" Loki snapped, raising his hands. "It's still bullshit, okay? We can't know for sure what started it. But there was a lot of talk that maybe it was Maynard's people. Purifying the city or some shit, trying to kill all of us."

"You're saying you think that's what's going on?" Anna looked askance at him. "Some kind of supernatural holocaust? Come on. It's not like you people are gonna die of the virus."

"What I'm a little surprised Loki hasn't explained yet," Tiaret interjected, "is that the Kindred community is very worried about this virus. Not that it could kill them, but that it could expose them. We're not kidding about a supernatural vector. Vampiric transmission is more than likely responsible for some of these deaths. It's certainly not in the interests of the Kindred to let such a thing go on. Am I right, Loki?"

"Yeah," he said. He looked from her to Anna. "That's right. We got as much interest in stopping this thing as anybody."

"You said according to the journal," the big, blond guy said. "What journal?"

"Oh yeah, sorry. That's where I got all this. It belonged to a Kindred named Dr. Nicholas Crain. He was in the city at the time."

"So this isn't personal recollection?" Mercedes asked.

"Oh, no," Loki assured her, "I'm not that old."

"And Dr. Crain isn't around anymore, I take it."

"Nah, he's long since ash."

"Too bad," said Gwyn. "Be nice if we could talk to somebody who survived."

Yeah, like that would help. "Not too many of those around anymore," Loki said. "Believe me, I tried."

Heartsblood reached into the duffel bag at his feet and fished around, coming up with something odd-looking in a plastic baggie. "If you do know somebody real old, we might could ask 'em about this here thing. I got it off a spirit we fought near one of the sewer grates down our way. The spirit, uh, vomited it up."

"Vomited?" That conjured some nightmarish images in Loki's mind, just the thought of something ghostly coming out of a sewer and upchucking shit.

What Heartsblood had found, as he was eager to explain, was an antique ink blotter, dating from the mid-1800s. It stank like it had been in the sewers a while, too. But what caught Loki's attention was the faded, tarnished gold initials and design embellishing the dark wood of its handle. "N.T.C—it's Nicholas T. Crain," he exclaimed. "It's in the journal, too, on the bookplate. And that—" He pointed to the faint design, a serpent twining around the shaft of an ankh. "That's a Kindred thing. That symbol."

"Crain knew something was coming," Loki launched back into his story. "The journal made that real clear. Whatever this Murder of Crows thing is, he was onto it, and there was something he meant to do about it. Only I don't think he ever got the chance before the Fire broke out."

"Specify, Loki," Tiaret asked.

"Like a ritual of some kind," Loki continued. "Maybe a sacrifice, though it never went into details. He and a few others created this Society of the Crow, and he mentioned somebody being in it who wasn't Kindred."

"Maybe these Maynard people infiltrated them?" Mercedes suggested.

"No, no." Loki shook his head. "I think it was a magician actually. He gave Dr. Crain the journal to start with. I found a weird gizmo with the journal, too. Like a pocket watch, only the inside was different than you'd expect. It had some kind of writing on it, and an extra hand, I don't know what for."

That caught Gwyn's attention. "A watch?"

"This mage have a name?" Baihu asked. "Even a shadow name."

"Aristede," Loki said, after thinking a second. "That was the guy who gave Crain the book, 'cause he signed it on the front page."

"Aristede!" Both Tiaret and Gwyn spoke at the same time, then exchanged a glance.

"You know the man?" Heartsblood interrupted.

"Know him?" Gwyn exclaimed. "He's my great-granddad—well, mystically speaking. His apprentice became my mentor's mentor."

"So you're heir to his teachings," Mercedes said.

Gwyn nodded. "Exactly. Aristede was one of the most influential magi in the city, at least till he vanished mysteriously in the Fire, quote-unquote. Like a number of us."

"Yeah, we had some convenient disappearances ourselves," Loki said, "Anyway. There was one thing on the watch I could read, dates in French. Twenty-seven July eighteen seventeen to fourteen October eighteen seventy-one. The rest was gibberish."

"Well, shit. Then he knew."

"Knew what?"

"The day of his death. It's not uncommon, at least among my kind, to have some vague inkling of how or when. For the lucky few, it's not at all vague."

"And he had it put on his watch?" Anna shuddered. "Talk about morbid. No offense."

"Didja say where you found this book?" Heartsblood asked.

Loki hadn't, of course, but it only made sense that someone would ask. "It was with a corpse," he admitted. "Buried in the woods. There was a whole chest of books, but I only took the one. And the watch-thing."

"Could you be a bit more exact? Which woods?" Glorianna asked, her PDA and stylus ready in her hands.

"The forest preserves," Loki said. "Not sure exactly where. I only found it because the fucking crows chased me right into the hole. But somebody'd already dug it up. No idea who."

"Was this body burnt up?" Heartsblood asked.

Loki shook his head. "Didn't look it to me. Nothing left but bones and the chest. Seemed to me like someone was taking advantage of the Fire to do some dirty work."

Heartsblood rubbed at his jaw. "You said the crows was chasin' you," he started.

"Yeah. Ghost crows. Damned things."

"So there must be somethin' you're meant to do. 'Course, this could be it right here. But somehow you're a part of it."

"Part of what?" Loki asked, suspiciously.

"Why, all this," Heartsblood blurted out. "The reckoning that's come—home to roost, you could say. I just wish I knew what I was doin' in it. I'm not even from here."

"Great," Loki muttered. The werewolf was back to babbling again. "Perfect. So what, do we need to do some kind of ritual like the journal was talking about…?"

"Hold the phone," Mercedes said and held up her hands. "We're jumping from like D to Z here. What kind of ritual?"

"It wasn't real clear," Loki said. "They were going to do a sacrifice… someone had even volunteered. But the shit hit the fan before they were ready, I think."

"And what was that supposed to do?" she asked.

"What, like I would know? Calm it down, I guess. Like throwing a virgin in the volcano."

"Dunno 'bout a virgin sacrifice, but the Murder sure wants something," Heartsblood insisted. "Otherwise it wouldn't be tryin' so hard to get ahold of us."

"They could just be spontaneous broadcasts," Gwyn mused. "A thing in pain will scream whether anyone's there to hear or not."

"No, it's been speakin' right to me. Besides—" He cast his arms around him. "I refuse to believe I got called from halfway 'cross the continent to be here for somethin' I can't do nothin' about!"

"I'm—inclined to agree with Heartsblood, actually," Baihu said, silencing Gwyn's retort with a look. "Aristede was a practical man living in a profoundly unsentimental town. If he thought the Murder would respond to propitiation, then he must have had reason."

"But what kind of propitiation?" Tiaret asked, then looked at Loki. "I don't suppose I could get a look at this journal."

"Already handed it all over," Loki said, looking away.

"Of course." Tiaret accepted his answer, but he was pretty damned sure Gretchen Mc-Bride knew a lie when she heard one. But she didn't call him on it, so it didn't matter.

"Look." Mercedes sat down again. "Let's start putting things together. Okay, you guys said you think the virus is being manipulated by a magician. That's bad. Then we've definitely got somebody poisoning kids."

"Actually, Baihu thinks it's the same person," Glorianna put in.

Poisoning kids? That was news to Loki. It took a few more minutes of listening to their discussion to understand how some strange waking dream—or perhaps a nightmare, given the description—had brought Baihu and Heartsblood together at the scene of a grisly ritual murder involving a bunch of teenaged would-be occultists.

Then he remembered a headline he'd seen in the *Tribune* recently, and the pieces fell into place. "You guys are talking about the high-schoolers who poisoned themselves a few nights back," Loki said. "Not a mass suicide then?"

"No!" several people answered in unison.

"So one guy," Mercedes continued. "One magician poisoning kids and dabbling in bioterrorism and who knows what else."

"Yes." Glorianna frowned. "I'm perfectly willing to believe it's all connected, I just don't see quite how yet. It's just a big mess, one problem after another."

"Then maybe that's the point," Mercedes replied. "Maybe it doesn't even matter what it is as long as it causes pain and death and strife, in this world, the spirit world, either, both. You heard Heartsblood. The more suffering happens the closer this thing gets to… conflagration. Whatever. Maybe not another Great Fire but something just as bad."

"And what good is that?" Glorianna argued. "I mean why would somebody want that?"

"Because it's what they want." Baihu spoke with absolute certainty, and a touch of bitterness. "There are two choices available to one who hates the world. Kill yourself or kill the world."

They? That was an odd emphasis, especially when the mages seemed so certain there was only one person behind it all.

"Make no mistake," the Asian magus continued grimly, "this is the work of a malice unfettered by reason. And it has found a perfect if unwitting partner in the Murder."

"So what if we took down this troublemaker?" Loki asked. "Would that cure the virus?"

"No." Gwyn shook his head. "At best, it might revert to normal encephalitis."

Shit. So much for that idea.

"Still," Loki continued, "we take him down and at least we don't have somebody poking this Murder with sharp sticks anymore, right? Buy us some time to figure out the rest. And if someone did have to be sacrificed, hey, kill two birds with one stone. So to speak."

"You're one disturbing little white boy," muttered Mercedes.

That, coming from a woman who could presumably turn into a hairy, oversized killing machine, brought him up short. Him, disturbing? What did they expect they'd have to do with this fucker who was poisoning people and encouraging the spread of a deadly sorcerous plague? It seemed obvious enough to him.

Or maybe that was the disturbing part right there. That the very idea of human sacrifice, assuming this plague-spinning magus was human to start with, seemed so obvious and plausible. The Circle of the Crone tended to see things that way. Mortals all died, sooner or later, and blood was the only true sacrifice, the only coin in which the ancient gods and spirits traded. The dark stains on the altar testified to that. He'd never witnessed the full ritual, but knowing it sometimes happened had ceased to horrify him. Perhaps he had become more one of them than he'd even realized. And that was a bit disturbing, too.

"—What about the virus itself?" Heartsblood was saying, and Loki snapped out of his musing. "It's his in a way, ain't it?"

"Yes, if we had live virus to work with," Gwyn answered. "Unfortunately, what we've got is all inert. I don't know if it's the refrigeration that killed it or something more mystical, like the fact that the hosts have died."

"Yeah, but come on, there's a damn epidemic going," the Lupine pointed out. "We can get us some live virus."

So, they were talking about tracking back to the magus using the virus itself? Clever, if it worked.

"Wait a minute," Glorianna interrupted, looking up from the tiny screen of her PDA. "You said the virus is inert either because the blood is cold or it's dead?"

Gwyn shrugged. "It's probably one or the other."

"Then how can vampires be transmitting it?" She gestured at Loki. "Think about it."

Shit. Loki really didn't want to be reminded of that right now.

janet trautvetter

"There must be some other kind of energy in vampire blood that sustains it," Gwyn mused.

"Kindred blood," Loki corrected him, almost automatically.

"Sorry."

"No problem."

However, something he'd said had evidently attracted the Lupines' attention. Loki looked up to see both Heartsblood and Anna coming toward him. Not attacking, no, but a lot closer than was comfortable under the circumstances. The Beast growled a warning, and Loki met their stares with his own. Among Kindred, this would be a challenge, a test of wills and strength of the blood where stepping back or looking away was submission. With werewolves, he had no idea, but he stood firm nonetheless. "How ya doin'?" he said, crossing his arms again.

"Fine." The werewolf's nostrils flared. "Just gettin' a better whiff."

"Yeah?" Loki shrugged. It still felt rude, an unwelcome intrusion inside his personal space. "Well, enjoy."

"Enjoy ain't quite the word," Heartsblood said, a scowl crossing his face.

Maybe Kindred smelled like carrion or something to werewolves, but this was getting way beyond rude now. "Then maybe you should give it a rest," Loki snapped back.

"I was wonderin' earlier why you got scared when you saw that girl's picture." Heartsblood's voice seemed to deepen a little, which was ominous enough even without understanding what he was saying. "And just now when Glorianna pointed at you, you got scared again."

The Beast snarled. Loki's fangs started sliding down again. *Enough already.* "Get out of my face," he said, barely holding on to his temper. "Or I'll show you scared."

"It does smell different in your blood, the virus. I didn't pick it out till just now."

Those words were an infusion of ice water through Loki's veins, chilling his temper down to something else entirely. He'd taken a step backward before he even realized and cursed himself for it immediately. "I don't have the fucking virus!"

"You have it," Anna said, coming around to his right, "and what's more, you know you have it. I should've known none of you mother-fuckers would dare come to something like this alone. But you've got a good reason to. If the others find out you're the carrier, your ass is grass, isn't it? How many have you infected? You even keep count?"

"The pledge," Tiaret said sternly, stepping forward. Loki imagined he smelled ozone, the scent of air right before lighting struck. Only now he wasn't sure if she was defending him or just trying to keep the Lupines from doing something stupid in another mage's house.

"We ain't touching him," Heartsblood growled. "We're all here to share information, right? That's all I want."

"Lick me," Loki retorted, regaining some of his equilibrium, and his temper.

The werewolf's lip curled up in disdain. "No thanks."

"Mr. Fischer." For a moment, Gretchen McBride was standing there, not Tiaret. With a little exhale of annoyance, she maneuvered herself into one of the pews. "Loki, that is," she corrected herself. "Loki. First of all, language."

He stared at her in disbelief. *Language?* "Like it matters?" he asked, incredulous.

"If this is true—" she began, her voice calmer now. Tiaret the magus was back again.

"Of course it's true!" Gwyn exclaimed, coming forward. "Just look at him!"

She held up her hand, never losing eye contact with Loki, and Gwyn subsided. "This new strain is extremely infectious," she said, seriously. "Anyone you used for sustenance, anyone, however healthy—"

"You think I don't know that?" Loki shouted, and turned away from her, even from the distrustful stare of the Lupines, only to meet the silent, reproachful gaze of the dead girl in the portrait. *Shit.*

He spun back around again. "What am I supposed to do? You have any idea what happens when we don't feed? How the hell do you think this works?"

Tiaret looked down, massaged her forehead with one hand.

"So you recognize this girl." Gwyn accused him. "Because you infected her. Good God, Anna's right. How many has it been?"

"I didn't know!" Loki cried out, flinging his arms wide. "I swear to Christ I didn't, not till just the other night. I, I don't even know how I got it." He didn't even bother to explain it was Raven who'd infected that girl, not himself. He'd let it happen, after all, and the result was the same. The girl was dead.

"Oh yeah? And whose death was it that finally tipped you off?" Gwyn demanded, his voice rising as well. "If your memory needs jogging, I could go get my files. We've been pretty busy down at the morgue lately."

"This is going nowhere useful." Tiaret stood up, and her voice took on something like her usual take-charge tone again. "Enough. We don't have all night here, especially not if we're going to do something, and I do suggest doing something." She glanced around, to make sure she had everyone's attention. She did.

Then she turned back to him. "Loki. I am going to assume that your… status as a carrier only sharpens your motivation to solve this whole problem. It certainly sharpens mine."

"Yeah," he admitted. His anger had drained away, leaving him bereft of defenses. "Yeah, it does."

"Then you are still willing to help us, and help yourself in the process."

"Hell, yes," he blurted out. "I don't want this. Believe me, I don't."

"I believe you." Her glance took in the others, including them in her statement. Not even Gwyn argued. Satisfied, she turned back to him.

"In that case, what we need from you is a sample of your blood. Hopefully, what Gwyn said will hold true, and the virus will live long enough for us to try to track it to its source."

Blood. Of course. Blood was the only true sacrifice, and this time he had no right to refuse. But what else could they do with his blood once they had it?

Tiaret seemed to grasp his reluctance. "I can assure you, Loki, that we'll get to the bottom of this quickly as we possibly can. What I hope you'll provide us with in return is a modicum of trust, and—" She hesitated for a moment. "And patience."

"Patience?" Loki echoed warily. Patience for what? Patience meant waiting—and then it dawned on him what she wanted him to wait for. "What're you saying? Don't feed?"

"I'm saying… hold out for as long as you safely can, yes," she said. "And if you can't, then let us know. We can make arrangements." She glanced over at Baihu and Gwyn, a

janet trautvetter

question in her eyes. Baihu nodded, and Gwyn scowled, unhappily accepting whatever those implied arrangements were.

"Are we agreed?" she asked.

It then occurred to him what arrangements had not been mentioned. "If I say yes, you'll take my word?" he asked, carefully. "No tailing me, no staking me and saying it's for my own good, no turning me in?"

She nodded. "I agree. Heartsblood?"

"If that's the deal, that's the deal," the werewolf said. "Long as everybody stays square, you'll get no problems from us."

"Yeah, what about the rest of you?" Loki asked, looking at the other four.

The big, blond guy took a step forward, to stand at Heartsblood's shoulder. "His word goes for the pack," he said. There was no argument.

The pack again. Well, that explained a lot, didn't it? Loki nodded. "Got it."

"Okay, then," Loki said, and stepped over to join the mages. "Shoulda known this wouldn't be over till I opened a vein. Where do you want me?"

"Well, fuck."

Loki surveyed the shambles of his haven and felt the Beast growling again, an anger that started somewhere in the pit of his stomach and left a bitter taste in his mouth, his fangs itching to come out and rip into the flesh of whomever was responsible for this wanton destruction the way they had apparently ripped apart everything he owned.

Not that his apartment had been especially lavish or anything. He hadn't even been staying here long enough yet for his current false identity to start receiving junk mail, much less get cable installed or have furnishings he hadn't found freshly abandoned in the alley or thieved from someone's back porch. This was where he slept, nothing more, but, as such, it had always been inviolable, secret, and safe.

Not so secret now. And clearly no longer safe. Every cabinet in the kitchenette had been opened, and several of the doors ripped off their hinges. The single easy chair in the living room had already suffered a few threadbare spots in its shabby upholstery, but now barely a handspan of that upholstery remained without deep slashes, the stuffing pulled out down to the springs and tossed around the room, the seat cushion shredded beyond repair. The end table had been broken and splintered into kindling and the stack of cheap paperbacks and magazines he'd accumulated for idle amusements had been ripped apart, littering the carpet with a layer of paper scraps.

His sleeping area in the deep closet was even worse—the futon and sleeping bag had been sliced open and pulled apart, the boxes he kept clothes and odd items in dumped on the floor, and it looked as though some of his clothes, at least, had also been slashed and torn.

Loki turned things over, dug under piles of shredded cardboard and futon stuffing and finally unearthed Aristede's gold watch, apparently none the worse for wear, but there was no sign of the Nicholas Crain journal. Clearly whoever had ransacked his apartment had stolen it—but why?

Then he remembered the pit in the woods, which someone had to have dug for a reason. Had it been the journal they had been digging for all along? That implied a Kindred had done this—worse, it all but shouted that a fellow Acolyte had done this, possibly one of those who had ambushed him four nights ago, or someone connected to them. Someone who wanted that journal very, very badly, and took advantage of his own troubles to come back here and rip the place apart to find it.

Except the journal had been sitting out in the open, not hidden at all. There was no need to rip the place apart like this—like someone had gone totally berserk, destroying everything he could get his hands on. Frenzied, perhaps, if he were Kindred, but why?

Heartsblood had seemed so goddamned certain all this shit was connected, the events of 1871 and now, and this Murder of Crows spirit-entity he kept talking about. There was a mystery here, that tied together the past and present, one he seemed tied into as well. Unfortunately, he no longer had the journal to sift through for clues. Maybe if he went back to the forest preserves, found the burial site again, some other clue remained that would give him an idea of where to go next, how it all fit, and who the fuck was screwing around with him like this.

The ticking started so softly, he wasn't aware of just when that was. But all of a sudden, he did hear it, clear and sharp, and it was coming from Aristede's watch. Very carefully, hoping that it wasn't a sorcerous bomb about to go off, Loki touched the release and opened the lid.

Inside, he could see the hands had changed position from before, and one of them was now moving, advancing counter-clockwise by one tiny slash mark for every seven ticks. As it passed over one of the other hands, it moved as well, though in the opposite direction. Gingerly, he put his finger in the moving hand's way. When it got to the ob-struction, it stopped, but continued again as soon as he took his finger away.

He closed the watch and slipped it into his pocket. Maybe Gwyn or Tiaret would know what it meant. But for now, he had to gather what he could that was still salvage-able, and find himself a new goddamned haven.

Loki spent the next three nights on his search, plus scouting out some additional emergency shelters should the need arise. He avoided the Skullery, Crobar, Metro—all his usual haunts. He told himself that he did so because the easiest way to keep his promise to Tiaret and Baihu was to avoid temptation. But, in truth, he was simply not ready to face either Moyra or Damien just yet, not after all he'd endured over the past few nights. And he did not want to ask either of them for shelter or assistance. He still didn't know who had vandalized his apartment, and, until he did, he felt considerably safer if no other Kindred knew where he was sleeping.

Unfortunately, without calling on his connections to either other Kindred or to mortals, his resources were limited. He finally had to settle, temporarily, for a makeshift shelter in a U-Store-It space, which he was able to secure from the inside. He'd want to find something else before the weather got much colder, but making it at least bearable as an emergency bolt-hole with an abandoned mattress, the stolen sleeping bag, and sufficient stacks of empty boxes for camouflage took the better part of two nights, and having a clear task to accomplish kept him from thinking too much of how hungry he was getting.

But by late Sunday night, when he had to catch himself on two different occasions from following mortals who happened to cross his path, and the Beast's growling was growing too persistent and demanding to ignore, he decided it wouldn't be entirely out of line to at least ask for a progress report.

janet trautvetter

He meant only to leave a message, realizing too late what time it was. But Baihu picked it up on the second ring.

"No, you didn't wake me," the magus assured him, though there was fatigue in his voice, which sounded deeper and slower than usual to Loki's ear. "I haven't been sleeping very well—well, hardly sleeping at all, actually. It's been a rough couple of days."

"Sorry to hear it," Loki said. "I just wanted to keep in touch. You remember you asked me to be patient, and I have been, but my patience is starting to run a bit low, if you know what I mean. And I was wondering how you all were doing with your part of it."

"Well." There was a bit of a pause after that, and then, "We do know where the virus came from now. And we know who the magus is."

"Well, that's good." Loki felt a glimmer of hope. "So you just take him out, and that will stop it, right? It'll revert to regular encephalitis, like Gwyn said?"

"Actually, it's a bit more complicated than that."

Loki's hopes dimmed again. "Complicated?"

"Yeah. Look. Can you be patient for just one more night? I have an idea, on how to deal with the virus directly, to unravel the making of it, but it's tricky. If I can get Jas—Gwyn's mentor to help us, though, I think we can do it. Just one more night, Loki. And if that doesn't work, we'll make arrangements for you again, okay?"

"Okay. I guess I can do that." Loki agreed reluctantly, wishing now he'd called a hell of a lot earlier in the evening, when it might have been possible to work out arrangements a bit sooner. "So I should call you tomorrow night to find out how it went? Or will you call me?"

"If it works, I won't have to call," Baihu assured him. "Trust me, you'll know."

Loki returned to the Skullery on Monday night. He promised himself he wasn't going to stay long, because to even make his way through the cluster of club-goers out on the sidewalk took nearly all the self-control he could muster. In truth, he wasn't even certain of his welcome. But he needed to know just where he stood with the others, especially his own coven.

Moyra met him on the balcony, just outside the loft. She was all in black tonight, something long and flowing, with a sheer black and metallic gold scarf wrapped over her head and around her neck. As he approached, his innate sense of her greater age and power hit him, harder tonight than he remembered feeling in years. He didn't fight it, but simply dropped his gaze, until she came forward and tipped his chin up with one gloved hand.

"Well," she said, looking him over, "you seem to have weathered the ordeal rather well, under the circumstances. Congratulations, Acolyte."

"Thanks." Relieved, he followed her into the loft, and took the seat she offered him. Better to be up here, away from the temptations on the dance floor. "So that was it, huh? The Gate of Fire?"

"That was your Gate of Fire," she said, sitting opposite him. "Others might experience it differently. We still need to initiate you properly, but you passed the test, that's the important part. And, actually, I'm glad you dropped by. I need to go out a little later, and I'd appreciate it if you could stick around and keep an eye on things here until closing."

"Me?" Loki echoed, a bit surprised. "Isn't Damien—"

"He's not here." She folded her arms over the tabletop. "You were right about him. The mortal he fed from last Monday night was in the hospital by Thursday. She died yesterday."

So Damien had been infected after all. But somehow that didn't make Loki feel any better about betraying him to Norris. "So now what are we going to do?"

"I don't know," Moyra admitted. "I haven't seen him at all, or heard from him. He said something about going nomad, perhaps he did. He hasn't been back here since Thursday, or his other haven either, as far as I know."

Shit. "What about Jed, have you asked him?"

"No, I hadn't spoken to him." Moyra gave him a puzzled look. "Why Jed?"

"Well, they were the ones hot on my trail most of the time. Jed had some kind of blood magic way of tracking me. I didn't know he even knew any Crúac. And they were riding around together every time I saw 'em."

"Jed, Crúac? I didn't know that either." She frowned. "He didn't learn that from Bella, that's for sure. What makes you think it was blood magic?"

He described what Jed was doing with his knife. "I guess maybe he was one of the ones who got me before I broke free. So he must've had my blood on his knife. I just didn't know you could do that with Crúac."

"It would have to be your blood, yes," she mused. "It's not any ritual I've ever seen before. Though I suppose that could work, in theory."

Shit. That probably meant that Baihu and the other mages could track him with the blood he'd given them, if their magic worked at all in the same way. Naturally, they hadn't mentioned that. Still, they'd made a deal, and he'd kept his end of it, at least so far. Even the thought of what he'd promised not to do triggered his appetite, and the Beast's complaints. His gaze drifted over to the windows overlooking the main club below.

But it was not mortals his eyes were drawn to. Marek Kaminski and the Earth Baines were making their way through the club below, on their way to the stairs. "Shit. Who let them in here?"

Moyra glanced over as well, then rose to her feet. "I'll deal with them," she said coolly.

"Mind if I'm not here when they come in?" Loki asked.

She adjusted her scarf over her hair, flinging one end of it over her shoulder. "I haven't seen you in a week, what are you talking about?"

"Thanks." He drew the shadows around himself and slipped out the door. By the time the Earth and Marek had made it up the stairs to the balcony, he was well out of sight in one of the side rooms. After Moyra welcomed her visitors inside the loft, Loki continued on downstairs and found a secluded corner back under the Loft in which to brood.

It could have been Damien who'd trashed his apartment. But it didn't really make sense. Not that Damien wasn't capable of violence if sufficiently provoked; he'd seen the Ventrue in a fight before. But what had happened in his apartment was different. And Damien had no reason to steal the journal. He'd probably be extremely interested in reading it if he knew it existed, but he didn't, at least as far as Loki knew. And there was no way Damien could have dug that pit in the woods, at least not the same night of the ritual.

He suddenly realized he'd left his corner, and was already walking toward the nearest table of mortals. He could smell their blood from here. In fact, he was acutely aware

janet trautvetter

of every mortal heartbeat within fifty feet of him. And every time he even let his vision focus on one of them, his gaze went straight to their throats, and his hunger deepened, almost beyond bearing. *Fuck.* There was no way he would be able to keep his promise if he stayed here much longer.

Focusing his will on that promise (and the reminder of what they could do to him if he broke it), he headed for the exit.

Somehow he made it past the mortals clustered around the door, fists clenched in his pockets, every muscle in his body tense, as the Beast strained against the leash of his will. But he couldn't control his eyes, which had to size up every mortal sitting on the low wall alongside the sidewalk.

And then he caught a glimpse of a long, burgundy velvet cloak, and a young woman with a white streak through her black hair. Sybil, that was her name, or at least the name Damien had used.

She recognized him as well, jumped down from the wall and intercepted him on the sidewalk. "Oh, hi. Loki. That's right, isn't it? I remember you—"

"Yeah—" Loki stopped, turned around. "Sorry, I'm in a bit of a hurry here—"

"Oh, okay, no problem," she said, though she didn't back away. "I was just wondering—do you know if Damien going to be here sometime tonight?"

She was standing too close. He was acutely aware of her heartbeat, the pulse under the delicate skin of her throat, the scent of her blood blending with skin moisturizer and makeup, the alluring warmth radiating from her living flesh. "He's—he's indisposed," he managed awkwardly. His fangs had emerged, making talking difficult without exposing them.

You could do it, she'd let you, the Beast whispered. *Take her into the alley. Take her, he'll get blamed for it anyway—*

"Gotta go, sorry—" Loki spun around on his heel and walked away as fast as he could without actually breaking into a run. He'd have to call Moyra from the El, apologize for running out on her—but compared to the probable alternative, annoying Moyra seemed the far lesser sin.

Baihu, you'd damn well better be working on this thing. Or at least be ready to ante up a refill.

It wasn't until he'd made it to the El platform that the real significance of seeing her hit him. Sybil had looked remarkably healthy, considering he'd seen her go off with Damien over a week ago.

Thoughts clashed together in his head, shifted, reorganized. Moyra had said the mortal Damien had fed from had died. But there was a problem with the process of elimination as a method of determining guilt, and he'd missed it entirely until this moment. It assumed that the Kindred known to have fed from a particular mortal was the only one who'd done so, and thus the only possible source of infection. But what if he wasn't?

The train pulled in, and Loki picked the emptiest car, sitting as far away from the mortal passengers as he could, slouching down in the seat and staring out the window.

What if there was another Kindred who was carrying the virus, and knew it? And to hide his own infection, was setting others up as scapegoats, feeding among their herds? Or as Loki had done himself, carefully targeting his victims so their deaths would not arouse suspicion? Of course, in order to cinch the case against Damien, that Kindred would have had to know he was under suspicion, know he had to insure that the Circle's own test came out the way he wanted it to.

Only one Kindred might have known all that, and had a possible chance to infect even Damien's test subject. And who knew where Loki's haven was, and had known when Loki was unlikely to be at home, so had time to steal the journal, and tear the place apart. Why he might have done that was a mystery, but opportunity? Hell, yes.

Jed Holyoak. Loki felt his fangs extending just thinking about it. Jed had been showing Raven around. And he'd teamed up with Damien pretty quickly, too, when Loki was the target. And now Damien was missing. Maybe he'd gotten on his bike and rode off to some other domain. Loki wished he'd thought to ask Moyra if Damien's guitar and shit were still in his room, or gone to check that himself. Or maybe Damien hadn't gotten very far at all.

It's all connected somehow. Glorianna had said it, and Baihu and even Heartsblood had agreed. Everything that was going on, all the weird shit, tied into this Murder of Crows: the deadly, tainted virus and the magus who had created it, the Fire, Dr. Crain's journal, the deliberate poisoning of a bunch of kids, the rain of black feathers, and some underhanded business that had taken place during or after the Fire over a century ago. And Aristede, who had seemed to have had a better idea than anyone that something terribly wrong was going on—

He heard the ticking then, surprisingly clear. *What the—?* Loki dug into his jacket pocket, found the watch, and pulled it out. The engraving of the skull seemed so appropriate now. He touched the catch so that it opened on his palm.

All three of the hands had moved since the last time he'd looked at it, slowly moving closer together. Whatever it was counting down to, there wasn't much time left. A few hours maybe. *Fuck. What am I supposed to do?*

The train pulled into a station. Loki shifted his position so he could better watch the door, check out anyone coming in. In doing so, he moved the hand holding the watch as well, and saw something else he hadn't noticed before: the third hand moved, so that it continued to point in the same direction, bobbing a little like a compass. It pointed west, as near as he could figure it. West and slightly south. What was west and slightly south?

The forest preserves. Aristede's grave. And the Circle's ritual grounds.

Fuck.

He dug into his coat pocket again, disgorging more black feathers, and pulled out his cell phone. Whatever Moyra's plans had been for later, he hoped they were subject to change.

It felt like the trip out to the forest preserves took forever. Loki ended up jogging the last stretch of it, because waiting for the bus would have taken too long, and he didn't know when Moyra would hear the message he'd left on her voicemail. Fortunately, Aristede's enchanted watch seemed to be as reliable a guide as Nicholas Crain's journal, even once he reached the shadowed depths of the woods themselves.

Extending his senses, pulling the shadows around himself so that he could move silently and invisibly as possible, Loki hurried through the forest, alert for any sign of his

janet trautvetter

quarry. He smelled the smoke from the lanterns first, the slightly acrid bite of burning kerosene, and then, a few minutes later, spotted the faint yellow light flickering through the trees. There was a drumbeat, low and steady.

Loki moved closer, circling around so as to get the clearest view of what was going on, crouching down behind the broad trunk of an oak.

Damien lay spread-eagled on the ground, a stake through his heart, in the center of a broad circle of evenly spaced stones. The similarly staked and spread out bodies of four crows lay at his head, feet, and on either side. Four hurricane lanterns, their flames safely ensconced in glass, hung from iron posts at the four points of a larger square, a comfortable distance from the circle's edge. There was no altar, just a low table set up off to one side that held ritual tools, laid out on a black rug.

A mortal, clad only in leather pants and a necklace of beads and feathers, sat off to one side, beating the drum.

Jed was walking around the outer edge of the stone circle, chanting in a language that Loki did not know. He wore the mask of the Horned King, a deer's skull with antlers and crown, horsehair wig, and a long patchwork cloak of leather and fur over his jeans and black T-shirt. As he chanted, he was tossing something from a bowl—from the way it floated on the breeze, Loki guessed it to be ashes. He wasn't sure he even wanted to guess where they'd come from.

As Jed continued his circuit of the stone circle, Loki started working his way slowly around the outside of the clearing, in the opposite direction, hoping to work his way around as close to Damien and the stake as possible. Assuming Damien would wake up once the stake was removed, he would be more than capable of defending himself, and probably pissed as hell, so freeing him would probably be the best way to fuck up whatever Jed had planned.

Jed put the bowl of ashes back on the table, and picked up a large leather pouch. Chanting again, he began a second circuit of the circle. But this time what he was tossing into the air were black feathers.

A chilling breeze wafted through the clearing, sending the lantern flames dancing even behind their glass chimneys. It caught the feathers as Jed scattered them, swirling them around in toward the circle's center. Once the feathers were drawn inside the circle of stones, they never left, nor did they settle to the ground—they kept being tossed about, as though the wind itself was trapped within the circle's confines and couldn't find its way out.

As Jed continued around, the wind followed him. A gust of it hit Loki, whipping around the leather jacket, catching at his hair, flattening the fabric of his shirt to his ribs. A flurry of black feathers erupted from the jacket's pockets, as if the wind was calling them to come and join the rest of the flock. Loki clamped his hands down on the pocket openings, trying to hold them in, but then the damned things started emerging from inside the jacket itself, whipping about on the breeze and out into the circle.

Jed paused, seeing the new arrivals drifting out of the trees, then turned in the direction they had come. He made a gesture at the drummer, who stopped immediately.

The Beast growled. Loki could feel its hackles going up, felt the prickling warning of another vampire suddenly aware of his presence. *Fuck.*

"Come out, whoever you are," Jed said, staring into the trees. "Let's not be rude. Show yourself."

Loki stood up, let the shadows slide away, and stepped forward. He braced himself for the vibe—the cold, sinking fear that hit him as soon as their gazes met, the urging of the Beast to back away, give ground before the more powerful predator. However old Jed Holyoak really was, he'd hidden it well, skillfully masking his power and true agenda behind a neonate's mask of ignorance and eagerness to fit in.

"You're about a week early for the Mabon rites, you know," Loki said, keeping his hands in his jacket pockets so Jed wouldn't see how tightly they were clenched. "Maybe you ought to check your calendar." He reminded himself sternly that he didn't have to actually win any contest of wills—all he had to do was get close enough to get the stake out. Damien could take care of himself after that.

"Loki. You keep turning up at the oddest times." Jed's voice held only mild surprise, but his colors in his aura blazed temporarily with a flare of anger. "And here I was certain the Unholy had finished you."

"Sorry to disappoint," Loki said, and managed one more step, sideways this time, closer to where Damien was bound. *That's right. One step at a time. Like she did—one forward, one sideways, approach with caution.* "Just what the fuck do you think you're doing?"

Inside the circle of stones, the wind seemed to be dying, the feathers slowly drifting down like so many snowflakes trapped in a globe.

"Stay back," Jed warned. "Don't even think of interrupting now, or I will boil the blood in your veins. Don't think I can't do exactly—" His voice faltered suddenly, and he stiffened.

Aristede's watch was suddenly ticking much, much louder.

"You had it." Jed's fangs were showing now. His voice had gone suddenly strained, and cracked in the higher registers. "You had it all along, all these years! Give it to me, Loki. Give it now!"

"What the hell are you talking about?" Loki demanded. "You stole the fucking journal—" He dug his left hand deeper into the pocket, suddenly aware that he should have felt the watch against his hand for the past few minutes, and didn't.

"Give it to me," Jed hissed, coming closer, tossing the feather pouch aside. "Give me the cursed thing—"

Loki took a step back and sideways, trying to keep a distance between them. "What, the watch?" he asked. "That old thing?" His hand dug around in the pocket, and found nothing. How the hell had it vanished like that? He had a sudden vision of Jed in his apartment, tearing the place apart in frustration, yes, even in frenzy—looking for a watch he could hear ominously ticking away but was unable to actually find.

Maybe it hadn't been the journal he was hunting for after all.

"Give it to me!" Jed reached up, pulled the Horned King's skull-mask and antlers down from his head, tossed them aside as well. "You miserable, deceitful little—"

Loki edged sideways a few more steps closer to the circle and dropped to a half-crouch, ready to make an attempt to get to Damien, when he felt a sudden burning sensation in the middle of his chest. "What the hell—" he managed to get out, his voice barely a croak. The burning intensified and spread, racing through his veins, as though his very blood was on fire. His legs buckled, and he fell to his knees. *You fucking bastard—*

Jed stumbled, one hand going to his chest, eyes suddenly going wide, fangs bared. "You—you traitor," he gasped. "You betrayed—"

black T-shirt. The cloak was gritty to the touch, and when he lifted it up, a cloud of ashes drifted out of it, floating away across the bodies of the crows.

Jedidiah, Loki guessed, had not been willing to surrender. Or perhaps the Unholy, having suffered the same agonizing cure without any understanding of why, angry at the death of her pets and followers, had not been in a mood to accept it.

Rowen had followed him. She took the cloak from his hands, examined it, and then let it drop. "That which is withheld shall be taken without mercy." She seemed grimly satisfied.

Loki felt a cold lump of fear settling into the pit of his stomach. Would that be his fate, a hundred years from now? Or had he done enough? Was the Murder satisfied at last? In 1871, all but one of the Kindred coven had given far, far more.

"Blood is the only true sacrifice," he murmured.

"Only when it is your own," Rowen said. "The blood that others shed is their sacrifice, not yours. A sacrifice that does not bring pain is no sacrifice. But sometimes another's sacrifice becomes your pain."

Loki wasn't sure if that made him feel any better or worse.

They wrapped Damien's body in the black rug and laid him carefully in the trunk of Moyra's car. She would find a safe resting place for him—though whether for a few weeks, months, or years was hard to predict. Loki would report to the Prince and Norris that Damien was no longer a threat to mortal health, and that the Circle would take care of its own.

Once Damien seemed comfortably settled, Moyra drew Crain's journal out of her robes and offered it to Rowen. "This should be kept somewhere safe," she said. "For the next time."

"Then you should find a safe place to keep it," Rowen said, and turned away, walking back into the woods, the rings on her staff chiming softly as she walked.

"I should have known better," Moyra muttered, and slid the book back into whatever pocket it had come from under the robes. "The night is waning, let's go."

Loki followed, sticking his hands into his pockets out of habit. The feathers had vanished, but the watch was there again. He drew it out of his pocket, flipped it open on his hand. It was silent again, all three hands frozen in position, no matter how he turned it around. It seemed to be neither timepiece nor compass now. Perhaps its purpose was done, now that Aristede's curse had finally been fulfilled. Or perhaps not.

Maybe Gwyn would know how to get it working again.

Birds of Ill Omen

by Sarah Roark

A man walks into a bar.

Sure, I know, but stay with me now. A man walks into a bar.

In old Chicago you wanted to pay attention to that kind of thing. You didn't want to go wandering through the wrong door. Ourselves were known to take the ears off Poles who came into our pubs, and if a Donegal lad fresh off the boat chanced to stumble into a Polish or, God help him, a German beer hall, well, you could safely say he was after writing his last letter home to mother.

Anyway, this man coming in doesn't look Irish to me. He's duded up like a Yankee in a morning coat and beaver hat, all starched and buttoned in the sweltering heat. But his skin is dark as an Injun's, and the brim of his hat lies low so I can't get a good look at him. Well, I don't like it and neither does Mike the barkeep nor anyone else. Still, we let him take a corner chair, and out he comes with a watch on a chain and lays it open on the table, like he's expecting company any moment. We like that even less, of course. Old Flaherty, he picks up a jar of pig's feet from the bar and makes as though to throw it, but the stranger doesn't so much as look up. So Flaherty puts it back down again. 'Twas all very queer. There was just something about the hot air and the quiet that sat on the nerves in a funny way, and all the stout in the world couldn't soothe it. Why that evening even Flaherty went home to the missus, sober as a priest at Mass. But I'm racing ahead of myself.

Well now, not a minute later, a second stranger bursts through the doors—a Swede, I think, his nose running blood—and another man chasing after him waving one of those big slaughterhouse pig-stickers. Up I get shouting and so does everyone else, except our Injun. But before we can get between the two of them, the Swede is falling to the floor with an extra hole in his throat. Men die quieter than hogs, I'll say that much for them. A lot of blood hit that floor in the years I had its acquaintance. Still, you must understand, hard as we all were then, it was rare for one man to murder another in broad daylight in such a way. Now, of course, they take these tommy guns and bang-bang—anyway, there we all stand gawping as this poor creature coughs his life out. And what does the Injun in the coat do? Closes up his bastard watch and lays it on the bar, touches his brim to Mike, and strolls out as cool as you please.

An odd tale, wouldn't you say? But I haven't told the oddest part. That was October the 7th of 1871. Sure, it was two firemen who carried the dead man out, having come to raise a brotherly pint to their victory over the big fire the day before. That fire was after burning up four blocks over on Canal, and a long hard fight they had to put it out. So the city gave the lads their pay and told 'em to take a well-earned holiday, and that's exactly what they did: holidayed to the horizontal.

And that very night, a certain cow kicked over a certain lamp….

We must learn, as a species, to distinguish between the evil and the merely uncaring. There are many things on Earth that were here long before us and will most likely remain long after we are gone. And perhaps the most frightening realization of all is that this place is as much their rightful home as it is ours.

— Lorraine Critten, MD, Ph.D., *The Good Fight: New Problems in Epidemiology* (doctoral dissertation)

A wolf and a human stood together in the musty air of an old wooden church. At least, Heartsblood figured that between himself and her, they added up to that much. It was just that each only had half of either.

"This ain't the kind of place I reckoned on findin' you," he said at last. He looked around, sniffing. Gallons of birdshit on the floor, in the pews. The rafters rustled.

"Oh?"

"Nope. Though it don't look like anybody's preached here in a year a' Sundays. It's whatchacallit, decommissioned."

"Deconsecrated, I think you mean." Doomwise ran a hand along the dusty altar railing, then suddenly twirled around, taking in the place with her wide-flung arms. Her long broomstick skirt spun out. He would've called her pretty if not for her flour-colored skin and hair, so pale she almost faded into the whitewashed walls. As it was, all he could think of was how the sun would fry her without that big poncho of hers, turn her cancerous and blind.

"Actually I don't know if it was ever officially deconsecrated," she finished. "They didn't need to. It was done in what I guess you could call a more organic way—the minister strangled his mistress right here by the altar, then poisoned himself. Look."

She pointed upward. He stared at the round stained-glass window that shone through the back over the choirloft. Jesus and the Apostles, it looked like, only the panes that had their faces had gone soot-black, while everything else was clear. He also saw that most of the bird guano had landed right on the altar.

"And you'll work in a place like that?" His body hunched and tensed with animal caution, but there was nothing to tell it which way to run. The building was just stale and empty, a little glum maybe.

"Why not? I set her free." She gave a tiny smile. "She was more than ready to go. As for him, we have an arrangement. With him around, the place stays quite clean of spirit and human traffic, just the way we both like it, and he's learned not to interfere with my work. Shut the doors."

He obeyed. When he turned back around, he had to quickly look away. She'd stripped down to the skin. Her breasts reflected the colors of the stained-glass light.

"We stand naked before truth," she said. It was an order, not an observation. He swallowed and unbuttoned his shirt. He smelled his own musk rising, and it only got worse as her chest grew furred and her legs crooked into hocks, her face stretching into a sly muzzle.

Down, boy. Piss-poor timing.

Now she spoke in the First Tongue, the spirit-speech. YOUR NAME.

He forced it out. "Heartsblood."

THAT'S NOT WHAT MOTHER CALLED YOU. NOR IS THIS PLACE AS FOREIGN AS YOU PRETEND.

"No," he admitted. "I was baptized Daniel Aaron Vickery."

THEN HOW DID YOU COME BY THE OTHER NAME? I'M CURIOUS.

He closed his eyes.

AND THE SPIRITS DEMAND IT, she added dryly.

"I…" He stopped. FROM MAMA. SHE ALWAYS SAID SHE'D GIVE HER HEART'S BLOOD TO SEE HER CUB SAFE, AND THEN LATER THAT'S JUST WHAT SHE DID.

He followed her into the wolf now, stopping partway as she had, right where the singer's throat of the wolf still used human lips and the First Tongue was as easy to speak as to think. Still, he couldn't put her moist nakedness out of mind. She was in heat—he could smell it, and she knew it—but did she seem to care? Hell no. That was a crescent-moon for you.

I SEE, she murmured. She made a noise, a cub's whimper for mother's side, and he realized that whatever he said, she really *did* see. He was naked in every way. AND NOW YOU BEAR THAT BLOOD?

— AND ALL THE VICKERY BLOOD THERE IS, THAT WAS EVER SHED OVER FARMLAND OR MINING-LAND OR WILDLAND, FOOT OR PAW.

QUITE A BURDEN. AND WHAT IF THE SPIRITS SHOULD FIND FAULT WITH SOME OF THEM? WILL YOU PAY THEIR DEBTS?

One had to watch one's mouth around spirits, crescent-moons, too. He shouldn't have said that about the Vickery blood. But even his little nieces and nephews heard it in their bedtime stories. The ancestors had paid, and they were owed. What else but their rotted bones made the green mountain home, fed its soul? More than his hide was worth to deny it.

He nodded. THEIR DEBTS I'LL PAY.

EVEN THOUGH WHAT BINDS YOU TO THEM IS FATE, NOT CHOICE?

— BECAUSE OF THAT. BUT WHY . . .

I KNOW THAT ISN'T WHAT YOU CAME TO TALK ABOUT, HALF-MOON. BUT THE SPIRITS WILL HAVE THEIR DUE, AND THEY ARE INQUISITIVE. IF WE DON'T TELL THEM HOW THE WORLD LOOKS THROUGH OUR EYES, THEY'LL MAKE UP THEIR OWN MYTHS ABOUT IT, JUST AS HUMANKIND IN-VENTED GODS IN CHARIOTS TO EXPLAIN THE SUN. She opened the font by the pulpit, took out a bowl, and sloshed its contents at the four corners of the altar, then replaced the bowl. His nostrils stung with the tang of salt.

"Dead Sea water?" he guessed.

NO. I USE ONLY LIVING TEARS.

"Whose?"

She looked at him and he felt stupid.

TELL ME YOUR QUESTION, HEARTSBLOOD.

— SURPRISED YOU DON'T KNOW.

I WANT TO HEAR IT.

— WELL, I… He fidgeted. I'VE BEEN HAVING THESE DREAMS.

THAT WASN'T A QUESTION.

— I WANT TO KNOW WHAT THEY MEAN.

WHAT DO YOU THINK THEY MEAN?

— FATHER AND MOTHER, WHAT DID I COME ALL THIS WAY ALONE FOR?

She chuffed softly. ALL TOO OFTEN I FIND MY PETITIONERS ONLY WANT ME TO CONFIRM WHAT THEY ALREADY BELIEVE. THEN THERE ARE THOSE WITH ONLY ONE WISH LEFT IN THE WHOLE WORLD—THAT I SHOULD TELL THEM I SEE NOTHING, THAT WHAT THEY FEAR WON'T COME TO PASS. IF ONLY I COULD GRANT THAT WISH, JUST ONCE.

Her wolf-ears flapped as she shook her head. I DISTRACT YOU WITH MY TROUBLES. BUT I NEED TO KNOW WHAT YOU WANT, NOT JUST WHAT YOU WOULD ASK.

— WELL. IT'S HARD TO EXPLAIN.

THEN DON'T EXPLAIN.

— BALANCE, he said.

THERE, THAT WASN'T HARD.

She picked up the cloth that draped over the altar, revealing a silver plate with bread and raw venison and a silver cup with something bitter-smelling inside. She fed him from each after taking swallows herself. The touch of the forbidden metal put the taste of a battery contact in his mouth, but he ate and drank. She'd spiked it, he couldn't tell with what.

LET'S SEE WHAT WE'VE BEEN SERVED, her voice sounded in his head. His legs buckled. He dimly felt his head hit the rail as he went down.

Running, running on wolf-legs through a tunnel with the smoke and steam of a roaring train chasing behind. Fluorescent lights blinked and buzzed, flooding their eyes with glare. Dirty puddles splashed up into their fur. Nails and broken glass stabbed their paw-pads. He could smell nothing but the boiling engine behind him, the rank oil of its joints and the clotted blood on its cowcatcher grill. But he could hear the shouting of the creatures that rode it, and if he glanced back, he could see their grinning heads leaning out of the windows. MEAT! they cried, or that was what he thought they said. MEAT!

Then the tunnel's end loomed up, opening out onto a bridge across a wide ravine. Far below, water churned through a gauntlet of rocks, and, even so, he would have jumped to escape the train except there was blood on the rocks, too, animal carcasses battered and rotting, cloying enough to make even a canine gag. He couldn't run forever, and he couldn't get off the tracks, and another tunnel was coming up now, one with a moving blackness inside it that croaked and squawked and fluttered.

Her face rose out of the dark, and they were back in the church. She pulled him to his feet and handed him a plastic grocery bag. It took him a second to figure out what it was for, but then he heaved into it over and over till every last drop in his belly came up.

MURDER. THERE'S A MURDER YOU MUST STOP, she said.

He gave her a bleary look, but didn't argue. Human violence was one of the worst stains on the spirit world. Columbine alone had done more damage than the whole Jurassic extinction.

— WHERE? he asked, tying the bag shut. He let his ginger-colored fur recede.

QUIET, she growled. She was still in the vision. Under her breath, she rumbled chants he didn't recognize, and her ears flattened and her thick teeth bared and he thought he caught the word BEGONE. Heartsblood listened as hard as he could to the still air, sizzling with occult static. At least one Something was definitely talking in here, but it all ran together and he couldn't make sense out of it.

THE PORTAGE, muttered Doomwise at last. RIVERS MEET AND MATE. ONE IS ANGRY AND WALKS BACKWARD... A PLACE IN THE MIDDLE, WHERE THE WATER MAKES ITS CHOICE OF OCEANS....

She fell into a monotone. COME COME FRIENDS, DO BETTER. YES, I SEE THE MEN IN CANOES, THE SWAMP, AND THE WILD GARLIC, AND THEN TWO WHITE FACES BURNT TO RED UNDER THE HOOD OF THE BOAT. NORTHERN FORESTS FALL AND GIVE WOOD, SOUTHERN PRAIRIES FATTEN CATTLE, A CITY RISES AND THEN—THEN THE MURDER, THE SICKNESS, THE FIRE. IT'S ALL HAPPENED BEFORE, HEARTSBLOOD.... THE CITY STANDS AGAIN. BLOOD AND FAT SWELL

THE RIVER, AND THE CITY DRINKS AND GROWS. NOW WHERE DO YOU LEAD ME? NO, I DON'T WANT TO GO THERE TONIGHT. AND THAT, THAT'S NOT ONE OF YOUR KIND. WELL, CHASE IT OFF THEN, UNLESS YOU WANT IT TO HEAR YOU TATTLING. OLDER THAN YOU? THEN YOU DON'T KNOW HOW OLD.

Heartsblood shivered and looked down.

YOUNGER THAN ME. OLDER THAN YOU, YOUNGER THAN ME. HOW IS THAT POSSIBLE? A KILLER NO ONE WANTS TO KILL. CAN YOU NAME THE WORD? IT'S ONLY HUMAN SPEECH. DON'T BE AFRAID. HIM, LET ME SEE HIM, THE ONE TALKING TO THE SUNBURNT PRIEST. 'PLACE OF THE WILD GARLIC' . . .

"Chicagua."

Startled, he glanced up and saw that she wore her woman's shape again. She shivered then, even in the close air, and went to pick up her clothes.

"Is that it?" he asked. "Chicago?"

She nodded. "Chicago. They were loath to just say it for some reason. They said the little scolds were eavesdropping."

He hopped awkwardly, pulling his jeans on to straightening legs. "They didn't say nothin' else about the murder?"

"Not that I could hear clearly."

"And they didn't say how… what's this got to do with, uh, with…"

"With you."

"Yes, ma'am."

"You weren't this unhappy the last time we met." She blinked at him. It was the first time she'd seemed to see him with ordinary eyes. "Did something happen? With the pack?"

"No." Suddenly his own vision blurred. Tears stung his eyelids. Shit. He soaked them up on the inside elbow of his sleeve. His fault. His own fault for taking off on this fool medicine hunt, for hoping she could somehow tell him his own business. "No. It's not the pack. It's me. And nothin' *happened*, especially—I'm just—just gettin' tired. Y'know?"

She stomped into the heels of her boots. "Tired." She lingered on the word, like she'd forgotten what it meant. "Tired of what? Imbalance? What else is new?"

He just stood there with his eyes brimming.

"I see," she said softly. "A half-moon always longs to set the world right, but it's your own equilibrium that's failing now. That's why both civilization and nature attack you in your dreams."

"Please help me," he croaked.

She sighed and fiddled with the tassels of her poncho. No more channeling, no more higher wisdom. She was just herself, whatever that was. "Daniel, this may not be what you need to hear just now, but you're one of the better-adjusted Uratha I know. You can run in the hunt like a born wolf *and* behave yourself at breakfast the next morning. Your family seems to have kept the old lore far better than most. You definitely set Elias a badly-needed example."

"I know, but—" He was whining like a puppy, but he couldn't help it now. Elias. Goddamn Elias. Good thing he wasn't here. Good thing none of them were. "But it's just such a *fight* all the time. They don't really get along, the man and the wolf. They don't *listen*. They just know how to beat each other down, so no matter what I do part of me feels wrong about it."

"It's always one conquering the other," she translated. "What everybody else thinks is your inner harmony is just the halves of your soul trading off defeats?"

"Yes, ma'am."

"And you don't know how much longer you can keep that war contained. Is that it?"

"Yes, ma'am." He wasn't going to sob, nuh-uh. Not here. And yet suddenly she'd brought him to it after all, the awful truth he'd come all this way not to ask her but to tell her: that it *was* a war and he was losing. Both of him. And only somebody like Doomwise could hear that, somebody with no dreams for him, maybe no dreams at all. Suddenly he felt as light as a soaring hawk, only it was despair instead of hope that lifted him up. Uncanny.

She pondered. "Heartsblood. Daniel. I'm talking to all of you now," she said at last. "You know that the Uratha were whelped in the world's dawning to guard the boundaries between flesh and spirit, waking and dreaming, so that neither would consume the other. So the oldest howls say."

"Yeah."

"Well—I doubt they would have been whelped unless they were needed. Think about it. That means Balance just wasn't happening, even back then. Maybe it never did. Or maybe trading defeats is what Balance is. Maybe that's all we can do. We are the Forsaken of the Moon, after all."

"Yeah. Yeah, I thought of that." He sniffled.

"On the other hand—you're Elodoth. The half-moon yearns for Balance, by nature." She shook her head. "And maybe you're also trying to be the waxing-moon your pack doesn't have, dreaming the impossible. Your life isn't my life. You sure as hell aren't a professional doomsayer. You probably shouldn't listen to me."

He shrugged miserably. "So you can't… can't tell me anything for sure, but Chicago, and a murder."

"I passed it on just as it came. I hide nothing from any of you. I don't think they were lying, but I don't know why they want you to go to the city, no. It might just be their price. I've seen them ask bigger favors for less. And they seemed frightened. On the other hand—anything bad enough to frighten them from that far away is our business, too. I'd be very surprised if there weren't something important for you to learn out there."

"Where the water chooses an ocean." The human part of his mind seized on that, worried it like a new bone. "The Atlantic or the Pacific, I guess."

"Yes. The continental divide."

"The divide." There was one word that sounded almost as true in English as it did in Uratha speech. Especially on a Southern tongue, where the long *i* opened up all hollow and sad. *Divide*: wolf from man, white blood from red, sweet Methodist hymns from the howls of a tribe that still saw Eden dying by inches. Maybe that was where he belonged right now. "That'd make it like a big giant crossroads, wouldn't it? Granny always said you could make a deal with the devil at the Bone Woman Holler crossroads, even on Sunday. And not just there, but anyplace two old roads met."

"Granny was right," Doomwise agreed. "Crossroads are the essence of choice, where Right and Wrong and Indifferent paths touch and people leading otherwise unconnected lives can meet. More than anything, they're a chance to get lost. That's why suicides were buried there. Watch out, Daniel. Nothing's more prone to mischief than a lost soul. Which is why I hope I've guided you well today." She touched his shoulder. Her hand was smooth but veined like an old woman's. He flinched a little. She noticed and took it away.

"One more thing," she said coolly. "You go alone."

Maybe there really was a crazy ghost haunting this place, because he felt the floor tilt. "Beg pardon?"

"Alone. There's no going home for you till this is finished. No pack." She barked a laugh then. "There's no going home for you right now anyway, is there? That's the only reason you're out here. And you're right, half-moon. They're far too fragile to see you break. But you can hate me for saying it. And you can blame me to them, too, for making a liar out of you."

"That your fee for services?" he asked bitterly. It was unwise, very unwise, but he wasn't thinking straight. "You get to put a curse on me? Misery loves company?"

"You can't conceive of what would happen to me if I broke my spirit-oaths and charged a fee. Don't speculate on subjects you don't understand. Curses are among them." Her irises were so pale they almost vanished, the pupils dark piercing points. "I do wish you well. Believe that or not."

It was the only time he ever walked out of church feeling dirtier than he went in.

"Don't promise them when you'll be back," she called after him.

It was the scorched dregs of a stale coffeepot, full of hard-water deposit and detergent. All the sugar in the world couldn't save it, and he didn't try. The dirty steam filled his nostrils as he lifted it, along with other scent-layers he sifted through without really even thinking. The diner was probably around thirty years old and definitely all-smoking for most of that. Wall paneling original, diesel-stained carpet still new and breathing manufacturing fumes. The broken cigarette machine in the corner had cigarettes in it. There'd been some kind of fight here at the bar, or blood spilled anyway, but it was at least several years ago, nothing to raise hackles. Somebody in the kitchen had a cold. The gal at the cash register was drunk but didn't look it. A newborn had been brought in and changed sometime that morning, and the single-serving half-and-halfs in the dish three stools down were sour. He'd long since learned this went faster if he let it all just swirl through his mind and settle out by itself. In a few seconds, the mess of smells was straightened up, laid out, and labeled for him like shiny presents on Christmas morning. The wolf grumbled, famished but otherwise calm. Things were safe, and that was all the man needed to know.

He shoveled in dripping over-easy eggs and ketchup and hash browns. The waitress lit a tiny flickering smile at him. She didn't know him, and strangers were rare here. But when he tucked into his plate like that, she seemed to think that was cute.

"You tell me if you need a refill on that coffee, hon. I'll brew some more," she said. He nodded and grinned back. Her pupils flared.

You ain't sired yet, the wolf reminded him pettishly, *and you ain't gettin' younger.* The trucker at the other end of the bar roused and sneered at him, baring stained dentures. He stomped down the wolf's lust-edged zeal (*ahh, we can take 'im, old SOB*) and turned back to his food. Elias could sprinkle bastards all over America, but Hearts-blood was a cautious hunter alone abroad.

Somebody'd left a newspaper on the seat next to him, and Heartsblood picked it up and unfolded it as he ate. The funnies first, always the funnies first, then Dear Abby, then the front section. A splatter of the last owner's ketchup drew his eye:

Crow deaths a harbinger for humans

HAMMOND, Illinois — Lorraine Critten doesn't believe in mincing words. "Looking just at the infection rates in Michigan, Illinois and Indiana," she says, "we've already met the definition of a pandemic. If the current situation persists into the winter roosts, we're looking at a fatality of 30 percent or worse — the equivalent of the Black Death."

Fortunately, she's speaking exclusively of the animal kingdom, and more specifically, of the Corvidae family, of which the best-known members are crows, blue jays and ravens. Yet Dr. Critten, an epidemiologist at Indiana University, insists that human beings have a stake in all this avian misery. Mass 'die-offs' among these species herald the arrival of certain blood-borne diseases known as arboviruses, including West Nile and the newly-dubbed Muskegon virus, which mosquitoes transmit to people as well as birds and livestock.

"As a community, we've both under- and over-reacted to Muskegon," she continues. "On the one hand, the frontlines of the obvious health crisis are secure. Despite the unquestioned tragedy of the handful of deaths to date, our hospitals and clinics are responding extremely efficiently, and the CDC is keeping the public informed—almost over-informed. On the other hand, we're still neglecting the earlier links in the chain of disease vectors, which is where we have the most power to contain it. It actually doesn't start with birds or mosquitoes. It begins on the level of the so-called inanimate, and that's why it's so easily overlooked."

If things were up to Dr. Critten, perhaps there'd be no pandemic to discuss. She was among the first to sound a warning note when West Nile made its U.S. appearance, reminding us that (as most natives know from stinging experience) Lake Michigan and its environs are replete with the stagnant water that breeds mosquitoes. This produces, in effect, thousands of tiny laboratories where the virus can mutate, grow hardier and adapt itself to new hosts.

Alas, politics and money have long clouded the mosquito-control debate. In Hammond, site of the most recent crow die-offs, officials plead civic poverty in failing to drain swampy areas and spray standing water for larvae. As we walk in the sweltering sun to a local café, Dr. Critten points out several children playing in the puddles of an abandoned lot — not an uncommon sight in this neighborhood. From the sidewalk, she spots a tiny black corpse in the grass and collects it with latex gloves and a plastic bag she carries around, just in case. She speaks to the kids, but whatever she says, it doesn't convince them to leave.

Nor is it necessarily possible to spray and drain our way out, she cautions. "Drained wetlands actually produce more mosquitoes," she explains, "because eggs can go dormant and then hatch months later in heavy rains, and more of those hatchlings survive because the predators are gone. Then, when they can't find a large body of water to breed in, they'll settle for smaller ones, like old tires and dog dishes. Needless to say, spraying for them becomes all but futile then. They'll just be everywhere." With this summer shaping up to be both the hottest and the wettest of the decade, her blunt words conjure up visions of Old Testament-sized swarms — a possibility she won't dismiss. And she admits her suggested solution, wetland restoration (which recently helped Massachusetts drastically reduce its mosquito population by returning natural predators to the area), is expensive and time-consuming.

Yet she won't abandon hope. "It may be too late for this year," she says. "Frankly, I'm expecting to see human deaths in Hammond, given the scope of the crow mortality here, and more in Chicago and Gary. To some extent, the real question is next summer. How many more will get sick? Will it be dozens or thousands? That depends on the number of mosquitoes, which depends on the state of the wetlands, and that state is not a good one. The crows are trying to warn us. However highly evolved, we're still just one animal species of many. We're not big enough to get around these circumstances. We have to choose. So let's choose. How do we want next summer to be?"

And, one can't help wondering, who may not be there to see it because of our actions — or our failure to act?

Mass die-off. The words rang in his head, crude and cold, with the unconscious poetry of human speech. He could picture it: the spirit of death silently passing under the roosts, laying its finger on bird after bird, not caring which fell today and which'd live for a little while yet, and the birds dropped like rain, landing with soft thuds, turning from black to ash-gray. No one cared. All nature fed on itself, and microorganisms always got dessert. No wolf could forget that. He'd dipped his muzzle in gore enough. One day it'd be his turn.

Still, the picture wouldn't fade. Or that strange sadness for the birds, falling by the thousands, each little body nothing but trash by itself, but the sheer number a mute witness to… what?

The crows are trying to warn us, doctor-lady said. *Trying to warn who?* he wondered. Not necessarily the humans who thought such things were their bailiwick. And the smell when he closed his eyes and saw the sick birds wasn't the rich web of sweet, sharp, and deep that rotting flesh gave off. It was the stark reek of fire, wood fire, and it put terror in his animal bones.

The phone in the diner was broken, so he walked out to the gas station parking lot and called from there. The temperature had dropped a good twenty degrees since sunset; his fingers were stiff as he dialed and fiddled with the volume button, and the night air crept in under his clothes.

She didn't pick up. "You have reached the mailbox for Desert Moon Web Services," her smooth business voice chanted over the miles. "If you're hearing this message between the hours of ten AM and—"

He hung up with a bang and dialed again. "C'mon, c'mon…. "

"Hello?" Now that was her real voice. "With what insistent person in Pennsylvania am I speaking? HB?"

"Yeah, it's me."

"You caught me in the mall restroom."

He blushed. "Sorry."

"No prob. What's up, you on your way back? You need a bus ticket?"

"I, no. I mean yes, I'm done with—I found her. I saw her." He realized, way too late, that he hadn't given a single thought to how he'd say it.

"So?" He could hear the scowl. "Does that mean you're on your way back? Hope everything worked out. You know what I say about looking for trouble. HB? You there?"

"Yeah. Kalila, listen. I need you to tell Elias. And everybody—"

"*Shit.* You're not serious." Too quick, that gal.

"It ain't for long," he blurted. "Just to Chicago and back. There's something I got to do there. But I'm supposed to do it alone."

"Do what alone? How long is not long?"

"Stop a murder. I don't have details yet, I'm sorry. Dunno, maybe a month or two?"

"HB! Look. You know I support your spirituality, but there's a t—I really think you don't—Okay, back up. Now I know what I'm saying. It's just this year that we've finally started feeling like The Pack, you know?"

"I know."

"Elias grasps the concept of a chill pill, finally got Dana not to go haring off all the time. Now *you're* haring off, and it's not like there isn't shit going on back here, HB, and Elias is gonna have fucking kittens!"

"I know. Kalila, you gotta tell him for me. I can't challenge him on this."

"You can't lose to him, you mean."

He leaned against the metal frame, feeling just a bit sick. Kalila always was a motormouth, but now her talk darted and wheeled like a cornered deer. She must've been expecting bad news all this time. Now that it was out, she couldn't get quite mad enough to hide how scared she was. And scared was catching.

"C'mon, Kalila," he mumbled. "It's killin' me already. Don't make it worse."

"How are you even going to get there, hitchhike?" She was back to the races. "You might as well paint a neon target on your ass for every tinpot bump-in-the-night and boogeyman along a thousand miles of interstate. Be sure to pack your vampire-bite kit and your exorcist equipment."

"I ain't gonna call him," he interrupted when she stopped to breathe. "You don't have to either. But I ain't gonna call him. So if you don't tell him… then he just won't know. 'Kay?"

"I want a word with that creepy bitch. You don't even know anybody in Chicago."

"No. I know I don't. But you do, don't you?"

"You *fuckhead*."

"Well, never mind then."

"Wait!" He heard a furious rustling. "Goddammit, Daniel, wait. You're really going, no matter what? You're going to hitchhike there and sleep on park benches, alone, trying to finish a walkabout you can't even find the manual for so that you can, what? What was it again?"

"I got to, Kalila." He let out a sigh. "That's why I won't challenge Elias. And it's why I ain't gonna argue with you. 'Cause, yeah, both of you'd beat me. And that's fine, I don't mind that."

"*Hnnh—*"

"Seriously. I don't. But this one thing, I can't roll over on. So—so I'm just not gonna call again till I'm done with it."

Another unbelieving little noise, but when she spoke he could hear a new note of reluctance. "Fine. Let me find my other PDA and get you a phone number. Storm Lord named Mercedes Childseeker. Her pack is the Hull House Haunts. I'll call her and let her know you're coming to town, and I can't promise she'll do anything but I'll tell her I'd consider it a favor. Lemme get the address, too, it's near the UIC campus…. "

Well, maybe in a way he had challenged them and won. Better not tell the wolf that, though. Poor SOB already thought the world was off its pole. He wrote the information on his palm in blobby ink from a ballpoint lying there in the carrel.

"I'm also gonna book your ticket online," she added. "So just go to the Greyhound station in Pottstown. It'll be there under the name we gave you for the Canada trip. You still have that ID, right? Unless you're going to be a dumbshit, asstard, married-to-your-sister redneck cracker."

Usually this was a good way to get a rare tussle out of him, but he translated it for the present situation: *please reassure me you're still one of us.*

"No, I won't." Sound set. Sound sure. "Not about that. I'll take the ticket. Thanks, darlin'. Oh."

"Oh?"

"If you're online, can you look somethin' up for me?"

"Yes. What?"

"I need to know what you call a flock of crows."

"Besides a flock of crows?"

"Yeah. 'Cause I think it's called a 'murder,' but I can't recollect exactly."

"Ah. Hang on." The tapdancing click of her laptop's keys, the good old soundtrack of his life. "Well. Sure enough. A murder of crows. A gaggle of geese. An exaltation of larks, ooh, I like that. A covey of grouse. Is that what you needed?"

"Yep."

"I won't ask why, I know it'll just piss me off. Look, you said you're not going to call, and if you don't, fine. But if you change your mind... I just want you to know I will pick up."

"I know you will."

"And I'll do it because I'll be missing you. Okay? We all will. So do whatever you have to do. Get it over with. And then get your red hindquarters back home where you belong." He thought he heard her sniff.

"I will. I promise. Tell Elias and Dana I said I was sorry."

"They won't give a shit how sorry you are. But I'll tell them."

"Thanks."

"You take care."

"You, too." There had to be something else he could say, something to tide them over, a winter kill buried under snow for lean times. But if there was he didn't think of it. Was that sound her hanging up? He hadn't said bye yet. "You, too. Bye."

"Bye." The word faded in as she quickly brought the phone back to her mouth. That made him feel better. Then click, and she was really gone this time. Bless technology and the sorta-clean goodbyes it made possible. No wistful cheek nuzzles, no jolt of the taboo as the familiar musk of packmates' markings turned into the alien smells of new territory.

But as he shouldered his backpack and headed for the on ramp, the hot meal that had gone down like manna was already turning into a hard ball in his belly.

A long bus trip was good practice for the city. Lots of time to get used to acrid stink of motor exhaust and hot road tar, the historical odor of crowds washed and unwashed, their pee and shit only partly muted by the chemicals in the blue-water toilet. Watching the puffy faces float by, your mental gears ground down and you started to feel like you knew them. You'd always lived here and nowhere else. These were your people. The cities he'd been to had that kind of way about them, and none of 'em were half Chicago's size. He'd have to keep his eyes peeled and his asshole puckered.

He stepped off the bus into a heat haze that just about knocked him over, which for a Carolina werewolf was saying something. A downtown canyon of concrete and glass swallowed him up, every building and windshield flashing afternoon sun into his eyes. He put on his shades. At least the station was cool and dim. He went in and called the phone number Kalila had given him. He got a computerized voicemail greeting, on which he left a carefully generic message.

That left him with just an address. But as he headed back out the door, he saw a big stand of tourist brochures and caught the words *Jane Addams Hull House* on one of them. Another had a mini-map with a dot marking the UIC campus. It looked like he wasn't far from the university, and the apartment was supposed to be right around there. He might as well walk and get his bearings as sit around the station waiting a decent spell to call again. He could head south on Halsted, 23rd should be a little piece after Cermak, and then the cross-street Kalila mentioned wasn't on his map, but he figured if he just cut west along 23rd he couldn't miss it.

He figured wrong, naturally. He'd only been in a big downtown a couple of times, and he'd forgotten how they worked. Even if everything *looked* like a neat little grid on your map, streets were liable to bend or change names or flat-out vanish on you. He kept south, still looking for a street that went through, and found himself crossing the river into China. China*town*, anyway, a shift that crept up on him as the signs went squiggly and the cooking smells took on a different savor.

His gut gurgled. He could sniff out raw fish and beef at the butchers' counters, but the tart, game meat the wolf hungered for was worlds away. His legs itched to run, and his shoulders hunched. He'd done the critter wrong with all this store-bought food and easy walking. A wolf who didn't work and kill and cache was a wolf who starved. Laziness made it nervous. The man had his own ways of foraging, but trusting in that could be hard.

Back home, the pack made time for hunting. Even if it was just a token run, small prey that Elias and Kalila didn't always stoop to actually eat, at least they agreed they had to keep fit. Run out the restless blood. He wondered if the Uratha of Chicago did such things. Supposedly, some in the Iron Masters tribe never even shapeshifted. He longed for it now. The wolf so rarely got lost.

Still, the charred flesh and spiced oils sparked his appetite. He stopped at a restaurant and got a bag of egg rolls, chomping them down as he wandered and tried to figure out if he had to double back or if there was some way to loop around. The bright colors and hanging streamers lured him, and the darkening sky made him feel a little safer. But something here still wasn't right. He peered up walls and down alleys, hoping to catch a flash of it. The wrinkled grandmothers wheeled their groceries home at too quick a shuffle. Most of the stores were closed, a good couple of hours too early. A paper lantern battered against a pole, but he couldn't feel any breeze. And the gutters and sidewalks were too clean, he realized, as though some busybody had come through with a leaf blower and swept it all off hither and yon. There should be cigarette butts and bits of stomped-on cabbage, losing lottery tickets. A stream of clear water ran in the gutter even though it hadn't rained that day. Yes, the spirits were nigh, as they should be. If he held his breath, he could see them. But his ears brought him a most unspirit-like silence. They were all hiding, in the echoes of buildings and behind enormous statues of Buddhas and goddesses that stood only in their world.

He slowed to a stop, suddenly much more anxious that he didn't know where he was. Just ahead of him, a weary man lugged something huge through a stiff-jointed glass door. Heartsblood started forward to help him. Then he saw what the man had: some kind of antique cannon, all salt-crusted and slimed with verdigris, but mounted on new wooden wheels.

It was a hell of a thing. Now he could hear a spirit-sound, huge gills laboring. The weight of centuries and millions of tons of cold water still lay on it. Death, too. *Too heavy*, it rasped in a dirty old man's voice. *Too heavy for a leaking boat, but Beijing had ordered us specially, so the sailors came with us, down and down.* The man glanced up at Heartsblood, startled, brown eyes dilating, and Heartsblood saw that he knew the cannon's story, too, that he was terrified of it. And that he was going to put it out on his doorstep all the same.

Heartsblood turned around and headed back north. This was probably just the kind of thing he should be poking his long snout in, but better wait till tomorrow when he'd hooked up with these other Uratha. ("Alone," Doomwise's voice nagged him.)

No sleek towers trying to out-Babel each other out here, just a couple of spikes of sooty old chimney stacks. Still, it felt pretty mazelike as he wound back out of Chinatown into what his map assured him was "Little Italy," though it didn't look Italian to him. Around and between the chalky islands of office buildings, public apartments faced out blankly, daring somebody to fuck with them, and untidy row houses hunched. If he squinted just right, he could see why they'd been built so narrow and close, could pick out their neighbors' ghosts—wooden spirit-tenements long gone in this world that still shoved and jostled for every square yard. The survivors eyed him through half-lidded dusty windows.

But somebody was knocking the insolence out of these projects, literally. Bright-colored cranes loomed everywhere. Huge brick piles and lone shards of wall stood like ancient ruins. He saw a big sign saying FEDERAL/STATE EMPOWERMENT ZONE by the sidewalk. Somebody'd sprayed black paint over whatever it was trying to explain about Empowerment, and there was nothing but a used rubber in the little plastic bucket that invited him to take a flyer.

Where the hell were the people? This was supposed to be a metropolis. Why couldn't he see or hear them and barely even smell them? Was it the virus? In the South on a muggy afternoon like this, even Columbia folks would be out on their porches with iced tea trying to catch a breeze or a wave from a passerby. Here, only the Washateria had any signs of life, and they were worn-out working poor more faded than their own laundry, too tired to even read *People*. He bought a gritty hot cocoa from the vending machine and drank it down as he got his bearings back. One thin skyscraper struggled up out of the landscape. The university must be that way. The local color had reached the end of its charm, and his shoes were starting to itch and squeeze.

A dank plywood tunnel covered the sidewalk and walls of the next block's buildings. He thudded down it and was halfway through the deserted intersection before a flash of green out of the corner of his eye made him spin and take another look at what he'd just walked through. A smile lit his face. The plywood on this side exploded with color—some kinda mural. As he came closer he saw the labeling: ABLA ARTS GUILD, FUNDED THROUGH UIC, and then a bunch of names and ages. Schoolkids. Painted over three days last spring, and probably supposed to have been torn down already. But with the promised, newfangled slum condo still unfinished, the mural had had a little stay of execution.

From head to foot, the panel buzzed with human activity. Meatpackers with bloody cleavers hacked at sides of beef and the cutting wheel of a big old McCormick reaper mowed right toward the viewer. Skyscrapers sprang past the rows of white pine that the loggers whittled down and dumped in the river, and a Ferris wheel circled the middle.

How proud they were of it all, the destroying as much as the creating. Well, why not? You could see the city lights from orbit. Meanwhile, the canoes and swamps and prairies that filled the left of the painting were so obliterated he hadn't even spied their ghosts yet. He couldn't even feel the stamp of the old watershed on the land. It was buried under yards of urban flotsam.

And yet it still had to be there. Somewhere, there had to be traces, unseen hosts that knew the story. Nothing vanished completely, not in spirit. The land must remember, it always did. Didn't it?

A riot of yellow and orange filled the middle of the picture. GREAT FIRE OF 1871, read the label under it. CHICAGO RISES FROM THE ASHES. He realized the flames were supposed to form the shape of a bird (just not painted very well), floating up from the black hulls of burned buildings, wings thrown wide and beak open in a scream. A phoenix.

He damn near cried then. That was the idea here, he knew. The neighborhood kids, walking to school past the slagheaps of their old homes while whatever money problem or other bullshit it was worked through the civic intestines—they were supposed to look at this and remember the city'd come back from worse. Maybe that was why there was a gummy brown splat across part of it, like somebody'd thrown a soda at it. His fingers brushed the blot.

And suddenly there was real fire there, sizzling where he'd touched the plywood and climbing up to cover the painted flames. It swallowed his hand in a pincer grip. He screamed through gritted teeth. That damn bird was *alive* in there. Its head turned sideways so that one beady eye could blink and scrutinize him, clicking its beak. Another talon came out and collected his shirt front, frying the cotton to a crisp.

WHATSTHISWHATSTHISWHATSTHIS, it hissed and steamed. He was afraid it couldn't even see him, couldn't tell what he was, and meant to kill him rather than find out. Then it blinked again, more slowly.

GOTCHA, it said happily. GOTCHA BOY. NOW WHATCHA GONNA DO? NOW WHAT? YOU EVER HEARD OF INJUN BURNING?

He couldn't answer. The pain was too bad. And somehow he knew that if it screamed, that would be it, he'd be prey.

EVER HEARD OF INJUN BURNING? it grinned, putting its eyeball so close he thought he could almost see through it to something else.

He snarled at it. It laughed. He put the strength of the Uratha in his arm and twisted his hand free. The fire vanished with a whistle, like somebody'd thrown a water bucket on it. Nothing was burned, not his shirt, not his skin, though his forearm hairs were a little curled.

He touched the picture again. Banged his hand on it. But the firebird was gone. He didn't know whether he was madder at it or at himself. He should've answered, should've asked. It was another test. He was sick to death of tests. He kicked the panel. It dented in the middle, squeaking on its nails, and fell halfway off.

No, wait. This was wrong. This wasn't his to tear apart. Pounding the shit out of some kids' art project wouldn't bring the vision back. He spent his tantrum in a flood of cussing that would've gotten him a Lava bar in the teeth from Pa. Then he stuck the panel back on as best he could. One of the firebird's feet had chipped off, and he couldn't find the missing piece.

Enough. The hell with the apartment, he could stalk down the UIC campus easy enough. Maybe if he went there and found Hull House, he'd catch a whiff of its name-sake pack. He found an El station and walked along the train line, north and then east. He distrusted the line map—names and dots with no sense of distance or ter-rain—but it delivered. He could smell the lake again by the time he got to the campus buildings. Of all the human ecologies he'd ever seen, he did like colleges the best. He'd never gotten the piece of paper from one of them, but he'd visited their libraries to breathe the musk of old leather book covers and whisper with the lonely knowledge-spirits, walked the footpaths under the gaze of watchful trees. Even the dark dangerous corners where somebody'd been mugged or raped or run over seemed a rightful part of the landscape, seemed to know their place and keep it.

He caught a skittering shadow out of the corner of his eye. It disappeared when he looked at it straight on, but then he let his sight move into the Shadow Realm and he found it again. It didn't move quite right to be a rat. It didn't move quite right for one of the Rat Hosts either. Those little shits always limped; their hive nature made them awkward on their own. He dared a quick change to the wolf and padded after the thing. Smelled like an old pork chop bone. Come to think of it, it looked like an old bone, too. It flitted from bush to grass, one hidey-hole to another. He wondered what the natural predator of the ghost of a chewed-up pork chop might be. He stumbled into curbs and bike racks that he couldn't see because his attention was on the Other Side, but he also found spirit-echoes that tempted his quizzical nose. Ancient beer bottles and high buttoned shoes. Rotted wood foundations. Dead, stiff alley cats that eyed him balefully as he skirted past. This hadn't always been university land, oh no. There was another history here, but only a nose close to the ground could catch it.

He lost the thing when it slid into the bushes at the base of Hull House. At least it had led him where he needed to go. And he saw at once why Uratha might take a shine to the place: it had a big spirit-presence, piercing the Shadow with high moonlit walls, ringed with outbuildings, and abuzz with noise. He heard kids shouting and somebody playing Joplin. Wild ivies and tangled trees leaned in, threatening to drown out the music with cricket thrums. He was downright crestfallen when he turned his sight back to the ordinary world and found only a single house there, dwarfed by stern university halls. It was clean and neat, that was all. And well-loved, with a gleaming plaque honoring it. People did remember some things.

He worried then about the critter he'd been following. It was only a piece of car-rion, but it had run here for safety, and that wasn't right. Well, nothing was entirely pure, he reminded himself grimly, neither here nor there. Not even the few places his tribe still toiled to keep sacred. There was always a snake in the garden, a bruise on the apple. As he snuffled around searching for it, he felt a hateful eye glaring down on him. But when he peered up, there was nothing in the sky. He suspected the house's windows. They were dark and sullen compared to the rest.

Still, that thing had gotten in from the bottom somehow. His paw nearly fell on something foul, and he jerked back. A stinging, garlicky odor laced with saccharine greeted him. He studied its source. Stained white paper, a coffee filter maybe, with a half-empty soda bottle beside it under the bush. Wolf eyes followed movement keenly, but they didn't see color so well. Nimble human fingers would suit better, too. He let his bones unfurl again. Once the man's eyes got used to the dark, he saw that it was a red stain, all right.

Just as he leaned toward the filter to pick it up, a scraping of cloth on cloth put him on alert. His head snapped up. His eyes refocused.

The boy was closer than he'd sounded—he crouched on the nearest bench, one hand resting lightly on the back to balance his coiled pose. He was somewhere in that long mile between child and man, his face baby-smooth and his armpits musky. Weeds of neon-blue hair stuck out from his head, except in a few places where beads, little pebbles, and daubs of something red and pasty weighted it down in clacking strands. His denim jacket glittered with hundreds of metal thingamabobs sewn on like scales— coins, bottle caps, hex nuts, washers, soda-can tabs. Chains of paper clips draped from shoulder to elbow. The left knee of his jeans was wrapped in what looked like a Hefty bag, and the rest was painted in swirls of color. Even his beat-up sneakers had a rim of brass and steel tacks pushed into the wall of the sole.

Despite the smell of sweat and French fries, Heartsblood couldn't quite decide if this was a real kid or some kind of kid-shaped city shade. It was the blade-glint gaze. But then the boy tilted his head at a familiar angle, and Heartsblood knew he'd been half right either way. It was another Uratha, barely grown but already strong in the wolf.

"Don't touch it. Get away," the boy said softly.

He was getting away, but he got away a bit more. He reckoned he must've done something wrong, something against the Law in these parts. "Looked like blood from a ways off," he offered.

"No." The boy scampered forward, untying the bag from around his knee. He wrinkled his nostrils. His left eye shone weirdly in the lamplight, filmed over with the reflections of stars that the light pollution had long since hidden from sight. "I said get back, unless you enjoy huffing burning ice gas."

"Burning ice gas?"

"Meth," the boy barked. "Toxic fumes from the cooking. They love to leak."

He put out his hand—silver fingernail polish—and muttered ancient words both soothing and warning. He tied some kind of tricky knot in the bottom of it. In went the coffee filter, then another big knot, then the soda can, and then another three knots. The whole time he carried on a conversation in the First Tongue with the little pieces of trash. He wasn't gonna hurt 'em as long as they minded him, he was just gonna put 'em back where they belonged, and this time they better stay. Things like that.

Heartsblood waited patiently for the crescent-moon to finish his witch talk. The boy got up, gripping the top of his plastic sausage chain. First order of business now finished, they both turned automatically to the next. The boy zipped his jacket shut and fiddled aimlessly with the bag. Heartsblood pretended to pick at his fingernails. It was the sizing up, and it had to be done out of the corners of your eyes because direct staring meant a challenge. He yawned, a peacemaking gesture.

"I reckon I'm the stranger here, not you," he said to the air.

"You saw our marks?"

"Smelled 'em."

"You didn't see the tags."

Visions of dog tags came into Heartsblood's head. But then he realized the kid probably meant claw-scratches, or little graffiti signs like he'd heard the city were-wolves used in places where scent marks got covered over too soon. "Wasn't lookin' for nothin' like that," he answered. No need to show off his ignorance. "Didn't have to. I got a shiver as soon as I set foot in your territory."

"And kept going."

Heartsblood nodded. He liked to leave a fact alone till he knew where it was headed.

"Ah reckon I know your name." The boy smirked, poking fun now. He was wary, but not so wary he couldn't tussle a bit verbally. "Is it Daniel?"

"Daniel Vickery. Or Heartsblood. You been lookin' for me?"

"You're hard to track. Like a tribe brother should be."

Not only a fellow Uratha but a fellow Hunter in Darkness, then. He never would've guessed from the boy's getup, but it was true that Heartsblood only heard him when he decided he wanted to be heard. Even with all those jangles.

"Well, I showed my belly button to your totem when I came in."

"You don't know our totem," the whelp retorted.

"No, but I knew you had to have one," he came back. "I woulda howled for it, but I didn't want to go a-stirrin' up a ruckus."

A new voice rang off the concrete. "No, that wouldn't have been a good idea."

It came from the direction he thought it would. No yearling squirt would sass an older, stronger interloper without his pack covering him. And sure enough, here they were, stepping out from behind an air molecule. There was a dark-haired, bronze-skinned woman in the last years of fertility, all tight sinews and rounded muscle under her T-shirt, and a broad-chested man with curly blond hair, a short, neat reddish beard, and a knife hilt coming out of his boot cuff.

"We spend most of our time trying to contain the ruckus," she finished. She played wolf games with her eyes, too, trying to catch his gaze, which he kept turned aside. She came forward, calm and slow, her hands swinging easily at her sides. Heartsblood ducked his head and let out a tiny, almost supersonic whine.

"That's better."

"I knew you was there." He didn't try to keep a note of wheedling out of his voice. In fact, he played it up. "I figgered I'd let you get a good look."

"Good for you." She didn't release her stare.

"Aw please, ma'am. Didn't Kalila call you? She said she would. And I left ya a message. I won't be no trouble. I can earn my own keep. Of course, if you're too busy, why that's fine. I'll find someplace else in the city to stay—"

"No," she cut in. One of many places in Uratha culture where adaptability had to prevail over instinct. Few *real* wolf packs would tolerate newcomers, however friendly. But the People had enough troubles already without picking fights with guests. "No, the last thing we need right now is tourists wandering around at loose ends. Come here."

He obeyed. She set her strong hands down on his shoulders. Dominance and reassurance at the same time: *I'm in charge, so don't worry.* She had to reach up to do it, but there was no question she'd had lots of practice. He felt the hardness drain out of the cords of his neck.

"Welcome to Chicago, I guess." She shrugged. "I'm Mercedes Childseeker. As you know. This is Erik Bleeding. That's Little Blue, our Ithaeur. That…" She nodded toward Hull House behind him. "That is our place."

"You can get in there after dark?" he asked.

"I have a key, yes. But I mean it's the home of our hearts, our locus."

"I like it."

"Well, don't like it too much. And don't wander around here alone again, because it's haunted and I won't approve."

Heartsblood didn't point, but he glanced upward. "Upstairs?"

She scowled. "Yeah. Our ongoing 'renovations.' You shoulda seen it when we moved in. Went all to pot without the velvet-gloved iron hand of Jane Addams protecting it."

"Oh, I believe ya," he said hastily.

"It takes time," she said.

"It does, it sure does."

"Let's get back to the apartment. I thought Kalila gave you the address."

"She did, but all I have is this little ol' map, you see, and it don't have—"

Mercedes snatched it away. "This isn't a map, it's decorated toilet paper."

She jerked her chin sideways. Her pack fell in. Heartsblood allowed them to surround him even though it made him feel imprisoned. They didn't walk right, or at least like he would have expected Uratha in the heart of their own territory to walk. Their legs ambled, but their shoulders were held stiff, their eyes scanning every shadowy patch.

"It always feel like this around here?" he asked.

"Like what?" Mercedes didn't look at him.

He tried to come up with a description that was vivid but not insulting.

"This."

She snorted. "Well, without any idea what exactly you're referring to. It's Chicago. How else should it feel?"

"I guess that's what I don't know yet," he said.

The pack's apartment was in just the kind of city neighborhood Heartsblood liked best, actually. It was a step up from the nearby projects, but lots of old construction, lots of streaky windows with bumper stickers or lightcatchers plastered across them, buckled sidewalks with weeds in the cracks. The burglar bars had at least four layers of flaking paint. Mercedes had to jiggle the key to make it turn. They slipped inside more like they were there to rob the place than to settle down for the evening.

"You know that, uh, mural at the apartments they're knocking down back north of here?" Heartsblood asked once they were safe inside. Blue kicked off his shoes by the door. Mercedes went into the kitchen. "On the scaffolding? Reckon you musta seen it."

Mercedes emerged with three shots of Scotch, which she handed out among the adults. She frowned. "Over where they're rebuilding Kennelly Homes? Place is a fucking DMZ. You went there?"

"Well, yeah," he stammered. "Like I said, I got a mite turned around. Anyway, there's this picture of the old Chicago Fire on it, y'know, and when I looked at it started in talkin' to me. Turned into a big ol' phoenix and grabbed me by the shirt front and asked me did I ever hear of Injun burning."

The frown deepened. "You're Cahalith, too?"

"No, ma'am. Half-moon. But even half-moons get visions sometimes, it's just we don't know what to do with 'em except worry." The joke sailed out like a lead balloon. "Anyways. The thing is I do know what Indian burning is—"

"There's no phoenix-spirit in Chicago," she interrupted. Then she almost smiled. "Don't ask me why there isn't, because Mother and Father know there should be. But nobody's ever seen one. And we've got a pretty active menagerie out here. It would have been spotted by now." She glanced at Little Blue, fact-checking. The boy nodded.

"Well, it might not a' been a real phoenix," Heartsblood hedged. "Maybe you got some spirits that are like to take on different shapes. But about the Indian burning. That's what they call a controlled burn, for clearin' fields and cleanin' out underbrush. Prevented forest fires, too, or some folks think so. I just go by what Grampa said, 'cause I'm Cherokee on that side."

"All right. That's good for Indians and people who live in forests to know, but why do we care?"

"Hell if I know," he snorted. "I was hopin' you might have an idea. I don't guess the city's been puttin' out any fire-risk warnings lately?"

"Um, no. Up until last week we were under flood warning."

"Then it ain't that. I dunno. The only thing that strikes me is the fire y'uns had in eighteen seventy-one definitely wasn't a controlled burn."

"Definitely not. But again, that was eighteen seventy-one."

He nodded, chewing on the ragged edge of a nail. "Long time ago. Good thing this ain't a forest, y'uns woulda been due for another one long since."

Eric, the full-moon, spoke for the first time. "Well, it was a forest." He sat. The puffy couch swallowed his rangy frame. "Just chopped up. The old city was all wood planks. Buildings, sidewalks, roads, bridges. And all along the river were stacks of lumber dry-curing to ship. Then you put a record drought and high winds on top of that. The fact is they'd already been putting out fires all week before the big blaze, the fire department was run ragged. That was half the problem."

Heartsblood could conjure it bright as noonday sun in his mind: one big tinder-box of a city just waiting for an excuse to combust. All the signs were there, but no one stopped it while there was still time.

"Not mistakes they repeated when they rebuilt," commented Mercedes. She skimmed the newspaper page Heartsblood had given her, holding it out at arm's length and tilting her head back as if she were a little far-sighted.

"No, they went on to make bold, all-new mistakes," Erik returned.

"Anyway, past an obvious bird theme, Dan, I don't know what if anything you've got a hold of here," she said. "This Doomwise is a big deal back East?"

"Yes, ma'am. She's got a real track record. I seen her visions pan out myself, more'n once." He didn't much care for her tone, and he didn't like being 'Dan' either, but when in Rome. "Ain't there no Bone Shadows tribe out here?"

"Of course there is. But they keep to themselves. Sarah Rainbringer speaks up in *ungin* occasionally, when they think they need to put in an advisory, but otherwise they're off doing—whatever it is they do. Most months, they don't even show up." She shrugged. "Besides, if we need the lowdown from the spirits, we just ask Blue."

Little Blue beamed but said nothing. He fiddled with some telephone cable, braiding and knotting it, every so often spitting on it and rubbing it in like polish. Heartsblood wondered if that neon hair stayed with the boy when he took the wolf.

"But you see what could happen." Heartsblood tried to iron some of the twang out of his voice, watch his conjugations. "Heavy rains you said, and now a heat wave. That means more mosquitoes. The city's set up to be ground zero for an epidemic of this Muskegon encephalitis. Maybe it's like the fire was, where just one more little thing has to happen and it'll blaze up, out of control."

"So maybe there'll be an epidemic." She tossed the paper down. "I don't know what you want me to tell you, Dan. It's hard to accept, but humans are more vulnerable to disease than we are. Especially kids and the elderly..."

"I know that. They're built to be." Trust a Storm Lord to lecture a Hunter in Darkness on biology. "But I don't just mean disease, not natural disease anyhow. You said there's an *ungin*? When's the next one?"

"Depends. If you mean the next big one, Lessner sometimes hosts an intertribal *ungin* at his Christmas party, after midnight. Other than that—well, Olivia Citysmith has open-door office hours every new moon. If I said I was bringing a newcomer we'd probably draw a crowd."

"Damn. That's a while from now," he mumbled. "Might be too late."

"Too late for what? This is what I'm saying, Dan, you have no idea what you're looking for."

"Not yet! That's why I need to talk to folks who know Chicago. Besides, maybe somebody's seen something they just ain't connected up yet, maybe what Doomwise said'll make more sense then. Can't we just have a whadjacallit, one of them ad hocs?"

She lifted her eyebrows as high as she probably wanted to throw her hands. "You want me to get you on over three dozen different and hella busy calendars at the same time, at short notice—"

"Three dozen?" His jaw literally fell open. "Three dozen werewolves in Chicago?"

"No, three dozen *packs* in Chicago," she corrected. "More or less, that I know of, that come to *ungins*. That's not counting the Pure Tribes, the Ghost Wolves, the dissidents, drifters, orphans, junkyard dogs, bane-ridden, and Mother Moon knows what other trash."

"Godamightydamn. What we could do with three dozen packs out our way." He knew it wasn't the reaction Mercedes wanted, but all he could feel was joyful awe at the thought of so many two-skinned folk in the same place. Just picture a hilltop covered with them, howling, tussling, chasing, talking. Why, he'd never feel like a stranger in the world again if he could see that even once. "We'd have the Pure and the Rat Host kicked out in a week."

"Really," she said, and her voice was like alum. "First, you'd have to get them to agree on the nature of the issue, and then you'd have to get them to agree on the scope of the issue, and just about the time you were finally down to arguing whether the scope of the issue was an issue, the whole thing'd have to be tabled because of some damn mess with some teenager's First Change phenomena getting caught on videotape." Mercedes stood up and stretched. There was a loud series of *crack-crack-cracks*. "Look, Kalila's a great kid, so you must be okay. But we can't take this forward on any kind of citywide basis without more to go on. I just don't have that kind of pull."

"Yes, we can," he protested. "We got to. We got to try at least. It's a citywide problem, and they can't argue that. That virus don't care whose turf it's on. And you got a right to complain about it, it's going to hit y'uns' neighborhood the hardest. You said it yourself, the kids, the old folks, the poor folks with no doctors."

Little Blue was making *shh-shh* noises and swatting his hands around. "Out with it, Blue," Mercedes said. The kid nodded and walked to the end of the kitchen bar where the garbage can stood, then picked it up and dumped it right on the floor. Mercedes stood up to field a skittering soup can.

"Yech! What the hell… Erik," she snapped. The Rahu jerked, as if startled awake. "Help me with this. Blue, I know Garbageman likes pantomime, but you don't always have to pass it on literally. Especially not indoors. Goddammit, point's made, whatever it is—now you can clean it up."

Heartsblood darted around collecting stray scraps. "Garbageman?"

"Our totem. You said you'd submitted to it already."

"I did. I submitted to something that was taking a gander at me. Felt like some kind of guardian, so I reckoned it was prob'ly yours. But it didn't show itself."

"Blue. No eating the garbage."

"Not eating it," the boy mumbled, but he was scraping the food out of cartons and rubbing it in his fingers, smelling it.

"You learn a lot from folks' garbage," Heartsblood ventured.

"As long as it lasts," said Little Blue.

"Some of it lasts a pretty long time." He wasn't sure whether he was talking with Blue or the totem or both, but either way it was probably best to keep on talking in little circles, the way spirits did. "Plastic, sody-pop cans, those'll hang on for five hundred years."

"Some of it lasts forever. And some of it even I won't touch."

"Obviously not a problem in this case," Mercedes said exasperatedly. She clicked her tongue as she found a wad of gum in fond embrace with her carpet. "All right, Garbage. What happens to the stuff you won't touch?"

"It stains."

"It certainly does," she grumbled. "And what else? Does it just stay where it fell?"

"Yes." The boy nodded sagely. "But it isn't forgotten."

"By who?" Heartsblood prodded. "Well, c'mon. We're listening."

"It remembers itself. And the things that scavenge on it get sick."

"Why, crows are scavengers," he said excitedly.

"I know that," snapped Mercedes. "Thank you, Animal Planet."

Heartsblood shut up, stung, but he didn't blame her. Her own totem was breaking ranks, talking to the stranger after she'd just given him a maybe that was two rats' whiskers short of a no. Still, maybe when she got over her annoyance she'd realize it had to have a reason.

"Garbageman is big on garbage, you notice. He's very demanding of us on the matter. But that's because Jane Addams was big on it." At least she was considering it now—that was a good sign. "Sanitation. No point giving the kids piano lessons if they're playing in raw sewage. The mosquitoes breed in it, the crows scavenge it, the virus spreads… dunno, Dan. Maybe there is something for you there, if you can sniff it out. Could be difficult, sounds like there's more to this than just physical garbage. Disposable diapers, disposable culture. That's what's wrong with this city. Things are done with, people are done with and they go out with the trash, the next day they're a footnote to a statistic." Her voice rumbled low, her eyes went hazy. "But Blue's talking about what doesn't rot away and disappear. No matter how badly we want it to."

"I'm bushed," said Erik. "It's two AM."

"Want to help me out, Blue? Never leave the thinking to the Cahaliths, we can chase our tails all year." Mercedes tweaked the kid's nose. He scowled.

"I just did help," he protested. "I'm tired, too." He darted a sharp glance at Heartsblood, then looked back to his alpha. "It's a school night, remember?"

"Blue's eternally in summer school." Mercedes smirked. "He gets a little caught up in his extracurricular activities. But he is going to graduate, dammit."

Blue panted. His features melted, thinned down, clothes disappearing into thickets of rowdy fur. He whined and nuzzled Mercedes, then trotted to the bedroom door, glancing back with the kind of pleading look canines had down to a science. (And yes, there was a shock of blue at his crown still.) He nosed the door open. Heartsblood caught a glimpse of mattresses on low futon frames, pushed all together. Den sleeping for the civilized werewolf.

Mercedes nodded. "G'night, Dan. You've got the room opposite the bathroom. I'll put out towels."

"Thanks," he mumbled.

"Sleep well."

"You, too."

He padded into the room. There wasn't a thing wrong with it. Nice twin bed, fresh sheets, polished bureau with a mirror. He took the wolf-shape. It was pissed—let out only to find itself in a strange house, and not allowed to mark anything. But he wanted to curl up. He tousled the bedclothes into a pile and settled himself on them. Too hot to sleep under covers anyway.

And too cold without other furry bodies beside him. He trod and lay down, trod and lay down but couldn't make it just right. Finally the warm stale air put him into a fitful sleep.

Lizzie tried to scream her husband's name, but the smoke stung her eyes, the ash choked her, and she could only see a few feet in any direction. Little Josephine huddled against her side. The stinking water came up to the girl's chest, and she shivered, her lips too dark, but Lizzie dared not take them any closer to shore because of the arcs of flaming debris that shot up out of the heart of the inferno and landed on the riverbank. The baby, on the other hand, was flushed, squalling hoarsely from a dry throat. Lizzie dipped her hand in the water and smeared it on the infant's face, where it quickly evaporated, and told Josephine to stay close, to keep her arms around Mother, not to let go. St. Jude, St. Bridget, St. Barbara, and St. Nicholas, the fire brigade, even the police, anyone—Lizzie would have cried out to the devil Himself if she were not convinced that this blaze could only have come from the devil's own breath upon the city.

Something brushed against the soaked knotting of her bustled-up skirts. Then she felt the touch of fingertips on her spine. She shouted, turning around. It was a hand, but it was the hand of a dead man, floating by on his back, his half-lidded eyes sleepy and staring, his jaw relaxed open, full of leaves that had caught in his teeth. She envied him fiercely: the way he drifted along uncaring, past fear and struggle. But then she thought of his soul. Such things were much on her mind tonight. It was her last night of life, she knew, and perhaps she would have to plead for her daughters, too, especially the infant, still unbaptized. She touched the man's chest, blinking out burning tears, and made the sign of the cross over him as he bobbed past. He must be one of those she and Josephine had seen earlier, knocked off the smoking bridge in the stampede. Even now, with the bridge lost to view, they still heard the splashes of things and people falling in. She did not need to know his name or trade, whether he was German or Polish. All were brothers and sisters now before the spreading blanket of wrath.

"Jo-jo, up on my back again," she urged the older child. "Move, girl. You'll be warmer...."

"I don't want to be warmer," the girl sobbed. "I want to stay in the water. I don't want to burn like Papa."

"You won't burn, you stupid creature," Lizzie hissed. "If you don't want to die, then get on my back and stay there. I can't hold you and the baby both. Do it now."

When the girl shook her head, Lizzie slapped her. "You had better hope your father's dead, because if he comes back and finds you defying your mother tonight of all nights, he will give you the biggest strapping you've ever had in your life and make burning up seem like a joy!"

Thank heaven, that did it. Still crying, Josephine took hold of her clothes and started clambering up, shoe-heels digging mercilessly into Lizzie's back.

And it grew hotter yet. Lizzie put the hem of her wet skirt over the baby's face to keep out the smoke (and to press down on just a little, some calculating corner of her mind whispered, when hope fades and mercy becomes more important). Then her eyes were drawn over the water, to an ever-nearing orange glow. Too near to be on land. As she watched, it spread left and right, racing like whipped horses. The years of hog and cattle butchering that had turned the river to bubbling offal had also made of it one long wick of fat and blood and oil, and now the fouled water turned vengefully on the people trying to shelter in it. The river itself was aflame.

He woke with his tongue out, panting. The window was open, not that it did any good in the lingering heat of the night. He thudded over anyway, trying to catch a fresh scent. A tree. A trickle of unfluoridated, unchlorinated water. Nothing. Even the lawn below smelled sour. As he sat there, a mosquito crawled through a hole in the screen. He waited for it to fly in, then swatted it against the wall. It must've just fed, because it splatted blood all over his paw. He scraped it off on the sill.

Attaboy. Now just do that thirty million more times, and maybe you'll have saved the city.

He could hear stereos, fights, sex, but none of it was visible from his lookout. The buildings hid it all behind their rocky faces. Nothing moved out there. It was all so wrong. Why'd he come here? What did he think he could do? He was out of his habitat. His dreams weren't even any better.

A ruckus started up outside, a fluttering and croaking. The light falling into the window flickered.

He jumped up on a chair for a better look and stared down into the parking lot. This was no dream. He galloped down the hall, stopping at the closed bedroom door.

Startling a pack of Uratha out of a sound sleep wasn't always a bright idea. But he could hear pages turning in there, breathing too deep to be unconscious. Somebody was awake. He put the man-skin back on and turned the doorknob as softly as he could, opening it a crack.

"What the hell?" came a low growl.

He opened the door a little wider. There was Erik on his futon, propped up with pillows and a paperback and one of those little clip-lights, staring back at him. "Oh. Dan. What is it?"

Thought you was bushed, full-moon. "Come on," Heartsblood murmured. "There's trouble outside."

"Trouble?" The Rahu switched off the light and set the book down open-faced. He got up, T-shirt and boxer shorts askew.

"Come on." Heartsblood led Erik back to his window. "See that?" he whispered, turning the 's' into a 'th' so as to be all the quieter.

Eric yawned hugely and ran a hand through his hair, changing it from an east-facing bramble to a south-facing one. "What?"

"The crows. They should be roosting."

"Oh yeah." Another yawn. The tornado of black feathers outside didn't tickle his nerves at all? The way their flapping wings made the lamplight jitter? "Fighting over food, I guess. It's okay, Dan. Go back to sleep."

"No." Heartsblood jostled his elbow. "Not food. Look at the crow down on the ground. Getting picked on. Picked apart, for Mother's sake. They're killing him."

"It's probably sick."

"Crows take care of their sick. That's one way they catch West Nile from each other."

"Fine, then something else is wrong with it."

Heartsblood squashed the urge to shake the man. Back home, just his tone of voice and posture would've been enough. Kalila'd be sniffing out the spirits. Dana'd be drawing her bigass knife. But this Uratha, this warrior supposedly—

"Something's wrong with all of them," he rasped. "Come on!"

"Come where?"

Heartsblood pulled off his old pajama pants and hunkered down on all fours. The Urshul was an ugly mutt of a shape, too large and lumpy for a wolf, too clumsy and crooked for a human. But it could run and jump like nobody's business. A wordless thought, and he was out the window without so much as brushing the drape, onto the fire escape, clattering down. He heard a clatter after him. Wolf feet. That reassured him, put spring in his leaps. The birds on the concrete below scattered as he bounded into them. The rainwater puddled on the cement had a foul stench, which led him to the nearby parking lot drain. He whined and scrabbled at the grate, but it wasn't coming up, not without more muscle.

More muscle needed more anger. Luckily, he had some going already. He did unto the grate as he would have liked to do unto Erik's knobby head. The stubs of his fingers stretched out. Thick hard claws—made of stuff more like cowhorn than fingernail—sprouted in answer to his need. His spine spread as his body grew to man-size and then far larger. Foot bones fused into hocks. Teeth and spit and hunger crowded his mouth. So easy. So wonderful and frightening at the same time, to be totally out of control and yet somehow safe beyond the reach of conscience or logic or even survival instinct. This was the Gauru, the rage-form. It couldn't be stayed in. It had one purpose: battle, and battle soon ended one way or another.

He tore the grate out of its well, bolts flying. A tide of filth roared up. Bags, rotted food, leaves, labels, bottles whirled out of the hole. He plowed into the slimy mess. It was piling up around him. It meant to bury him. That, too, stoked his fury. He only realized how deep in he was when a massive talon reached through the flood and grabbed his shoulder, tumbling milk cartons onto his head.

NOT HERE, Mercedes howled in the First Tongue. She'd taken the Dalu, the near-human form, but her expression wasn't too human at all. Her sharpening snout whipped back in an arc. OVER. CROSS OVER.

The rage didn't like this at all. Stop. Listen. Change direction. All roadblocks in its path. But as he clung to her shaggy arm, he felt her moving across, and he had enough brain working to know he wanted to stay with her. *Feel the light from the dark side of the moon*, that was how Aunt Lou had put it. You let that light shine on you and melt you, change you from flesh to more-than-flesh.

On the spirit side, the garbage was heaped up even higher, and he found himself wading in bile—thick, stinging yellow bile spraying from the mouth of a humongous Thing that squatted in the shadow of the parking lot.

Along with the mouth, the Thing had a backbone and eyes—lots of little beetle-black eyes—but past that, it wasn't about to settle into any taxonomy Heartsblood knew, and he wasn't in a mood to sort such shit out. Its skin seemed to be just the clotted version of its bile. It spread its maw wide and a wind started up, blowing inward, toward the billowing throat. The bile started flowing back the way it'd come, and it was trying to take the pack with it, down the Thing's gullet.

"Fuck," Erik shouted. It got garbled in his thorny mass of teeth. "Whafuck…" But the Rahu didn't stay in shock for long. He plunged a plate-sized hand into the maggoty flesh of the Thing's side and came out trailing strings of gore. It convulsed. He stuck his arm even further in and started rooting around.

Some full-moon, Heartsblood thought as he fought the current. He was used to seeing them turn into whirling dervishes of pain. But there was lunacy in the Rahu's slitted eyes all right. It was just goddamned focused, the mindless intensity of a sperm drilling into egg-membrane, only with the aim of killing not merging.

Heartsblood caught one of the—arms? tendrils?—of the Thing as it tried to wrap around him. It lifted him in the air. He sank his fangs in it and just as quickly pulled them out in disgust. Still, it was enough. It let go of him. But he didn't let go of it.

THAT'S IT, Mercedes yelled. KEEP IT BUSY. LET BLEEDING WORK.

Little Blue danced with another of the arms, snapping at it and harrying it, then darting away. Now there was a wolf tactic. It did Heartsblood's soul good to see it. But then the Thing knocked Blue off-balance, and he crashed muzzle-first into the bile. It picked him up and dashed him into Erik, once, twice. Erik got up and tried to catch the younger werewolf, but only managed to get himself airborne, too. Heartsblood dropped down to the ground and whined in Mercedes' direction. The alpha had a big, long knife out but wasn't budging from the spot she'd chosen, clinging halfway up a twisted streetlight pole.

DIVIDE ITS ATTENTION, she growled at him. DO IT!

Divide, attention. The Gauru was not getting input it understood. It felt threatened. If things went on like this much longer, it might have to *think*, and then it could die. He turned away from her and back toward the Thing, which was about to eat his fellow Uratha (a notion the rage had far less trouble working with). He jumped back onto on the writhing arm he'd let go of a second before. It slammed him into the concrete. Something much harder than the Thing drove into his shoulder blade, almost impaling it. He grabbed at it wildly as the Thing lifted him up again, and it came out of the muck with him.

It was a chimney mast with a bristly old UHF antenna on top, but what he knew about it in that moment was it was longer than his arms and sharper than his claws, and if he swung it hard into that Thing's mess of eyes it would probably hurt. He was right. The Thing gurgled as the tines popped several bubble-like eyes. Then it shook him like a rat. His head flew sideways at the wrong angle, and his neck snapped. He just kept flailing with the pole till the Thing finally threw him down and batted it out of his hands. He tried to stand up. The current pulled on him, dragged him to his knees. The nerves in his hands tingled, and his neck labored to heal itself. The pain soaked into the edges of his rage, nagging at that flip side of instinct that decided when to crawl away in defeat. He moaned.

The Thing was mewling, too. It dabbed at its gouged eyes with one arm while it tried to scoop Erik into its maw with the other, using Blue as the spoon.

And now Mercedes moved, running across the roofs of a row of Model Ts and Detroit Electrics that had apparently broken down for the final time in this very lot. As she landed on each rusty ghost-car, its roof crumpled in, but she didn't stumble or slow down, just raced on with her knife out in front of her like a lance.

Heartsblood yelped and started to follow, but she was already gone, straight down the Thing's throat, letting the suction carry her. Meanwhile, Erik had finally managed to wrench Blue out of the Thing's grasp. Erik hefted his packmate and tossed him into the air. Blue landed on top of the Thing, chanting. Then suddenly Erik was snorting around—looking for his alpha.

CHILDSEEKER! he screamed. His yellow eyes fell on Heartsblood. Even with the ragged edges of the Gauru anger still warming his blood, he felt it freeze. The Rahu was bounding toward him.

The gale blowing into the giant tunnel of the Thing's mouth reversed itself and blasted them both off their feet. A sound like the barking of a mountain-sized seal rapped out twice, three times. A fountain of green and purplish-black shot up and rained down on them. Mercedes came with it, flying out of the Thing's mouth and slamming against the lamppost, which hissed and dropped its glass globe into the slime.

The Thing started to… boil, was the best word for it. Its skin looked like the surface of water at full boil. And yet it was shrinking. No, draining. Falling in on itself and sinking back down into the sewer grate. Blue snarled and swiped at its eyes a few more times, irritated to have his revenge cut short, but then he leapt down, dodging through the waving tendrils. Erik had Mercedes on his shoulder. The alpha was shrinking, too, back into her human form. But she was alive and awake. She waved her hand frantically—away, away. They slogged back to a safer distance and watched the mess slowly recede.

"What the hell was that?" Erik rumbled. His muzzle drew up, nostrils flaring into the spur of a human nose. But his eyes were still wolfish.

"Gag reflex," Mercedes said. "He didn't much like me tickling the back of his throat with a klaive."

"No, I mean what the hell was that thing? What's it doing in our backyard?"

"It ain't the spirit of the gutter?" Heartsblood rolled his neck around till the joints popped back into place.

"That's what it looked like," Mercedes allowed, "but a real gutter-spirit shouldn't be crawling around aboveground. Or driving bird flocks nuts. It should just be lurking down there with its mouth open to catch whatever flows in. Of course, maybe that's what it's been doing up to now. Maybe that's why we've never seen it before. Put me down, Erik."

Heartsblood glanced at Little Blue. The Ithaeur sniffed the yellow slick that remained on the concrete, swabbing it up, shivering and chanting. "Spirit vomit," he announced. "It was sick."

Mercedes shook her head. "Not good. Especially if it's contagious."

"See, now that's what I'm talkin' about," said Heartsblood. "And what if there's another heavy rain and the drains overflow?"

"Then it might get into the river," she said grudgingly.

"We got to call the *ungin*."

"I told you, I don't have that authority."

"Then we better call somebody who does."

"Easy, cowboy. It's supposed to be sunny all week."

He kicked at a piece of trash. It was heavier than he expected, stubbing his toe. He bent over and looked at it. "Hey," he said. "Hey, look-a here." He picked it up. It was an old rocking ink blotter made of dull gray metal, molded with a design of twisting snakes. He wiped the slobber off it and read.

D.B. & S. Patent 87

NTC

"It's monogrammed," he said.

"Nice," said Erik. "Probably get several hundred for it once you polished it up."

"Yeah, but think—that thing throwed it up, and I just tripped on it. Maybe it means somethin', huh? And it belonged to somebody."

"Everything belonged to somebody once," Mercedes said flatly. "How would you trace it?"

Heartsblood squinted to see if there was some little spirit hiding in it, sniffed for a hint of True Scent. Nothing but the reek of bile. He shrugged. "The normal way, I guess," he said. "I can look up the manufacturer. Coincidence is the spirits' telegraph line. I got to work with what I'm given and have faith in the reward."

"Faith." She said it like a foreign word.

"Well, that's how it works, right?" he asked, almost plaintively.

"You seem to be the one who knows, you tell me."

"Nope. Never been on my own spirit-quest before."

"All I know is that people usually don't get what they deserve. Not very often." She was fully human again, small and tired, and naked as well. Erik took off his T-shirt (clean as a whistle; it must have had the rites that permitted it to change with its owner) and slid it on over her head. She let him. Blue was bare-chested, and his jeans were unbuttoned, thrown on. Heartsblood himself was down to his boxers. But once you'd let somebody see you nine feet tall and flaring blood from a hairy snout, standing around in your birthday suit didn't feel too exposed. They slipped across the veil between worlds and stole back into the building silently, anger and fear spent. Even Heartsblood, still worried about the meaning of it all, couldn't really think past the cozy twin bed he'd found so unrestful a little while back.

"Sleep good," he told them.

"You, too, Dan," Mercedes said. "All clear now. No more watching out the window. It's the only way to rest in the city. 'Kay?"

"Yes'm."

"Hurry up eating, Daniel." Mercedes stuck her head out of the hallway and called to Heartsblood, who perched at the kitchen bar working his way through bacon and the paper. "We've got a job."

"A job?" Heartsblood echoed. It was Saturday. Little Blue got up, switched off his game console and headed back to the bedroom.

"Yes," she said. Heartsblood saw that she was pushing bullets into a revolver. She turned back down the hall and pounded on the bedroom door. "Eric! Come on, drag it out, and throw a pair of jeans on it!" The door opened. There was a heap of back-and-forth snarling, then a banging of furniture drawers.

"What kind of a job?" he asked calmly when she came back. He started lacing his boots on.

"I told you our totem was demanding. Especially about things near and dear to Hull House."

"Yeah."

"And you remember my deed-name?"

"Childseeker."

"So, we're seeking a child. He's been kidnapped."

"Glad I got breakfast then," Heartsblood remarked. "Well, let's go. Can we get hold of something to scent 'im from?"

Mercedes held up a small child's shirt. "Done."

Heartsblood blinked. "That was fast." He hadn't heard anybody leave either—she must've already had it.

"Not that we need it," she said dryly. "We know exactly where he is."

Eric put his foot up and kicked the door right alongside the lock. It flew open with a crack of breaking wood, slammed, and rebounded against the inside wall. Mercedes was there to catch it as she strode in. Heartsblood followed in a position he knew from second nature, just behind and to the left, so that anybody in there could see their numbers right away.

It was a grungy one-bedroom, littered with used paper plates and magazines. A man in a faded shirt and papery boxers jerked up from the couch.

"You learn slow, don't you, Carter," Mercedes said, leveling the gun at him and cocking it. "Last time I gave you a count of ten. Today you get five. Next time you don't get a count. Five, four—"

"Holy shit. He's in back," the man started blubbering at once. "He's in back, he's just sleeping, go ahead and take him."

"Blue. Dan." Heartsblood nodded and fetched the little boy, who was out like the proverbial light in the dank bedroom. Five years old, maybe, twisted up in his sheet with the blanket half-fallen down, probably shrugged off in the sticky heat. He carefully laid the sleeping child over one shoulder and came back.

"Now, Carter." Mercedes stepped closer to the man, who dropped down on the floor. She brought the gun close to his head. Heartsblood could smell cordite wafting out of the barrel. She had fired it, not long ago. He wondered if the man smelled it. "You've been told many, many times that you have no legal or physical custody of Calvin. You are not allowed to see him outside of your supervised visitations. At all. Ever. You understand that, don't you?"

"Oh, Lord. Oh, Jesus Christ."

"Answer me."

"Yeah, yeah, I know that. She keeps bringing him late, and the staff's all on her si—"

"Quiet." She sounded bored, and it wasn't an act either. Was she fucking bored? "I don't wanna hear it. Personally, I think your ex-wife and the courts have been overly generous. Though I should warn you, last time April begged me not to get mad and kill you, and today she issued no such caveats. Everybody's getting very tired of your shit, Carter. Do you understand why you may not take this child?"

"Because she says I slapped her," he whined. Heartsblood was torn between the instinct to accept a bared belly and an urge to throttle the man before any more noise came out.

Mercedes sighed. "No, obviously you don't understand. Here, I'll help you. Repeat after me: It's because I'm an abusing piece of dogshit and I don't deserve to be a father. Say it."

"Oh, come on." Tears streaked down into his scraggly beard. "Come on. I oughta called the police on you before. My own alimony checks are paying for some psycho bitch to pistol-whip me—"

"You want me to make sure you don't call the police?" she rasped. "Say it. I'm an abusing piece of dogshit.... "

"I'm an abusing piece of dogshit.... " Almost inaudible.

"And I don't deserve to be a father."

"And I don't deserve to be a father."

"Now you say that in the mirror every morning when you pull your stinking ass out of bed, a thousand days in a row, until it finally reaches that bowl of rotted menudo you call a brain, and maybe there'll be hope for you. If not—"

She fired into the sofa above his head. He dove under the coffee table. She turned on her heel and strode out, not bothering to shut the door. Heartsblood did it for her.

"Take it you folks don't worry about the police much."

"For gunshots in the projects?" Mercedes snorted. "There are kids here who can't fall asleep to anything else."

"His breath smells wrong," Heartsblood frowned as they got in the car. "Calvin's, I mean."

"Yes, Daddy likes to keep him drugged up on these little father-son weekends, so he's not too noisy."

He absorbed that for a minute.

"I find that goddamned disturbing," he said at last, but he chickened out on the second part: *so why don't you?*

She didn't even seem insulted. "Well. Believe me, the shock wears off after the first couple of hundred times."

That ain't all that's worn off. Heartsblood wondered if they'd have even come if it weren't for the totem, if it weren't for the money—he'd put that down as a scumbag lie, but maybe not. He glanced at Erik, back off in la-la land now his services were no longer required, and Blue mumbling under his breath.

They can't have always been like this, he told himself. *Kalila'd never put me in with such folk if she knew.* Or would she? Maybe they really were the best she found in Chicago. Maybe the city made them all this way. Or else it was just the opposite—the city was this way because they were.

He just hoped he could get his whatever his work was done on it before it got to do too much work on him.

Calvin was a hard sleeper, Sudafed or no Sudafed. He snoozed on Heartsblood's arm the whole time they stood in the muggy El station sweltering and looking like tourists—well, fine, he was probably the only one looking like a tourist, but he was enough for all of them—and Mercedes read somebody the Riot Act over a pay phone.

"On file. You've had it on file for six months. You know how I know that? Because I was there when she hand-delivered it to you. Remember? But listen, this actually isn't about you for once, it's about your Holstein of a school nurse. Now either she's ignoring the law, or nobody's told her that Calvin is not to be released to Mr. Carter. Which is it? Yes, I am Ms. Terrell's advocate, do you see anybody else doing it? Tell me, I'll be overjoyed. My point is because your people fucked up, she had to call me and I had to go out again and—well, you shouldn't even have his phone number. It should have been whited out of the contact information. Why was it not?"

"Hey, Blue," Heartsblood whispered.

"Little Blue," the boy muttered.

"Oh, sorry. It's just Mercedes calls ya Blue. What's a tag again?" When those flat blue irises just stared back at him, he turned to Erik.

The Rahu shifted his weight and kept his arms crossed, but he answered under the barrage of Mercedes' tirade. "Different packs use different kinds of marks, because it can't stick out too much," he said. "Like in our territory, spray-can graffiti's just wallpaper, but in the Gold Coast over there it'd get noticed by the wrong people. So they put little logo stickers in bus stops and places like that, like what rock bands use for street advertising."

The wrong people. "And this is your territory."

"Yeah…?"

"Oh." Heartsblood hitched up the sliding kid. "I was just wonderin' about them scratches on that there telephone pole."

"What-where telephone pole?" Erik blinked. Not the answer Heartsblood had hoped for.

"Not that one. The one back at the corner. Five lines, four foot up, definitely an opposable thumb, so I... you saw 'em, right?"

Eric looked to Mercedes, who seemed about ready to jump down the receiver and strangle a vice principal. She flapped her hand at them both.

"Well, just so long as it's nothin' we need to worry about..." Heartsblood trailed off, resigned.

"Exactly," she exploded. "Now if you've lost the court order, then get another copy, but you're still liable for anything that happened to Calvin while he was with his abuser. Are we communicating? If you need me to come speak to all his teachers and all the staff and the TAs so this doesn't happen again... no? You'll take it from here? Good. I hope I don't hear any different." She slammed the phone down. The cord came out of the handset and bounced around like a spring.

"Cell phones," remarked Erik. "I can only say it so many times."

"Right, because we all know who'd get the most out of the family plan," she said with startling scorn. "And what we really need is to put on little radio collars for any Iron Master who's ever kicked the ass of a telecommunications-spirit to track us whenever it feels like it. This way, Dan."

He was glad to follow. The station felt like a car trunk, and the stink of things people preferred to do in the dark was heavy despite the old wooden floor's grayness from repeated scrubbing. At least the platform above was open air. Little Blue threw down his skateboard and raced ahead of them, weaving around and between the weary commuters. He flipped it up and caught it at the train doors.

"There's another one," Heartsblood warned Mercedes quietly.

"Another what? Here, gimme Calvin, he knows me." The boy stirred as Mercedes took him. She whispered in his ear, lilting words in the First Tongue, and he settled back down.

"Another mark—"

"Get on, move."

The train was as bad as the station. People wilted like summer grass in it. They were in their own little worlds, trying to distract themselves from the metal tube's boiling heat with newspapers or Game Boys or their own reflections in the windows. He felt sweat trickle down the middle of his back. He longed to scratch it, *really* scratch it, put out a wolf's tongue and pant. He wanted to tell them all that it was a good week to go on vacation out of town. Goddamn, couldn't they feel it?

The PA squawked something or other. The doors whooshed shut.

They'd pulled out and hit full speed before he smelled it. First a musk wafted in through the back. Then she entered, following in the wake of her own scent. She was a spare rib of a woman, small and bony and bent in a sullen hunch. For some reason, she wore a long-sleeved mock turtleneck jersey, and she'd put her hair in a ponytail but it was too many different lengths and needed a plaster of bobby pins to keep it together. Heartsblood glanced sideways at her. Her lip curled. The tooth that showed was sharp and yellow. She stared right at him. *Challenge.*

Heartsblood turned to Mercedes, desperate—if Chicago alphas couldn't catch that much when it was right in front of them, then he was up Shit Creek. But thank heaven, she was on it. Her nostrils flashed. Her brow corrugated. She sat forward in her seat. Little Blue still sprawled, but every little stringy muscle on him had tensed. Erik was the only one whose alarm wasn't dead obvious. He just sat there being big, which was plenty. None of them spoke. Neither did the strange Uratha. But when they got off at the transfer point, she followed them at a distance, not even trying to hide among the passengers.

"Uh…" He finally couldn't stop himself from making a noise. Part question, part growl.

"Ghost Wolf," Mercedes said under her breath. "She'd better not follow us any further."

"So we weren't in her territory."

He said it as neutrally as he could, but he still got a snarl back. "She has no territory."

Well, that explained a lot. But the Ghost Wolf did keep following, and in fact she sped up, like she meant to catch them before they got on the next train. Mercedes suddenly whirled in place, teeth bared. This station was pretty dead, but there were still folks around, students mostly. On her shoulder, Calvin's head shifted.

"Look," Heartsblood said hastily, "I'm not one of y'uns. Take the kid on home, I'll stall her."

"Stall her? She's on our turf," Mercedes retorted, but her heart wasn't in it. Neither honor nor instinct would let the pack face this threat without turning it into a full-on fight (which was probably why they had the policy of ignoring her as much as possible), and now was a bad time for that.

"Go on," he urged her, and after a moment's hesitation she did, and the others with her. Heartsblood loped forward to meet the Ghost Wolf, who stopped short.

"Who the hell are you?" she barked.

"Their guest," he said. "I'm new in town."

"Well, I'm not, so get out of my way." She stared over his shoulder at her escaping quarry and started to push past him. He stepped in front of her and reached for her arm. That got her attention. She rounded on him. He was now the enemy.

He kept his voice smooth and calm. "Now looky here, ma'am. They're on the train for home. You really gonna follow 'em all the way there?"

"You gonna stop me?" She planted her hand on his chest and shoved. He let it carry him back a step. She seemed happier with him there.

"If you got somethin' to tell 'em, you can tell it to me," he said. "Ain't no skin off my nose to carry the message. I'd be happy to do that."

"Oh yeah? Fine. Bend over and I'll give it to you."

He scratched his jaw. "Well, all right, ma'am, but that'll be three days processing and delivery—"

"You goddamn—" She shut her mouth and blinked. "Processing and delivery." She fought down a crook of the lip. "Hyuk hyuk. What's your name? Bubba?"

"Daniel. Daniel Aaron Vickery." He put out a hand, hoping to move things more on to the human side. She took it, squeezed it quick and hard.

"Like Elvis Aaron?" She gave the doorway to the other platform a last wistful glance. "Fine. I'm Anna Urchin. I don't suppose they've mentioned me."

"Nope. They haven't. Those were your marks on the poles and the doorframe of the station, I reckon?"

"No shit. How big do I have to make them? You tell that woman that Division's off her map and she knows it."

"So you claim that whole… business then, Cabrini Green and all?" he frowned.

"Fuck no," she exclaimed. "That's just it. Nobody has Cabrini, nobody *can* have Cabrini. Every time your friend comes out here, it's like taking a pooper scooper to a toxic spill. All she's doing is stirring up shit, and then it leaks out into my neighborhood."

"Really? You got spirit trouble? I didn't see anything too bad.… "

"You haven't been out here at night," she grumbled.

Well, now there was a thought. She must've seen it on his face, too. "I mean it. You people need to stay the fuck out!"

"All right, all right, I'll tell 'em."

Her eyes narrowed now. "You haven't said what *you're* doing here, Elvis. You another hero? What's your tribe?"

"Why do I have to have a tribe?" he shrugged, but she wasn't buying it.

"Bullshit. You've got beta smell all over you."

"And you've got loner all over you. That's why they don't care about your marks, darlin'—"

"Don't darlin' me, and what the hell is your point."

"I'm just sayin', if it's that bad a neighborhood I'd want at least want a pack to back me up."

"You complete motherfucker." Her eyes lit up like a struck match. He knew that look. It was the beginning of *Kuruth*, a Death Rage neither canine nor human (in fact, both sets of nerves screamed to run, run now for dear life). *Kuruth* hailed from that part of the Uratha born entirely beyond flesh—a primal blackness that swallowed Mother Moon and didn't return Her, the claws of Father Wolf's children still lodged in His heart, bleeding infection into Eden. Blind with hate, *Kuruth* didn't know friend from foe or predator from prey. Just like that, every life in the station was in danger, but he was the only one who knew it. Yet.

"If I had a pack to back me up, would I be here in this toilet bowl?" she demanded. Her voice was strange. It cracked and sizzled, and his head was suddenly abuzz. "Is this a place where people with friends end up? Shut your mouth, Heartsblood. In all your petty little life, you've never been alone. Not once."

She said Heartsblood. His throat closed up. *I never said it, but she just did.* Oh, if only Kalila were here she'd figure it out from that one clue, and Elias and Dana wouldn't even need to figure it out to do something.

He bit his lip accidentally, drawing blood. This thing he faced saw it. A line of spit appeared on its lips. In the spaces around and between them both, he felt something else smelling the blood, too, a milky-sweet presence that seemed to cool and darken the air. Mother be praised, the Choirs of the Moon were with him.

Why? Why now? Over the years he'd begged their wisdom many times. The moonbeams shared their Mother's pity for their misbegotten brothers and sisters, teaching the People secret ways of surviving in a fallen world. The half-moon spirits knew how to smell a lie, how to keep rivals from each other's throats, how to ride out a Gauru fury. But why did they crowd around him when he hadn't invited them, in broad daylight? Why did they savor the spilt blood like an offering but say nothing?

He stared back at the woman's distorted face. Time went by, he had no idea how much. When he did finally open his mouth, he had no idea what might come out. It was like he was no more Heartsblood right now than she was Anna.

"That's true," he said. "It's all true. I'm sorry."

The flint-light in her eyes guttered. He felt the floor heave, heard a creak of metal from the walls, as if the station itself had gotten all wound up holding its breath and now could let it out. Or maybe it was the train.

She gave him a tired look. "Whatever, Elvis. 'Sorry' is only valuable in Scrabble.... "

"You been seeing things?" he blurted. "At night?"

"No. No heroes."

"I don't mean just at that Cabrini place, I mean anywhere in the city. Is it just Cabrini?" When she didn't answer, he jogged her elbow and pointed at the hot dog stand at the mouth of the station. "You want a hot dog, ma'am? Lemme buy you one. I'm gonna get you a big one with those big ol' chunks of pickle in it."

"Fuck off."

"Well, shit. I'm hungry anyway." He started off toward it. She grabbed him.

"You're not getting one either."

"Don't see your tags on this station," he protested.

She rolled her eyes. "Not from that guy. His stuff'll give even you the shits. Come on, I'll show you where to go." She started down the street. He trotted along, encouraged.

"I bet it ain't just your turf. And I bet whatever it is, it's been gettin' worse."

"Oh? What else would you bet?"

"I bet you get around to lots of places you ain't supposed to be."

"One of the dubious perks of my social position."

"You know what they say, right? They say a little knowledge is a dangerous thing. Well, guess what, that's me right now."

"Understatement of the century." She glanced sideways at him. "The Haunts aren't showing you the ropes?"

"Well…" Admit it or not? "They're kinda doin' a favor for a packmate of mine."

"Aha."

"You could at least tell me where not to go."

"How about anywhere out of Mercedes Bitchmaster's sight?"

"Too late." He grinned. "And you ain't talked me out of nothin' yet."

"Your problem is you know you can slide by on cute. You still haven't said why you're in town."

"Well, all right then. I'm here about the crows." He watched for her reaction. Nothing. Just a slight pucker under the eyes.

"You mean the ones dropping dead of Muskegon virus? Crows are bad news birds in these neighborhoods anyway."

"How come?"

"They keep some bad company."

"More than one kind?"

"I'm not sure."

"Are they Spirit-Ridden?"

"Not quite that kind of thing," she said, a bit too quick. "But it's all old news."

"The virus isn't," he pointed out.

"Yeah." She sucked in one cheek. "So you're interested in the birds, or in the human cases?"

"Both," he said. "You got a lot of sick ones in your neck of the woods?"

"It does occur to me about the one they lost," she interrupted him.

"The one who lost?"

"The Haunts. Y'know, Kyle?" She seemed surprised at his blank look. "Their packmate. They lost him this spring."

He slowed almost to a stop. "They did?"

"Yeah. Kyle, Kyle Wolf-at-the-Door. They didn't mention that either?"

"Shit on a shovel. How'd they lose him? What do you know about it?"

She shrugged. "That he disappeared. And that the four of them were way too tight for him to just leave. And—I heard them howling one night. Tried to drown it out with the stereo, but I still heard it. Never saw him again after that."

He looked at her. She looked away, and he knew she saw what he was thinking: he was thinking she kept an awful good eye on her neighbors.

"You said somethin' occurred to you? What did?"

"The night they howled. That was the same night I found the first sick crow on my turf. Dunno if that helps you out, but I'm sure the Haunts could pin down the date for ya."

"Yeah. I'm sure they could." One hell of a question to ask. And they'd know who'd suggested he ask it, too.

"All right, I'll bite," she said suddenly. "You actually figured anything out about what's going on? What the crows mean?"

He shook his head. "Not much. I think they're trying to warn us. But I don't know about what yet."

"Maybe that they're going to kill everybody."

"Now what makes you say that?"

She shrugged again. "Because they could, couldn't they? If the geniuses don't get this thing under control. They say in the *Trib* you don't have to worry unless you have a 'compromised immune system.'" She sneered. "I remember when they said in the *Trib* you wouldn't get AIDS unless you were gay. Viruses don't care. They take it wherever they can, like the rest of us."

"Got any suggestions?" he asked. The whatever-it-was that got into her earlier seemed long gone, but still, if he'd been picked to hear the message, she'd been picked to say it.

"For what?" She gave him a funny look. "The virus?"

"Yeah. Like if you was mayor."

"Yeah, me the mayor."

"If you was."

She snorted, but a little more energy came into her scrawny body. "You really wanna know? I'd throw everybody who even sneezes this summer behind a barbed-wire fence, put a twenty-five dollar bounty on every dead crow brought in, and drop a DDT bomb out of a plane flying over the city. And there you have it, the reason I'll never be anybody's mayor."

He stuck his thumbs in his belt loops. "You wouldn't be new-moon by chance, wouldja? I mean, virus don't seem all that contagious to humans. Yet."

"Enough shit already happens that nobody can do anything about. When something comes along that you can actually prevent, you don't fuck around. You get busy and pay the toll."

"Like a controlled burn?" he ventured.

"Exactly," she agreed, but he didn't hear any special ring in her voice. Oh, well.

"Listen," he said. "I know it pissed you off, but I'm kinda glad they stepped over the dotted line today. Good to meet another Uratha in the city." He put out his hand again. "I do mean that."

"I know you do, Elvis. Crap. I forgot your real name now. Something Aaron."

"Daniel Aaron Vickery. Or Heartsblood."

"Heartsblood. Well, that's vivid." She took his hand, a little quirk tugging at her lips.

A hoarse scream ripped through the air, not ten yards away. A young black-haired woman rose from the bus stop bench they'd just been about to walk past. She was pregnant, fluttery maternity top stretched tight across her belly. She got up and then crumpled, trying to stand, moaning. Her mouth contorted, pulled into the wrong shape by a face taut with pain. Heartsblood smelled blood. And another smell, ripe, wet and promising: the smell of birth itself, the juices of the womb. But it was the wrong time. A good smell at the wrong time was a bad smell.

He came out of a moment's frozen shock with a shudder. Anna whipped her hand out of his. He started toward the woman, who had turned to them with a wordless plea, but the Ghost Wolf snarled. Her head sailed a few inches higher—still not as high as his, but her bared teeth and forward lurch were signal enough that if he didn't back down she could get one whole hell of a lot bigger.

"Get out," she ordered him. Her throat was gravelly with the beginnings of the change. "Go, I never want to see you again, go!"

A dozen things rose in his throat (*I didn't do it, please believe me, what's happening, I want to help*), but not one of them was any good to anybody. He ran.

The city didn't defeat you in a day. It was more patient than that. It had a thousand little ways.

Getting you lost was a big one. Blotting out sun, moon, and stars, blocking the four winds, it could wind even a lifelong tracker round like a ball of yarn. But there were other things. The hard cement. The restaurants that smelled good from a block down but served up plates of what you'd swear was medical waste. The spiral garages with their urine puddles and the purposeless folk loitering shiftily nearby.

He didn't go back to the apartment for hours. There was too much he wanted to say that he knew he couldn't defend. He thought about Anna. Maybe she saw more because she was alone, vulnerable. He was supposed to be alone, too, and being with the Haunts sure as shit made him feel alone, but maybe that wasn't enough. Maybe he had to forget just a little bit about his own pack, stop having imaginary conversations with them. He didn't want to, of course.

He jerked as the sound of flapping wings exploded behind him. A mass of birds swooped off the telephone lines and disappeared behind the roofs of the buildings across the street. He instinctively ducked behind a car. Something was moving in the street. It had no scent and no sound. The only way he knew it was there was by watching the roosting flocks rustle, hearing windows close one by one as sleepers woke in the dead of the night and suddenly decided their bared flyscreens were too drafty. *Nature abhors a void*, he'd heard. That's what this was, a moving void. It trailed crows after it. All other critters rippled like water, scampering or flying away for a moment and then stealing back. The neighborhood dogs started up a howl in its wake, but the ones that still lay ahead of it didn't dare so much as a growl.

He crept closer, morbidly fascinated. There had to be something of it he could sense. But the moment he finally heard it—a *thok-thok* of hard leather boot heels on pavement—he withdrew again. He could tell by the tread, measured and just a little too slow to be simply ambling from here to there. It was a predator going by, and it was higher up the food chain than he was. He doubled back over his own trail for quite a ways before he turned back toward the Haunts' place.

Dewan hated these alleyways. Still, the more he used them the less chance Naomi would catch him so close to Elly's apartment. He just knew the nutty bitch was lurking out there somewhere, she was off work after all. And, of course, *she* had the restraining order on *him*. Hustling was not turning out to be the career option it'd been for the old man.

He heard the clink of a bottle hitting pavement and froze despite himself.

"Naomi? Baby?" Jesus, what did he say that for? Dumbass. Last thing he needed was to *engage*. Especially in that scaredy-cat voice.

He made himself turn around. In the heavy heat still reflecting off the concrete and brick, sweat instantly beaded up on his upper lip. His vision blurred.

Stupid. Stupid. His body's alarms all started clanging at once, and he wasn't even sure if it was Naomi or some tweaked-out methhead or crazy homeless dude but he was suddenly quite sure it'd been a mistake to walk down a South Side alley in the middle of the night, whatever made him think he could do that more than once or twice without his number coming up?

He heard the slow tapping of shoe heels now, *thok-thok*. He couldn't tell which way it was coming from, but it had to be nearing him because the echoes came louder and faster. Then he saw her: a tall figure in raggedy jeans and a duster and a dark beat-up cowboy hat, hands stuffed in oddly bulging pockets, a vast, gleaming black bramble of hair bristling around her like dead twigs or a stray cat's tail. Her head was down, eyes on the ground, but he didn't doubt she knew his every move.

"You can run, rabbit, if you want," she said. "I don't mind."

Her voice was so raw he didn't know how he even understood it, but he did. It was like her throat had something stuck in it or was just shaped completely wrong.

Her head came up, and she grinned at him. The only thought that came to him was at least it explained the voice. Nobody could talk right through that many teeth.

"Fact, I kinda like it," she added.

He wanted very badly to oblige her, but he'd forgotten how.

The flashlight batteries had run out for the last time years ago. She'd never replaced them because just the threat of using it was usually enough to keep them in the shadows, and when it wasn't, she didn't want to see anyway. But she held it tight in her hand.

She also counted the ticks of the clock. She was one of the few people on Earth who could tell you exactly how long she slept each night, because for every five minutes she was awake and counting she slid a coin from one corner of her bedside table to the other. Numbers were good. They took concentration. Sometimes, when she subtracted it out and found she'd gotten three or more unconscious hours she rewarded herself in some little way. It'd been a while, though.

They were excited. She could tell. Usually they were a constant murmur. Usually they spoke more to her than to each other. When something was up, it became more sporadic. There were jagged patches of silence and then bursts of urgent, staccato debate. It actually bothered her now to think they might be saying things among themselves that she couldn't hear.

Mustn't stop.

The unholy one is back, with her crows. That will help.

Not if she realizes.

None must realize.

Long drop, short stop. Long drop, short stop. Fingertips cold, how can I be dead if my fingers are cold?

The blood calls from the ground.

It cannot ignore.

Its tongues will cry out.

None must hear.

Black rain. Poison quills. It is well, but more is required.

Should have been ours long ago.

No one cares if you scream.

Gonna touch you. Almost touching you.

Dare you to look.

She turned to stone, always, always. It didn't matter how angry she got. She couldn't lift the cover. She couldn't not lift it. She saw her own hand moving as a silhouette stirred outside. She had to know which one it was. She whimpered quietly.

The covers flew away and she saw that it was *her* leaning over the bed, dark eyes with a rim of yellow light like the crescent moon. From the mummy-wrapped mouth came a wet moan. It took her a second to recognize the mockery of her own whimpering, to see the cruel crinkle of laugh-lines. She grabbed the covers back and wrapped them tight around her, refusing to move until the soft steps retreated into the corner again.

Bandaged Mouth Girl, the worst of them. They only sent Bandaged Mouth Girl when they were really hungry.

She didn't have very long.

The hot dog vendor blew a strand of her hair out of her face, caught it in midair, and tucked it behind her ear. She shoved a giant soft drink cup at one customer and held a commanding finger up at another one. They piled up around her, streaming

"Mommy, wanna tennis racquet." "No, those aren't toys, honey. We're going to watch the bridge open, won't that be neat?" "No, wanna toy!" "Jordan, don't yell. Your brother wants to see the bridge open." "Yeah, stop whining, little baby." "David. Zip it."

He knocked again. The boats below were getting ready to come through the drawbridge, engines firing up, yachters retreating into their pilot's cabins and sailboaters hauling up anchor. The one boat that wasn't a pleasure craft, looked like a freighter to Heartsblood, pulled out to lead the pack. On the bridge, the cars had packed up like sardines, all trying to make it on. A guy in a convertible stood in his seat trying to see over the tops of the taller vehicles and shouting, like that'd help. Harried working folk hunched at their wheels, willing their neighbors forward with sheer force of gaze.

He told himself not to lose it. They were just busy operating the bridge controls. Then again, if they were busy doing that, shouldn't it be opening? Shouldn't the damn barrier be coming down?

He looked down again. That freighter was getting close. There were men on deck, but one was at the stern and he couldn't tell if the two on the foredeck were aware of a problem. They didn't move, just stood close together with their heads bowed over something. He almost hooked a leg over the rail to jump off right then and there, but then he stopped, torn. Once he hit the water, that was it for the bridge house. He couldn't be both places at once.

"…world's first double-decked, double-leaf trunnion bascule bridge," the guide said proudly. "One pivot on each end. Both spans so perfectly balanced and counterweighted, they can handle two levels of rush hour traffic and yet fully clear the channel in under sixty seconds…"

"Hey!" Heartsblood yelled down at the boats, cupping his hands around his mouth. "Hey, hey! Up here! SOS! Mayday!" He broke into the tour crowd and shoved up to the guide. "Sir. Sir, ain't the bridge s'posed to be openin' up?"

The man shifted, blinking owlishly through his bifocals. "Yes, sir, any minute now. If you want to join the tour, it's fifteen dollars a ticket—"

"No, it's not openin' up, and the boats are comin'. Can you get up in the control room, can you call up there, is there a phone?"

He was being as polite as he knew how to be, but the man was still picking something up, ancient human instincts waking at exactly the wrong time, chasing the color out of his cheeks. The other tourists edged away, drawing their children close. From the way they eyed Heartsblood, he wouldn't have been shocked to see them pull pitchforks and lit torches out of their pockets. "Sir, I'm going to have to ask you to calm down—" the guide stuttered.

"Goddammit!" He could rip that door open. He could kill everybody here before they could even get off hold with 911. He had such power.

He flung off his shoes and socks, jumped onto the bridge railing and sprang several yards straight up to grab the lip of the control room window, catching the top of the door with his toes, ignoring the gasps and shouts behind him. He pounded on the glass till it shook like a drumhead. At first he didn't see anybody. Then the black man's face popped up from somewhere below the sill, already bloodless and frightened. He knew right then it was too late.

"Just get it away from me," said Gary. "I can't think about this shit now." He put his glasses away and went back to the rail, squinting to adjust his focus. "Where the hell's the buoy?"

"Whaddya mean, where is it?" Narciso joined him. "Isn't it where it always—that's the wrong one."

"We musta passed it." He glanced up at the drawbridge. The lights were still solid red. He picked up the phone and dialed the pilothouse. "Ken? They said they were opening up? Well, something's off, 'cause they're not. Yeah okay, but—hello?" He blinked at the phone and then hung up. "He's gonna hail 'em again."

"Fuck that shit," blurted Narciso. "Look above the lights. There's still traffic on the bridge. The gates aren't even down."

"Shit.… " He grabbed his walkie-talkie. "Ken? Come in." Then he picked up the phone, waited for what seemed like a hundred rings. "Ken! There's cars on the bridge. We gotta back down. Well, didn't they answer? We passed it. We passed it already! Jesus, just back it down! I'm sounding the whistle." He hung up. "Narciso, turn to! Get the captain!"

He grabbed the whistle chain and gave five short blasts that nobody in the channel who wasn't dead or deaf could fail to hear.

Felicia, swear to God, thought it was an earthquake. SoCal spinal cord. Anything that made the floor wave was automatically an earthquake. But the sound was like nothing she'd ever heard before, a volcano boom and an extended scream of metal on metal and a labored ratcheting. She heard hundreds of voices cry out, muffled by their car windows. Tyler woke out of a sound sleep and burst into wailing. She looked around, blinking. It took her a few moments to put the facts together.

Something hit the bridge. Something big. A ship?

People around her were quicker on the uptake. Motors revved, bumpers spanked bumpers, and gears whined as people started trying to push the vehicles in front of them forward. She heard a PA or a bullhorn squawking somewhere, but she couldn't understand it. She rolled down her window, but the sound was still echoing too much.

"Stay calm… police… on the bridge… evacuate in orderly… cars in Neutral…"

"Calm!" she screamed. "Calm! Neutral!?"

At least the traffic was moving now, inching along at maybe three miles an hour instead of two. She coasted and stopped, coasted and stopped, scrabbling in the passenger foot well for her purse and her phone. She speed-dialed Curt. *"We're sorry. All circuits are busy. Please try completing your call another time. We're sorry. All circuits are busy. Please try completing your call another time. We're sorry. All circuits are busy.… "*

She told herself she wasn't going to ram the car in front of her no matter what, that it wouldn't help, that she was not that much of an asshole or that much of a panicker. But as she crept over the midway point, her noble resolve broke. A vehicle labeled both "sport" and "utility" had to be good for something sometime. She let her foot slip off the brake, just a bit, as if accidentally. And then she thought of Tyler still belted in his car seat, and how hard it would be to get to him and free him if the bridge crumbled out from underneath them, and she started tapping the gas.

Heartsblood's fingers and toes slipped free when the freighter struck, and he fell sidelong to the cement, scraping his arm open. He didn't even feel it. He sprang up, leaned over the railing, and stared down. Oh, the ship'd *tried* to stop, a cross-eyed bat could see that. It'd come up on the bridge sideways, flipped partway around from the change of thrust. It had a massive dent where it'd struck, but he couldn't tell whether it was taking on water. The bridge beside him had suddenly gone musical. Honks and screams and tire squeals blended into something almost hymn-like, strangely muted by distance and number. But at least they weren't all falling in the water, like the cattle.... *Of course not,* he sneered at himself. That size of ship against that size of bridge? It'd take more than that. No, it must be the ship he was meant to tend to. He swung to the outside of the railing and got ready to drop down into the water.

Then the sound of grinding metal—blossomed, that was the only word for it. It had been coming from the place where the ship hit, but now it seemed to be all around. Past the still-raised gates, past the unopened break, he saw the opposite span shudder again and then suddenly rise up with the easy grace of a giant bird wing, arcing up toward the late afternoon sun just like that was what it was supposed to do. Which, of course, it was, but not *now. Not now,* his mind shrieked, but not a single power in Creation was listening.

It felt like the start of a roller coaster, that drop in the stomach, that momentary sense of flying, and this time Felicia knew at once what was going on. The rubber of the SUV tires clung to the pavement a good long while—seemed like minutes, must have been at least ten seconds—and up to a surprisingly steep angle. Felicia was looking straight down the pivot joint through the windshields of the cars in front of her and rather startled to find herself having the time and brainpower to think *goodness, we're still stuck on, but that can't last, we can't possibly stick at a ninety-degree angle . . .*

And she was right. Shock notwithstanding, there was nothing wrong with her grasp of physics.

They were curled up all snug and safe in their little den when Heartsblood returned. Erik was buried in his latest medical thriller, Mercedes was cleaning and oiling a pair of handcuffs and slapping them onto her wrist to check the action, and Blue was playing some kind of zombie-shooting game on the living room computer, headphones on.

He gave them a second to react. Nothing. Pathetic. Then Mercedes glanced up, but he was already moving across the apartment. He found the power strip to the computer and yanked its cord out.

"Hey!" The Ithaeur yelped and whirled around. Heartsblood ignored the boy and strode over to the TV, jabbing the switch. It came right on to the news. There was a shot of the bridge with its one leaf up and the other leaf down and a text banner blaring *MICHIGAN AVE. BRIDGE DISASTER.* But the sound was turned way down. He went digging in the sofa for the remote.

"What's the matter with the bridge?" Mercedes set down the bottle of lubricant and stood up. Heartsblood just scowled and fiddled with the remote, accidentally changing the input and turning the screen blue. She tried to take it from him, but he wouldn't let it go at first. "No, give it here, Dan. Give it here."

She got the broadcast back and turned up the volume. "…Death toll stands at a confirmed eighty-five and is expected to climb dramatically as bodies are recovered, with at least twenty-three more victims listed in serious or critical condition at Northwestern. Rescue workers comb the wreckage and the water in a desperate race against the failing light. The city is asking people in the area to refrain from unnecessary cell phone use. The mayor has also activated the Emergency Information phone bank to provide information on street closures, alternate routes, and other disaster-related inquiries.…"

"Yes, Martha, and that number is 312-745-INFO. However, if you're a relative seeking information about a victim or, or a possible victim, the number to call is the Red Cross hotline, 1-866-729-8222. Now you've said one of the bridge tenders suddenly collapsed, apparently from Muskegon encephalitis, and that helps explain the failure at the control center, if not the locking mechanism failure. But have we learned what happened on the, with the ship?"

"Not really, Trevor. Seaward, the company that owns the vessel, has stated that all on board survived with minor injuries, and it will be conducting a full inquiry. But they're declining to speculate on the possibility of negligence by the ship's lookout or officers."

"This is going to raise major issues of… of legal and financial responsibility, I think, where, incredible as it seems, there were apparently problems on the bridge and the ship simultaneously…"

Heartsblood made a noise deep in his throat. Mercedes quelled it with a glance.

"Undoubtedly, Trevor. Now I have with me a former merchant marine who witnessed the accident. Sir?"

"Yeah. I never seen anything like it. I mean, my God, the ones that fell in the water were the lucky ones. At least they had a chance, not like the ones who hit the pavement or each other—"

"Yes, now, sir, you were saying that the ship was well past the warning buoys for its class before it sounded the whistle or reversed engines?"

"Yeah, she was picking up speed as she went by, like they didn't even know. I don't understand it. I see the *Adamant* on the river all the time when I'm out boating. I, 'scuse me, I just wanna let Mom know we're all okay, Heather's okay—"

"Back to you, Trevor."

"Dear Christ," Mercedes said.

"Eighty-five confirmed dead," Heartsblood repeated tightly.

"I caught that." She studied him, nose wrinkling. "And you're wet. You were there?"

He nodded.

"Helping?"

"Trying." He didn't dare unclench his jaw. He was aware of the other two Uratha, getting up and circling toward their alpha. "Pickin' jumpers out of the water."

"That was good of you. Easy, Dan." A talk-you-down, singsong voice. She was trying to work that waxing-moon juju on him. She'd locked eyeballs with him, too, but those eyes looked soft and brown and human to him just now.

"Easy, my ass."

"Look. I'm missing something here? Let's hear it."

He exploded. "Somethin'? Sugar, you done missed ever'thin'! You ain't caught a single motherfuckin' ball! Oh no, we don't have to take a thing that hillbilly says seriously. What does he know?"

"Nobody's called you—" she began heavily. He plowed right through.

"Well, how come the hillbilly was there instead of you? Whose town is this? Why am I the only one who gives a shit? Where the fuck were you?"

She crossed her arms. "In our territory. Where we belong. I'd expect a Hunter in Darkness to understand that."

"Don't you turn that around on me. A Hunter in Darkness knows when the enemy's creepin' up. He knows the wind can warn him while it's still a hundred miles off, and he fuckin' well pays attention when it does!"

"All right, so if you knew the bridge was going to crack up, then why the hell didn't you tell us? I certainly don't remember you walking out the door saying 'Bye, everybody, I'm going to go try and stop a major disaster all by myself, don't bother getting up.' A heads-up would have been nice."

"Heads-up! If y'uns' heads was any further up—whyja think I stopped askin' you along? How many times you think I got to be told to fuck myself? If you'd-a come you'd-a seen it. It was just the crows that tipped me off. I keep tellin' ya to watch the crows!"

"Oh, I see my mistake now." Her voice climbed. "I should have been wandering aimlessly around downtown waiting for a bird to shit on my head."

"I wasn't wanderin'." He felt it coming, the change, burning at his cuticles and the roots of his teeth, the joints of his face. It was coming, and he couldn't stop it, but he dug in and tried to delay it. *Wrath is for enemies,* said the howls. "I was huntin'. I was lookin', and you shoulda been lookin', too! I needed the pack, goddammit. I couldn't take on the boat and the bridge at the same time. I had to pick."

"So you picked, and it didn't work and that's our fault. Or at least you've decided it is. I guess that is easier than taking responsibility."

Venom-words, aimed at the heart. And they struck. He gave a strangled roar and felt his frame distort with the power of the suppressed fury. The leather of his shoes strained and threatened to split—if he went any further into the wolf, they'd relent to the charms Kalila had laid and melt into his shifting flesh, but this was still the wary border between.

"We have neighbors," Mercedes said softly, though she didn't look too scandalized. Her eyes gleamed. "You want to watch it, Danny-o. I'm still alpha here."

"Then lead," he snarled. "Your city's in danger, and you know it. Stop pretending you don't. You know damn well how bad it is. This goes way past making fat pedophiles piss themselves."

"Ah, then I'm afraid, is that it? I'm a coward?"

"You tell me."

It was a thin evasion, and she knew it. The Thunder Lord had the ozone smell of a storm around her. Her face twisted into an ugly sneer. "You know what? I'm looking forward to *ungin* now," she said through sharpening teeth. "You're this disappointed in me, I can't wait to see the big shots react to your diarrhea. They'll pile on you like farmboys on a new goat, and I will laugh and laugh and laugh. You have no fucking clue."

"Oh, I can guess," he shot back. "Just from watchin' you in inaction. At least the humans can say they didn't see it comin', but I wonder what y'uns' excuse is gonna be before Mother and Father."

Her lip curled. "Mother and Father? What, this is a religious issue now?"

"Yes," he said. "It is. That's what I figgered out today. This ain't just my spirit-quest. No way could this much be happenin' just for me. It's comin' for all Chicago. And if it falls on your territory, where your totem stalks and your marks are read and your rites are howled, then shit yeah, you better believe you're gonna answer for it."

"You're rabid. At least that explains a lot. You're a fanatic."

YOU KNOW NOTHING ABOUT ME, he shouted, and he didn't even know it was coming out in the First Tongue. At home he was the peacemaker, the voice of sanity and family-feeling. Nobody there doubted that. What'd this woman done to him, that he was suddenly the one pushing and threatening and boiling over? How dare she accuse him of being his own opposite?

She picked up a book on the coffee table and dashed it to the floor. LOOK WHO'S TALKING, she growled. YOU BARGE IN UNINVITED AND START TELLING US HOW WE SHOULD TEND OUR OWN GROUNDS, LIKE WE WERE BLIND, TIT-SUCKING PUPS?

YOU'RE NOT BLIND. YOU CLOSE YOUR EYES ON PURPOSE, WHICH IS WORSE.

SANCTIMONIOUS—YOU HAVE NO IDEA WHAT WE'VE GIVEN TO THE BATTLE. IS THIS WHAT I GET FOR MAKING A SOFT PLACE IN OUR DEN FOR YOUR UGLY HINDQUARTERS? I SHOULD THROW YOU OUT IN THE STREET RIGHT NOW. SEE HOW LONG IT TAKES THE *idigam* TO FIND YOU, OR THE PURE!

OH YES, SCARY, he snapped, spraying spittle. AS IF I HAVEN'T BEEN WALKING THESE STREETS ALL ALONG! AT LEAST THE PURE HAVE SOME FIGHT LEFT. I'D PROBABLY GET MORE HELP FROM THEM!

Even in the depths of her indignation, her mouth fell a little more open. WHAT? WHAT DO YOU PUT MY NOSE IN? YOU PRAISE THE PURE TO SPITE ME? WHAT DID YOU SAY?

He'd just realized what he'd said himself, but it was out and some nasty part of him didn't even want to take it back. I SAID I'D PROBABLY GET MORE HELP FROM THE PURE THAN FROM YOU.

THEN LET ME DELIVER YOU TO THEM, she said. Her flesh ran quicksilver across her bones, and black fur enveloped her. She filled her side of the room. I CERTAINLY KNOW HOW NEAR THEY ARE. WOULD YOU LIKE TO KNOW HOW I KNOW? THEY KILLED OUR PACK BROTHER A FEW MONTHS BACK.

Mother save me from myself, Heartsblood thought in sudden agony. This wasn't what he'd meant at all. Erik and Little Blue were showing signs of the Change, too, but they backed off now, slowly, to an outer orbit. Erik pulled the coffee table along with him. The challenge was made. All other tasks of a wolf's life were done as a pack, but not this one.

TRY IT, Heartsblood growled.

She flew at him like electricity down a wire. He met her, bowling into her with his heavy shoulder. In the war-shape, they were closer matched in size, but he was still heavier. She slid. The rug bunched up behind her feet, and she fell to the floor where the table had just been. But she somersaulted over backward and was back on her haunches a split second later. She sprang again, caught him by the mane-like fuzz that was left of his head-hair and wrenched his neck downward. He heard cartilage pop. Then her jaws closed around his throat, pressing in hard. He froze. She'd stopped just short of breaking skin. Usually that was a signal—go limp, submit, end this. But her teeth trembled with the effort of holding back. He wasn't really one of her pack, and he'd stung her hard. What if he turned his belly up and then she lost control?

Another thing came to his fevered mind then, something that'd never even studied the notion of crossing it before. *And why submit when you could win?*

It was like just thinking it was enough. Her jowls twitched. He felt his blood seep warm around her fangs. With a roar, he tore away. Some of his hair came off in her fingers. She jumped onto his back. Her massive arms circled his collarbone. He swung around trying to fling her off, but no luck. The bitch was flypaper. He pulled one of her arms away and sank his teeth deep into it, then finally threw himself backward on top of her, slamming her into the floor with all his weight. The room shuddered. Her ribs buckled underneath him with a loud crack, and her grip loosened. He turned over. She snapped at the soft flesh of his gut, tearing it—little pain reached him through the foaming battle-frenzy, but he knew it was a wound he should be upset about. With a gloating bark, she got her rear paws under him and shoved him sideways, then rolled over onto him. She drove her elbow into his throat and eye. A flood of green-black washed across his vision. Her caved-in chest was already filling out again, goddammit. He kicked her away from him.

She lunged again as he got to his feet. Her head drove into his mending belly and kept going. He skidded and toppled into the futon with her still propelling him. The wooden slats cracked from the force of the blow. He was trying to get a breath in, and she was savaging him, biting his snout and chest. He picked up the lamp from the side table and shoved it in her face. Somehow he was able to get his rear legs into her and catapult her off with a rabbit kick. She landed against the easy chair, snarled, leapt up, and picked the chair up.

"Shit—Merce, no," Erik exclaimed, but she threw it at Heartsblood anyway. He caught it like a pro and dropped it to the side. Elias was liable to hurl things when he got mad, which was often, so his packmates got lots of practice. She was on him again before the chair even touched the floor, hitting him in that still-bleeding gut.

Quick. She was used to winning on quick, damn her. He grabbed her leg, yanked it out, and stomped down on the knee until it bent the wrong way. Let her scamper around on that. She tried to scrabble away, but something had finally let go in him. In that moment, she was no different from any squealer of the Rat Hosts or sneering whelp of the Pure Tribes that he'd ever ripped up. The harder she squirmed and snapped, the harder he gripped, and he lifted her off the ground upside down, shaking her furiously until the pain of her compound fracture cut through the adrenaline. He was still shaking her even as she began to dwindle.

STOP… STOP…, she croaked. "Pax!"

"Dan. Daniel. Heartsblood!" Somebody was calling his name. But it wasn't until he saw her bloody woman-face and the locks of black hair hanging down that he realized it was over. He put her down. Erik started for her side. Heartsblood almost let him, but then he suddenly realized something else. It wasn't just over—it was over and he'd won. He set his claws on Erik's shoulder. The full-moon looked murder at him, but drew back.

Mercedes grimaced and felt at the broken bone, trying to help it knit straight. Heartsblood bent down and carefully fitted his open jaws around her throat. A warning growl shuddered through his chest.

"Fuck," she coughed, and then, "Uncle. Uncle. You win."

He exhaled into his human self and staggered down to one knee.

"Leave her alone," Erik said tightly. "You're done."

"No. I'm-a help reset that," he said. "Scoot over. Hold her still." Erik stuck a rolled-up magazine in her mouth for her to clamp down on. Heartsblood eyed the break and then pulled the leg taut as he could before shoving the end of bone back through the torn flesh. It quivered and roiled under his fingertips, starting to heal.

She looked at him strangely. He felt triumph, but it was a dirty kind of triumph that put the same tang in his mouth as an oncoming *Kuruth*. Yeah, he could beg, he could orate, he could prove. He could even leap in their cesspool of a river to drag up escaping corpses. But it was only pain that made her respect him finally, his power to cause her pain.

He realized he'd always known this, too, about the People. It had always been his reality. He'd just gotten to ignore it because he let Elias do all the ass-whooping (they all did), let Elias be the designated sadist. Now Elias wasn't here. So if this was the way the Haunts wanted it, he was the only one left to oblige.

He wouldn't forget it again.

(From a paper currently buried under a layer of ash and debris, three feet under the floor of a kosher butcher shop in Hyde Park.)

To Whomsome ever finds this.

I Jeremiah Lawson Maynard, formerly of 52nd Rgt of Ohio Infantry D Brigade, beeing of sound mind & also Body (but for 1 Ball that staied in my leg from a Rebel shot in Apr/62 and pains me yet in Bad Wethar), do attest here in Writting to the fallen State in wich I leave the City of my Father's birth, so that if the Almty. sees Fit to strike me ded on my Journy or the Wile of Satan snear me some word of Truth shall remmain.

What the Temperence gazetes tell (bee it ever so Horrid) is But a sliver of the Wickednes of Chicago, for along with Mans vices of Wrath, Venery, Drink & Opium-pipe & Lozzenge are the evils of a World Beyond wich I first witnessed in the long siege of Chatanooga, when I saw a black Mist come each Nite to smother the Horse & Mules so that near 10 Thousand dyed. The ofcrs. thot it was Starving that kilt them all but they never saw the Mist. It took many Men too, who was in perfect Health (tho hungry) in the am & laied down with a Fevre to dye in the pm. I thott I had seen the worst of my Life then But when I come to Live here I lernt that Nitemares in flesh suck the Blood of poor womens babes & lay Curses on Riteous heads, & even the crows on the roofs some times dont wait anymore for a critur to die before they devower it.

Please gentle Rdr. I Beg you to Study these pages and search out Others to beelieve tho God Above knows such are few, and begin my Work agin if need bee. In case of jepordy the hon. & galant Gen. Sheridan and Rabbi Joachim Mayr will asist you as they may. I fear I shal not be Mustered out of this War But if a man will lay down his Life to stop the Secesh from tearing our Country apart, then he can do no less now that a secrete Brotherhood of that other World plots to tear us from our verry Souls....

"That's the western border of our pack's territory, right there." Erik nodded at a partial wolf-print in the long-dried cement of the sidewalk slab. Heartsblood crouched to look at it. Not a step but a single, deliberate dab of a paw—dead giveaway to anybody in the know. "Next couple of blocks are kinda no man's land. Sometimes, when they're trying to start something, one of their teenagers'll come in and piss on the fireplugs or whatever, try to get a rise out of us."

"They haven't been in there for months," Mercedes said. "They backed off a lot, actually. Probably expecting reprisal." Even with whole pieces of thoughts missing, Heartsblood could guess what she meant.

"But there wasn't any."

"It wasn't a good time… there was trouble with the *idigam* up north." To his probing look, she answered, "Cateria promised her pack'd help us with a real offensive once the lakefront was secure, take the Pure down once and for all. At least on the West Side."

"And then forgot all about it?"

"I doubt she's forgotten," she said, and the deadness in her voice broke his heart. "Anyway. We can go in. I'm sure it's fine."

"No. No point going in if it's fine." He took in a deep breath. "Besides. Think you're right. Not smellin' any recent traces."

"We could go check out the projects again."

"Naw. Let's just knock off for the night, go on home." They didn't need to be told twice. But Mercedes noticed him hanging back a bit, not taking up his lead position right away.

"You're not coming?" She tilted an eyebrow.

"I was just thinking," he said. "We ain't had dinner. I'm-a go get takeout from the Thai place and carry it back. Whatcha hankerin' for, medicine man? Pad Thai? Green curry?"

Little Blue perked up. "And swimming rama," he added with a quick checking-look at Mercedes. "Oh! And an order of spring rolls for Erik."

"Yeah." Unless you asked him something directly, Erik didn't so much talk as bookmark the conversation around him. Probably to make you think he was listening.

"No problem," said Heartsblood. "Saw a whole herd a' spring rolls scampering by a piece back. Bring one right down for ya."

The smile he waved them off with faded almost before they turned away. Fighting them'd been bad, but not doing it was starting to feel worse. At least the Thai place was a few blocks off, far enough to get some thinking time. For a Hunter and an alpha, he sure wasn't bringing in much game. The virus wasn't leading him like he'd hoped it would. He wasn't doing any better with the pack than he had been alone, and that was the real kicker.

He sat down on the curb. A photocopied flyer was half-ground, half-cooked by rain and heat into the gutter beside him, along with a flattened soda cup and a black banana peel. *ODDLY ENOUGH* it blared, and then under that, *Giant Sunspots Visible Only in Chicago: Omen or Mass Hysteria? Hundreds report seeing massive moving solar shadows out of 'corner of eye'; 20th Muskegon Fatality: Human-Human Vector—or WORSE?; Don't be Fooled: Phony 'Herbal' Pest Repelle . . .*

The rest disappeared under the banana peel. He reached down to move it. As he did, a fly lighted on his knuckle. He smacked it with his other hand, then recoiled. He'd broken open the abdomen and it was full of live, squirming maggots. It wasn't a housefly, but a flesh fly, the kind that needed rotting meat to lay its young in.

"You fuckhead," he told it. "You're way off-target, and you just killed your kids." But then he wondered. Was it off-target? If the fly thought it smelled Death nearby, it could always be right. Its senses for that were even better than his. He closed his eyes.

Please. Please, I beg you, Chicago. You got so many friends you don't need to pay me no mind? Honest answer now. Look, I ain't havin' much fun either. Lemme finish this, help me help you, and I'll leave you alone. I promise.

"Yo. Got a smoke?"

He started and shot to his feet as a wiry hand jogged his shoulder. He turned. There stood a thin, old black man in a dusty overcoat and broken sunglasses—one of the lenses was knocked out, showing a plaque-yellow eyeball with a dark iris.

"I don't smoke," Heartsblood blurted back. "You shouldn't scare folks like that."

The man bared his gold-plated canine in a grin. "Well, I can't help that, boy. 'Dja buy me a pack then?"

"Buy you a pack?"

"From the store there." He nodded at the grubby, steamed-up liquor store across the street.

"Yeah, but looky here, sir—"

"I'm not from here, ya know," the man said, just like Heartsblood had asked. "I come from t'ousands of miles away. I come for my own people, but maybe I help ya. If you're nice."

Heartsblood noticed then that the man's shoes were polished to a high shine. Nobody could sneak up on an Uratha in squeaky new shoes like that. Almost nobody. He had a strange accent, too.

"All right," Heartsblood said. "What kind?"

"Unfiltered." That eye was steady and cold despite the grin. "And a flask of the rum, too, if you'd be so very kind."

"You got a name, sir?"

"Do you?"

"You can call me the Rest of the Hairs," he said, thinking fast. Best way to avoid giving your real name without offending a spirit was to riddle it.

The man chuckled. "Well, all right." He took in a deep breath. When he let it out, a cloud of smoke came with it. "Papa Guede show ya what ya lookin' for. But I don't give no charity. I got a job to do, some holes that need fillin'. You get me my vices so I can work."

When Heartsblood came out with the liquor and cigarettes, the old man took them, laughing greedily. He put two cigarettes in his mouth, where they lit by themselves, and swigged the rum.

"That's better. Turn around now. Quick, before I change my mind and kick you into your mama's grave for a visit!"

Heartsblood gave a warning snarl, but he obeyed. The man shrugged off his moldy-smelling overcoat and draped it over Heartsblood.

"Put it on, ya mutt. There ya go. Now you find it. Be sure and pass my compliments to the host.... "

Heartsblood didn't like the feel of the thing, starting with the way it pulled too tight across his shoulders and ending with the fluttering that started up in the pit of his stomach. "Host? Now hold up," he said, not at all sure what bargain he'd just struck. He turned around. The man was gone.

"Shit."

Smoke and ash were drifting out of the overcoat. No matter how he flapped and beat it, it just kept coming, rising around him in a haze. It made his ears tear and blur up.

Papa Guede. Papa Guede. Damn, why didn't I finish that comparative religion book?

The nasty cloud blunted sight and smell but sharpened hearing, or maybe it just seemed like that because it was the only sense working. He blundered in the direction of the sounds he heard, putting out his hands in front of him.

Many voices pounced from the smoke, some shouting at him, some muttering right by his ear, some chanting in the distance. "Death to the plutocrats." "Death to the Pinkerton men." "Death to the criminals." "Death to the cheerleaders."

He didn't understand, and he wasn't even willing to bet there were any real bodies attached to the voices, but he followed them anyway down a good number of city blocks. He had no idea how far in what direction because they seemed to keep turning around.

"I hope they burn up and die." "I hope they get Muskegon and die." "I hope he's the blister." "I hope I get a seat at the hanging."

Heartsblood fell into a racking coughing fit. When he stood up straight again, the smoke had cleared.

I ain't peeking across, he thought wildly. *It ain't me. Once again it ain't me.* For some reason, he still had trouble believing it. But it was right in front of him.

He was staring at about one-tenth of a building. A fire station, according to the sign outside. He could see firefighter coats and hats hanging on one of the remaining inside corners. The left end of a desk supported itself impossibly on one foot, its sliced middle resting on nothing at all, and the amputated halves of long fluorescent bulbs somehow stayed lit in their amputated fixtures.

As for the other nine-tenths of the building and whoever was supposed to occupy it, they just weren't there. The thick walls and floor linoleum ended abruptly, randomly, and rough wooden planks and concrete walkways from some bigger, taller, seemingly much older building began. A dark juice seeped from the few points of contact between the two. Most places, they simply didn't match up, leaving huge, jagged gaps where Heartsblood could peer into the building as if it were a clumsy dissection project.

This was no thinning. Something had gone and slashed the Veil open, tore this horror from wherever its native place was, and grafted it onto the here and now. He crept, silently, holding his breath, to a better vantage.

The walkways ended in midair, but that didn't stop drab men in drab uniforms from pacing up and down them, and when they reached the edge of the concrete they simply vanished. Down below, in what looked like a fragment of courtyard, wood planks seamed together into a wide scaffold. Figures robed and hooded in yellowing muslin dangled from ropes partway through its open trapdoor. And there was an audience, too, sitting in front of it—dressed in mourning mostly, or black anyway, but they sure didn't sound like mourners. Most of them were cheering, or standing up and shouting curses both gleeful and angry.

"Death to the beautiful." "Death to the bombers." "Death to Alicia." "Death to Trent Young!" "Death to the Italian murderers." "Death to the white devils." "Death to the crows!"

That was a popular one. Several voices took it up. *Yeah, where are them crows?* Heartsblood wondered. *They're runnin' late.*

He didn't have long to wait. It was a hanging after all. Flight after flight of crows descended out of the sky, landing on the heads and shoulders of the hanged corpses, pecking holes through the fabric and pulling at the flesh underneath.

"The crows, damn them," one of the corpses cried, twitching violently. His voice was hoarse, but it carried like a scream. "They eat of us, they eat of us. Can't rest."

"Persecuted," another moaned.

"It must stop."

"Falsely convicted!" A leather strap broke with a loud squeak. The rightmost corpse's hands reached up to seize hold of a fat bird working at his eye. It died with squawk of protest as he squeezed it. Then he ripped off his hood and began stuffing the crow into his mouth, beak-first. He couldn't move that skewed head of his, but his livid hands were full of the strength of the angry dead. Soon the corpse next to him had done the same thing, breaking free of his wrist bonds and turning on his tormentors with a will. Heartsblood's beast-soul shuddered. Anything that started right off turning the natural cycle of life and death, scavenger and carrion, on its ear could only get worse.

What he was supposed to do about it, though, he couldn't fathom. The vision of the old bridge stampede hadn't helped him much with stopping the accident on the modern bridge— in fact, it'd half crippled him. And this was even stronger. Not shades, vague feelings, and ghost-smells, but what a preacher would call *manifest*, real enough to grab hold of. Real enough even to totally blot out the things that should rightfully be here.

Something bad must be about to happen again. Another test? Was there any way for him to pass it this time, or was something torturing him for sheer fun, blowing trumpets of doom in his ear always just a little too late?

He whimpered and made himself take in the scents. They were sharp, stinging, wet. There was the smell of encephalitis, oh yeah, lots of that. Most if not all of these crows were sick. And the smell of decay and the vermin that attended it. But there were other smells he'd only ever caught in the furthest depths of the Shadow Realm. Some he didn't even know.

One, however, he did recognize, and it was a smell that shouldn't belong here. It took him a few seconds to pick the living man out of the crowd. His exercise pants were gray, but the tank top was black, camouflaging him. As Heartsblood watched, the man wove through the back rows of the audience calmly, slowly, like he had important but not urgent business elsewhere.

A massive creaking took Heartsblood's attention back to the scaffold. The dead were freeing themselves of their ropes now. Their hands and fingers had grown enormously long, spreading out into spokes, and their faces were even more distended, streaked with feathered gore. Their noses and mouths were stretching into sharp, bony bills. They chewed at their own nooses with their bills, and others were coming up from below the trapdoor to catch them as they fell, clambering up onto the stage. They all wore the pale, stained robes of the condemned. The crows dove at the new-comers, but couldn't seem to turn the white tide. One after another of the birds disappeared down crooked throats and were replaced by brothers who followed right after.

Well, the one thing Heartsblood was sure of was no normal person should be here. The man in exercise pants was about to walk by him. He took his chance and sprang, dragging the man into the shadow he'd been watching from, putting a hand over his mouth to stop a scream.

But there was no scream. The man didn't even fight. He was almost limp in Heartsblood's arms.

Let me go, I'm all right. It wasn't quite like the mind-to-mind speech some Cahaliths could do, it didn't come to Heartsblood in the First Tongue, but the idea was clear enough. He stared at the man in confusion.

The man looked back at him. "Haymarket hangings," he said. "Yes, I recognize it. This was the old Hubbard jail. Others were hanged here, too, of course, but I doubt most of them were innocent. I suppose nobody thinks he deserves to die. They all look angry. Is that what you're trying to show me?"

"Beg pardon?" Heartsblood managed.

"I didn't realize this went so far back." The man shivered a bit as a breeze picked up and brought the carrion stench their way. There was something wrong with his eyes, Heartsblood realized. They were unfocused, cloudy, like he was asleep. Almond eyes, surrounded by pale, yellowish skin and dark, curly hair.

Werewolf tolerance wore thin. "Shh. Beats me all to hell how you got here, but you got to get gone. Ain't nothing sweeter to the undead than the taste of real life."

"But I think there's something I'm supposed to see."

"Yeah, that's what I thought, but now I'm thinkin' I seen enough. You comin' or do I have to carry you?"

"I can walk," the sleepwalker said serenely.

"Great. Come on." He took the man's hand and pulled him along. Was he imagining things, or was the audience growing, filling up the courtyard, and spilling out into the alleyway beside the station/jail? And some of these black-draped figures didn't look too humanish either. He guessed he shouldn't be surprised—the crows and zombies were putting on a hell of a show, of course it was drawing an eager crowd. But now he had to walk through them to get away, and if they smelled Uratha breath in their midst, they'd probably go berserk. He hunched himself into the overcoat, turning up the collar.

"Hold on to my arm, don't look anything in the eye, don't speak, don't even breathe if you can help it," he whispered, and then he plunged them both into the throng. *Yecch*. The smells of the skid rows of the spirit world. At least none of them'd noticed him yet.

Then a light brown arm floated past him through the tangle of clamoring black. *Issues* said a tattoo on it, and it had a picture underneath of a cartoon cat in a straightjacket. He froze. Another human? Mother and Father, how many more were there? They were all going to catch the goddamn virus if they didn't get eaten first. Too late, he changed direction and tried to dive after it. It disappeared. And he felt the hand on his own arm loosen.

He turned. A boy in knickers had stepped right in front of them, but Heartsblood knew right away it wasn't a real boy. The blood running from its scarred forehead, down its nose, into its teeth was a strong hint.

"Found you, Isaac!" the boy-thing cried joyfully.

To his horror, the sleepwalker was staring right at it, lifting up his hand as though he meant to touch it. It was reaching back.

"No, not in the eyes!" Heartsblood howled. "Don't touch 'em!" He bodily picked the man up, moving partway into the wolf now for speed. The overcoat that had pinched him so tight seemed to give way without splitting. Weird.

"Don't touch who?" the man asked vaguely.

"The boy! Shit! Never mind!"

"Boy…?"

The black shapes had suddenly stopped milling aimlessly and started pressing around the two of them, crushing. Arms and other kinds of limbs reached out for him. Oh yeah. The word was out.

SALT ON ITS TAILS. SALT ON ITS TAILS.

SO CLOSE NOW.

WHAT'S THIS? WHAT HAVE WE GOT?

A LITTLE BOY THAT THINKS HE'S A BIG BAD WOLF.

WE'RE NOT AFRAID OF WOLF-BOYS, NO. NOT IF THEY EVER CRY IN BED.

NOT IF WE'VE TASTED THEIR NIGHTMARES.

NOT WHEN WE KNOW THEY'LL NEVER WIN.

LITTLE BOYS WHO KILL THEIR MOTHERS MUST LOSE AND LOSE. THEY'RE CURSED, JUST LIKE THE FIRST URATHA, THE KINSLAYERS.

YOU DO KNOW YOU KILLED HER, YES? OH THEY TOLD YOU AND TOLD YOU IT WASN'T YOUR FAULT, BUT WASN'T THERE ALWAYS THAT FUNNY TIGHTNESS IN THEIR VOICES?

And the image blotted out his sight completely, Mama turning the way he forever saw her turning, caught in the camera flash of moonlight and then dashing out the broken door, and if he'd just gone in the store and dialed home when he first saw the man in the suit following him it never woulda happened, but he'd been scared it was really nothing, he was just being a big ol' baby, his cousins would all tease him for being as chicken as a normal kid—

He called out an old howl in the First Tongue, a rhyme of banishing and vexing. He didn't even know if he was still in that hole ripped into the firehouse or outward bound somewhere, headed wherever the fuck these things came from.

Can't get out!

He tried to bring the Gauru, but it wouldn't come, he was too afraid. And then there was no lynch-mob of spirits, no cackle of voices at all. The different shades of cloth black mixed into one utter black, and he was in what felt a lot like a cave the size of China, cold, smelling of nothing but minerals and water and possibly fish and silent except for a very slow drip somewhere.

"Hmm," said the sleepwalker in a tone of calm puzzlement.

"Goddammit. Goddammit. Shitalltofuck. Toldja not to look at 'im. You've fucked us up, you—weirdo—" Words were useless and getting more pathetic by the second, so Heartsblood shut up and just trembled in a panic, unable to move, terrified to stand still.

"Weirdo…" The word echoed. And then, the topper. "Is this what you wanted to show me?"

"Show you? Show you, I'll show you, I'll show you something…." The Gauru wouldn't come, but he was amazed to find himself grabbing the man anyway and shaking him. He'd had no idea he had it in his human heart to do such a thing. Hard enough to bruise, to break something, maybe even hard enough to—Then something flashed in the dark, sending a huge magnetic push through his bones. He was forced a step backward. His hands flew back, too, and they were numb for several minutes after.

"I see," said the sleepwalker as if nothing special had happened. "Then this isn't the right way."

"No!"

"Then you need me to show you. Is that it?" He seemed to take Heartsblood's consternation as a yes. "Close your eyes."

"What the hell for? It's pitch dark."

"Maybe for you. But I see a way out. If you want to come, you have to follow; if you want to follow, you have to trust. So close your eyes and take my hand."

What it came down to was, he didn't have a damn choice.

The sleepwalker moved slowly but surely through unseen tunnels. Heartsblood couldn't even feel the wall beside them or the man's hand over his own because of his numb hands. The man could let go, and he wouldn't even know it.

"The path through here is identical to the shape of a medieval Amerindian earth-work twenty-five miles southwest of town," the man commented. "We always theorized it was either a map or a passage. Evidently both. It's visible in satellite photographs."

That was good, if completely bugshit. *Keep babbling, then I know where you're at.* He decided to keep the conversation going. "So, you still asleep?"

"Of course. This is a dream, isn't it?"

"Shit. Maybe for you." Well, if he was dreaming, it was worth asking him. "You know what the crows mean?"

"I know what the black feather rain means. Open your eyes, we're going out."

He did. Still pitch dark. "Going out where?" he said lamely.

"You assume a lot," the sleepwalker observed. "Maybe you're meant to represent instinct: I need to ally with it, but sometimes lead and sometimes follow. But you could just as easily ask 'going out when' or 'going out whom,' because that may be more the issue…. Anyway. Don't let go."

They fell upward, into a light that grew colder every second until Heartsblood was sure his partner had to be dead and even Uratha circulation might give out. And then, just as he thought he felt his heart arresting, they were back.

The fire station was back in one piece. Its blank smooth side stared at them all innocent, like *What? What'd I do?* There was no whiff of the scaffold, the corpses, the monsters. Even the crows were almost gone. Just a quartet of them perched on the streetlight above.

But there in the alley lay seven bodies.

They were all pretty young. That was the first thing Heartsblood noticed. Teens, maybe early twenties for a couple of them, but he doubted it. Three male and four female, one black, one kinda Greek-looking, and the rest pale Caucasians, but all dressed in black. Black leather, black lace, black jeans, black cotton. That must be how they'd blended in. And they were most certainly dead. Heartsblood could smell the tiny changes that come over a corpse the instant the blood stops and the flesh starts to digest itself. It seeped out of their pores. That and something else.

The sleepwalker gasped and pried himself out of Heartsblood's grip. He fell down on his knees to pick up the sprawling forearms one after another. He felt their wrists, checked their pupils. Then he looked up at Heartsblood with hollow, shocked eyes. His face was almost livid enough to match the dead ones.

"You're here," he said at last. "You're real."

"Yeah." Not news to Heartsblood, but he guessed it was to the sleepwalker (who would have to have some other label in Heartsblood's head now that he was awake).

"I—I thought I was asleep…. "

"You was. You told me so."

He didn't argue that, but it didn't seem to calm him much either.

"Where did they come from?" he mumbled.

"They was here, too, all along," Heartsblood answered wearily. "In the audience."

"Audience?"

"The audience. The things in black. You saw 'em, right? Goddamn hard to miss. You didn't see the boy—"

"No—" The man shook his head.

"The bloody-headed boy. You remember when I said don't touch him because you started—"

"No, no, there was a—"

"He was in knickers."

The man just kept shaking his head harder and harder, till Heartsblood feared he was going to shake something out. "No, I saw hanged men. I saw the crows. I saw you. I didn't see these…" He blinked back tears.

"Well. You and me're together on that," Heartsblood said ruefully. "I only saw this 'un." He reached down and turned the arm of the black girl so he could find it: yep, there it was, the *Issues* tattoo. Nice to know he was doing such good for the world as well as himself on this sojourn of enlightenment. As he touched the girl's skin, the coat on his back crumbled into ashes and he felt something pass through him into the body, then back out through him again—something eel-shaped and guileful. He thought he heard a laugh, soft and thin as cigarette paper. *I come for my people,* he heard the old man saying again.

"Shit." He flailed at the ash, trying to get it off himself as much and as fast as possible. *Spirits. Fucking spirits.*

The man watched him gyrate, frowning. "Are you all right?" he asked.

"Shit. Yes. It's fine."

"I take your word." He drew up into himself, hunched over. He looked cold despite the warm night. His arms were goosebumpy. He probably was in shock. "I just didn't see them. I don't know why I didn't. I didn't think I'd really walked out. I thought I was still… but I don't know why I didn't know."

The last thing in the world Heartsblood wanted to do was stay in this corpse-filled alley and listen to exactly the kind of talk he was trying to push out of his own head. Especially since the man was getting louder as he soared toward panic. He took hold of the man's shoulders.

"Hold on now," Heartsblood urged. "Just listen. We got to scat. There's prob'ly fire-fighters in there on duty—if they ain't dead—and if one of 'em comes out for a smoke or somethin' we're gonna have one hell of a time explaining this."

"No," said the man. "I mean yes. But we can't just leave them! I, I have to find out who did this."

"No, you don't." Heartsblood started to argue, but then he thought about the way the man had floated so serenely through the pitch dark, thought about spirit-quests and crow-mysteries, and realized he couldn't say any such thing. "Or fine. Maybe you do, but we still can't stay."

"Let me at least take this." The man removed his tank top and used it to pick up a wooden bowl that lay spilled almost empty on the pavement beside one of the boys. "I know I've smelled this liquid before. I think these kids died of poison, not the virus. The bowl might have impressions."

"Impressions?"

"I think." The man shivered. "I think—we probably have a thing or two to explain to each other."

Heartsblood nodded. "Let's find a better place to talk."

"And just leave them for the police?"

"That's what the police are for," Heartsblood said as gently as he could manage. "You can always call nine-one-one after."

"I know where we can go," the man said after a moment.

Wolf-wariness kicked in. "Someplace public."

"No, just the opposite. Something's still watching us. It has to be a place I can ward."

"You mean ward off things?"

"Ward against eavesdropping."

Heartsblood didn't look up at the crows over their heads, but he hadn't forgotten about them either.

"Yeah, okay. But quick now. I don't want us seen."

"Understood." The man wobbled up to standing, and Heartsblood pulled him out of the glare of the streetlights.

If the man had been any steadier on his feet, Heartsblood would have really felt suspicious. The path he led them on was almost as bad as the one in the pitch-dark cave, definitely as bad as any maze of streets and alleys Chicago had ever tried to lose a little red wolf in. He took them around back of an old. brick powerhouse, down an access shaft with a long, damp metal ladder, and through a puddle-filled zigzag of low tunnels. The man had keys to unlock a couple of padlocked gates along their way, but he couldn't open the switchboxes mounted up high on the walls to turn the lights on. Heartsblood had to tear one open, which made the man wince.

"Watch out," the man said just as Heartsblood tripped over something hard under the water. "There's old rail lines on the bottom. This way." The man's teeth chattered in the underground cool. They went through another metal gate into a suddenly wider, drier space filled with racks and crates and pallets, lit only by the red bulb of an emergency exit.

"They were built for coal-hauling, for the furnaces," the man explained. "Utilities still run lines through. They're all over downtown."

"Where we at now?" Heartsblood asked as the man found a switch and flipped it on. Buzzing fluorescents came to life.

The man looked over himself, clucking his tongue. There were forming bruises in a couple places where Heartsblood had grabbed him. He massaged the spots. The bruises melted away under his fingers. "I don't feel any security guards around, but keep a lookout. Oh… right near where we were. The old Shriner temple. Now, of course, it's a department store, what else? Still, all those years of Masonic ritual have tuned the building pretty well—damn. I don't have anything but my coin tassel on me. I need a pen and paper. Hurry."

Heartsblood picked a clipboard up off one of the stacks of boxes. "This-here work?"

"Yes." The man grabbed the paper, folded, and tore it, then wrote Chinese on the scraps and placed them very deliberately on the floor. Out of his pants pocket, he took a knotted and braided red silk cord tied up with gold coins and jade. He hung it from the handle of one of the pallets, which he rolled up near the constellation of paper scraps. Then he started moving his hands in the air, chanting in a language Heartsblood couldn't be sure of, though it did sound more or less Asian.

It seemed wrong somehow, what the man did. Heartsblood only knew two ways to deal with spirits: either you bargained with them or you tore them down to ribbons of shadow. You didn't change the physics of their whole world out from under them. But as this man worked, that's just what happened. The spirit-reflection of the room warped, becoming something more curvy than rectangular. Spirit presences that had been zooming through the building, ignoring walls and doors and even flying right through the man's body, now moved in a bent path around them. What was stranger, they didn't even seem to notice being rerouted.

"So you've used this place before," he said when the man seemed to be finished

"Yes. Well, not me so much as my… teacher." The man sighed and looked around. "We should be safe now. Thank you for agreeing to come. I'm Baihu." He extended his hand. Heartsblood took it and gave it a single shake.

"Daniel Vickery."

"Interesting. That wasn't the name I had for you in my head."

"Well, Baihu wasn't the one I had for you either. And I thought the boy called you Isaac. Well?"

"What?" He was jiggling the coin tassel, adjusting it.

"Your name ain't Isaac?"

"Oh, it is. My birth name is. Baihu is my name among my—colleagues."

"What was the one you had in your head for me?"

"Redheart."

"Shit. Close," Heartsblood allowed. "So you read minds, too. Who the hell are you? I mean."

"You mean…" Isaac turned to him with a wistful smile. "…what the hell am I?"

"Yeah, what are you. Some kinda occultist, looks like?"

"I'm going to pretend I didn't hear that word. In our circles, it implies a wannabe."

"And you're an is."

"Yes. Though I don't quite read minds. My senses aren't that developed yet. Or they're usually not." He frowned. "On the other hand, I can usually sense the presence of minds around me, which is why I don't know how I missed those—children. They didn't register on me at all."

"You was dead asleep," Heartsblood said. Sorcerer or not, it was Elodoth nature to want to say something.

"But I registered you."

"I'm a werewolf."

"Yes…" The man nodded reluctantly. Plainly not the most comfortable notion he'd ever taken up.

"Though the right name is Uratha," Heartsblood finished.

"I've never dealt with… Uratha before. I've heard stories, that's all. So I'll have to ask you in advance to excuse my ignorance." He picked up the bowl he'd taken from the alley, still using the tank top to hold it. "I know I've smelled this before. It's one of the sedatives. You didn't see them drink it, did you?"

"No, but it was comin' out of their skin. Gimme that," he said suddenly. The sorcerer handed it over carefully, leaving room for Heartsblood to take it by the cloth. Heartsblood sniffed it. "Why, I recognize this. It's plain ol' jimsonweed. Stinkweed, Granny called it. She tole me not to eat it, but Lord, with that smell I don't know why you'd wanna."

"Jimsonweed." That seemed to jog something in the sorcerer's brain. "Man-t'o-lo. *Datura.* My granny—" He cut himself off. "I should have gotten that right off the bat. I stay away from it in my own preparations because it's treacherous. But it's a poor man's hallucinogenic. It also causes tachycardia, convulsions, coma." He stopped again. Neither of them wanted to think about that too much. "And sometimes people try to use it for asthma, brewing it in a tea like this, and end up dead."

"So they poisoned themselves on accident?" Heartsblood asked. He couldn't quite scrub the doubt out of his voice. The whole damn Shadow Realm didn't go rising like that for stoned teenagers. At least not normally.

"Possibly," Baihu allowed. "Or maybe that's just what the police are supposed to think." He picked up the soggy leaves in the bottom of the bowl. A little stained paper strip came out with them. "Aha. Or it was a ritual." He read the strip. "It says *Trent Young.* Mean anything to you?"

"Yeah, that was one of the death-chants."

"Death-chants?"

"You didn't hear those either? The voices?" Heartsblood prodded him impatiently.

Something flickered through Baihu's eyes, but he said, "I heard the hanged men. What voices? Did the crows speak?"

"Uh-uh, they don't talk, not these crows. Wish they did, I'd have a thing or two to say back. No, this was from the audience. Or the kids, or both. But there was definitely voices."

"Saying what?"

"Death to this, death to that."

"And?" Heartsblood felt something like a cool breeze brush the across the top of his brain as Baihu said that. *Damn mind readers.*

"Stay outta my head, and I'll stay outta your… business," he growled.

The man actually blushed. "Sorry. Bit flustered here. Control isn't what it should be. Please tell me, what else did they say?"

"Well." Heartsblood scowled. "Never you mind exactly what. But it was personal. They tried to make me believe again—somethin' I ain't believed since I was a boy. Somethin' as used to keep me up nights. There, hope that helps."

"Ah. It might." Baihu seemed to know he was on thin ice. He turned back to the bowl. "Here's another name. *The whole fucking cheerleader squad.*" He fought off a quirk of the lip. "Ambitious. Completely amateur, but ambitious. These were occultists. And they paid the highest price for their ignorance."

He sighed and glanced at Heartsblood. "Well. I was sleepwalking when I came to that place. I thought I was still meditating at home. What was your excuse?"

"I was just followin' the death-chants," Heartsblood said ruefully. "Been tryin' to piece out what the hell's wrong with this town for weeks. Chasin' my tail. But I don't buy that this was just a stupid accident. Somebody there knew what they were doin'. And it's got to relate—" He wondered how much it was safe to tell. *Who was this man really? How much would he tell his 'colleagues'?* "You know. To the virus. To all the other shit goin' on."

"Yes." Baihu was checking him out with those almond eyes of his. No fog of trance now, no sir. "I agree there's been plenty of that. I think we should meet again, Daniel. In a better, or at least better-dressed context." He put his shirt back on. "I have friends who might be very interested to get an… Uratha take on this whole mystery. Fair's fair. You could bring others if you want. There are some in the community whom I know have caused trouble for your kind in the past, but it wouldn't be anybody present. Still, I wouldn't blame you for wanting backup."

"Yeah, I'd most likely be bringin' a few folks." Heartsblood tried to say it confidently. "Well, looky here, I'll just have to think about it. I'm interested, too. But it ain't exactly breakfast at Denny's we're talkin' about here."

"Definitely not." Baihu nodded. He tore off another paper scrap, wrote on it, and handed it over. Heartsblood stared at it. After all this, a plain old phone number seemed like downright odd.

"So all I do is call? I don't have to do nothin' special, like…"

"Like cut a calf? No." The sorcerer chuckled. "Come on, I'll show you back out."

The handset of the pay phone smelled like smoke and gasoline. *A lonely smell,* he thought. Did anybody ever make a happy call from a pay phone? They were for stranded drivers, runaways, drug deals. Folks far from home.

"At the tone, please say your name." *Boop!*

"Daniel."

Burring ring tones, the sudden urge to hang up. "Hello?"

"This is an AT&T collect call from…" "Daniel." "…Will you accept the charges?"

"Yes." Kalila's voice came extra-crisp for the computer's sake, then softened. "HB? HB?"

He blinked back tears. He'd almost gotten used to callous Chicago voices. Now he suddenly remembered what it felt like to talk to his pack—his true pack. "Kalila?"

"HB! My God. This was the first morning that my absolute first thought of the day opening my eyes wasn't *Oh my God, I wonder if he's okay,* and poof, it's like magic. You must have felt yourself losing my undivided attention. Admit it."

"It's good to hear your voice, darlin'. You got no idea. Everybody okay?"

"As okay as we get. Trouble in Denver again, Elias wants to go, but Dana won't hear of it until you're back. You catch that? Dana won't hear of it."

"So she's trainable."

"I'm starting to think so. So does this mean you're done? How'd it go out there? Did the thing with the crows turn out to mean anything?"

"No. I mean, uh, yeah, the crows are definitely the thing, but I'm not done yet. I… uh." He scratched furiously at his half-shaved jaw till he almost raised a blister. "I got a problem. I've kinda wound up bein'… alpha of this whole project and, uh."

"Alpha?"

"Yeah, I know," he blurted. "I was hopin' maybe Elias was around, so's I could ask his advice."

"Elias is observing the *Uratha shall cleave to human* part of the Oath of the Moon just now," she said dryly.

He grinned. "Goddamn. New girlfriend?"

"Status is speculative. He's let her into his car, she's petted Fenris Dog, he has not, however, cooked for her." She paused. "Anything lowly little me could help you with?"

"Well, maybe," he said. "It's these Hull House Haunts you sent me to. We ain't been gettin' along too well, and I really need their backup. 'Cause like f'rinstance, there's these other folks I wanna meet with."

"Not getting along? I thought you said you were alpha."

"I am, but I—I guess they're unhappy about how it happened. See, Mercedes and me, uh, we got in a fight about somethin' I said, and, uh, I won. So I'm alpha, for now."

Just from the silence he knew what the look on her face was. "You forced Mercedes Childseeker to a challenge. Actual fisticuffs with a strange Uratha."

"Well, I didn't know what I was doin' until I was already into it. I was kinda het up about that bridge accident…."

"Yeah, I've been telling myself you weren't on that thing when it went, thanks so much for not calling to let us know. And now you're using your victory to take control of the pack. Am I getting this correctly?"

"You don't know the whole story yet, Kal," he complained. "I'm tellin' ya the thing's just too big. It's gonna take more'n just me, and they plumb refused to take a single word I said seriously! Now these are your friends."

"All I can say," she said calmly, "is this is turning out to be one hell of a walkabout. HB the tyrant is a heretofore nonexistent concept. Maybe Spookygirl was on to something."

That went through him like a spark of static. It was true, he barely recognized himself lately, but it all felt wrong and out of balance. He was supposed to scare himself shitless? That was enlightenment? "Yeah. Well. I'm havin' trouble with it. Like I said, there's these folks, occultists or—somethin' like that, and they want to meet up and compare notes. I'm thinkin' that could help me finish this a lot quicker. The one guy seems smart as a whip. But I don't wanna go if the pack ain't behind me."

"What exactly did you say to Mercedes?"

"It was pretty bad. I did apologize, later on. Listen, did you know Kyle Wolf-at-the-Door?"

"Kyle? Of course, he's a doll." Her voice suddenly dropped. "What do you mean 'did' I know him?"

"Shit. I'm sorry, darlin'. I shoulda told ya. He's passed on. Killed this spring in a skirmish with the Pure."

"Oh. Oh, no. Oh, Mother be with him. Oh, that's sad."

"Yeah. I think they're really missin' him bad. They won't talk about it though. What was he like?"

"Well, no wonder you're having trouble with them. He was practically the soul of the pack. The barometer, you know. Major smartass, could turn anything into a laugh. It's hard to imagine them staying together for very long without him. Kinda like imagining us staying together without you," she added, subdued. He tried to ignore the guilt pang. "But he was Irraka. He did it in his own way."

"And I'm not Irraka. And I'm a stranger. I can't take his place. I almost wish I could."

"No, you don't," she returned. He smiled, though he knew the sudden burst of jealousy was dead serious.

"No, no, I don't. But y'know what I mean. I'd like to see them… whole. Even if it didn't have a thing to do with me or the goddamn Murder."

"Murder? Oh, of crows. Heartsblood." She usually didn't say his whole name. "That's your incredible compassion talking. Maybe you should listen. Even if you took charge of them by force, that doesn't mean you can't bring your whole self to the alpha role now. You don't have to do it like Elias, and you probably shouldn't try."

He nodded, then remembered she couldn't see him. Goddamn, he missed her. "Yeah. Yeah, you're right. My whole self."

"So what does your compassion tell you?"

"Well." He let out a wintry sigh. "An Irraka shows the pack the secrets of their own hearts. Now they got no one to do that for them. They might learn to do it for themselves, in time. In the years to come."

"It's possible. We manage without a Cahalith."

"I still say we'd be a lot better off with one."

"Of course. That's what an Elodoth would say," she teased.

"But their real trouble is they're lonely. They're hurtin' too bad to be there for each other. And Mercedes," he said suddenly, "keeps puttin' me off from goin' to *ungin*. I reckoned it was 'cause she didn't believe me, but maybe it ain't so much that. No, that ain't it at all! Now that I think of it. She don't want to see the other packs."

"Yeah. That sounds like a good instinct. Go with it. Go on."

"They don't want to watch the others enjoyin' bein' together. And I'm no good to them, I'm just a bother. I'm gonna be gone anyway, soon as this is over. Go back to my real pack. It's too bad they don't see…"

He trailed off. After a second, Kalila prodded him. "See? See what?"

"Not what," he said. "Who. Ooh, they're gonna hate my ass."

"And this is a good thing?"

"She's right there," he said. "And she cares. They just don't know it yet."

"I'm just going to keep assuming it's enough for you to know what you're talking about."

"And she even knows what's goin' on. Yeah, I got a notion now. Thanks, Kalila. You're a pistol. I really 'preciate the help."

"Well, I'm not totally sure what I did, but you're welcome. Look, HB. You know we're right here if you need us. You do know that, don't you?"

"Yeah, I do know that." (*Alone.*)

"Oh, here's Elias. He wants the phone."

Heartsblood buried his dread. "Hey, Heartsblood," came Elias' cool voice over the thousands of miles. "I feel like we need to take out one of those personals. *All is forgiven, please come home.*"

"I'm comin' home as soon as I can," he promised.

"All right. Here's a neurotic question. To which I know the answer already, but I'm going to ask because I just need to hear you say it. This isn't about you being mad at us, is it? Or at me?"

"Hell, no," Heartsblood yelped, shocked. *Elias worrying that he was mad at him?*

"That's what I needed," the Rahu said. "Good boy. What—?" Muffled sounds from the receiver. "Oh. Kalila said you've gone alpha out there?"

"Yessir."

"Well, don't get any big ideas. When you come back, I may have to beat your ass just to remind you who's boss."

Heartsblood laughed and laughed.

"You think I'm kidding?" Warning tone. Poor alpha. So hard to dominate over the phone.

"No, sir." He wiped his eyes. "No, I know you ain't, Elias. I'll start applyin' the ass liniment now so it don't get bruised too bad. Lookin' forward to it."

"Well." He could hear a smile, no matter how hard Elias might be trying not to. "All right then. You want Kalila back?"

"Naw, I gotta get goin'."

"Do what you gotta do. Good hunting, Hunter."

"Thanks. Talk to ya later."

He hung up, feeling better and worse at exactly the same time. Somewhere inside the gas station were a hundred thousand potato chips, and one of those machines rolling Chicago franks. That's what he needed: a big helping of partially hydrogenated soybean oil. It wouldn't be one of Yolanda's, but since she didn't seem to be running her cart anymore (because she finally put her foot down about the mosquitoes, hopefully), it'd have to do. He put his thumbs in his belt loops and headed over. Hell, maybe there was a city boy in him yet.

She took it pretty well, for Mercedes.

"What the hell?" She jumped up from the dinner table as Heartsblood strode in the door, acting like she'd flat forgotten she wasn't alpha—hunched forward, lips curled, nose flattening.

"I'm guessin' you don't know her name, though she knows y'uns'," Heartsblood interrupted her. He stood aside and coaxed the Ghost Wolf over the threshold with a nudge of his hand. "Folks, this is Anna. Anna Urchin."

"Delighted—" Mercedes sneered.

"Yeah, right—" Anna shot back. Heartsblood called for order with a snarl.

"Now what's she doing here?"

"She's your next door neighbor," Heartsblood said. He couldn't help putting on his best shit-eating grin.

"So are the Pure."

Eric stood up as well. Little Blue was fishing in his ten thousand pockets, never a good sign. Heartsblood pretended not to worry about them.

"Well, she definitely ain't Pure. And she's been havin' a lot of the same problems we been. And she's kindly agreed to join forces, so I signed her up. Temporarily, like myself. Any other questions?"

"Yes. Why," said Mercedes. "Nothing's happened for days."

"Nothing's happened to you. Anna, you tell 'em what you saw yesterday."

"It was about five blocks out of your territory on the east side," the Ghost Wolf reported, standing her ground passably well. "Four or five different cars out on the street just suddenly started going nuts. Going up on the sidewalk, knocking out fireplugs, crashing into storefronts. Road rage, the news said, but I saw this guy in one of the trucks trying to jump out his driver's side window. He got caught on the mirror and was hanging half in and half out, but the truck just kept going around bashing into things. Nobody was driving it."

"Well, that's fucked up," Mercedes agreed. "What'd you do about it?"

"Oh, wrapped my teeth around the bumper and pulled it to a stop," Anna retorted. "Then I put all the rioting techno-spirits down with my solo-guitar rendition of 'Kum-ba-yah,' negotiated peace in the Middle East, and spent the rest of the afternoon delivering sushi platters to the homeless."

Little Blue let out a little high-pitched giggle despite himself.

Mercedes' eyebrows flew up, but she kept her mouth in a tight scowl. "That was in the nature of a question, bitch."

"I watched real close," she shrugged. "I can show you the place for your shaman to check out if you're concerned at all. But I warn you, it's attracted attention. The media reports were all pretty damn groomed, the only one that had his facts straight was that *Oddly Enough* guy. They're finally catching on to all the weird shit."

"Who is?"

"The *others*," she said defiantly. "Just so you know, the Pure and me aren't your only neighbors. Though I doubt they've dared show themselves to a whole pack."

"Speakin' of others—" Heartsblood raised his voice, but then just as quickly dropped it. *Mother be with me*, he prayed, and Her children answered. The light in the room changed as the harsh kitchen fluorescents and reddish lampshine were lulled by an outpouring of soft moonlight from his own body. Blue gave him a grateful look. Even Mercedes' shoulders drooped a bit. *Balance.* This was one of his few real achievements in that journey so far, that the half-moon-spirits came at his call to calm a brewing fight with their beauty.

"Save it, Mercedes," he went on in his smoothest, firmest voice. "She's in, and we got things to do. So let's just skip the traditional pissing contests—"

"What's your moon, Anna?" Erik asked it mildly. But it put Heartsblood on notice in a way Mercedes' pushing and cussing hadn't. He'd never heard the Rahu interrupt his alpha, neither Mercedes nor himself.

"My moon?" Something pricked Anna's instincts, too. She was shifting warily all of a sudden.

"Yeah, your moon," the Rahu repeated. "You know your moon, right?"

"Yeah," she said. "Of course. It's new moon. Irraka."

"That's what I was guessing." Erik looked at Heartsblood. The hue of his eyes slid toward yellow. "I see what's going on now."

"You got a problem, Bleeding?" Heartsblood said, but he was disappointed at how it came out. "You take it up with me."

"Oh yes, I'll take it up with you. You know they think red wolves are part coyote?" He smirked humorlessly at his packmates. "Well, you think you're just going to fix everything, aintcha, little clever clogs? Fix the virus, fix the spirits, fix the city. And as long as you're in the neighborhood, you're going to fix us, too. Is that it?"

"Oh, hell no, I can't do that for you," snorted Heartsblood. "Alpha or not."

"I don't recall your even asking if we want to be fixed." Erik stood still. His breathing was even—consciously controlled. Heartsblood found it hard to hear whatall the full-moon was saying; the wolf was too distracted by body signals. "You ever lost a packmate? Oh fuck, don't even answer that. Has it occurred to you that maybe it's not time for us to get all better? You ever heard of a mourning period?" He started blinking rapidly, and his voice broke. "It's not even his birthday yet.…"

Little Blue clapped his hands over his ears. "Stop," he whined. The next second he seemed to decide he couldn't trust anybody to do that and pelted out of the living room. A door slammed and a stereo came on at full blast. Heartsblood often forgot lately that he was a teenager.

"Jesus Christ, Erik!" The unexpected explosion was from Anna. "Listen to yourself. You talk like somebody seriously expects you to take me as a replacement for Kyle and that's just stupid."

"There is no replacement for Kyle!" Erik roared. The handle of the cup of coffee that he held burst into white powder, and the rest clattered to the floor.

"Oh yeah?" She was about the coolest in the face of the arriving Gauru that Heartsblood had ever laid eyes on. She arched her back like she was trying to stand against a headwind and stuck her hand in her back jeans pocket. "Well, who here doesn't know that already? Who needs convincing? Ya know, I think you're scared shitless that you might actually be ready to go back to your life and your work someday. I think that's the real agenda here—"

The next instant Heartsblood and Erik were in a ball together on the floor. Erik howled, incensed at being denied his target, but Heartsblood soon forced him to change focus. The Rahu was even huger in Gauru than Heartsblood remembered. That in itself wasn't the problem. He was heavy, too, and he knew how to use his weight, centering it on one spot to lodge in your flesh and crack bones. Heartsblood reached up with human hands and grabbed Erik's ears, wrapping them around his fingers to hold on tight. His enemy reared back, but ears were sensitive, yanking too hard on them hurt. So he raised his arm and smashed it into Heartsblood's face instead. Heartsblood felt his teeth slipping into the back of his throat. He gagged and tried to swallow. The tang of blood filled his mouth.

Anna'd given him the key. He had to hold on to that no matter what, and he begged the moon-spirits to help him remember it, not to let him slide into *Kuruth* himself. Stoking the fury of Bleeding's war form was a sure ticket to losing. It was the fear and sadness hiding right under it that he had to reach. Not an honorable way to win a challenge—at *ungin* such dirty tricks would get an Uratha torn apart—but this wasn't *ungin*, it sure as shit wasn't a proper challenge, and anyway there was more than one fight at stake.

Am I the Pure to you now? he gurgled at Erik through blood and snot. Am I killing him again?

The full-moon let out a horrible noise, half howl, half scream, and picked Heartsblood up and drove him into the floor time and again.

Shut up! Shut up! Shut up!

Heartsblood heard ribs snap and waited for the pain he knew was coming. He had to keep talking somehow. Even with his soul screaming at him to surrender or fight, freeze or flail, *something*, he had to keep talking. That was how he'd hold on to the man when he needed him most. Jibber jabber.

I DON'T WANT TO KILL HIM, BLEEDING. He drew in a ragged breath. I'M NOT ASKING YOU TO FORGET. JUST TO FORGIVE. IT'S NOT YOUR FAULT YOU LIVED.

It IS!

Dimly, through a wash of honeycomb yellow in his eyes and bee-buzzing in his ears, he felt himself being lifted up and thrown. He didn't know what he landed on but at least it was something strong enough not to break under him.

YOU THING OF NO PLACE, Erik yelled. It was the closest the First Tongue had to an obscenity, and even hearing it made Heartsblood feel as if he'd gone all wispy like a spirit himself, like he wasn't even there. He gave a hoarse cry, letting his body prove without words that it existed. The Rahu grabbed him again.

YOU KNOW NOTHING. Erik slavered on him. His breath smelled like Scotch, blood, and ammonia. I TOLD HIM I'D ALWAYS PROTECT HIM. I TOLD HIM NO ONE COULD HURT HIM WITHOUT GOING THROUGH ME. I SWORE IT!

Heartsblood felt himself wilting. It beat all, but he was finding it hard to stay awake. Still, he knew what to say. Maybe it was the moon-spirits. Or maybe he really could come to his own rescue once in a while. THAT WAS A FOOLISH THING TO SWEAR, he answered. YOU SHOULD ONLY HAVE SWORN TO LOVE HIM, BECAUSE THAT IS THE OATH YOU'VE KEPT.

"Oh shit." A crumbling, on every front. Abyssal growls in the First Tongue melted into threadbare English, muscles dwindled to flat human ribbons. The Gauru fled like a fox into the night, leaving the man far behind. Erik dropped Heartsblood on the floor and sobbed like it had just happened that very second, like it was right before him all over again. "Shit. Shit. Shit. It's no good. It's just no good."

Mercedes was there almost instantly. She wrapped her arms around her packmate, murmuring to him, soothing bullshit, not caring who heard. "Eric. Come on, baby boy. Come on. I've got you. Shh. You're gonna make it. Shhhhh." A *miracle*, Heartsblood thought dizzily. *A damned expensive one.*

He heard the door that slammed earlier open, smelled Little Blue's junior aftershave and the salt of tears. His vision kept blurring, but he could hear that a lot of things were being said over his body now, intimate things, good things. He wished some of them could be said to his body, but he'd shake the hand of the fairy godmother who could make that happen.

"Lemme take him." Anna's voice. Heartsblood felt himself being picked up and laid down on the sofa. And there was the pain at last. Those bones did not want to be shifted. Even sinking into the cushions made vomit climb to the top of his throat.

"I've got an idea," the Ghost Wolf said uncomfortably, once a minute went by with no sound in the room but grief. "We'll put it to a vote."

Heartsblood tried to rise up on his elbow. "No."

"Hang on, hero," she broke in, not unkindly. "You guys might as well get the facts. Heartsblood wants me in for extra support, so we can go meet with this cabal of sorcerers, show of strength or some shit. Yes, they want to meet. They claim to have information on this whole Murder of Crows thing. So anyway. I'm here because I'm interested, because I thought I could help. Beats just waiting for the sky to fall on my head."

She snorted. "I'd like to say Heartsblood's plan seems like the best I've heard so far, but actually it's the only. In fact, he's the only one I've met in this whole city who's even trying to do anything about what we all know is coming. But if you guys really don't believe that, really don't want my help or his help, really don't give a fuck, then there's just no fucking point, because it won't work. So let's vote."

"No." Heartsblood had a couple of teeth budding back into place now, but he still sounded a lot more like Grampa in the early morning than he would've liked. He forced his eyes to refocus. "A pack ain't a democracy."

"I understand that," Anna returned. "I do know the basic shit, Elvis. But I haven't joined up yet, have I? No. And you really can't make me. And I'm saying, I'm not coming in for even a day unless we're all gonna back each other up. So. We each vote. Blind ballot, majority wins. We'll just take this dish of M&M's." She picked out some of the candies. "Yellow, I join you guys, and we move on Heartsblood's plan, talk to the sorcerers, see what we can all figure out. Brown, we say fuck it, and I go home and pretend none of this happened. That work?"

When no one answered, she said, "Heartsblood. We can assume you're yellow?"

He nodded (*ow*). Two candies landed with a plink in the empty coffee cup she'd picked up. She handed each of the other Uratha a brown and a yellow. Three more plinks. Then she dumped them out into her hand and showed it to Mercedes. Both women blinked in surprise.

"Three to two," Mercedes said. "She's in."

"Fine," said Erik. "This meeting isn't tomorrow, is it?"

"Shit, no," Heartsblood coughed from the sofa.

"Good." The Rahu went into the kitchen. There was the too-familiar sound of liquor bottles being jostled.

So one of them'd broken ranks. Which one? Heartsblood turned over and squinted at their faces. Mercedes was hugging Little Blue some more. Poor squirt. He'd already seen war and death, but he was so young that a family fight was still worse. Still, something had finally joggled loose tonight. Constant touching and nuzzling was normal pack behavior. A wolf needed to mix his scent with his fellows. He had to feel of their fur to know they were all right. The almost total lack of that among the Haunts had put Heartsblood's hackles up from day one. Now it was back, and it seemed Heartsblood might be the only one in the room who was still all alone. He guessed that was an improvement.

"I hope for the love of Mother and Father that you know what you're doing, Heartsblood." Mercedes looked at him. "I really do hope you know. I hope you have something to show for this when it's all done. Because otherwise, I can only conclude you were sent as our punishment."

Heartsblood shook his mending head but nothing worth saying would come out. She wasn't joking.

He wanted to bathe in the light of his moon, the half-moon.

He went down to where land and water met at the old Chicago Harbor. Once, so Mercedes' encyclopedia said, there'd been nothing there but a patch of marsh to slog through as quick as you could with a canoe on your head. Now it was all fancy park with a bigass fountain full of seahorses and shooting water. Two bronze statues on pedestals stood lookout at the park entrance: mounted Indians in warbonnets, one hefting a non-existent spear and the other pulling on a nonexistent bow. Heartsblood took the wolf, curling into a glum, ginger-furred ball on the soft grass. It felt good to slip into smallness, to get rid of all the bunching and pinching of human clothes, to be unnoticed.

It might've been wishful thinking, but he felt the tiniest breeze stirring from the lake. Maybe it was the moon peeking through the overcast sky, pouring radiance out onto the bay. The dark water rippled.

And was that music he heard in the distance? He swiveled his ears. Yeah, somebody was sawing on a fiddle somewhere all right, and a lot of other somebodies were clapping and clopping on a wooden floor. Then a wolf howl started up across the water. He jerked to his feet, but it wasn't Uratha howling. It was a real wolf howl, a pack's rendezvous-howl. That couldn't be right. There couldn't be packs of natural wolves living this close to Chicago. Most would rather starve.

A flurry of noise and glimmer and virus-smell drifted down to the ground on his right side. The crows. The goddamn crows, swirling in a kind of pillar like a living dust-devil. They mostly faded into the night air. It was only by the reflected light from their eyes and beaks and feathers that he saw them at all. Some landed to make a stab at hunting around in the grass, then took off again. Others just wheeled around, spying for some invisible carcass.

He held very still for a long time, but they didn't go away.

There you is, he thought at last, careful to watch them only sidewise. *It figgers that the minute I sit down to take a rest, you show up.*

The birds on the ground seemed to regard him curiously, cocking their heads up and down and letting out little *graaaks*. But they didn't stop in their rounds for long.

You worrry me, he went on in his mind. *Might as well. Time to call and turn the cards over. Know why? For one thing, you ain't even a real crow-spirit. I've met lots of those. They answer when I talk to 'em. Fact I can never get 'em to shut up.*

"Real crow-spirits also shit. Voluminously. Ask the statues." This was a strange voice to the left of him, low and husky. On its breath came the stink of oily water and clotted blood.

Oh sweet Jesus and Mother Moon. He buried his nose in his paws, but it was too late to block it out. And he knew the hunched mass was right beside him, so close he could feel the chill. She could lay a hand on him if she wanted, and if she did that he just didn't know what he'd do. Go plumb crazy, maybe. *You better not be what I think. Look, I tried to stop it. I tried, but I made the wrong choice. I'm sorry.*

"I tried, too," she said distantly. "For all I know, that was the problem, all of us trying. Maybe it was my fault. I pushed an inch further than I should have and that pushed the guy in front of me and that pushed the one in front of him, till there were just too many of us on one side of the pivot. I only wanted to save myself and my son. I didn't know."

You couldn't know, he moaned. *Please.*

"Neither could you," she said, and paused. "Still. Here you are, and you have to go on. It's out of my hands now at least. Maybe that means I've made my last mistake?"

He wanted to say something comforting, something to lay her to rest so she'd leave, but he couldn't sit under his own moon and lie. *Dunno,* he finally answered. *Prob'ly not.*

"I guess not. Or else I could find Tyler. I guess you haven't seen him," she added, not too hopefully. "He'd be in his car seat still. I didn't have time to unstrap him."

Mother and Father, lady. Please don't haunt me. I'm sorry, I'm sorry I'm not enough for all this, I'm sorry.... Wolves couldn't cry, and he needed to. Wolves could mourn their lost cubs, but they never learned regret. He couldn't hold on to this innocent skin. He felt it escaping from him, and yet the man-skin wouldn't feel any better, and the Gauru was no shape for doubt. There was no right shape, no answer. His bones and tendons melted and wrung themselves trying to find it anyway. He couldn't stop them.

A monumental creaking and ringing of metal—not unlike the sound of a major bridge failure—rose up behind him and the crows and the dead woman. He remembered what it must be just before they hove into sight, the Indian statues dismounting from their bronze horses. As he watched, their bronze Sioux-style headdresses shrank, changing into turbans. Their almost-naked bodies sprouted bronze buckskin leggings, bronze cloth shirts, bronze vests, bronze beaded necklaces. They walked forward into the shallows at the bank of the lake, becoming silhouettes in the moonlight, then stopped and turned west.

Another two figures appeared to face them—Heartsblood couldn't tell whom, but they wore white man's clothes. Items changed hands between the four. The Indians seemed to sign, or mark, a big roll of paper. Then the pairs paced past each other in opposite directions like they were about to start up a duel. But they never turned and fought. The Indians stumbled away, leaning on each other, and finally fell into the water. The white men just disappeared. The music and clapping and wolf-howls suddenly stopped.

"They don't remember," the dead woman said. "The statues I mean. Not really. It's just the crows have roosted on them so long, they believe they remember. They do this every night, and nobody sees. Except me, I've started coming to watch. Sometimes I think there's something I'm meant to do about it. I don't know what. It happened so long ago…." She trailed off. He thought she might disappear then, too, but no such luck.

"Sometimes, I think if I could help them I could save my little boy," she went on more quietly. "I think they must be appearing for a reason and the reason must have something to do with me. That's a stupid idea, I know."

He tried to put together a way to tell her—that she was both completely right and completely wrong—but he couldn't speak or even think straight anymore. The confusion of his own body swallowed him. If this was wisdom or Balance or whatall, then he'd been wrong to hunt it. It hurt. And it was too much to understand. Too much to bear. Too much to hold.

The flapping of cool, dark wings folded around him. The crows moved from their station beside him to surround him, lifting him and covering up his stunted nakedness. Whether they meant it as a mercy, he didn't know and didn't care. He just felt glad. So he wasn't the only one in pain and poisoned, the only one with too many souls crammed inside. Even if they tore him apart for learning it, he'd die with the satisfaction of knowing that much. For a plugged nickel, he would have joined them and turned into a carrion bird of ill omen himself.

He didn't know quite how he got home that night. It was possible the crows carried him there.

"So why do they want to meet at a funeral home? Pure creep factor?" Erik grimaced as he got out of the car and scanned the grounds. His nostrils flared, reluctantly taking in the odor of chemicals Heartsblood had looked up years back purely to have names for the unnamable: cadaverine, putrescine, adipocere, formaldehyde. The garlicky smell of old arsenic embalming fluid penetrated the softer rot of moss and loam. Even in human form, Uratha noses couldn't ignore the sheer mass of it.

Sarah Roark

Heartsblood shrugged. "Dunno. Nice and private, I guess. Ain't nobody gonna come callin' at this hour of the night."

"Oh? Think so?" Mercedes nudged him. Flashing lights approached up a far driveway, toward the back of the old frame house that towered over the private cemetery grounds. An ambulance and a police car, sirens silent.

"Well. Nobody alive anyway," he allowed.

A flare of orange cigarette ash glowed on the porch as they walked up the stone path. It was attached to the pale, spidery hand of a young man in loose jeans. He gave them a casual little wave, but his sweat smelled sour and nervous.

"You're in the right place," the man called. "Don't worry."

"You work here?"

"No, I work for the county medical examiner. But my master Dr. Poole runs this place and agreed to lend it to us for our meeting tonight. It's very well protected." He ground out the cigarette in an old-fashioned ashtray stand.

"Yer master." A weird phrase to be coming out of such a modern mouth. "Right nice of him, then."

"He's got his moments. I'm Gwyn. Don't know if Bai mentioned me."

"Heartsblood. Or you can call me Daniel. This is Mercedes, Erik, Anna, and Little Blue's our shaman. Which is why he's, uh, doin' that." Blue was deep in negotiations with an oak tree beside the path, tapping it threateningly with what looked like a big rib bone.

"Stands to reason. I know I'd be curious about one of your places. Come in."

"Everything all right?" Heartsblood nodded in the direction of the ambulance lights.

"Hm? Oh yeah. Just a delivery. It's not true what they say about death kindly stopping for anyone; it just keeps on trucking." He motioned them into the house and upstairs. Unlike the grounds, the house was almost sterile in its lack of smells. Not even lemon oil on the old furniture. Sample cremation urns, from the 'Dignity' model to the go-to-hell-just-for-wasting-money-on-it model, sat in the hall on pedestals. Each was neatly labeled with a price.

"I got donuts, and there's coffee over there, if you want a snack before we go inside." Gwyn opened up a set of double doors. They were the doors to a chapel, dimly revealed by stained-glass light from an upper window and fake gas-bracket lights. There was a bier, too, empty, but the space behind it bristled with potted plants. A stack of leaflets, a guestbook, and a photo of a smiling young woman on an easel stood up front.

"Dear Christ," muttered Erik.

"That's for a service tomorrow morning," Gwyn explained. "A little theatrical, I know. But this is a well-loved ritual space, so the point is once we shut the doors I can ward it nice and tight. Dr. Poole's only request is that nothing be disturbed. I'm sure even the dust has been arranged to his specifications, so try not to breathe too hard. Oh. Actually, there's a second request. Traditional among us so it goes without saying, but I don't know about you guys. No violence, at all, period, no matter what. If something happens, it's for the master of the house to decide how to handle it. I actually need your oath on that," he added apologetically.

"I promise, on behalf of myself and the pack," said Heartsblood in what he hoped was the proper solemn tone. He even put his right hand up.

Blue made a beeline for the refreshments in the reception room. Meanwhile, three figures stood up from the pews inside the chapel—Baihu, a stout black lady in a gray pantsuit, and a redheaded, freckled girl no bigger than Blue and not much older either, in a ribbed tank and denim skirt. They looked even less wizardly than Baihu or Gwyn did. But they showed no surprise at the Uratha's entrance or their names, and when the black lady opened her mouth, it was clear she was fully briefed.

"Welcome." Her handshake was crisp and cool. "I'm Tiaret. You know Baihu, and this is Glorianna, who's visiting from out of town but kindly offered to assist us. Wait a minute." She stopped in front of Mercedes. "You said Mercedes? I've seen your face."

"I don't know about your face, but…" Mercedes frowned. "Have we talked on the phone or something?"

"Possibly." The woman hesitated. Then she opened her mouth again, but Mercedes cut back in.

"You're with CPS! What is it, McSomething."

"McBride."

"Devlin case. They take him out of his stepfather's house where he is not being abused and put him in a foster home from which his mother kidnaps him." The Cahalith's voice rose. "Then when I call his caseworker, you're the only one who calls back, a month later."

"I'm afraid his caseworker was taking a long-overdue vacation at Tinley Park Mental Health." A calm blink behind thick eyeglasses.

"I guess that makes you the resident cleanup artist." Mercedes stepped forward and started to circle around, her eyes narrowing. Challenging gestures. Heartsblood tensed, unsure if the human woman was catching it. "But hold it. What's a magician doing in civil service? Can't you just turn lead into gold or whatever?"

"It's an excellent vantage point," Tiaret returned, stiffening. "Great suffering often awakens Arcane talent, especially in the young, and it's important that someone be there who knows what she's looking at." She paused again. "For what it's worth, I'm not one of your detractors at the agency. You do good work. Work that's all too often necessary."

"Especially when official channels fuck up."

"No argument here."

Always worth remembering that one way to win was to not play. Mercedes turned away, satisfied.

"On the phone, you mentioned…" Heartsblood decided to take charge of the conversation before somebody forgot who was alpha again. "Is he not comin'?"

"Your guess is as good as mine," said Baihu. "But it's getting late. We should probably get started, Gwyn."

"All right then. Last call for donuts." Gwyn waited gamely while Blue made one more quick trip out and back, then shut the doors. "No one touch the walls or doors." He put his hands up on the dried wreaths that decorated the upper panel of each door. They wriggled and sent out tendrils of thorns, which started to curl outward.

The opening notes of "Fly Me to the Moon" tinkled somewhere in the room. Baihu snorted. "Naturally. Hang on."

Gwyn straightened with an annoyed noise. The tendrils withered, decayed and blew away. Baihu flipped his cell phone open. "Hello? Yes. No, it's fine, that's how all Doc Poole's customers arrive. I'll meet you out front."

"Pasty made the scene after all?" Gwyn remarked as Baihu hung up.

"Yeah. Be right back. Talk among yourselves."

No one seemed eager to follow this advice.

"Well kick my ass," said Heartsblood after a long silence went by. "This is a Muskegon victim." He held up one of the flyers for the funeral service.

"Yes, she was, as is the new guest downstairs," said Gwyn quickly. "Twenty-two years old, tragic, please don't even touch those."

"Oh shit." Heartsblood replaced it as near as he could. "I'm a lunkhead. We can sit down though?"

"The pews are fair game, yes…" The mage stopped mid-sentence as the door opened and Baihu came in with a skinny little weed of a young man. Or something man-shaped, anyway. In the fluorescent glare from the outer room, his skin was a jaundiced off-white (the 'gaslight' of the chapel was a lot kinder), and dark smudges circled his eyes. He smelled of limestone, mold, and dust. Under that was something a little like shellfish blood. Grampa'd always insisted you could know a vampire by that odor, but the few Heartsblood had ever run into had been too full of human blood for him to tell. Something had ripped a gash in the sleeve of the vampire's leather jacket and several holes in his shirt, too. That was where the blood-smell wafted most strongly.

"Except for you," Gwyn finished. "What the hell happened? Trouble on the way here?"

"Nah, I just got the message late. I had to—I, uh, had my cell phone off. Sorry." The vampire stuck his hands in his pockets. He started edging fitfully around the room, almost tripped over the girl's photo stand because he was too busy watching the rest of them, jumped, and scooted even further around. Heartsblood felt the other Uratha contract around their alpha. He had to resist the urge to fall back into beta position behind Mercedes himself.

"Well, just don't get mud anywhere. I won't be responsible for the results, safe conduct or no. Folks, this is Loki. He's a, a representative as I understand it, of the, er…"

"Kindred," the vampire supplied.

"Right. The Kindred of Chicago."

"You look like you been rode hard and put up wet," Heartsblood commented. He kept his distance though. No need to get on the critter's nerves. "You quite sure everythin's all right?"

Loki gave him a wet-cat look. "You're sure as hell not local."

"No, Heartsblood's from out East," Mercedes said. "But he's with a pack of… well, they've got a good reputation back home. And he's come specifically to help with this."

"Yeah. And these are the Haunts, a pack with a good reputation here." Heartsblood gestured around. "Mercedes, Erik, Little Blue. And this here's Anna."

"Pack?" Loki chuckled with a shrug. "Interesting way to put it." Then he squinted at them again, and his mouth dropped open, tiny triangles of white already showing under his chapped lip. "Fuck. Fucking shit."

In an instant, he was clear across the room, as far away as he could get without actually flying through the wall.

"You didn't say that! You didn't fucking mention!" He flung an accusing finger at the frowning mages. "You set me up, you motherfuckers!"

"Loki," Gwyn said loudly, "if you're gonna tell us werewolves are the freakiest or the scariest thing you've ever met, especially this week, I'm going to let Glory here stick another stake in you for pure mercy's sake. Stop being a pussy."

"Gentlemen," began Tiaret icily.

"Use that word again," interrupted Glorianna, "and I'll show—"

"Pussy, hell. You left out a relevant fucking detail!" Loki snarled at Gwyn.

"I left out a relevant detail," said Baihu. "Yes. I'm sorry. But frankly, we were already worried enough that you might decline, and we do need your help."

"Just hold on, son." Heartsblood felt dumb the second he heard himself saying it, but he was Elodoth and somebody was panicking. Instinctively, he held his hands up, palms out. "Nobody's here to do anything but talk. You got no call to worry."

"Exactly," Tiaret agreed. "This is a situation that affects all of us, Loki. We've all got a piece of this problem, and I personally believe our best hope lies in putting the pieces together." She crossed her arms. For some reason, that triggered a shift in the vampire's posture. He uncoiled a little.

"Besides," she added, "the nonaggression pledge binds all of us while we're under this roof, and our host is not a magus to be trifled with. Therefore, there will not be so much as a whisper of the word 'stake' or anything else even slightly similarly discomfiting, is that clear? Gwyn?"

"Just trying to calm him down," the other mage shrugged, making a piss-poor stab at an injured look.

"Well, that was a pretty spectacular failure, even for your social skills. Let's proceed."

Gwyn put his fingers into the wreaths on the doors again. This time, the twisting vines spread fast and wide, looping around the chapel and meeting themselves in a huge knot over behind the empty bier. Heartsblood also saw the vines reach out to gently touch a couple of small hexagonal mirrors set up on stands on the side cabinets in the room. Baihu's work probably.

"There. Protections are up." Gwyn sat down, already looking a little winded. "Who's going to do the honors?"

"Well." The girl Glorianna stood with a pile of stapled papers in her hand. It was supposed to be a businesslike tone, but Heartsblood couldn't help thinking of a high school kid about to deliver a book report. "Let's distribute the handouts first. This is a comprehensive analysis of the Muskegon virus. As you'll see, it's pretty apparent that the new strain circulating is not a normal mutation."

"And that tells us...?" Mercedes puzzled over her copy, flipping the pages. Heartsblood read biology books and articles all the time, but even he got lost in the flood of fifty-cent words and strange diagrams.

"What the hell is a 'gnomonic autonymic/antinomic elaboration'? Don't make a lick of sense."

"That's just what it means," Gwyn said. "Something that both feeds on itself and generates itself, which doesn't make any sense. According to natural law, it shouldn't exist. The point is that it couldn't have gotten that way by accident. Somebody's deliberately twisted it, made it a hundred times more virulent."

"How? Genetics?" Heartsblood was trying to figure out one of the graphs but just staring at it gave him a pain in the left temple.

"Not unless you're talking about a geneticist who also happens to be a major Adept of the forces of life and death."

"Then this falls on your doorstep," Anna realized.

"It might," Glorianna admitted. "We're not aware of any other way such a thing could be done, though we're obviously open to suggestions. But it was done with purpose. Specifically altered not only to be more deadly, but to spread more easily through more vectors—including supernatural ones. That's on top of the old vectors of mosquitoes and crows."

"Yeah, the crows, that's the key," blurted Heartsblood. "The Murder of Crows."

The vampire, who'd been slogging through the handout like everybody else, looked up. His gaze narrowed on Heartsblood, the instant pupil-adjustment of a carnivore. "What do you know about the crows?"

The look made Heartsblood skittish, but the words were encouraging. "You noticed 'em, too?"

"I know there's some spooky-ass crows around lately, and they love dropping dead on my balcony. You got an explanation?"

"They're the ones trying to warn us." Weeks of observations jostled in Heartsblood's mouth, refusing to come out in order. "I mean *it* is, the Murder is. I guess it ain't so much warn as—well, it's what they are. They can't even help it."

"Okay, that was persuasive," remarked Anna. He glared at her. She put a sly hand to her mouth. Irraka.

"Shit. It's like a rash, all right? You scratch at it and scratch at it and all you're doin' is spreadin' it around, but the rash can't help it. It's immunological, y'know what I mean?"

"The rash is just the symptom." Baihu came to his rescue, Mother bless him. "The real problem is underneath."

"Perzactly. I mean exactly." He turned to the Asian sorcerer excitedly. "See, they came to me last night. I finally understood. It ain't like a regular spirit. I don't even know what it is, but it's always been here. This is its home. And anytime somethin' happens, somethin' bad I mean, why the crows take it up. They try to take up all the carrion, but there's too much. They been takin' it up and takin' it up till they're full to the gullet and can't hold any more. For Chrissake, you were there, you know what I'm talking about."

A weird silence fell.

"Yes," said Baihu finally. "It's really hard to explain, especially in a way that doesn't make you sound crazy. But there's a… force of some kind. And the crows are its way of manifesting, expressing. And it's in pain."

"And it's supposed to be here," Heartsblood added.

"Wait. I thought we were supposed to stop it," Erik argued.

"We are! Just not the way I thought."

"It is supposed to be here." Baihu spoke slowly, in counter to Heartsblood's frantic spouting. "But it's not supposed to be this way. Something went wrong. Now it's trying to right things as best it can, but, uh, let me see if I can put it into words. It is kind of like an immune response, in that it can go overboard. It can kill the host trying to cure it."

"Like the encephalitis." Heartsblood tapped the handout. "It's the inflammation that squeezes their brains to death. We got to bring the inflammation down."

At least now he had company. The rest were staring at Baihu the way they'd stared at him.

"Great," said Gwyn. "So the crows aren't the enemy, but they might kill us anyway, so we have to figure out what's bothering them and stop it?"

"Yes."

"Anybody else awed at the sense of progress?"

"Well." Loki hesitated. "Actually, we might be getting somewhere now. If we can figure out what set it off the last time."

"Last time?" Glorianna reached into her backpack. She took out a shiny PDA and a foldable keyboard, plugged them together and started clattering on the keys.

"Yeah. This has happened before. You guys don't know anything about it?" The vampire looked around. He straightened, plainly satisfied now that he had something they didn't. "Eighteen seventy-one. The Great Fire. Weird shit went on back then, too, and a lot of it had to do with crows."

Heartsblood nodded. "Yep. The Fire's part of it, too, I just ain't figgered out how."

"Care to expand on the phrase 'weird shit'?" Gwyn prompted.

The vampire thought. "Well, lots of fires, a couple a day, 'cause of the drought. Lots of violence. I guess that's not too weird by itself, but then the crows were acting up as well, and some really bizarre rumors floating around. Slaughtered livestock standing back up. More hauntings than usual. Black feathers appearing out of nowhere, and I know that's happening again—"

"The black feather rain," blurted Heartsblood. Baihu actually stumbled when he said that, and Gwyn looked like somebody had slapped him.

"That's right," Baihu said a bit faintly. "Black feather rain on a dead city."

"And the Maynard party," Loki finished.

"Maynard?"

"Maynard, Maynard. That rings a bell." Mercedes broke in. "I think Sarah's mentioned it. But it was back before any of us were born." She gave the vampire a wary look. "Something to do with somebody finding out too much. The People almost being discovered."

"Everything almost being discovered," Loki corrected her. "Us, you, you guys, everything that goes bump in the night. Maynard knew, and he tried to expose us. Most people didn't believe him, of course, but he did wind up with followers. According to the journal, they kept on even after he left, headed up by some witch-hunter named Talley."

"But what's that got to do with anything?" Anna demanded.

"Well, that's the thing. You know how everybody says it was Mrs. O'Leary's cow that started the fire?"

Heartsblood grinned. "The one who winked her eye and said—?"

"It's gonna be a hot time in the old town tonight," several people finished together in several different keys.

"Fire! Fire! Fire!" Blue was the last one to quit.

"Okay, I was born here, I know the fucking song!" Loki snarled, throwing Blue a baleful look. Didn't care much for the word fire, obviously. "It's still bullshit. We can't know for sure what started it. But there was a lot of talk that maybe it was Maynard's people. Purifying the city or some shit, trying to kill all of us."

"You're saying you think that's what's going on?" Anna looked askance at him. "Some kind of supernatural holocaust? Come on. It's not like you people are gonna die of the virus. Fire, yes."

"What I'm a little surprised Loki hasn't explained yet," Tiaret said, "is that the Kindred community is very worried about this virus. Not that it could kill them, but that it could expose them. We're not kidding about a supernatural vector. Vampiric transmission is more than likely responsible for some of these deaths. It's certainly not in the interests of the Kindred to let such a thing go on. Am I right, Loki?"

"Yeah," he said. He looked from her to Anna. "That's right. We got as much interest in stopping this thing as anybody."

"You're still not gonna die of it."

"Hey, if what Miss Genius says is right, we don't even know that for sure—"

"You said according to the journal." Erik sat heavily down on a pew. "What journal?"

"Oh, yeah, sorry. That's where I got all this. It belonged to a Kindred named Dr. Nicholas Crain, he was in the city at the time."

"So this isn't personal recollection?" Mercedes asked.

"What?" He blinked. "Oh. No, I'm not that old."

"And Dr. Crain isn't around anymore, I take it."

"Nah, he's long since ash."

"Too bad," said Gwyn. "Be nice if we could talk to somebody who survived."

Oh yeah, nice little chat, thought Heartsblood, but then another thought interrupted. "That reminds me. Hang on." He picked up the duffel bag he'd brought along and rummaged through it. "If you do know somebody real old, we might could ask 'em about this here thing. I got it off a spirit we fought near one of the sewer grates down our way. It, uh, vomited it up."

"Vomited?" Loki grimaced.

"That spirit vomited up a whole lot of crap," Mercedes said.

"Yeah, but this is the only thing I stubbed my toe on." He held up the plastic baggie with the antique blotter in it. The skinny vampire gave him a blank look, so he glanced at Baihu instead. "Look-a here, I bagged it. See? I learn quick."

Baihu took it gingerly. "What is it?"

"It's an ink blotter. Britanniaware, made between eighteen thirty-eight and eighteen forty-five by Du Bois & Smith. I looked it up."

"Nasty." But then Loki got up on his toes. "Tilt it forward a bit, there's something on the top."

"A monogram. Couldn't figger out whose."

"NTC… Nicholas T. Crain!" Loki exclaimed. "It's in the journal, too, the bookplate."

"I'll be dipped in shit," said Heartsblood proudly. Vindication at last.

"Well." Baihu took a pair of gloves out of his shoulder bag and removed the thing from the baggie. The smell came out in a wave. Even the mages noticed. Their noses wrinkled anyway. "I don't know much about antiques, but this thing's survived a long time, given where it's been. Probably a lot longer than it should have."

"And that." Loki pointed to the handle's snake-design. "That's… well, that's a Kindred thing. That symbol."

Baihu rubbed at it with his gloved thumb. "We might be able to get something off it with proper examination. I think this is soot."

"Yeah." Heartsblood nodded. "I can't smell much on it but spirit-bile, but I was hopin' you people had your own ways."

"Well, that is freaky." Glorianna stepped closer. "But why's it showing up now?"

"Crain knew something was coming," said Loki. "The journal made that real clear. Whatever this Murder of Crows thing is, he was on to it, and there was something he meant to do about it. Only I don't think he ever got the chance before the Fire broke out."

"Specify, Loki," Tiaret said. He got a cagey look on his face.

"Like a ritual," he said. "Maybe a sacrifice. I dunno. He and a few others created this Society of the Crow, and he mentioned somebody being in it who wasn't Kindred."

"Maybe these Maynard people infiltrated them?" Mercedes suggested.

"No, no. I think it was a magician actually. He gave Dr. Crain the journal to start with." Heartsblood smiled at Baihu. "Ball's back in y'uns' court."

Baihu frowned. "This magician have a name?"

"I found a weird gizmo with the journal, too," Loki went on. "Like a pocket watch, only it was wrong inside. It had some kind of writing on it, and an extra hand, I don't know what for."

"A watch?" said Gwyn suddenly.

"A name," repeated Baihu. "Even a shadow name."

"I'm thinking." The vampire snapped his fingers. "Aristede. That was his name, the guy who gave Crain the book, 'cause he signed it on the front page."

"Aristede!" Tiaret and Gwyn stared at each other.

Anna jumped practically out of her skin, then shot them a resentful look. "Spiral-cut Jesus on rye. Don't *do* that."

"You know the man?" Heartsblood interrupted.

Tiaret ignored him. "Are you absolutely certain of that name, Loki?"

"Yeah. I told you, it was right in the book."

Gwyn waved an irritated hand at Tiaret. "Know him? He's my great-granddad—well, mystically speaking. His apprentice became my mentor's mentor."

"So you're heir to his teachings," Mercedes said.

"Exactly. Aristede was one of the most influential magi in the city, at least till he vanished mysteriously in the Fire, quote-unquote. Like a number of us."

"Yeah, we had some convenient disappearances ourselves," Loki offered. "Anyway. There was one thing on the watch I could read, dates in French. Twenty-seven July eighteen seventeen to fourteen October eighteen seventy-one. The rest was gibberish."

"Well, shit. Then he knew."

"Knew?"

"The day of his death. It's not uncommon, at least among my kind, to have some vague inkling of how or when. For the lucky few, it's not at all vague." Heartsblood slipped Gwyn a questioning look at that. The bastard gave a thin smile back that translated as *wouldn't you like to know.*

"And he had it put on his watch?" Anna snorted. "Talk about morbid. No offense."

"None taken."

"Didja say where you found this book?" Heartsblood asked. He knew the answer was no. It was just a polite Southern beat-around-the-bush. Even so, the vampire hunched his shoulders.

"It was with a corpse," he finally said. "Buried in the woods. There was a whole chest of books, but I only took the one. And the watch-thing."

The mages exchanged glances. "Could you be a bit more exact? Which woods?" Glorianna asked. She was already getting out her little doodad.

"The forest preserves. Not sure exactly where. I only found it because the fucking crows chased me right into the hole. But somebody'd already dug it up. No idea who."

Heartsblood pondered that. "Now I admit, I'm not up on these things, but it ain't usual for folks who die in city fires to go traipsin' off to the woods miles off to get buried, is it?"

"No, not generally," agreed Gwyn. "Besides, if he did die on the fourteenth, that's a couple days after the Fire ended."

"Was this body burnt up?"

Loki shook his head. "Didn't look it to me. Nothin' left but bones and the chest."

Anna put in, "Well, more to the point, somebody buried him. And his stuff."

"Flammable stuff, too. So it wasn't just vampires taking advantage of the Fire to do some dirty work." Loki smiled grimly.

"Especially since his house did burn down." Baihu looked to Gwyn. "We could visit the site of the house, see if there are echoes of foul play there."

Something new had occurred to Heartsblood. "You said the crows was chasin' you," he started.

The vampire nodded. "Yeah. Ghost crows. Damned things."

"So there must be somethin' you're meant to do. 'Course, this could be it right here. But somehow you're a part of it."

"Part of what?"

"Why, all this. The reckoning that's come—home to roost, you could say. I just wish I knew what I was doin' in it," he added ruefully. "I'm not even from here."

"Great." The vampire crossed his arms. "Perfect. So what, do we need to do some kind of ritual like the journal was talking about…?"

"Hold the phone." Mercedes' eyes widened. "We're jumping from like D to Z here. Ritual?"

"It wasn't real clear," Loki said. "They were going to do a sacrifice… someone had even volunteered. But the shit hit the fan before they were ready, I think."

"And what was that supposed to do?"

"What, like I would know? Calm it down, I guess. Like throwing a virgin in the volcano."

"And, for all we know, just as effective," Tiaret said.

"Well." Loki shrugged. "They never got to do it."

"Dunno 'bout a virgin sacrifice, but the Murder sure wants something." Heartsblood looked at Baihu. "Otherwise, it wouldn't be tryin' so hard to get ahold of us."

"They could just be spontaneous broadcasts," Gwyn mused. "A thing in pain will scream whether anyone's there to hear or not."

"No, it's been speakin' right to me. Besides—" He cast his arms around him. "I refuse to believe I got called from halfway 'cross the continent to be here for somethin' I can't do nothin' about!"

"That's a stupid idea, I know." He put the ghost-woman's voice out of is head as quickly as it came in.

"Well, at least we know your bias right from the start," Gwyn began. Erik snorted. Heartsblood started toward the skinny magus, but Baihu stopped him.

"I'm—inclined to agree with Heartsblood, actually," he said. "Aristede was a practical man living in a profoundly unsentimental town. If he thought the Murder would respond to propitiation, then he must have had reason."

"But what kind of propitiation?" Tiaret scrutinized Loki. "I don't suppose I could get a look at this journal."

"Already handed it all over," Loki mumbled.

"Of course."

"Look." Mercedes had sat down again. "Let's start putting things together. Okay, you guys said you think the virus is being manipulated by a magician. That's bad. Then we've definitely got somebody poisoning kids."

Glorianna nodded. "Actually, Baihu thinks it's the same person."

"I didn't sleepwalk into that murder scene by chance," Baihu said uncomfortably. His gaze unfocused. "I was meditating on the disease spell, the shape of it. Kind of a double-scroll. Maybe the eyes of a dolmen deity or the roll of the Severn Bore as it passes into Annwn…. After a while, I didn't know whether I was moving or it was. Talk about an uneasy chair."

"It reminded me of the strange attractor generated by Chua's circuit." He seemed to have pulled Glorianna into a trance with him. "Fractally self-similar, but then it rolled in on itself, another spiral."

"Keep it undergraduate, people," Gwyn murmured. "And let's stay off the spirals right now."

Baihu shook himself. "Apologies. The point is, I started walking its contours, and it bodily led me to that alley. So if it's two magi, they're working in such close concert that their workings interconnect as though they were one. Which is rare."

"You guys are talking about the high-schoolers who poisoned themselves a few nights back," Loki said. "Not a mass suicide then?"

"No," echoed back from more than one direction.

"All right then," Mercedes said. "So one guy, even better. One magician poisoning kids and dabbling in bioterrorism and who knows what else."

"Yes." Glorianna fidgeted with her handout, rolling it into a tight tube. "*Why* is a whole different question."

"No, I'm sure it's a very related question."

"I'm sure it is," the girl snapped back. "I'm perfectly willing to believe it's all connected. I just don't see quite how yet. It's just a big mess, one problem after another."

"Then maybe that's the point," Mercedes said. "Maybe it doesn't even matter what it is as long as it causes pain and death and strife, in this world, the spirit world, either, both. You heard Heartsblood. The more suffering happens, the closer this thing gets to… conflagration. Whatever. Maybe not another Great Fire but something just as bad." She must have seen the grateful look dawning on Heartsblood's face, because she scowled. "Well, we're all here, we might as well try to figure this shit out."

"And what good is that?" Glorianna argued. "I mean why would somebody want that?"

"Because it's what they want." Baihu said it like he was handing down the eleventh commandment, a harder edge in his voice than Heartsblood had heard yet. "There are two choices available to one who hates the world. Kill yourself or kill the world."

Glorianna paled.

"As much of it as you can, anyway," he finished. "Make no mistake. This is the work of a malice unfettered by reason. And it has found a perfect if unwitting partner in the Murder."

Loki cleared his throat (*weird thing for a vampire to do*, thought Heartsblood, *what could be stuck in there?*). "So what if we took down this troublemaker? Would that cure the virus?"

"No." Gwyn sounded totally sure of it. "At best, it might revert to normal encephalitis."

"Still. We take him down, and at least we don't have somebody poking this Murder with sharp sticks anymore, right? Buy us some time to figure out the rest. And if someone did have to be sacrificed, hey, kill two birds with one stone," Loki pointed out. "So to speak."

"You're one disturbing little white boy," muttered Mercedes.

Heartsblood was going over everything he could remember, everything everybody had said. "We got any kinda bead on this magician? Any good suspects?"

"Magus," said Tiaret. "And no. It's no one whose work we recognize."

"Then how do we find 'im?"

"Excellent question. In our case, we could track him down if we had something of his, a personal link."

"The bowl he used in the—" Heartsblood began, but Baihu shook his head.

"Must've had gloves on. No fingerprints, no psychic resonances except for the victims themselves."

"Well." He scratched at his stubble. "Shit. What about the virus itself? It's his in a way, ain't it?"

"Yyyyes," said Gwyn, "if we had live virus to work with. Unfortunately, what we've got is all inert. I don't know if it's the refrigeration that killed it or something more mystical, like the fact that the hosts have died."

"Yeah, but come on, there's a damn epidemic going. We can get us some live virus."

"Wait a minute." Glorianna roused at that. "You said the virus is inert either because the blood is cold or it's dead?"

"It's probably one or the other," Gwyn cautioned.

"Then how can vampires be transmitting it?" She gestured at Loki, who flinched. "Think about it."

"There must be some other kind of energy in vampire blood that sustains it."

"Kindred blood," corrected Loki.

"Sorry."

"No problem."

Heartsblood moved closer to the vampire. Anna did, too. He glanced uneasily at both of them but tried to stand his ground. "How ya doin?"

"Fine." Heartsblood didn't back off. "Just gettin' a better whiff."

"Yeah. Well. Enjoy."

"Enjoy ain't quite the word." Heartsblood let the scents completely sift out this time, not trying to name them till they'd all bloomed and died in his olfactory lobe. The wolf would tell him what he needed to know. Sure enough, a few patient seconds later, it did.

But the vampire's patience was out. "Then maybe you should give it a rest," he exploded.

Heartsblood grunted. "I was wonderin' earlier why you got scared when you saw that girl's picture. And just now when Glorianna pointed at you, you got scared again."

"Get out of my face," the boy snarled. "Or I'll show you scared."

"It does smell different in your blood, the virus. I didn't pick it out till just now." The other Haunts read the change in the tilt of Heartsblood's shoulders and head and went on alert, ready to follow his cue. No, he wasn't the scared one. For once, the pack was with him.

"I don't have the fucking virus!"

"You have it and what's more, you know you have it." Anna's yellow teeth were locked in a wide grin, but her eyes were hard and bright. "I should've known one of you motherfuckers wouldn't dare come to something like this alone. But you've got a good reason to. If the others find out you're the carrier your ass is grass, isn't it? How many have you infected? You even keep count?"

Tiaret was the first mage to get her tongue back. "The pledge," she reminded them severely. There was a waver in it though.

"We ain't touchin' him," Heartsblood said. It didn't come out too gently. He was top dog in the room for the moment, and he knew it. "We're all here to share information, right? That's all I want."

"Lick me," was the vampire's response.

"No thanks."

"Mr. Fischer." Tiaret maneuvered herself into one of the pews. "Loki, that is. Loki. First of all, language."

"Like it matters," Loki retorted.

"If this is true—"

"Of course it's true! Just look at him," Gwyn said.

"This new strain is extremely infectious." She was choosing her words less nimbly than usual. "Anyone you used for sustenance, anyone, however healthy."

"You think I don't know that?" He finally looked at the girl's picture full on, a hostile glare, and turned back to Tiaret. "What am I supposed to do? You have any idea what happens when we don't eat? How the hell do you think this works?"

Tiaret rubbed her forehead.

"So you recognize this girl." Gwyn moved toward the picture, as though to protect it. "Because you infected her. Good God, Anna's right. How many has it been?"

"I didn't know!" the vampire fairly howled. "I swear to Christ I didn't, not till just the other night. I, I don't even know how I got it."

"Oh yeah? And whose death was it that finally tipped you off?" Gwyn's voice rose. "If your memory needs jogging, I could go get my files. We've been pretty busy down at the morgue lately."

"This is going nowhere useful." Tiaret left off massaging her head. "Enough. We don't have all night here, especially not if we're going to do something, and I do suggest doing something. Loki."

The vampire looked to her.

"I am going to assume that your... status as a carrier only sharpens your motivation to solve this whole problem. It certainly sharpens mine."

"Yeah," he said, subdued. "Yeah, it does."

"Then you are still willing to help us, and help yourself in the process."

"Hell, yes. I don't want this. Believe me, I don't."

"I believe you." She gathered herself. "In that case, what we need from you is a sample of your blood. Hopefully, what Gwyn said will hold true, and the virus will live long enough for us to try to track it to its source."

"All of us," Heartsblood asked, "or you mean just y'uns?"

"I mean a working," she said at once. "Just myself and my colleagues here."

"Well." He considered whether that was worth a tussle. "Fine. But I wanna know what happens. We ain't half bad trackers ourselves. You figure out where this guy is, we'll help you run 'im to ground. I'm determined to do whatever I can."

"Understood." Tiaret nodded tersely. Then she turned back to the vampire. "I can assure you, Loki, that we'll get to the bottom of this quickly as we possibly can. What I hope you'll provide us with in return is a modicum of trust, and—and patience."

"Patience?" Loki echoed. He took a couple of seconds to translate that. When he did, disbelief flooded his face. "What're you saying? Don't feed?"

"I'm saying… hold out for as long as you safely can. Yes. And if you can't, then let us know. We can make arrangements."

Heartsblood tried to seriously picture Loki squeezing out one of those blood-donation bags into a glass and drinking it. Fat chance—from everything he'd ever heard, vampire bloodthirst made Uratha stalking look downright tame. But he guessed it didn't hurt for her to try.

"Are we agreed?" she asked.

Loki looked like he didn't know whether to run, shit, or go blind. He darted a quick testing glance at the assembled pack, then at the mages. His shoulders fell.

"If I say yes, you'll take my word? No tailing me, no staking me and saying it's for my own good, no turning me in?"

She relaxed, too. It wasn't till she relaxed that Heartsblood realized how tensed up she'd been. "I agree. Heartsblood?"

"If that's the deal, that's the deal." Heartsblood shrugged. "Long as everybody stays square, you'll get no problems from us."

"Yeah? What about the rest of you?" Loki said warily.

"His word goes for the pack." It was an unexpected burst of loyalty from Erik, who unfolded to full height beside both his old alpha and his temporary one. Well, he was Rahu after all. Even the vampire seemed to sense that, sense what it meant.

"Got it." Nope, no more argument from that boy.

Loki stepped uneasily toward Tiaret.

"Okay," he said. "Shoulda known this wouldn't be over till I opened a vein. Where do you want me?"

Step on a crack, break your mother's back. He hopped from one sidewalk block to the next. Hard on the ankles. The cracks were getting awful close together, and where was the stupid general store? He knew damn well it was still there selling Spam and foam beer cozies with OLD SMOKEY printed across them and 'hillbilly shot mugs' made of bark, and if he just went inside this time and asked Mr. Tyburn to use the phone, then none of it would happen. After what seemed like forever, he finally reached the store's dirt parking lot and ran in the doors crying with relief. But it was pitch-dark inside, and something reached out to grab him, threw him down on the dusty tile floor.

"What happened happened," it growled. He tried to scream, but it put a stinking hand over its mouth. A hundred more hands took hold of him.

We're with you forever, was the sound that the scrabbling of the hands formed. One of the world's more perverse creators had ordained that even things with no mouths could speak the First Tongue, but he wished it wasn't so, he wished it in vain. We're yours forever. Can you carry us forever, Daniel?

No, he screamed through the rotting fingers. No, go away, stop it, leave me alone.

They chittered, clicking their fingernails together. He knew with the surety of dream-wisdom that it was their way of laughing.

What will you give us? they asked.

"Anything," he sobbed. He woke up sobbing it. "Anything."

Eric half-rose up on his futon, leaning on an elbow. His eyes pierced Heartsblood through.

"Anything? Anything what?"

Heartsblood turned on his bedroll. It was good to have Uratha bodies around him when he woke now at least, even if they were the wrong bodies. "Nothing. Nightmare."

"If you say so."

"I wake you up?"

"No."

"You wanna drink?"

Eric considered. "Yeah, sure."

"Scotch, straight?"

"Works."

Heartsblood got up, twisting his boxers back around frontways, and went in the kitchen. He got out the shot glasses and poured. The phone was in his other hand and he was dialing before he even realized it. He blinked and stopped one number short, argued with himself, then delivered himself up to fate and finished.

"Hello?" The voice that answered was so raw and suspicious he barely recognized it.

"Isaac? I mean Baihu."

"Yes. Daniel?"

"I—thought I better check on y'uns. Sorry if I woke you up. How'd it go? The, uh, tracking. It's been two days, I figger you musta tried by now. Did ya?"

"It's four AM."

"I know. But did ya?" He waited. And waited.

"Yes. It… ah… it didn't quite go as planned."

"What's that mean?" He wondered if it'd be jumping to conclusions to ask if everybody was still alive.

"It means," the mage said tightly, "that we still don't know who it is."

"All righty then." He tried to put the bottle up quietly. "So now what?"

"We haven't decided."

"Well, we got to try somethin' else. We can't let up."

"Agreed." A sigh. "Sorry. Well, Glorianna wants to do some more research and Jason left. Probably headed back to the morgue."

"The morgue?"

"Yeah. Maybe there's something on the victims, I don't know. It's a long shot, but at least they've been preserved for evidence. Maybe that's what he's thinking."

"Well." Heartsblood didn't much like the idea of a morgue at four AM, but hell. "I could help with that. You know. I pick things up, especially by smell."

"I wouldn't vouch for Gwyn's state of mind just now. I wouldn't vouch for any of us." Another sigh. "Gah. Never mind me. Look, I don't guess you're afraid of facing possibly lethal levels of snark, so do what you want. His cell is 773-555-9970."

"Thanks. I 'preciate that. I don't think I'm gonna be able to get back to sleep anyways."

"And I do appreciate your help, even if I don't sound like it right now. I've got to go try to get some rest."

"Okay then. You sleep tight." Heartsblood started to hang up.

"Heartsblood—" The voice from the phone suddenly shifted from weary to anxious. Heartsblood brought it back to his ear.

"Yeah?"

"My granny."

"Your granny?"

"She, ah. She died today."

"Oh." He blinked. He vaguely recalled Baihu starting to say something about his granny the night they met, but he couldn't remember what. There was a strange note in the man's voice. "Shit. I'm real sorry to hear that, Baihu. Real sorry. What was her name now?"

"Xiao-Chen Tsu."

"Well, I'll tell you what, I'll get down on my knees and pray for her, pray she finds her way to wherever she wants to go. 'Kay?"

He wasn't sure whether the quiet on the other end of the line was a good thing or not. "Werewolves pray?"

"Shit, everybody prays at least once." *(What will you give us?)*

"True. Who answers is what differs, I guess. G'night, Daniel."

"Night, night." He hit the button, downed his shot, and picked up the other glass to take to Erik. He'd meant to wash his clothes before wearing any of them again, but hell with it. Any mage who moonlighted at the morgue couldn't be too prissy.

"Don't touch anything," were Gwyn's only words at the door as he let Heartsblood in.

"You say that a lot," Heartsblood commented.

"I trust I don't need to explain why."

"I do watch *CSI* y'know."

"Great." Heartsblood followed the man obediently through two or three keycard doors, until they came to a cool, dark room with a wall of metal lockers along one side and several standing rolling fridges, some of which were plugged into outlet strips.

"Yeah, we've had to break out the portables. One wonders how close we are to tripping the building's circuit breakers. Over here." He ushered Heartsblood into the next room. Three bodies lay naked on examining tables, a boy and two girls, all unfortunately familiar. They all had big Y-shaped cuts on the fronts of their bodies that had already been sewn up. Beside them sat plastic bags holding their clothes. There wasn't even a cloth over their privates or anything.

"Goddamn. Can't think what it was like for the families."

Gwyn snorted. "Feel sorry for the families of the bridge victims. We had to ask a lot of 'em whether they wanted to be notified every time we found a body part, or just the first time. These kids—well, let's just say I've been where they were and worse, and at least I never stooped to hexes. If their little hedge-witching had gone the way they meant it to, the only change would be I'd have a different pile of corpses. Okay. I got out what seemed to be the most promising of the subjects. I'll open the clothing bags first. You let me know if you run across anything unexpected, anything you don't remember being at the scene, et cetera."

He pulled on purple latex gloves. He already had a splash apron and shoe bags on. He offered the glove box to Heartsblood, who shook his head. Then he started opening up the bags one by one.

"No. There's vomit, but I guess you know that. Oh. Shit. This 'un was pregnant."

Gwyn nodded. "Yeah, I'm glad I don't have to be the one to tell her parents. And this is the boy."

Heartsblood put his nose as close as he dared, then stood back to sneeze in the opposite direction. "'Scuse me," he said. "I need to… hang on."

Quicker to just do than to explain. He let himself move toward the wolf, just a little. Stiff hair prickled and muscles strained under his clothes. He saw Gwyn step back uneasily. The smells sharpened and deepened further in his changing nostrils.

"Gimme the girls' bags again."

Gwyn had a question in his eyes, but he didn't ask it, just obeyed.

"Nope. It ain't neither of them."

"What's not either of them?"

"There's a tiny little bit of perfume on his stuff. Not aftershave, perfume. And female scent. But it ain't from these two."

"Oh? Well, hang on." He went out into the fridge room and came back with some more bags. "These belonged to the other girls."

Heartsblood lingered over each of them. He wanted to be sure. Finally, he shook his head again.

"Nope. It wasn't none a'them."

"You're absolutely sure?"

"Pretty sure."

"Then there's a living girlfriend. Not unlikely, I guess. I don't have their police files right here. Maybe Glory can track them down."

Heartsblood was already approaching the boy's cool corpse, slowly, as if he could still take fright and leap away.

"Don't," Gwyn yelped as he saw Heartsblood reach out.

"Well, all right!" Heartsblood snapped. Preservative and germicide odors made him irritable. "Then you handle him."

"Handle him how? Dear God, you're not serious." But Gwyn talked more squeamish than he acted. He lifted the boy's scrotum, pulling the penis back and forth so that Heartsblood could check it out without contaminating it.

"Y'uns get anything off it?" he asked the mage.

"The girls were checked for assault, so we know none of them had sexual contact prior to the poisoning. I don't remember about the boys. Lemme look…. " Gwyn went over to the computer on the counter, took off his gloves, and started typing.

"Well, this boy sure had some major contact, and it wasn't with none of these gals."

"Here we go. The boys were checked for anal assault, all negative. Nothing about consensual sex." He chuckled. "Obviously been a while since high school for this prosector. I can take a swab, maybe get some epithelial cells. Erm. Before I do that… I don't suppose you could give an estimate of how long ago?"

"Well." Heartsblood circled around. "I can't give you nothin' exact. But… wait a sec. Hard to talk and scent at the same time."

"Take your time."

"It can't have been much 'fore he died," he said after a minute. "'Cause the front part of his hair smells more like shampoo than skin oil, so he was fresh from a shower, and then the hanky-panky had to come after that, and he didn't get another chance to wash up."

"You said the front part of his hair." Gwyn pulled a notepad down from a shelf and scribbled in it.

"Back part smells like rainwater and concrete."

"Ah." The mage came back over, still scribbling. "Strange though. Not very good magical protocol. Even teen pagans should know it's better to abstain right before a major working."

"They should? Thought half the fun of bein' a witch was the sex orgies." Heartsblood shrugged at Gwyn's expression. "Well hell. Like you said, we ain't all forgotten high school. Maybe he was all set to abstain and the little head just took over."

"There is that, yes." The haughty look melted into musing. "He gets primped up for the ritual and then has sex… that suggests it most likely happened there at the scene or nearby, doesn't it, instead of earlier at a girlfriend's place or whatever. Which is suspicious. Everyone we know to have been in that alley is here. No survivors have come forward."

"Get his clothes out of the bag." Heartsblood nudged Gwyn's elbow. The man started. "Shit, sorry. Forget what I look like sometimes, I'm so used to it."

"It's not so much the look. It's more a feeling—never mind. Here." Gwyn got another pair of gloves and laid out the boy's clothes out on a metal table one by one. Heartsblood snuffled the front of the jeans. "And I think it's a sparkle on my personal halo that I'm not laughing hysterically while you do this."

"Shut up," Heartsblood growled. He knew exactly what the little fuck was thinking of. Gwyn fell silent.

Heartsblood straightened. The wolf gratefully slunk into its hiding place, taking its power and senses back with it. The mage watched the change with undisguised curiosity but still said nothing.

"He had her with his jeans on," Heartsblood reported. "Standin' up'd be my guess. Her legs were wrapped around him. I can't tell if he was leanin' on anything."

"Right. Again, that suggests it happened near the crime scene. Someplace you wouldn't want to lie down anyway. Maybe he showed up early, before the others. There was just enough time." Gwyn closed his eyes. His gloved hand went to rest lightly on the eyelids of the boy, thumb and middle finger. "Tell me again how they were."

"She was wrapped around him," Heartsblood said. "Just unzipped his fly and went. Prob'ly done before they barely started. I don't think—I don't think she was all that het up, actually. Maybe it was his idea."

Gwyn's head dipped and his jaw fell open. *"No, it wasn't,"* he croaked, and the voice wasn't his voice at all.

Heartsblood had to deny every instinct from the base of his spine up to not fling a dissection tray at the mage and bolt. He gripped the side of the examination table. It took him a good while to get any words out, to dare the possibility of those eyes opening and looking at him. Ghosts were tolerable on their own. When they took over living flesh, though, violated the boundaries of Shadow, that made Uratha skin crawl.

"It wasn't?" he managed finally.

"She said… would help." The eyes didn't open, but the throat and jaw labored, like they'd forgotten how to work and had to be forced. *"She said… I… too nervous…"*

"Baihu." Heartsblood had to make the call because Gwyn was in no shape. Or Heartsblood assumed so, anyway—he wasn't keen to find out. As soon as he'd come out of his medium trance, the mage had chased Heartsblood out of the autopsy rooms and shut the door, muttering something about "recovering himself." All Heartsblood knew was that locker doors were still opening and shutting in there.

"Daniel." Baihu sounded damn alert for a man who'd supposedly gone to bed an hour ago. "Something's happened?"

"Yes."

"Why are you whispering?"

"Uh. No reason. I just wanted you to know, Gwyn and I figgered out there was a woman at the poisoning. I mean who didn't die. The high priestess of the coven, he thinks. We didn't get no fingerprints or nothin' like that, but I know the smell of her now."

"Good. Actually Glorianna's been up all night in cyberspace with Watson, and that fits with her findings." Baihu stopped, yawned hugely, then went on. "Somebody was definitely playing mentor to these kids. Whetting their unhappiness, teaching them to work in circle. And both she and Tiaret are convinced they felt something feminine in the resistance we met when we tried to trace. Hold on."

There was the rustle of a hand going over a mouthpiece, muffled voices.

"You said you know her scent?"

"Yeah. He was able to get a few cells, not a lot to go from. But if I smell it again, I'll know it."

"Glorianna says she has an idea."

"You're hitchhiking on every source of input in the city now," Glorianna explained the next morning. She wound the cord around Heartsblood's ear and tucked in the hearing aid. It felt like a chigger burying itself in his flesh, like a live thing. He squelched a whimper. "Every ATM camera. Every radio antenna. Every phone line."

"Except none of those things can smell," he protested.

"It's synesthetic. Don't worry about it. The principle here is simple. Watson has the reach, you have the sensitivity."

Heartsblood sent a pathetic glance to Mercedes. She raised her eyebrows in a *Well, I'd sympathize if this wasn't all your fault* kind of look. Anna just laughed.

"Well, your gadget just better behave itself while it's plugged into me. No taking over my brain."

"Watson is a digital assistant," Glorianna said just a bit harshly. "He doesn't take over anything. He assists. Now relax, you're going to need to concentrate."

Heartsblood closed his eyes. "And do what?"

"Just… scent the air. See where it takes you."

Heartsblood stepped out the front door into the blistering sunlight bouncing off the white concrete of Gretchen's driveway. He breathed in. The air was hot on his lips, but it tingled on his palate like he'd just chewed a mint. The smells came in, and he barely had time to notice them before they were snatched away from him curiously, eagerly. Disturbing how ready the thing was to commandeer his senses, no matter what the girl said.

"No." He turned suddenly. "I don't like this. Not this way."

"Bullshit." Gwyn pushed in front of him. His eyes were red-rimmed, and he looked about as close to an animal as anyone who wasn't Uratha could. "Bullshit. Not after all this. You know what we've been through to get this far? All of us? What Bai's been through? Bai, tell him."

"I'm not going to tell him anything," Baihu said wearily. "It's up to him. Why waste energy?"

Heartsblood stood there with his ear feeling as though it were going to bleed any second, wanting to either rip out that wire or rip off Gwyn's little tousled head. He settled for snarling. "Move."

He started off across the street. He wasn't at all sure it was his own decision which way his feet turned. The thing just reacted so fast that he honestly couldn't tell which of them was reaching the conclusions first. Maybe that was what mages liked. It was damn near effortless. If he didn't watch out, he could start to think it was his own mind that made those incredible calculations, that had a million feelers out, that was somehow picking up the traces of a unique set of pheromones from an infrared gate sensor three miles from here and matching it against the strength of the same signal at a neighboring cell tower. To him, it was too much like possession.

"Where are you going?" Gwyn asked.

"North," he growled. "Apparently."

Any other summer they might've gotten a lot of stares, a bunch of people who didn't look like they belonged together all striding purposefully to none of them knew the hell where. But all the panicky newscasts of the past few weeks had started to sink in. Nobody sat at the sidewalk tables of the cafes and restaurants. No kids played Frisbee or touch football out in the neighborhood streets or park playgrounds. The few folk whose business kept them outside reeked of sweat under unseasonably long-sleeved shirts and pants. Heartsblood even saw a hasty sign in one drugstore window, marker on neon-colored paper, saying SOLD OUT OF REPELLENT—COME BACK THURS. Behind it stood a ransacked end shelf. It was a city that was holed up now, waiting, ready to die of heatstroke rather than open one window more than it had to.

The buildings got cleaner and fancier, the signs snazzier, and still no people. But the air started to cool—a breeze was coming in off the lake. They'd gotten to the waterfront now, and to the elegant kinds of homes people built near water. Millions of dollars apiece, he reckoned, all going to waste right now despite the clear sky. Nobody was going to be taking out their yachts or eating on their sleek patios or cooking on their car-sized gas grills. Not unless they thought they were just too important to die.

"This is the Gold Coast." Tiaret looked more uneasy the further they walked. "Not sure how someone this formidable could be operating out here without Eleagia or her little bloodhounds noticing."

"You haven't joggled the connection, have you?" Glorianna nagged.

"Of course not, Glorianna," the PDA answered in an Alistair Cooke voice. It sounded put off, if such a thing was possible. Receiving excellent signal quality on all channels and triangulating as instructed.

"I didn't mean *you*, Watson. I meant Heartsblood."

"I ain't joggled nothin'," he returned. "Itches like a diaper rash wiped with poison ivy though. Why ya think I got my hands in my pockets?"

"Vivid." Glorianna stopped him and examined the transmitter anyway, but after a minute she grunted. "Let's just keep going, I guess."

"Good. It's thisaway."

"You picking up anything yet, Blue?" Mercedes asked.

Little Blue pushed along on his skateboard. His left eye was full of starlight again. "Something," he mumbled. "Hard to describe—nothing ever seems exactly right in this neighborhood. And we lost Garbageman," he added suddenly.

Mercedes snapped to attention. "Hold the phone. When did we lose him?"

"Just now. He's leaving."

"Tell him not to!"

"No, he has to go."

"Why?"

"He says it hurts too much."

"What's Garbageman? A spirit? Maybe he's run into some kind of warding." Tiaret slowed and took a thing that looked like a compass out of her purse.

"Well?" Anna hunched her shoulders. "Come on, we shouldn't be just standing out here. Neighborhood rent-a-cops'll get up our asses."

"There isn't anyone like that in the immediate area," said Baihu. Tiaret was doing some kind of math problem under her breath.

"No, there's no formal ward," the older sorceress said after a minute. "Not the kind I'd recognize anyway. But there's definitely a radiating aura. And… Yes. It gets stronger going this way."

"Like I said, thisaway," Heartsblood repeated. "Goddamn, fuck, and shit." The cussing defused his urge to knock heads, so he said it again a few more times. Nobody asked him why.

"This 'un," he said at last, stopping in front of one of the houses.

It was a stately, big, almost plantation-like place with red brick and ivy-covered pillars on the porch. Talk about building way back on the lot—you could practically hold the Super Bowl on the front lawn. In fact, hoops for cricket or croquet or something were set up on the green grass in the middle of the circle driveway.

Sarah Roark

"So they're not only evil and supernatural, but rich, too?" said Gwyn. "Wonderful. I'm assuming you can disable the security with a dirty look, Glory."

Glorianna snorted. "You're sure they're in this house?" she asked Heartsblood.

"Ask your little doodad if you don't believe me."

"Not to be punctilious, but my virtual processor is nearly a quarter mile cubed and could hardly be described as little."

"Oh, well, shit, I stand corrected."

"The 'doodad' I'll grant you."

"Can I get this thing the fuck out of my head now?"

"And the origin of the signal is twenty degrees to the west and sixty-eight degrees up, at a distance of approximately seventy-three point forty-five meters."

"Like I said—in the house!"

"Pardon me. I'm merely confirming your organic data to my notoriously stubborn mistress."

"Organic data…"

"It's just that once I take this off I doubt we can get the connection back," Glorianna interrupted, hastily unwinding the cord and removing the metal business from his temple. Heartsblood couldn't stop himself from immediately scratching the shit out of the spot. Good thing Uratha didn't have to worry about brain cancer.

Baihu had barely turned his head the whole time, but now he stirred. "Um, people. I'm not sure about this."

"What's up?" Gwyn asked.

"Well, there are people in there, and… I don't know, they just seem like ordinary people. Nothing sinister at all. A man and a woman."

"Look, we don't have to hurt anybody. We're just checking it out. If the radar's off, we just leave. They don't even need to know we were here. They're not right by the origin point, are they?"

"The 'radar's' not off," Mercedes grumbled. "Or if it is, it's your equipment. The nose of a Hunter in Darkness is damn near infallible."

"There might be something in there the people don't even know about," Heartsblood pointed out.

"I'm not saying don't go in," said Baihu. "I'm just saying something doesn't fit."

"They could be brainwashed," said Little Blue hopefully. "Like the *Manchurian Candidate*. Or robots like the Stepford wives."

"Jesus Christ, Blue. You meet your first wizards and suddenly anything's possible." Anna bapped his head. He bapped her back.

"Well, isn't it?" the boy protested.

Baihu shot that down. "Anything's possible, but brainwashing would be fairly noticeable."

"Keep a lid on the party back there," said Glorianna crossly. "Okay, Watson. Change of program, we're breaking into this house."

They went around to the back door. Mercedes fished out a little leather folder and opened it up to reveal a set of locksmith's tools.

"Some lost children aren't so much lost as kept prisoner," she said bluntly, and set to work with Erik touching the locks every so often and whispering in her ear.

"I think that's it." She pushed down the latch.

"Okay, wait." Glorianna turned Watson toward the door. A line of white light flickered up and down it. A few seconds later they heard a soft *beep* from inside. Tiaret looked to Baihu, who shook his head.

"They didn't hear. They're downstairs watching TV."

"Well, keep a bead on them."

Blue was already through the door. Mercedes and Heartsblood followed, then the mages. Erik came last, scanning the yard one last time before closing the door behind them.

Blue shrank into the wolf-shape and started sniffing down the hall. He growled and snapped his jaws at something.

"Shh," hissed Glorianna.

"You shh," said Mercedes. "The shaman does the spirit-herding."

"Well, the signal's this way."

Heartsblood kept his hands in his pockets. This was the kind of house where fragile things leapt off tables and dashed themselves to pieces on the floor next to him just to be spiteful.

"Hot," said Gwyn. "Getting real tired of the hot." He opened the door Glorianna almost walked into, then followed her inside. Heartsblood shuffled in after. Glorianna didn't look up from Watson's screen till she was in the dead center of the room. Then she looked up, frowning.

"Dear Lord." Tiaret frowned, too. She turned around and around.

"This is it," said Baihu.

"But this is a child's room," she protested weakly.

And it was. Not a small child's. Looking at the size of the jeans and skirts on the floor, Heartsblood would've guessed maybe fourteen. The gewgaws of a younger age still lay around the place, though—a lamp with a yellow, ruffled lampshade, a row of porcelain dolls, a box of crayons. A backpack sprawled half-open on the bed. Pubescent sweat and a sickly-sweet floral perfume. Hair goop. Acne zapper cream.

"I can't figure out where the rotting meat smell is coming from," Mercedes said very quietly. "It seems to move with me."

"Victims were schoolkids, too," said Heartsblood. "Guess it makes sense."

"But it's just a room. Just—a room. I don't smell anything." Tiaret flustered was a rare and unwelcome sight. "My niece has these albums."

Blue nosed the box of crayons off the bedside table. It spilled and dumped out on the floor. Red and black crayons scattered across the floor, most worn down to stumps.

"If this is the place, it's the place." Baihu turned one of the porcelain dolls around. It had a steak knife plunged into its back. He quickly turned it back again.

Anna grimaced. "Holy fuck. What other shit is in here?" She opened up the closet and started picking through the pile of clothes on the floor.

"Nothing visible from the front." Baihu turned around the other dolls. They were all mutilated on their backsides, ripped or marked up with obscene graffiti. Heartsblood followed a pungent smell under the bed and dug out several shoeboxes full of different things. Here was that jimsonweed all right, and some candles made with fat, and one box had nothing but hundreds of dead spiders in it. Here was a flashlight with a dead battery, but when he touched it he got a little *zing* like a static spark.

"So her parents don't know. They can't know, can they?" Glorianna's voice shook a little.

"Not if they didn't come any further than the door," said Baihu.

"Very teenaged." Mercedes sighed. "See me, don't see me. See me, don't see me."

"I resent that," muttered Glorianna. "This goes way beyond—"

"I didn't say it was dumb." Mercedes cut her off. "Just teenaged. The girl's obviously pretty damn cunning."

"Don't handle that, Heartsblood, give it to me. It's pretty strongly linked to her. We may need it." Baihu had his gloves on. He reached for the flashlight. Heartsblood gave it to him.

"Wait a minute," Tiaret broke in.

Heartsblood held up a shoebox. "Found the jimsonweed."

"So I see."

"Dead crow in a Tupperware," reported Anna from the closet. "Dead and bloody. And there's something else in it. Smells like… " A rush of odor, even though Heartsblood guessed she'd barely cracked the lid. "Whoo, there's a nostalgia smell. D-Con."

"Anticoagulant," said Baihu. "She knows her poisons."

"Easier to work with the virus if the blood doesn't clot," Glorianna agreed.

"There has to be more to the story," Tiaret insisted.

"There is," murmured Baihu. He was holding a piece of paper he'd gotten out of one of the desk drawers. Then he tilted his head. "They're coming this way. We'd better go."

"We need her name," said Glorianna. "At least her birth name."

"The backpack." Baihu grabbed it up and put the paper and the flashlight inside it, then zipped it up.

"Let's go." Mercedes whined briskly at Blue and urged the rest of them toward the door.

Tiaret's pumps made a sharp echoing *tick tick tick* on the linoleum of the deserted office hallways. Compared to it, all the rest of their footfalls were almost eerily quiet.

"Thought your office was on the other end, McBride," Mercedes commented. "You get promoted?"

"The day I'm promoted you can expect Wormwood to fall out of the sky, burning as if it were a lamp and turning the third part of the waters bitter, and the four Horsemen will be saddling up." Tiaret didn't even crack a smile as she said it. She took out a key ring and unlocked the door to an office marked H. Schwimmer. "No, my boss' computer has much better access. Close the door."

She set her heavy shoulder bag down on the desk, took out a laptop and turned it on, then sat down at the desktop computer and typed into the login screen.

"Dammit. He changed his password. Hang on a second." She opened the drawer, pulled out a pen and a pad of sticky notes, wrote down HAROLD IVES SCHWIM-MER and started doing equations under it.

"Numerology? Jesus, how medieval," said Glorianna. She set the PDA down on top of the tower case. "Watson, get his passwords, please."

"Done."

"Now which files are we looking for?"

"We just want the main database," Tiaret said, miffed now. "We can do a search on the address or the last name."

Windows popped up onto the desktop screen. Tiaret hunted-and-pecked at the keyboard.

"And that is?"

"According to her U.S. history book, Regina Howe," Baihu said soberly. He'd become keeper of the backpack. He flipped the textbook open and then put it back. "H-o-w-e."

"My God." Tiaret opened up the full entry. "Here she is."

They all looked over her shoulder except for Erik and Little Blue, who settled on the floor in the corner for lack of anyplace else to sit. Blue played with the anatomically correct dolls he'd found sitting on one of the bookshelves.

"Fourteen, and she's had four different diagnoses," Tiaret read. "Parents cooperative… Initial diagnosis pediatric-onset schizophrenia, with some symptoms of PTSD but no positive evidence of inducing trauma or abuse. Second opinion produced the bipolar I diagnosis, but she didn't respond to Lithium or lamotrigine, so they changed their minds again, nothing like reasoning backward from cure to disease. She's supposed to be taking olanzapine now."

"That's serious shit to be giving a kid," Gwyn said.

Baihu shook his head. "She's not taking any meds. That'd cripple her workings."

"What about the jimsonweed?" asked Heartsblood.

"No, she wouldn't be taking the jimsonweed either. The last thing someone like her would want is to induce hallucinations."

Heartsblood eyed him. "I meant, could the jimsonweed be causing her troubles? But you seem awful sure about her. Something happen I don't know about?"

Baihu gave him a terrible look, a kind of dreamy horror he'd only seen before in the eyes of dying folk. Then he handed Heartsblood the piece of paper from the backpack. It was covered with words in black and red crayon, arranged in circles, stars, spirals, thick shapeless crosshatches. *Voices must stop. Voices must stop. Voices must stop.*

"Voices?" Heartsblood glanced from the paper to Baihu and back. Something sat burning at the back of his throat for a few seconds before it burst out. "This's got to do with the death-chanters, don't it? The boy, the bloody-head boy, and the rest of the ones you said you couldn't see or hear. Those voices."

"The Voices in the Dark," Baihu broke in. Gwyn stepped closer to his friend, whether to protect or restrain Heartsblood didn't know. "I'd rather you didn't refer to them individually, especially that one. But yes, I know what they are."

He took the paper back. "I remember, rather."

"I knew he had to mean somethin'. You was ignoring me every time I brought him up."

"Not ignoring. More of a psychic blind spot. An unintentional one, on my part anyway. But it seems I'm not the only child to have received these things' attentions." Baihu brought his hand up toward his face and then put it down again. Heartsblood noticed the nails were all bitten down. "This girl would have been luckier if she really were schizophrenic. The Voices aren't hallucinations. They're all too real. And they can't be drugged away."

"Hm. Interesting. I found an additional file on Regina. Shall I bring it up?"

"Definitely," said Glorianna. A word processor window appeared. Tiaret's finger froze in midair.

"Hey, that's not from the database." Glorianna scooted her chair closer.

Tiaret glared at her. "No, it's from my laptop."

"Correct. My apologies, I searched the entire network to save time."

"So you had a file on her all this time?" Gwyn peered at the screen. "What the hell!"

"I guess I must have. Wait a minute. I remember this girl." Tiaret scrolled down. "This is from when she was six. That's right, she had a ligature bruise on her neck."

Heartsblood got a picture of that in his head before he could stop it.

She kept reading as she talked. "There was an argument about whether we should even follow up, because she said it was from a suicide attempt and the parents were complying. But suicide wasn't her original explanation. That's why I put her in here. Here it is. She originally said a sweater in her closet tried to strangle her. Then she changed her story in the psychiatrist's office. I remember thinking six was exceptionally young for a serious suicide attempt."

"And you haven't updated it since then?" Anna said wryly. "I guess that's about right for government work."

Tiaret whirled in the office chair, pulling off her glasses. "You know how many kids I have on this hard drive? You realize how much preternatural activity there actually is in this town?"

"It happens," said Gwyn, holding up a hand. "Nobody's perfect. Let's not start down this road."

"So she was seeing haints all this time." Heartsblood chewed on that. "All this time. I guess she just knuckled under finally? Went crazy for real?"

"She's not crazy," Gwyn corrected. "And she hasn't knuckled under, she's joined forces. See, the Voices don't just threaten. They also entice. Isn't that right, Baihu?"

Baihu answered grudgingly. "The most enticing thing they ever offered to me was their absence. They promised to go away if I would do a certain thing for them. I always said no, but… I didn't have to hold out for fourteen years either."

Heartsblood almost asked what the thing they requested was. (*What will you give us? Anything, anything.*)

"So she's cut some kind of deal with these things, is what you're saying."

"That's my guess," Gwyn nodded. "And her end of it seems to be to provoke the Murder of Crows into fully waking, by hook or by crook. Whether it's the Murder itself they want or just the general banquet of horror it'll bring with it is harder to say. Hardly matters, does it?"

"Hell no. Either way, we can't let it happen. Especially not if they can actually take the Murder." He tried to logic forward from that. It was hard to imagine. "That'd do to Chicago what—what knockin' the moon out of orbit would do to Earth."

"I agree."

"So what do we do?" he prompted.

"Nobody's doing anything yet." Tiaret held up a finger. "We're gathering information."

"No. We're not." Mercedes hadn't spoken since the files first came up, just scanned them over Tiaret's shoulder. But now her tone brooked no argument. "We have all the information now. The only thing left to find out is where she is."

"Behind a ward, probably," said Gwyn. "Or else our triangulation would've led to her instead of the house. And if she's behind ward, that means she's working and we don't have much time. But now we know her real name, her date of birth. We have her things—"

Tiaret closed all the files up on the screen. "No. There's been a change of plan."

"What plan? There was a plan?" Heartsblood looked to Baihu. Suddenly there was a lot of talking around shit. Never a good sign.

"There's no time," Gwyn argued.

"Somebody wanna to let us all in on the plan?" Heartsblood raised his voice. "Hello? I'm 'bout ready to crack some magical heads till somethin' informational falls out."

"We've devised a working," began Baihu. "Or at least the basic outlines of one."

"Which was designed with an adult object in mind," Tiaret finished.

Gwyn shrugged. "Yeah, but it shouldn't require any adaptation."

"The hell with adaptation. That's not what I'm talking about and you know it. I'm talking about the one fact everybody suddenly seems eager to ignore, which is that our opponent is a fourteen-year-old child."

Heartsblood no longer needed to have the plan explained to him, at least not the important part of it. He had the whole argument with himself that Tiaret was having with everybody else, only he got through it much faster. He'd seen too much by now.

"Jesus Christ, Tiaret! Do you think any of us aren't fully cognizant of that?" Mercedes snarled.

Heartsblood would have sworn to Mother and Father that he saw lightning flash in the sorceress' eyes.

"What did you say they call you?" Tiaret threw back. "'Childseeker?' You of all people…. "

"Me of all people." Mercedes started to put her fingers to her temples and wound up yanking her hair instead. "Me of all people, unfortunately, understands your problem and unfortunately also knows that it doesn't make a difference. Look here."

She went and hunkered down by Tiaret's chair, almost in a kneel.

"She is a child, yes," she said. "But she's not an innocent. Not anymore."

"Yes, she is! It's these Voices. They're the ones behind it. She's just their pawn."

"Ask your friend." Mercedes turned toward Baihu, who was facing the wall to hide his tears. Heartsblood took him by the shoulders and forced him round. "They wouldn't be helping her if she hadn't bargained with them. Now maybe they drove her to that choice, maybe it wasn't a fair choice, but she made it. It's made. Baihu. Tell her."

Baihu sucked in a slow breath and let it go. Heartsblood had never met anybody able to shed so many tears so fast, so silently. He kept a steadying hand on the mage's shoulder.

"The Voices… are part of Chicago's architecture," Baihu said at last. "Much like the Murder. If we destroyed them, something else would have to take their place. She's the one who gave in. She's the problem."

Tiaret got up. "Well, wouldn't it be a treat to see your Granny hear you saying that," she said coldly. It was totally on purpose, a grabbing of the first obvious weapon, and from the flinch on Baihu's face it struck home. "If it weren't for her, if it weren't for the working she did, if she hadn't blocked out the better half of your childhood like you're so mad at her for doing, it could just as easily have been you. I'd like to see how you would have held up against those monsters alone. Don't you understand there was no one here for this child? No one who saw? My God, even I didn't see. The only difference between you is you got your rescuer and she didn't."

Baihu's tears didn't stop. "I know."

"And now you're going to blame him for having even that little bit of luck?" Mercedes retorted. "Listen to yourself! Tiaret! You're a social worker, you work for society. You have got to put your own ego aside."

"My ego—" Tiaret's eyes bugged, and she almost couldn't get the words out. "I'm pleading for a little girl's life, and you call it ego? How much do you charge these poor women for your 'retrievals'? They could probably call the Mafia and get similar service at a slightly cheaper rate, maybe I'll start recommending that instead. Or maybe I'm the one undercharging."

"I thought I did good work 'for what it was worth,'" Mercedes snapped. "Anyway, stop trying to jump up everybody's ass. I'll admit you've turned out to be a hell of a lot more than I suspected, and I'm sure you're a very skilled... wizard. Mage. But you're not omnipotent. And too much is at stake here. If you can't accept that you didn't save this girl when it was possible and you had the chance—"

It happened so fast. He heard Mercedes saying it, his reflexes kicked in, he was moving, and then there was a noise that was almost too loud to be heard, and Anna was lying up against a dent in the metal filing cabinet with her shirt laid open and her chest reddened in a scorching sunburn. Mercedes stood back, breathing shallowly, pupils dilated, staring at her unwanted packmate. Everyone else had frozen solid.

Tiaret was sitting back down, trembling.

"I didn't mean. I—I wasn't thinking."

"Like hell," Heartsblood yelped, finding his voice again. He fell down beside Anna and picked her up. Her chest was already starting to heal, but she was still out, from the sheer backwash of blood on impact probably. Erik moved quickly to catch Blue in mid-leap and hold the boy back as he growled and barked, flinging spit from his half-changed snout. He whispered urgently in the crescent-moon's ear.

"You're right. You're not thinking. You're reacting." Mercedes couldn't stop blinking, but she was getting her wits back, too. She turned her head. Heartsblood followed her gaze, out the window to the twilight moon.

Yes. *Gibbous moon now.* He thought it at her as hard as he could. *Wake up, old girl. Time to wake up.*

Mercedes touched Heartsblood's head—not a beta gesture, but he wasn't about to pull rank just now. She was Cahalith, and her light was on her. It was for the pregnant moon to say the right thing at the right time. He was tired of trying to be everything to everybody.

She pulled a chair up beside Tiaret. She took the woman's shaking hand and put it onto her own lap, then spoke to her in a voice that was soft but relentless. She sat very straight.

"You are doing exactly what Regina is trying to do," she said. "Shift your problem onto someone else. Only you don't have the excuse of being a child. This has to stop. Do you understand? It can't be paid forward anymore. And Regina..."

Tiaret nodded tearfully. Mercedes didn't let up. "Regina's already lost. You know that, don't you? Yes. That's the worst part. Already lost."

"And not just her," Tiaret said. The words had to tear free one by one. "Trey, too. Loki. He was one of mine, I wanted to help him, and it's too late."

"I know." Mercedes held her hand tight. "I know, honey. But you have to answer, can you help us stop this girl?"

"Kill her, you mean."

"If that's what you all have ready to go, yes. And I don't mind telling you, if you're against us, if we can't trust you, then we'll do whatever it takes to restrain you while we take care of business. And your friends will help us, I think." She glanced up at Baihu and Gwyn. By the unhappy looks on their faces, it was true. "So we need to hear it from you right now. Can you do it?"

Tiaret didn't answer. When Mercedes spoke again more sharply, Tiaret flinched. "Can you?"

The call came at about three-thirty in the morning. Revenge was sweet, Heartsblood guessed—he was almost asleep when the phone rang.

"Sentinel Point, Haig Park," Baihu said. His throat sounded dry. "It's a little private park on the lakefront, Glorianna has the address… Get there fast as you can, I don't think it much matters how at this point."

Heartsblood took the man at his word. Any natural pack of wolves would have been terrified to make the run they made, taking Urshul shape for maximum speed and not giving a damn who saw the monster dogs (or dire wolves, or hellhounds, or however human sight was inclined to interpret it these days) on the way. Much less how many pack-marks they trespassed. Of course, this wasn't Heartsblood's town and he was leaving it soon, he dearly hoped, but it was a sign of the Haunts' growing determination how they never blanched or slacked. He took the nearest path to a beeline he could, reckoning by what he could see of the sky and what he could smell of the water.

As they came up on the bridge-tunnel that led to the park, Heartsblood stopped. The pavement in the dark, man-made cavern looked alive. Then he realized it wasn't alive, just full of living things, spiders, roaches, frogs, rats, all jumbled together in defiance of species, flooding down the road in a squirming carpet that rushed toward them. He steeled himself and ran through anyway. He felt squishings and crunchings under his paws but ignored it. Why not? It was only right. The only proper end to all this was the complete abandoning of both instinct and common sense. Of course, he was going to go the opposite way from all God's other creatures.

Clouds raced to cover the sky, impossibly quickly. The pack raced against them, trying to find wherever it was they needed to be while it was still bright enough to see. He saw a lone car's headlights pulling into the parking lot and steered the pack toward it.

The mages were getting out just as they ran up. He heard Glorianna cry out and saw the others turn and reach into their bags. It flashed through his mind that if they didn't have a whole lot of experience with Uratha and didn't quite know what they were looking at in the dark it could go pretty badly, but then he heard Baihu give a bark of relief. "Heartsblood!"

He changed hastily, the others following suit. "Yeah. Yeah. We got her?"

"Probably. We got something."

"She's not moving," said Glorianna, staring at Watson. "It looks like she's closer to the lake than to the road."

"Yep. She is, not too far away either," Heartsblood said. The wind had changed and brought with it a powerful female scent, a young scent, and the smell of sickly crows. Even if he hadn't smelled either before he might have guessed it was important just by the sudden strength of it. He nodded at the pack, knowing that they were making it theirs as well.

"Heartsblood." Baihu took his arm. "She'll have protection while she's working. Nasty ones. Can your people handle them while we handle here?"

He snorted. Whether they could or not…. "That's what we're here for," he answered.

"Good. Let's hurry, before she gets too far along."

They found the girl sitting on a breakwater railing right at the so-called Point (which was a little on the small side to warrant a name all its own, but rocky and treacherous-looking). A good thing Heartsblood's nose told him she was the one, because his eyes never would have. Yes, she was dressed all in black, with black feathers sticking up out of her dark hair, and something long and silvery and snaky draped across her back. Yes, it was clear she didn't belong here, that the air seemed too thick for a slender, little thing like her to breathe. But the way she sat was so relaxed, so unworried, and, dammit, so childlike. She leaned back on her hands and crooned softly into the breeze, and it sounded like a lullaby. The crows gathered curiously around her, listening. They were coming by the hundreds now, by the thousands maybe. He had no idea just how many there were except where they actually moved. They were in the trees, in the bushes, on the picnic tables, on the rocks.

Then she stood up. Her song changed. Was it because she heard him and the others coming, or just because it was time? There was a growing urgency in it anyhow.

She spread her arms. The crows fell dead. All of them. At least, all the ones he could see. They dropped silently and simultaneously, with one mass exhalation. He cried out and started to charge. The wind picked up and blew into his chest, slowing him and then forcing him backward. Just as he stopped fighting it stopped, too, teasingly. When he moved again, it blocked him. Meanwhile, it plucked the dead crows' feathers and puffed them up into the air, leaving increasingly pale, tiny corpses behind, then turned and hurled them down at a slashing angle. It was the whirlwind again, the same circle that the crows always flew in, he realized, only bigger this time. Much bigger.

"That's enough, Regina," said Tiaret. Her voice was quiet, but it carried the way low thunder carried.

The girl turned slowly, with no sign of surprise. Her eyes were filmed over with something oily and black. When she blinked, it bubbled and dripped down her cheeks.

"It's coming," she answered simply. Her voice carried the way the whirlwind carried, a vicious thing that pummeled the ears with both noise and force, blasted into orifices where it wasn't invited. "You should run for your lives now."

"That's not possible anymore, is it?" Tiaret seemed not to be getting the wind, somehow. At least it didn't keep her from stepping forward. "You've made sure of that. We know what you're doing, Regina. We can force you to stop—maybe that's what you want, it's probably what you've needed —but I warn you, at this point there's only one way for us to do that. Think. There might be another way out for you, we could help you try to find it, but not after this. There's nothing after this."

Regina's fingers danced. The feather rain pelted harder, slingshotting into all of them. It was difficult to keep your feet—the wind was trying to pick Heartsblood up by his flapping clothes now, so the whole time he had the strange sensation of having to reach for the ground to stay touching it.

"Nothing." The girl's face curved into a smile. "Yes, nothing. Now you understand. No one else could finish it, but I can. And that's what it needs, too. Look at it. Look at its pain. Carrion-flock!" she called out. "Meet our eyes. Do you see? Yes, even you can end. We've made it possible. Come."

She raised her hands and cupped them together, light shining through them, as if she'd caught a lightning bug, and the feather torrent pulsed and railed. She was squeezing it down. More and more force crammed into a smaller and smaller space. Soon it would have only two choices, buckle or burst. Heartsblood was more afraid of it buckling. He'd tasted the Murder's heart now. He knew how oblivion would seem sweeter with every new torment she inflicted on it.

And somewhere in the wind the Voices, Regina's and Baihu's Voices, were whispering again. He recognized them now. This time they spoke seductions instead of torments. Tiaret had turned away from the hypnotic sight of the girl's face and seemed to be talking to him, but he couldn't hear her. She couldn't be saying the words that reached his ears. Could she? It had to be the Voices. Only they knew what to say to a little red wolf inflamed with the alien savagery of the spirit world. Even a sorceress couldn't know how his throat closed when he heard *Yes, solve everything, you know this'll solve everything. When your right eye offends you, you pluck it out, when the world sins against you, you flood it, you rain down fire and brimstone, you teach 'em, you make 'em sorry. It's someone else's turn now, someone else's after all this time.*

Most spirits really were like that deep down, hard and hungry. In ages past, when the Veil between was thin and lightly guarded, they'd gotten used to drawing on the living world whenever the whim took them, sucking the marrow right out of its bones. They felt cheated of their due now. And the Uratha had some of that, too, that rage like the fury of an Old Testament God. He wasn't the one who'd killed Father Wolf. He wasn't the one who'd turned the stars inside out to become black holes. None of it was his fault. Why should he be denied?

No. The black feather rain. The ghost of Chicago. That had to be more revenge than his grubby little soul deserved. And it was sure as shit more than the Voices should get. He grabbed at the sooty quills that pierced his skin. Fistfuls of it gathered in his hands. He tried to reach through them, find that connection he'd found before at the lake.

DON'T GIVE IN, he begged it. Them. DON'T LET HER HAVE YOU.

A hand touched him. It felt almost hot in the chill of the storm. "Remember, you're on the side orders," said Gwyn in his ear. "We've got the kid. No matter what she does, you focus on the others."

"Others?" Heartsblood muttered feverishly.

"The Voices. Can't you hear them? The second we go for her, you'll see them, too, trust me. They'll come out of the woodwork. Keep them busy."

He nodded. "We can do that."

"Especially…" The mage hesitated. "Especially the bloody-head boy. You keep him off us and off Baihu. You understand?"

"I'll try." He shook Mercedes' shoulder and growled at the pack in the First Tongue. GET READY.

The mages had strayed apart from each other, which made Heartsblood nervous, until he realized why. They were taking up the points of a square. The instant Tiaret stepped into her exact place in it the air suddenly crystallized and shattered. Gaping holes opened up in the storm of black. The feathers banged into the edges of the holes but bounced back off again. It was like invisible tubes were reaching in through the vortex, straight toward the girl. She felt it, too, whatever it was they were sending at her. Her eyes opened even wider, and her lips, pressed shut in concentration, split in a grimace. The mages walked slowly, counterclockwise, opposite to the whirlwind.

Blue swelled into the Gauru and leaped up in the air. Instead of landing, though, he just hung there, and then Heartsblood saw something appear under him, a lump in a stained and ripped bedspread. Mercedes tackled it, too. It tried to pull away, the bedspread starting to slip. Heartsblood yanked it the rest of the way off. It melted like butter in a pan, draining into the ground, but more monsters rose up from the same spot. "Voices" was a bad name, Heartsblood decided. Even if they got a lot of their power by being unseen most of the time, they definitely had bodies, and those bodies were the kinds of things only dreaming humanity could conjure up.

The pack refused to be outflanked. Heartsblood led Erik and Anna around behind something that looked like two scorpions grafted back to back. It kept flipping end over end, but Erik hung onto it while the other two worried at its legs, biting off joints until it collapsed in a pool of ichor. Out of its shadow floated a woman all veiled in white with black eyes and hair the only things showing through the gauze. She never raised a hand—her weapons were the Spanish curses that seethed around her. *("Llorona. Chingada. Traidora. Profanadora. Maldecida.")* Every time the werewolves hit her, a skull dropped onto the ground from somewhere in her skirts and she withered a little, but the curses got louder and didn't stop until they stomped every skull to shards. Wherever a monster rose up, the feathers assailed it. They didn't seem to give a shit. It took the whole pack just to bring each one down. The damn things were in their hour of strength.

Shit. Heartsblood spotted the bloody-headed boy squirming through the growing mass of Voices. He left off snapping at the pile of moving masks that the pack was trying to fight and scrambled forward. His paw fell onto something—the flashlight from Regina's backpack. He instinctively changed, picked it up, and flipped the switch on it, shining it where he'd seen the boy last. He heard a hiss, a grunt, and a sizzle.

Then it came to him. If this was the flashlight, where was the backpack? Where was Baihu? Who had the backpack?

He who hesitated was lost in this feather rain. As he stood still, a fucking bargeload of the things collected on him, falling into his hair and covering his eyes and nose. He brushed them away to find a skeleton in front of him: not lying on the ground but bleached and wired together and hanging from one of those medical school stands. It had a stained wedding dress on.

ENOUGH, HARRY, it said to him. He reached back, trying to grab hold of Mercedes, Erik, even skinny Blue. The shaggy fur of Mercedes' shoulder slipped through his fingers and he was flying, up and up. He was alone in the dark sky above the city, clutched in invisible talons. And he could see it starting, the blackout. Lights in one building after another sputtered and died. He heard the cannon sound of transformers blowing.

This is the way the world ends, he thought dizzily. Well, why not? A perfect angel of doom for the new century. Turn off the air conditioners, turn off the hospital equipment, turn off the TV and the radio, turn off the bridge lights and stoplights. He could feel it in his bones already, the thrum of mass surprise and annoyance. Soon it'd turn to fear and anger. The sensation pulled him out of the sudden strange apathy he was slipping into.

Why show me this? He tried to pitch it loud enough to be heard over the roaring wind, but every time he opened his jaws the breath was ripped from between them. Why if you've decided it's too late?

The answer, what answer there was, came as a scent. Maybe because the Murder had finally figured out that was the clearest way to get through to him. Or maybe because it only had that much to spare. Wolf-scents and Uratha scents could say a lot about the important things in life—*I'm hungry, I'm afraid, come fuck me it's time, walk no further into this wood*—but this was a whole different thing. This was nature smells and city smells, animal and human smells, life and death smells colliding in a rioting tapestry. Still, they made words, or a feeling in his heart that he translated into words.

What is given freely shall be accepted and blessed. What is owed and withheld shall be taken without mercy.

What do you want? he screamed with the last air he had.

But that was a stupid question. It wanted. That was all. The specifics didn't matter. What mattered was that it got its due. It might even be waiting for him to choose. And he was at the goddamn epicenter now, far too close and too late to escape. Besides, every step he'd taken for months had been leading here.

I'll do it, he pleaded. Anything, anything, whatever you want, I don't care anymore what the reason is. Whatever you think I owe you, I'll give. Just stop it.

His desperation whetted something in it. Its scattered focus narrowed to him. Oh yes, something about that it liked. It didn't ask, not exactly, but a moment later he *knew*. His gaze fell on something, and it wasn't accidental. The something was Baihu, moving from his spot in the mage-square far below and walking slowly but steadily toward the bloody-headed boy.

Baihu looked up as Heartsblood dropped out of the sky like a stone. Hurtling closer, he saw the mage's eyes had become like Regina's, covered in polluted oil-slick.

"Oh fuck no," he breathed. "Fuck no, you ain't doin' that."

But he was. And Heartsblood got the message in his head, too, somewhere between handwriting and a voice, the words of Baihu the sage rising out of the babble of other Voices.

I see what's needed, Heartsblood. They've always wanted me. I can distract them, break their grip on the Murder. But I must not be interrupted.

So calm. Just like he knew it was gonna be all right, that Heartsblood could take it from there. Heartsblood never thought about hitting the ground until he found himself jerked up short just above it, dangling crooked for one sickening second, and then let go. He tumbled into a heap. Erik ran to pick him up. He warned the big Rahu off with a growl.

By now the other magicians felt the ripple in their configuration. "What is it?" Gwyn shouted. "Baihu!"

"Oh God." Glorianna's hands dove into her pockets and she pulled something out. "Gwyn, take my hand! Tiaret!" They clung together to make a better shield against the unnatural wind and started toward Baihu.

It's got him, snapped Mercedes. She looked to Heartsblood, straining with the urge to lunge.

He knew he was standing there looking confused. He couldn't connect brain to tongue fast enough. She was on the move. With a snarl of command, she gathered up the rest of the pack and they fell in instantly.

"No." But they didn't hear that. He melted into the wolf and darted in front of them, barreling into Mercedes and bringing her up short. He tried to get his jaws around her muzzle in the ancient signal—*stop, submit.*

She grabbed hold of him and rolled him over with a baffled whine. WHAT THE HELL? Then she charged forward again. It was desperation that sent him into the war-form, not anger. There was no anger. He just didn't know anything to say and it was still ringing in his head, *I must not be interrupted,* and the urgency filled and swelled his bones. He'd never known the Gauru could be anything but a shape of rage. That was all it was meant to be.

She croaked as his sudden weight bore her to the ground, but a second later she was flipping him over again with her own hairy mass. He snapped at her face. It was pack-tussle stuff and she knew it, she started to stand up and shake him off. Again, it wasn't anger. He just didn't know what else to do. He dug his teeth into the ropy flesh of her neck and drew blood. That she'd have to take seriously.

And she did. She roared. Her eyes met his, full of puzzled pain.

He realized what he'd just done then. An alpha did not turn on his own pack. Fuck the Oath—that was a law predating any human speech. Whether or not he deserved it, he was the Haunts' leader right now, their protector. And they'd followed him here. Their lives were in his hands. The sacrilege yawned under him like a land-slide. Then the moment was past before he'd barely felt it, and the shock of the void it left behind was almost bigger than the feeling itself.

And the Murder was there to take it up, gleefully, to claim his pain before he hardly got to know it. It was probably taking up her pain, too. After all, she was bleeding for its sake even if she hadn't chosen to.

What moved him now was a step even past desperation. As it had so often before, the wolf saved him. Once the law was forfeit, it was forfeit, and once blood was shed, it was shed. Its instinct turned to the new problem of surviving. The man-mind submitted with rare grace, readily taking the chance to go numb. It was out of its depth, and it knew it.

Mercedes threw him aside. He jumped up and tackled her again. The three mages were getting nearer to Baihu. Fuck. He tried to get loose—easier said than done. Just because he'd decided to stop fighting her didn't mean she agreed. She dragged at him, grasping his fur. Staying upright was hard enough in the gusts. At last he reached the huddling humans, caught hold of one of Tiaret's sticklike legs and pulled it out from under her. She stumbled. The others tried to help her up. He roared at them. He saw Glorianna's pretty face drain to white.

You better be doing it, bastard. His hate turned to Baihu. He'd never realized how much he'd needed the one mage he liked to be all right in the end. Especially since the little girl had to die. Especially since it seemed no one else got to be all right.

Tiaret wrapped her hand around his arm. Her fingers sent tendrils of cold into him, freezing him from the inside out. His blood slowed in the veins. Shards of pain drove into his bone joints. His head rang. He felt the frost sliding up his shoulder, down his chest, reaching for his heart. He struggled, but it didn't do any good. He tried to think, but the panic of the beast drowned it out. He strained toward her with jaws open. She flinched and the cold faltered, but it didn't stop.

"Get Baihu," Gwyn yelled hoarsely at Mercedes and the others. "Get Baihu! Can you understand me? Pull him back. Vales of Death! Please understand me. Is there anyone in there?"

Mercedes moaned, dwindling out of the Gauru into a more human shape, but then she and the other Uratha shot off. Heartsblood followed them with his eyes, silently pleading after them. He knew they'd never rescue him now, but he couldn't help it. They'd been the pack. As he watched, they ran right up to Baihu and then right through him, tumbling with surprised whimpers to the ground, sliding through the bloody-headed boy. It was a hell of a thing to see, because they and Baihu and the boy still looked solid as ever. But the pack scrabbled and nipped to no good. Where their muzzles closed on Baihu's hand or the boy's legs, there was a faint violet glow, that was all.

The cold stole out of Heartsblood's bones, retracing its path. Tiaret's hand loosened on him.

"Baihu," Gwyn wailed.

"Don't get any closer," said Tiaret. She looked and sounded like some abandoned stone idol from a forgotten culture. "It's done."

"Oh *shit*." The younger mage started to get up. Tiaret took his hand.

"No closer," she repeated.

"I can stop it." He was hoarse almost to muteness, but Heartsblood heard him fine now. "I see what he's doing. I'm Moros."

"And that's why it's especially dangerous for you." She didn't let go of him. "Listen. You know how yours comes. This isn't it."

Gwyn clenched his free hand. Heartsblood saw something gathered in it, a kind of anti-light. It radiated like light, but inward instead of outward, leaching the color out of its surroundings. Whatever it was, it seemed to take all his strength to hold it.

"You only have to wait," she added quietly. "Do nothing."

Heartsblood felt himself slipping back toward the human. Was it possible they understood?

"That's the worst." Gwyn's hand began to seep the clear yeasty-smelling stuff that comes out of a forming scab.

She nodded. "I agree."

Baihu's outlines blurred now, a change that terrified Heartsblood. Wolf, man, or in between, at least there was always a boundary where an Uratha knew he ended and the world began. He could never have tolerated just *dissolving* like that. The mage didn't seem to notice. The bloody-headed boy stood rooted, one hand up. A mound of feathers was building up around it. Its mouth grimaced, and blood showed in the cracks between its teeth. But the portals of its eyes opened wide, its irises expanding.

Baihu walked straight into it.

Something jangled in the heart of the storm. The Voices had always been a babble, but still there'd been a pattern to it, a resonance beneath the surface chaos. Heartsblood realized it now that the resonance was disturbed. The next instant the Voices ceased. Completely. Baihu and the boy both disappeared, no fuss, no light show, just winking out like a TV screen.

Heartsblood lurched up with a yell. The feather rain turned wet against his skin.

YEAH, YOU FUCKING THING. NOW YOU CAN CRY, NOW YOU'VE FUCKING TAKEN EVERYBODY'S EVERYTHING. HAPPY NOW?

No, of course not. It would never be happy. That wasn't in its nature, if any feeling even was. It could be appeased for a little while, that was it. That had to be enough. He brushed the feathers off, but more came. He would have clawed them off if he could have, torn his own flesh.

Blue was digging furiously through a flood of feathers with his wolf-paws, Anna beside him. They pulled up Regina's body from underneath. The black slick had left her eyes—they were bloodshot and empty of life, but human. Something clear and watery that wasn't snot ran from her nostrils. Heartsblood hurried up. Anna snatched the girl away, but not before his hand brushed up against her dead flesh and found it hot instead of cool. It was the strongest scent yet he'd ever gotten of the virus, hanging around her like a haze. But it was changing, too, going sour very quickly.

"Fuck you," the Irraka said to him. She was almost vibrating with outrage. "Don't touch her. And don't touch me."

The other Uratha gathered behind her. Mercedes laid a torn, bleeding hand on Anna's head and stared at Heartsblood.

Fuck Balance and fuck the Elodoth moon. He would've traded them both to be Cahalith, to know how to explain.

"But it's over now," was all he ended up saying.

"Yes, it is," answered Mercedes. "That means you can leave. Now."

"No. I can't leave him."

"Who? Baihu?" She blinked down at her feet, at the feathers that almost completely covered Baihu's body there, then at the mages who instinctively stood a safe distance away. "Fine. I guess that's appropriate, in a twisted way. Let them deal with you then."

"My things," he protested weakly.

"I'll mail them to Kalila." Her body was deceptively relaxed, but her eyes watched him intently. He didn't blame her. A Hunter in Darkness rarely let himself be ambushed once, and would die before it happened again. He doubted Storm Lords were different. "I don't know what was going through your mind, Dan. I'm sure there was some reason, you've had a reason for everything so far. But I don't care what it was."

She turned away. The pack instantly moved to follow. Then she seemed to have an afterthought, and stopped.

"You can have a day," she said. "If you're still here after that, I'll charge you as forsworn under the Oath and call the hunt."

"I won't be here," he assured her.

They left.

The feathers stirred. He thought for a second Baihu might be alive and breathing after all. But no, it was just the breeze, tame and spent. He laid his hand over the mage's, not even bothering to clear the feathers away, wanting one moment of private communion before the other mages got there. Then he changed his mind and slipped into the wolf, all the way into the wolf. There was no better shape for mourning.

She must've gotten one hell of an earful, because Kalila insisted on meeting Heartsblood at the train station in South Bend. Tackling him, was a better way to put it. If she noticed he didn't run to meet her halfway, it didn't curb her energy. She got a few funny looks from the other travelers by picking him up off the ground till he was two heads above her instead of one. There was a lot more muscle under that T-shirt than you would have thought just looking at her.

"HB, HB, HB, HB," she kept saying. Her beaded dreadlocks clicked as she bounced up and down on the balls of her feet. After a while, he couldn't help smiling a little, even if his stomach still felt like lead. He let her get a whiff of his hand, his hair, the spot behind his ear.

"Come on, we have to board soon. I, uh… need a cuppa coffee."

She rolled, smushed, and fiddled with her wrinkled dollar bill, trying to get the machine to take it. "I tried to bring Elias," she said more quietly now, "but—can you believe it—he said the alpha doesn't come to the beta, the beta comes to the alpha."

"Well. He would know," Heartsblood shrugged.

"Think he's still a little ticked."

"You, uh, tell him and Dana about what all Mercedes said?"

She frowned. That was one fascinating dollar bill. "I decided I'd better get your version first. Am I going to hear it?"

"Yeah. Dunno if you're gonna like it any better than her version."

"She did say the Murder was taken care of."

"As much as it can be in one lifetime, yeah."

"So does that mean you fulfilled Spookygirl's prophecy? You're done with your spirit-quest?" She took a sip and immediately started stomping around flapping her arms and making muffled noises of pain. "Shit. This shit's scalding. Yegh. Shake me if I start popping out stubble."

He'd almost forgotten that as far as his pack was concerned, this was all about him and them: when *he'd* be done, when *he'd* be back with *them*, being *their* Elodoth again.

"No. I mean, yes, I fulfilled it. But I'm not done."

"Not done?" she spluttered through her burnt tongue. "What the hell's left? Aren't you Balanced enough to suit yourself? Mother and Father. Let's get on the train. I brought some of your clothes."

"Thanks, darlin'." He followed her. "Um. It wasn't quite like that. I did figger out somethin' about Balance, mostly that it's a lot more of a pain in the ass than I thought. I'm gonna have to be a lot braver than I am."

Kalila snorted and shoved her suitcase into a nook in their roomette. "If you're not brave enough… yegh. I should stop talking, I'm pissing myself off. Or stop listening, one of the two."

He watched her fish around with her familiar bustle, getting out all her city-girl gadgets, MP3 player, phone, adjusting the air vent, finding the ends of her seatbelt. He realized she was just like she always was.

He wanted to let her be that way. It was soothing right now, though he knew that couldn't last. He'd changed a lot recently, possibly for the better, just as likely not. Of course he had. That was what he'd set out to do. He'd changed before leaving the pack, too. He'd just been too chickenshit to show it. He'd hidden it oh so nobly, set off on walkabout, let them think whatever they wanted to about his reasons, knowing damn well they'd err on the admiring side. He'd been going to do the right thing: come home having saved both himself and them, all without their even having to know about it.

Then Chicago had learned him better. And so, whether Kalila realized it yet, she was going to have to learn better, too. They all were. Maybe in the long run it'd help them. But whether it helped or hurt, it had to happen.

He wondered if Doomwise would be proud of him for figuring that out, or if she'd just ask what the hell took him so long.

"No." He forced the word out. Kalila stared at him.

"No? No, what?"

"No, you can't stop listening. There's something I need to tell you."

"Right this second?"

"Right this second, yeah."

She twined her long brown hands together and set them on her knees to keep them quiet. She held herself straight and stiff, not sure what direction whatever it was was going to come flying at her from.

"Okay. I'm waiting."

Oh, yeah. Nothing could be taken back, nothing was forgotten, and deeds had consequences way beyond what anyone could guess. But what power was in the soul of a werewolf, if not the power to change anyway?

"I've been in a lotta pain for a real long time," he said finally. "Not body pain. Soul pain. The kind we're all afraid of, that makes a lot of us insane after a while. I know I ain't said so. There was things I didn't want you to know about me. Maybe things you didn't wanna know either, and maybe you still don't want to, 'cause I know things're hard enough already, and… and I'm sorry, darlin'. But I'm about to make 'em a whole lot harder. Because like it or not—the time has come for you to hear all about it."

SHADOWS AND MIRRORS

by Myranda Sarro

Part 1

The Hotel Monaco billed itself as the best hotel in Chicago for the discriminating traveler, offering a host of amenities for a by-night price tag just short of outright extortion. At the moment, Tamara Hollister didn't care about the amenities or the price tag attached to them. She could have been walking into the sleaziest roach motel in the nastiest, most underdeveloped part of the city, and she would not have given any sort of crap. It was thirteen hours' flying time between Tokyo and Chicago, with one stopover in San Francisco to take on passengers and fuel for the second leg of the trip. Landing in Chicago in the it's-so-late-it's-early hours of the night, Tam had expected a cursory trip through customs and security. She desired, passionately, to be wanded down by some mouth-breathing security company troglodyte, who would use the opportunity to look down her shirt, possibly cop a feel, and then send her on her way. She wouldn't even have taken the theoretical trog's name or badge number, or called her employers to complain loudly or anything, that's how little she cared right now.

But, no. Of course not.

No, instead, Tam found herself being pulled aside for an "interview" with the night-shift security chief, whose mouth-breathing subordinates found her cleavage too unremarkable to warrant a pass given the contents of her carry-on bag, which had, she was forced to point out, been cleared at Narita Airport just thirteen short hours before. It took the senior troglodytes in charge an hour and a half to confirm her story—that she was attending a robotics and technology convention for senior graduate students and research fellows at various international universities—by which time Tam was ready to call their employer and have all their jobs before she left Chicago again, a fact that she informed them of with the bluntness of a very tired, very headachy traveler who wanted to be in her very expensive hotel's bed ninety minutes before. She had not received an apology but, instead, a lecture about the suspicious nature of a young woman traveling alone with large amounts of consumer electronics in her luggage, and, well, from there things sort of fell apart in Tam's recollection of the incident. She departed O'Hare with the names and badge numbers of four trogs, all of her luggage and other personal possessions, and an admonition ringing in her ears that the city was under a health advisory by the CDC due to an avian encephalitis outbreak, and that, even though she was in the middle of a major city, she should make use of insect repellent when she went outside and report any unusual headaches, faintness, or dizzy spells to a local hospital at once.

The sun was technically up by the time Tam left the airport, not that she could tell. To add insult to injury, it was raining. Correction: it was unbelievably warm and raining, two conditions that a quick consultation of her guidebook informed her were extremely unnatural for this time of year. Normally, Chicago was kept cool in the summer by the same winds off Lake Michigan that made its winters a tundra-like frozen hell. Stepping out of O'Hare's pleasantly climate-controlled concourse was like walking into a sauna. Before she could successfully flag down a cab, Tam's clothes were stuck to her by a combination of drenching rain and instantaneous, humidity-provoked sweat, and she was longing for an umbrella and a return ticket to Tokyo, which in her memory seemed to be balmy and temperate in comparison.

By the time Tam finally reached the Hotel Monaco, she was, perversely, wide awake again, and so headachy and miserable that she wanted something to go wrong with her reservations just so she'd have an excuse to bite off the concierge's head. The universe continued in its perversity by denying her even that amount of relatively righteous

release. The suite she'd booked had actually been vacated a day early by its previous occupant and was ready for her immediate occupancy, the concierge was utterly pleasant
and personable, the porter actually took a great deal of care with her bags, and, once
again, she was given quite adequate warning about the CDC advisory. There was even
a complimentary bottle of some New Agey all-natural, herbal, nontoxic insect repellent
in a seventh-phase recycled plastic bottle in the bathroom and a flyer listing the major
symptoms of encephalitis infection and a list of the local hospital emergency room
numbers on the desk.

Tam, who had spent much of her youth slathered in Off! brand-related products in
exotic locales around the world and who had had more mosquito bites than dates, realized that the universe was conspiring against her desire to indulge in thorough self-pity
and personal malevolence. She took some prescription-strength acetaminophen for the
headache, put some of the complimentary coffee in the complimentary coffee maker to
brew, and took a shower. Twenty minutes later, restored to the semblance of humanity
by cool water and spa-provided bath products, she had her first cup of coffee of the day
and was restored to a semblance of sanity by the recalibration of her caffeine-to-blood
ratio. At eight AM, she called room service to order breakfast, dressed, and unpacked her
collection of suspect personal electronics. It took a while, particularly once she began
assembling and reactivating the hibernating power supplies and restoring all the connections that would allow her to charge and use all of the system's peripherals, most
importantly the Watson laptop and its companion PDA handheld unit.

A soft, three-part tone announced that the system had finished its startup processes
and was ready to come online again. Tam, who was not going to any sort of robotics
and technology convention whatsoever, opened the hood of her laptop and activated it,
punching in her passwords and setting it on the bed next to her to finish warming up.
After a moment, the screen resolved into the image of a genial older man with snow-
white hair and a grandfatherly smile, seated in a wing-backed chair and being orbited by
a selection of program and file icons that seemingly moved in three dimensions around
his person. Behind him, a huge room full of books stretched off into the horizon.

"Good morning, Watson. I hope you enjoyed the trip." Tam picked up the handheld and
activated its wireless mouse function, adjusting the volume of the laptop's speakers.

"Good morning, Glorianna. Indeed, the trip was quite lovely. What brings us to
Chicago today, dare I ask?" Watson, as always, spoke in a perfectly modulated and natural
voice, with a noticeable British accent. First thing in the morning, he rarely had much
in the way of personality but, then, Tam didn't, either.

"We'll get to that, Watson. The hotel has high-speed wireless connectivity—get online
and do your startup exercises while I pull up Daddy's contact list for this city…" Watson
was not Tamara's creation, but he was her companion/assistant in all her endeavors, a
gift from her father. She had personally built the system that supported him to his own
specifications shortly after receiving him, shortly before her father's disappearance.

C. Jeremiah Hollister was an extraordinary man in many respects. A self-made
man of business, he had made and spent at least one fortune before the birth of his
only daughter and the tragically early death of her mother, and then had proceeded to
make another, even more substantial fortune. A genuine polymath, Hollister the Elder
had traveled the world in pursuit of his political and social goals, his business interests,
and other, even more esoteric pastimes. His daughter, reared by a series of nannies who
had attempted to instill in her a proper degree of traditional femininity, educated at a

series of private schools usually populated only by the scions of the social as well as the economic elite, regarded him as the center of the universe, the sun around which she had always revolved. She could admit this because Tamara Hollister was brutally honest with everyone, including herself. Her father was all she ever had: all the family, all the support, all the friendship, all the guidance. Everything and everyone else was, at best, a distant second.

And then he vanished, just after her sixteenth birthday. Her whole world changed with a phone call, informing her of that fact. A few days later, her whole world changed again, when she went home to the family estate where she'd barely spent more than a few days of her life since she was old enough to walk, and there discovered that there was a great deal about her father, and herself, that she'd never known.

Since that day, Tamara's life had become extremely complex. She graduated from her expensive private school, but, instead of entering immediately into college, as everyone had been expecting, she elected to withdraw her applications from the several Ivy League schools she'd considered in favor of a "less structured educational model." Her teachers were stricken, and her few acquaintances dumbfounded. She traveled a great deal. She sought out instructors who could teach her more about her heritage, but rarely stayed with such mentors for more than a few months.

Mostly, though, she hunted—for some sign of her father anywhere in the world, for some person or some clue that could point her in the right direction. C.J. Hollister had disappeared in the "Far East," a term vague enough that it irritated Tam significantly, especially since she couldn't get any more information about where in the Far East out of her father's associates. Much of the last year had been consumed in a lengthy sojourn through Thailand, Korea, China, and, finally, Japan. Along the way, she'd acquired some clues, some new contacts, but nothing substantial, nothing concrete, no one who had seen her father in the years immediately preceding his disappearance. In China, though, she'd met an old, old man, who'd pointed her in the direction of his granddaughter, Grandmother Feng-huang, who lived in America and who had known Tam's father.

Running short on reasons to stay in the East, where all her efforts had met, at best, a dead-end, Tam had decided to return home, by way of Chicago. Grandmother Feng-huang lived there, and if she had even the slightest bit of information, dragging herself all over every bit of snake-and-mosquito ridden jungle in Asia would be worth it. If not, Tam would simply have to cry.

"I've finished my startup exercises, Glorianna. What would you like me to do?" Watson inquired courteously, jarring Tam out of her woolgathering.

"Oh! Just a minute…" The handheld unit had the speed, processing capability, and data retention capacity of a NASA supercomputer. Tam occasionally got the feeling that the handheld considered being used as a PDA somewhat offensive and beneath its dignity. It took less than an eye blink to pull up the dossiers and contact information for every colleague of her father's in the greater Chicago area, a list that was, admittedly, not very long. "Start making calls. Use the standard recording if you get voicemail. Route live responses to me."

So saying, Tam lay back to let her companion do some of the work while she let her tired eyes rest. Her second wind was fading, and her mind was reminding her slightly wired body that, were she elsewhere just now, she'd be getting ready to cycle down for the night. Distantly, she listened to her own prerecorded voice, giving her shadow name, her reason for calling, and her cell number, to a half-dozen voicemail boxes….

"Hello?"

Tam sat up suddenly, startled by the intrusion of a real, live voice into the proceedings. She picked up the handheld and activated its cell phone function. "Hello, this is Glorianna." She glanced down at the flat screen display and found that Grandmother Feng-huang's number was highlighted. The voice on the phone, however, was young and male. "I'm calling on behalf of my father, and I was wondering if I could speak to Grandmother Feng-huang?"

A lengthy pause followed this question. Tam wondered, for a moment, if she should rephrase her question in Chinese.

"I'm afraid that you're a little late." The voice on the other end of the line said, quietly. Tam's heart sank. "My grandmother is in the hospital—she's very ill." Tam's heart rocketed back into place with a startling lurch. "Could I ask why you need to see her?"

I want to interrogate her about my father's disappearance. "She and my father are… colleagues," Tam admitted, after an inner struggle to avoid blurting out the unvarnished truth. "My father is missing, and I wanted to consult with her about anything they might have been jointly involved in, or if she had any knowledge of his whereabouts."

Another pause, shorter this time. "I'm… almost sure I've seen the name Glorianna in my grandmother's papers." Pause. Tam held her breath. "My name is Baihu—and if your father is my grandmother's colleague, I can assure you that he's probably mine, as well." Tam let her breath out. "Is there someplace we can meet?"

"There's a restaurant across from my hotel… the South Water Kitchen, I think it's called. Would that be adequate?" Tam really wished she had a phone cord to twist nervously at moments like this.

"That's fine. Say, in a few hours? I have some things I need to deal with here, first."

"Lunch is good."

"Okay. I'll meet you in front of the restaurant." She could almost hear the smile attached to the voice. "You'll know me when you see me."

Gretchen McBride was not having a good day. In fact, her bad day had technically begun more than twenty-four hours before, when she received the first of several phone calls from Natalie Sheridan, the elder sister and legal guardian of one of Gretchen's more recent, more special cases. Under other circumstances, Gretchen might have put Natalie off. The girl had obtained legal custody of her younger sister within only the last two years, and was still prone to fits of new parentish nerves and the occasional bout of less-than-perfect confidence. Gretchen could fully understand these reactions—they were only natural, after all—without necessarily feeling it was her place to backseat drive in Natalie's evolving relationship with her little sister. Offering advice when advice was solicited (and occasionally when it wasn't), yes. Mentoring as seemed necessary for both sisters, of course. Being a 24/7, all-hours-of-the-day-and-night-plus-weekends source of endless moral support? Not so much. Eventually, Natalie and Jillian would simply have to start getting along entirely on their own, or else Jilly would end up back in foster care or with another relative. It was that simple.

So when Natalie started calling, declaring in a faintly over-nervous manner that Jillian was listless and headachy and running a fever, Gretchen did what she thought was best: she told Natalie to get a doctor's appointment and not to panic. She administered a minor lecture about a parent's natural tendency to think the worst (and occasionally indulge in the odd hypochondriac tendency) when a serious disease was all over the news. She reminded Natalie that there were plenty of other ailments that could cause those symptoms and that Jillian probably just had a normal cold. Natalie, ultimately, agreed, and Gretchen spent the rest of the day out of the office, paying visits to a substantial chunk of the rest of her clients—many of whom, like Natalie, were worried and all of whom, like Natalie, wanted their fears comforted. By the time Gretchen made it back to the Department of Children and Family Services offices, it was past eight PM, raining like it never intended to stop, and even Super Social Worker Woman had had enough for one day. She'd glanced at the stack of messages piled on her desk, half of them from Natalie, dropped her stack of waterlogged case files on top of them, and had gone home with the firm intention of not worrying a damn bit about anyone else until she was fully dry and had some food inside her.

Perhaps, if she'd been ten years younger, she'd have followed up with Natalie immediately. If she'd been twenty years younger, she would have followed up immediately and possibly would have even made the necessary phone calls to arrange Jillian's doctor appointments herself. Gretchen McBride was no longer the young woman who had emerged from college, bright shiny master's degree in social work in hand, afire with the desire to change the world for the better, from the ground up if necessary. She had gone home, and gotten a shower, and eaten dinner, and been awoken at one in the morning by a genuinely hysterical call from Natalie. By the time it had penetrated her head that Jillian was in the hospital, that Jillian was *very sick*, that Jillian had the goddamned Muskegon variant of encephalitis that was putting the fear of mosquitoes into Chicago, Gretchen was already out of bed and half-dressed and wondering where the hell she'd put her car keys.

By the time she reached Northwestern Memorial, it was already over. Natalie was in the family waiting room, sitting there numb with shock at the suddenness of it all, and Jillian was dead. Gretchen was shocked pretty numb herself. Jillian was not one of Gretchen's normal clients, not one of the literally thousands of young girls who passed across her desk in the course of a single year at DCFS. Jillian was a special girl—special in her sensitivities, special in her interests, special in her raw potential. Gretchen hadn't known it from the moment they'd first met, more than two years prior, shortly after the death of Natalie and Jillian's parents. It was almost impossible to know with a child that young. But there was something about her that caught Gretchen's eye, even then, and she'd made a point to hold onto Jillian's case across her brief stint in foster care, after she'd gone to live with her mother's older sister, through the legal battle by which Natalie had finally attained guardianship of her sister. By then, Gretchen was sure—the little spark of "special" and "different," the spark she had once looked for in every child she'd met, was definitely there, and flickering at the edge of jumping into a full-fledged flame. The girl was close, close to making the transition, close to waking up all her sleeping inner potential, and Gretchen had watched and guided as best she was able.

Now, all that potential was dead. If she'd been run down by a drunk driver or shot by an idiot jealous boyfriend or mugged in the park, that would be one thing. Those were the normal hazards of urban life just about the world over. But, no. No, Jillian had somehow managed to contract a disease that had found its way across the Atlantic Ocean and, from there, into the body of a mosquito and, from there, into her bloodstream and… it was completely unreal. Gretchen knew that she did a piss-poor job of comforting Natalie at the moment when the woman needed her the most, just because she herself could hardly believe this situation was actually happening.

Gretchen's sense of pure unreality deepened when, shortly after she'd put Natalie in her car, her cell phone rang with a number she hadn't seen in quite a number of months. Baihu was also one of her special kids, though, in Baihu's case, it had been a damned long time since he could accurately be called a kid.

"McBride. Baihu, do you know what time it is?" As always, she had to forcibly resisting adding *young man* to the end of any sentence involving him.

"It's 2:23. I'm at the hospital. Granny has encephalitis."

Seven words, and the world had stunned Gretchen McBride—Tiaret—again.

They met upstairs ten minutes later, in the cafeteria rather than the ICU family waiting room, because Baihu wanted to talk somewhere more private. He arrived before she did and managed to banish any loitering night shift nurses by pulling the plugs out of all the vending machines.

"I really could have used a Twix, you know," Gretchen informed him, looking for a chair large enough to fully accommodate her no-longer-twenty-year-old keister and failing. "And, no, I don't need a lecture about the adverse effects of refined sugar on the human body because I still remember from the last time we sat down together. What's happened?"

"Granny woke up yesterday with a headache." Baihu looked like he'd gotten precisely zero sleep in the last twenty-four hours or so. "She took some Tong Qiao Huo Xue Tang to invigorate—well, okay, she took it to get rid of the headache, and she seemed to feel better for a while after that. By afternoon, it was back and she was running a fever. We wanted her to lie down and rest, but she had appointments…. " He looked up, eyes bright with tears. "Aunt Mel found her unconscious in her workroom just before suppertime. I'm sorry, Tiaret, I didn't know who else to call."

"Jesus. Do they have any idea how she was exposed?"

"The doctors are assuming it was a mosquito bite." Something in Baihu's tone made her eye him sharply. "I'm… not so sure I agree. Tiaret, please hear me out before you call me crazy. I think there might be something going on here beside the biannual encephalitis outbreak."

Gretchen resisted the urge to groan aloud. "Baihu, I know this was sudden, and it's a terrible shock, but what—"

"My grandmother hasn't been sick in almost forty years. Not a bug, not a sniffle. Not even the flu. She's never said as much in so many words, but she might not be able to *get* sick anymore, that's how profound her skills have become." Baihu, damn his pretty eyes, was born with more powers of earnestness and confidence than any human deserved. "I'm not saying that a natural, organic explanation is impossible—"

"That's good, because, the last time I checked, your grandmother was also over a hundred years old, incredibly skilled maga or not."

"—but it strains credulity just a little to ascribe solely natural causes to something that came over her so quickly, too. She is, as you so kindly pointed out, an elder maga. She is not only highly skilled but she is also wise in ways that both you and I can only guess at." He reached out and caught Gretchen's hand tightly. "There are already more people in ICU than died in the last encephalitis outbreak, Tiaret. Almost twice as many, in fact. My... instincts... are telling me that something's wrong here. I felt as much even before Granny got sick, and I think she might have thought something was wrong, too."

"You think—she didn't talk to you about it?"

Baihu hesitated for a long moment. "No. She was acting pretty secretive for the last couple of weeks."

Gretchen snorted. "Where have I heard that before? All right, for the sake of argument, let's say I agree with you that something weirder than average is going on. What do you think it is?"

"I don't know. But I can guess." Gretchen gave him a Get On With It, I Have To Be At Work In Two Hours Look. "A magically tainted version of the encephalitis virus that we've had the last couple of years. It killed forty-one people last year, and the gods alone know how many crows. It's not beyond the bounds of possibility, you and I both know that."

"No, it's not beyond the bounds of possibility—but what motive would anyone have to do something like that?"

"I did say I didn't know."

Gretchen sighed. "You realize how insane and grief-stricken this sounds, right?"

"Yes. I'm also not saying it's the only possible explanation. I am saying that anything—any disease, any virus, any infective agent—capable of hitting my grandmother this hard and this fast has got to be something special, in the worst way possible." Baihu stood up. "I'm sorry to drop this on you, Tiaret, but there's not a whole lot of people I trust enough to even suggest this to. Yes, I'm probably a little crazy right now. But that doesn't also mean I can't be right."

"If you tell me that's your personal key to enlightenment, I'm going to run screaming." Gretchen started to massage her temples, realized what she was doing, and stopped. "Look, I have to be at work very soon, and it's liable to be a bitch of a day. I'll make some calls to people I know who might have some expertise that'll prove useful. Why don't you dig up what you can, and we'll talk to exchange notes? That's the best I can do right now."

"All right. I'll give you a call. Thanks, Tiaret."

It wasn't until she was out of the hospital and back in her car, driving toward a very early start at the office, that Gretchen remembered that she hadn't told Baihu she was sorry to hear about his grandmother.

The Ninefold Lotus Healing Arts Academy occupied a four-story building on one of the less touristified streets in Chinatown. There was some creep, of course—a handful of plain red brick façades done over in faux-traditional "wood" painted a shade of cinnabar red offensive to human eyes and nature in general, highlighted in garish contrast paint and carvings—that stood out even more dramatically against the tastefully restrained storefronts to either side. Isaac Tsu didn't suppose he could blame the proprietors for going that route. Tourists and even most city-dwellers expected Chinatown to look "authentically Chinese," and were prone to dropping a good bit more cash in places where the waitstaff and cashiers wore skin-tight red cheongsams and chopsticks in their hair than others. The questionable nature of the authenticity never seemed to register to anyone laying down his credit card, and the remuneration no doubt helped ease the pain of their neighbors' scorn.

Isaac, who was only half authentically Chinese himself, didn't generally waste his energy on ethnic correctness but also didn't feel the need to kiss the community redevelopment committee's ass, either. The facade of the Ninefold Lotus was painted in cool shades of pale green and pale yellow, to accentuate the curtain-bordered picture window that carried the store's name in both English and Chinese. The canvas overhang was a similar shade of green, decorated around the edges with hanging baskets of live flowers. The first two floors of the building were the Healing Arts Academy itself—rooms for consultation, massage therapy, homeopathic medical treatments of all kinds. The upper two were family apartments and workrooms, containing three aunts, an uncle, six cousins, his grandmother, and his grandfather. Granny and Grandpa Tsu and his oldest aunt were at the hospital. There were no other lights on at the hour he finally arrived home, for which he was grateful. He wasn't sure how well he'd handle the rest of his family just now, particularly a couple of his more irritatingly teenaged cousins.

Isaac wanted desperately to sleep. He didn't. He slipped through the back door of the Ninefold Lotus and made his soft-footed way upstairs to his grandmother's private office/workroom, too tired to sleep, too driven by urgency to even try.

Granny Tsu's private room was as she always left it—compact and not precisely cluttered, but organized in a manner that only she could fully comprehend, indexed as it was according to her one-hundred-plus years of life experience. All four walls were lined in bookcases, chests, filing cabinets. There was no real desk, only a low, rosewood-and-marble writing table with one flat pillow next to it and one candle lamp on it. A cup of tea still sat on the edge of the table, along with a handful of brushes, a half-complete handwritten recipe or prescription, a now-dry bowl of fresh-ground ink. Despite the carefully maintained untidiness, the room's energies were profoundly well-balanced, guided into a state of harmonious flow that perfectly matched the rest of the building and which could not fail to edify the chamber's occupant. Isaac, attuned as he was to the spirit of this place, could sense nothing at all amiss, nothing out of balance, no sign of internal disorder or external assault, and that aggravated the living hell out of him.

"Of course there's nothing visibly wrong. If there were, I could figure out what the problem is and fix it. That would be too easy." Alone, he talked to himself, preferring any sound, even his own voice, to silence.

Granny Tsu's newest papers occupied a small rosewood correspondence chest situated next to her writing table. Inside, he found a dozen carefully inked recipes with accompanying instructions awaiting dispersal to Granny's personal clients, some of the oldest living residents of Chinatown, with whom she shared certain perspectives and experience and who trusted her more than they did any of her children or her grandson. These, he set aside to bring to Aunt Mel's attention when she got back from the hospital. Also stashed away inside was a handful of fairly recent letters with postmarks and return addresses primarily from points in Asia, which he bundled together and laid aside for the moment. At the very bottom was the object of his search, his grandmother's most-current personal journal, linen-rich paper pages, bound in a simple cover of dark blue silk and hand painted in her elegant calligraphy, marking the number and name of the year.

Isaac paused for a long moment before opening the book. There were some things one simply didn't do lightly, and invading the privacy of your mentor was one of them, even if she was also your direly ill grandmother. Given another choice, he would have taken it in a heartbeat—but, of the members of the family, only Granny Tsu and he were sorcerers, and there were some secrets she kept even from him, much less from the rest. With a silent plea for forgiveness, he opened the book and paged quickly through it to the most recent entries, trying to read no more of it than he had to. The last entry was dated two days earlier, and, as it happened, reading it wasn't much of a problem because he couldn't. Oh, the characters were all correct, perfectly drawn and perfectly arranged, into sentences that made no sense at all. A quick scan over several randomly selected pages showed him quickly that it was the same throughout, not just the most recent entries, and so the nonsensical but otherwise readable sentences were not the product of her illness, but likely some sort of code. A code that she had never taught him, and the key to which he had no immediate method of discerning. He let his head fall forward with a sigh.

From that angle, looking down on the book with his eyes half-focused, it leapt out at him—the characters for "golden" and "hart," which he'd missed in his rapid scan. The "Golden Hart" was a reference he did know. It was Granny Tsu's pet name for his best friend, Gwyn, who was, among other things, extremely blond and apprenticed to one of Granny's own colleagues.

Granny kept her office phone hidden under her table. Isaac fished it out, punched in Gwyn's phone number, and got a generic mechanical answering machine message in response. "Gwyn, you should really change that thing to something with more personality. It's Baihu. Call me—Granny's in the hospital, and I need to talk to you about a few things. Make it soon, okay?"

It didn't disturb him overly that Granny was in contact with Gwyn. He'd practically lived with them most of their freshman year in college, and Granny Tsu was the only person on Earth Gwyn treated with even a modicum of genuine personal respect. It did, however, seem somewhat odd that Granny wouldn't have mentioned talking to Gwyn to *him*. They weren't fighting, they weren't avoiding one another, and they weren't on bad terms, as they'd sometimes been over the years. At least, Isaac didn't think they were, and Gwyn in a snit wasn't particularly ignorable, and so he doubted that there was any problem in that direction, either. Granted, the reference might have been something completely innocuous, but, if so, why write in a working journal, in code no less?

As he sat thinking, the phone rang in his hand.

Despite the renewed enthusiasm talking to a live person brought her, Tam was realistic enough to assess her need for sleep as fairly desperate. She drew the curtains, set Watson on the desk with instructions to search out and collate a decent street-level map of the locations in the handheld's address database along with any information pertinent to the areas in question, and lay down to take a nap. She drifted off to the sound of her computer humming slightly off-key to himself as he went about his business and woke far too short a time later as her travel alarm went off, muddled and cranky and only marginally rested. Tam wasn't one to give much credit to the mystic nature of dreams—she'd read far too many studies on the science of brain function and had one too many dreams of walking into something important in her underwear—but that didn't really help when her overtired mind insisted on dancing across the border between lucid waking and lucid sleeping.

"Watson." Tam addressed the system, hoping she didn't sound too bad-tempered. "No one entered the room while I was asleep, correct?"

"That is correct, Glorianna. Housekeeping came by, but when you didn't answer the door, they moved on to the next room."

"Housekeeping. Okay, that makes sense. Just a dream, then." Tam sat up, rubbed the remaining grit out of her eyes, and went to the bathroom to wash her face. "Did you get the information I wanted?"

"Of course." It sounded mildly affronted that she even bothered to ask. "The print-outs have been prepared, and I had the browser save all the relevant links in a separate file."

"Thank you, Watson, that was good of you." Tam decided that she looked like crap and there was likely nothing she could do about it short of getting twelve uninterrupted hours of sleep. She settled for brushing her hair and putting a little Visine in her eyes.

A ream and a half of paper awaited her in the printer tray. "Watson, what's all this?" She picked up the top third of the pile and scanned through it quickly. The first few sheets were the maps she'd requested, but the rest was something else entirely. "I didn't ask for information on... the Leopold and Loeb trial... famous serial killers of the Chicago area... the World's Fair... Where did all this information come from? Tangential searches the browser worked out?"

Watson was silent for a long moment. Tam flipped open the laptop hood and was treated to the sight of her companion actually frowning as he considered the answer to her queries. "I am... sorry, Glorianna. I cannot trace the origins of several of the search strings the browser function executed."

"What do you mean?" Tam frowned herself and pulled up the browser manually, opening the file in which the salient websites the browser had consulted while compiling the information she'd wanted. A quick glance through them showed her nothing too bizarre—a good number of online route mapping sites, several links to various Chicago Chamber of Commerce pages, the UIC main website, a few local blogs of interest. "The browser saved all the links it followed, right?"

"Yes."

Tam sighed. "Look, my meeting... was four minutes ago, actually. I have to get going. Run your diagnostic processes while I'm gone. I want to know if the browser might have been hijacked somehow."

"Oh, now really, Glorianna. That's simply insulting."

"I'm fully prepared to admit that your internal security protocols are entirely capable of dealing with any normal form of malware, Watson, but I'd just like to make sure." The handheld unit went into its waterproof carrier and the courier bag she carried in lieu of an actual purse went around her waist and a quick glance out the window showed her that it was raining. Again. "Remind me to buy an umbrella before I come back."

"As you wish." Oh so very prissily. Tam rolled her eyes heavenward and asked for strength in the face of easily insulted computers.

Amazingly enough, it had got even hotter and more disgustingly humid. Tam felt her hair frizzing into an unruly mess the instant she stepped outside, and she was half-drenched by the time she made it across the street and to the doors of the restaurant. Fortunately, the air conditioning was working. Not so fortunately, it was packed to the walls with skirt-and-suit clad downtown workers who nonetheless made her feel distinctly underdressed in a pair of khakis and a short-sleeved Oxford. A quick glance around the lobby showed a handful of business types waiting for their tables to come available, but none of them stood out. Certainly not the way she thought the man she talked to would.

Someone tapped her on the shoulder, and she turned around to find herself looking at that someone's T-shirt-clad sternum. "Hello... Glorianna?"

Tam blinked, and looked up, and found herself staring into a face that would cause at least six of her former classmates to squeal like Japanese schoolgirls. He was like the platonic ideal of the exotically cute boyfriend that your parents wouldn't be threatened by, all gorgeous dark eyes and a winning smile married to an utterly dorky haircut. "Baihu, I presume?"

"That's me." He offered a hand—a strong, long-fingered hand, Tam couldn't help but notice—and gave a nice firm shake. "I got us a table. I hope you don't mind."

"Not at all." There weren't any particularly isolated booths or tables in the restaurant but, somehow, he'd managed to score one that wasn't located in the middle of a cluster of office workers. "It was good of you to take the time out to see me."

"It's the least I could do." He actually pulled her chair out for her. "After all, you came all the way to Chicago to see my grandmother. Dare I ask for the story behind that?"

Tam took a deep breath, and gave him the encapsulated version of events: her father's disappearance, her several years of searching along the trail of his many interests and acquaintances, the encounter in China that led her to Chicago. He didn't interrupt, just listened, which impressed her greatly.

"Great-grandpa." Baihu shook his head, a little smile lurking at the corners of his mouth. "My grandmother hasn't spoken to him in years, I'm afraid. He didn't approve of her second marriage."

"But they may have shared a colleague in my father." The waitress arrived and delivered their drinks, water with lemon for him and iced tea for her.

He glanced away. "I'm sure they did. I found your name and what I think is your father's in one of my grandmother's old contact books, and she's written of him several times in her journals."

Tam forced herself to swallow the surge of excitement that rose in her at those words. After all, she'd heard variations of them at least a dozen times before. "I think I hear a 'but.' Were any of the journal entries recent?"

"Semi-recent, yes. Within the last five years. The problem is that I can't read the substance of the entries. My grandmother writes her journals in several different codes, some of which she's never taught me how to break." He sounded deeply and sincerely aggrieved by that.

"A cipher?" Tam perked right back up at that. "I can help with that. My father didn't write everything in code, but he certainly didn't take chances with the majority of his sensitive documents. After he disappeared, I spent most of the first year just going through his papers and tearing out my hair."

He looked, for a moment, extremely torn. "Well... there's the rub, I'm afraid. It's not that I don't want to help you. Believe me when I say that. I understand how painful it is to lose a parent. But the references to your father occur in my grandmother's private journals—the books in which she recorded things that, by definition, were never intended for public consumption. I'm not sure she'd particularly appreciate me letting someone else look at them."

"Oh." Tam had, quite frankly, not even thought of that possibility as far as objections went. "But... what if I just decode the entries you *let* me look at? The ones that pertain to my father?"

"I'll have to think about that. If it's possible, that might be an option. But, for right now, I'm going to have to say I'm not sure if we'll be able to do that. I need to talk to... someone else about that." He looked intensely guilty, which didn't precisely mollify her. "How long will you be in Chicago?"

"A few more days, at least." Tam managed to get out, after spending a moment disciplining her temper. "I have a few other people I need to contact before I go back home to Boston. Can I at least give you my cell phone number and email? In case you change your mind?"

"Of course." The waitress arrived to take their order. "Lunch is on me if you'd like to stay... ?"

"That would be nice." Tam ordered the most expensive thing on the restaurant's decidedly upscale lunch menu and made a point of enjoying it thoroughly as they sat and talked around each other, carefully avoiding any potentially personal topics. He was full of good advice about how to get around the city and whom she might find amenable to helping her in her search, which Tam found almost unbearably nettlesome given the circumstances, and genuinely didn't mind paying, either. That made her regret the pettiness somewhat, though he waved off her attempt to pick up her half of the check.

"It's okay. I can write it off as a business expense." Baihu, she decided, had a very nice smile when he chose to employ it. "I'll be in touch, Glorianna. I'm sorry I couldn't be more immediate help."

"It's okay. I understand." The damnedest thing about it was that she did understand, even as she was eaten alive by irritation. Most of their kind were, at best, secretive to the point of stupidity, with or without the trained obscurantist tendencies instilled by many mentors and "professional organizations." At least she didn't get rained on again crossing back over to her hotel. The sun was actually peeking through the clouds, though it didn't look like the weather was anywhere near over yet. Despite herself, Tam felt the uncontrollable and unworthy urge to call someone and whine—not Movran, because he'd be far more likely to bust her chops than offer anything resembling sympathy, and not Watson, because whining to a computer was significantly less comforting than complaining to a real, live human being.

She settled for going back upstairs and settling down with the enormous mess of papers that Watson had produced. He was still deep in his diagnostic cycle when she entered, not even responding to her greeting, the laptop screen hibernating to conserve system resources as he worked. Sorting produced a small pile of completely useful maps and information culled from local websites about good places to eat and points of interest/concern, including the very newest bulletin from the CDC, and a large pile of documents of decidedly dubious and somewhat morbid interest. Tam supposed that every city had its seedy nastiness, past and present, that the suitably perverse would naturally seek to learn about and preserve, but Chicago seemed to have considerably more than its fair share of serial killers, environmental disasters, ethnic strife, and general corruption. The city also had its own local weblog and newspaper columnist, the quirkily anonymous *Oddly*

Enough to chronicle the apparently ongoing weirdness, several pages of which Watson had insisted on printing out.

What, exactly, statues that allegedly predict death had to do with the substance of her request for useful information, Tam couldn't guess. She tossed the printout aside, rose to stretch—and froze in mid-motion as Watson's speakers came on with a quiet burst of static that resolved into a single word:

"*Glorianna.*"

A shiver crawled up her spine. It wasn't Watson's voice. It didn't sound like an even quasi-human voice, synthesized or otherwise. The laptop screen flickered, irregular streaks of vivid color, black, white, and gray, flickers that almost resolved into a face, or a form.

"Watson?" She firmly resisted the completely irrational urge to ask if he was okay, or still in there. Of course he was. She crossed the room and jiggled the attached mouse. In a moment, the interference on the screen cleared, resolving into the familiar image of Watson, sitting in his chair, as his processes functioned around him. She let out a little breath that she hadn't realized she was holding. Then, her mouth fell open.

At Watson's feet, unmistakable despite the low-res pixellation of the image, was a black feather.

The silence woke him. Isaac had lived every moment of his life in Chicago. As a child, he'd lived in the crime-infested slum that provided the only apartment his parents could afford, and had learned how to sleep through the sound of gunshots, screams, and ethnically varied music. A part of him suspected he'd even been comforted. Then, after he'd come to live with Granny and Grandpa Tsu, he'd learned how to sleep through the sound of diesel-belching delivery trucks rattling up and down the streets at all hours of the day and night, and people yelling at each other in at least three Chinese dialects with a little English thrown in to further clarify or obfuscate any given point of argument—and that was in his own house.

So when the sound-no-sound of profound silence finally penetrated his sleep-sluggish mind, it woke him up as quickly and thoroughly as an air horn right next to his ear. For a long moment, he just lay still in his bed, staring up at the ceiling of his room and listened with all the senses physical and mystic at his disposal. It was mid-afternoon by the quality of the light in his two-room apartment—a gray and rainy afternoon—but there should have been plenty going on.

And there was nothing. No soft murmurs of consultation, underlaid by some soft and relaxing New Agey music, from the shop downstairs. No sound of his cousins at the PlayStation 2, arguing viciously over whose turn it was to play something next. There wasn't even the constant and ever-present hum of the building's mystic protections, a sound so subliminally low that it rarely registered at the level of conscious awareness, even in the Awakened. Isaac rose slowly and put on his glasses, went over to the window and looked out. There was nobody in the alley his window fronted on, not even a waiter or cook from the restaurant next door taking a smoke break, not even a delivery truck dumping a fresh load of linens or vegetables. He craned his neck further, and saw that the street out front was likewise empty, devoid of the tourists who could be counted on to throng Chinatown no matter how nasty the weather.

A quick trot around the building showed him that the weirdness wasn't confined to outside. The lights were on, but there was nobody home, not even his youngest cousin and her newborn daughter. All the apartments were empty. The shop downstairs was empty. The restaurant on one side and the butcher next door to him were both abandoned. Up and down the street, the shops and homes on his block were as devoid of life as the Chicago River. There weren't even any pigeons, none of the local cats or dogs. No traffic sounds, either, from elsewhere in the city.

Firmly repressing the urge to panic, Isaac climbed into his battered old Honda and set out to see if the weirdness, the zone of silence or whatever it was, was localized or all over. It didn't take him long to realize that, no, local it most definitely was not. There were no cars on any of the roads, not even the major city thoroughfares that were always choked with traffic at this time of the day. He parked and sat watching an elevated train platform and its tracks for a half-hour—even if there'd been passengers to pick up, which there weren't, no train ever passed by. The Loop was as silent and deserted as an Old West ghost town.

The urge to panic was getting a couple of orders of magnitude harder to ignore. As he drove past Lincoln Park Public Library along Fullerton, it finally occurred to him to see if he had cell phone reception, which he did. The first three numbers he dialed (the hospital, Tiaret, and Gwyn) terminated at the switchboard and two answering machines. Adding frustration to the growing urge to freak out, Isaac disconnected his last call and nearly jumped out of his skin when the phone rang in his hand, for the second time in as many days. Juggling the cell, he managed to punch the receive key and got it to his ear without dropping it. "Hello?"

And then he jerked it away, as a sleet-storm of static, punctuated by a chorus of hundreds of babbling voices, all speaking at once, all trying to talk over one another, poured out of the speaker. A glance at the screen showed him no connected number, none at all, and as he registered this, the storm of voices resolved into a single word: "*Baihu.*"

The voice was genderless, almost toneless. It didn't even sound human, unlike the voices babbling on after it. Those voices sounded human… and weirdly familiar. As he listened, the voices became *a* voice, a childish voice, a boy's voice, a low whisper gradually increasing in volume.

"*Peekaboo, I see you…. Peekaboo, I see you…. Peekaboo, I SEE YOU…*"

Even pressing the disconnect frantically didn't cut off that voice.

"*Shall we play hide-and-seek again, Isaac? I know you always enjoyed that game….*"

"No," Isaac forced his own voice to work, though it barely reached above a whisper. "I never liked that game."

Then, very simply, he woke up. Opened his eyes. Took in the familiar interplay of shadows and light falling across his ceiling, the way the night lay in his apartment. It was three-oh-three in the morning, according to his bedside clock, and he decided, abruptly, that he'd slept quite long enough. The cell was right where he'd left it, on the bedside table next to his glasses, and he punched for the first preset before he even finished wiping the sweat out of his eyes. Got the answering machine, again. "Gwyn, look, I really need to talk to you. Call me, okay? Something weird just happened."

We must be careful—the others are blind but that one… that one is different….

All HIS fault, couldn't keep hold of his little toy….

We could still put out his eyes, if it comes to that.

"Shut up, I'm trying to think."

No.

What do you mean, NO?

Really, it's not as though he's YOURS anymore.

You can't control him, you can't use him, you can't—

You're wrong.

"Shut up, shut up, shut up!"

Momentary silence fell. A very thick silence. The girl brushed her hair out of her face, finished the sentence she was working on, and clicked Send. Soon. She'd check back later—she knew everyone was waiting for her call. They'd write back as quickly as they could. It would be soon.

Watson's internal diagnostic produced no results, indicating no outside intrusion into the system whatsoever and no logical origin point for the system browser to have turned up more than half the information it had. Tam was simultaneously concerned and more than a little displeased by that result, but didn't think having Watson run two diagnostics in two days would really accomplish anything but take him offline when she needed him most. Instead, she put him to work contacting the people whose numbers Baihu had given her the day before: Tiaret, Nuad, Airyaman, and Protagoras, in Baihu's words, "probably the only contact person for the local Consilium that you'd want to deal with. Trust me on this."

Tam had trusted him, and, as a consequence, she ended up having a very pleasant conversation with both Protagoras and Airyaman, who were in close enough quarters that one could pass the phone to other. Yes, they would make her presence in the city known to the local Hierarch, and, no, they didn't think she'd need to present herself formally, since she was only going to be staying for a few days. They'd also mention that she was looking for her father, and what was the name again…? Protagoras had a very pleasant British accent that put her immediately at ease, and Airyaman, though he sounded a bit on the spacey side, said he'd check his cabal's records to see if they'd had any dealings with her father in the past, though he couldn't remember any right off the top of his head. That was disappointing, but not totally unexpected, given her luck in this city thus far.

Calling Nuad resulted in a message directing her to call one of two other numbers: Poole & Updike Funeral Home, if the need was professional, and a cell phone number if the need were personal. The cell phone number dumped into a generic voicemail box, at which she left a not-particularly-hopeful message. Calling Tiaret got a live person. Tiaret was wary until Tam indicated that she'd been referred by Baihu, which smoothed some of the tension and resulted in an invitation to lunch, which Tam accepted, despite the recent history of unproductive meetings. Tiaret specified a place downtown, "close to my office—we've got a lot of stuff on our plates just now, so I can't take much time out of the office," and gave Tam some time to get herself in order beforehand.

The restaurant Tiaret wanted to meet in was a hot dog stand with pretensions, complete with Formica tables and mismatched chairs and a scent compounded of equal parts grease and cigarettes. Tam immediately felt the need to shower upon entering the place, her dripping new umbrella in hand.

Tiaret was, as promised, sitting at a table just inside the doors. She rose, an imposingly tall and wide black woman in her mid-forties, her graying hair pulled back in a tight bun, dressed in a determinedly nondescript business casual pantsuit. "Glorianna, I presume?"

Tam took the offered hand and shook it. "Tiaret. It's a pleasure to meet you."

"Have a seat." Tiaret reseated herself. Tam couldn't help but notice that she oriented herself to keep one eye on the rest of the diner and one eye on the door. "How can I help you?"

Tam took a deep breath and, for the second time in as many days, gave her encapsulated spiel: missing father, searching the world, in need of help. Much like Baihu, Tiaret listened, nodded, and, at the end, said, "I'm afraid there's not much I can do to help you."

Tam rubbed her eyes, which were watering in response to the arrival of a platter of chili-cheese dogs with extra onion. Her own lunch, three domes of egg, ham, and tuna salad on a bed of greens and tomato, gazed up at her dolefully. "I admit I expected that was the case. But when Baihu referred me to you, I sort of hoped—"

"Baihu referred you to me for one reason and that was because he didn't want to see you sucked into our local problems by one of the others." Tiaret took a sip of her soda. "What sort of research did you do before you came here?"

"Uhm." Tam considered how to answer that for a moment. "I looked up the municipal website to see what the weather was like at this time of year and bought a couple of travel guides…? I was coming from Tokyo."

A sigh. "I thought as much. I dearly wish you'd called your mentor before you came—"

"I don't have a steady mentor. Not really. Most of what I've learned, I've learned on the fly." Tam stuffed a forkful of egg salad in her mouth under Tiaret's quelling look.

"That's even worse, I'm afraid. If you'd had a mentor, he or she might have been able to tell you that Chicago is not the sort of city you want to go poking around in without someone to watch your back." The older woman took a handful of paper napkins out of the dispenser and a ballpoint pen out of her purse. Tam thought she was writing phone numbers or addresses on them until she dropped one next to her chair, one at each end of the table, and handed one across the table. "Please put that on the floor next to you, dear."

Tam did so and, instantly, felt something happen—everything seemed slightly distant, the smells less immediate, the sounds softened to a low murmur. She somehow suspected that, from the outside, nothing looked particularly different. "You've made our conversation harder to overhear…?"

"Yes." Tiaret flicked a glance past Tam's shoulder. "Did you see that man sitting four tables back when you came in—brown hair, navy blazer, looks like he hasn't shaved in a couple of days? No, don't look. He can still see us. He just can't hear us without doing something himself."

Tam wracked her memory. "Sort of."

"That's Mimir, the first chief legbreaker for the local Consilium. He usually effects to be as unmemorable as possible, with or without any tricks. He and his staff have been making themselves annoying to me for several days now. Have you been in contact with the Hierarch?" She took a bite of one of her hot dogs, keeping her expression as open and pleasant as possible, just two girls out having a casual lunch.

"I've spoken to a representative of the Consilium. He told me that I wouldn't need to do anything special since I was basically just passing through." The hairs on the back of Tam's neck kept trying to rise, much to her annoyance. "Was that a lie?"

"Not really. The Hierarch and I don't agree on many issues, but he rarely harasses visitors unless they do something to negatively attract his attention. Unfortunately, you might be walking down that road right now." Another sip of soda, another bite of hot dog. "You've been trying to find your father's old colleagues. Do yourself a favor and look somewhere else. Most of the older cabals in this city were destroyed in the 1980s. Most of the wizards who lived here then are either dead or... elsewhere. Left the city. Some even left the country."

Tam swallowed another mouthful of salad with some difficulty. "Destroyed?"

"Yes. It was... stupid. Based on nothing but a rumor," an extremely expressive grimace, "about a powerful artifact. One of *those* artifacts. It was enough to bring on a full-blown war between the people who wanted to find said artifact, and the people whom they thought were hiding it. As it turned out, no artifact. But that doesn't make the people who died less dead, or the situation more stable. The Hierarch's one of the ones who thinks the artifact is here, it just hasn't been found. And you'd do well to remember that he and his kind are willing to use any warm body they can get their hands on to further their efforts in that regard. If there's even the remotest chance that your father might have had some connection to this artifact hunt, you may very well be in some danger."

"Oh." A chill started a long, slow slide up Tam's spine. "I... I don't even know if my father might have had anything to do with it."

"Neither do I. Likely neither does anyone else, with only a couple exceptions."

"I've already been in touch with Grandmother Feng-huang and Nuad, but I haven't been able to speak to them. I've also spoken to Airyaman, though he said he didn't remember my father right off the top of his head." Tam surrendered to the urge to look over her shoulder and found Mimir sitting just where Tiaret said he was, glancing down at his watch.

"Airyaman has forgotten more about this city than most people ever know—which, in his case, means he might just have written it down someplace for later consideration." Tiaret steepled her fingers. "It might be all around safer for you just to stay in contact with him remotely and—"

Tiaret's cell phone rang. Almost instantaneously, the handheld unit in Tam's courier bag began vibrating. The public pay phone on the wall next to the emergency exit also starting ringing, as did the store phone behind the counter, and, within moments, the entire restaurant was filled with at least a dozen clashing ring-tones as various cell phones went off, more or less simultaneously. Tam dug out the handheld and, even as she was processing the fact that the flat screen display wasn't registering an incoming call, Tiaret said, "What the hell...?" and clicked her own receive button.

A storm of a thousand voices, all speaking, screaming, babbling, wailing at once poured out of her phone. Before Tam could hit the disconnect on the handheld, her own call connected, with similar results. Up and down the tables and the snack bar closest to the grills, people yelped and dropped their phones. Within moments, the babble of lunchtime conversation had been replaced by the eerie, hissing, screeching pouring out of the phones—every phone in the restaurant. Then, just as quickly as it started, it stopped. The phones all cut off at once, some in mid-word, going silent. For a long moment, nobody said a word, Tam and Gretchen looking at one another, wide-eyed. Then:

"Can you hear me now? Good."

Nervous laughter greeted this statement, coming as it did from the lips of the tall, broad-shouldered man in the blue blazer, whose face no one would remember later. Mimir swept out of the restaurant and speared Tiaret with a look in passing, as conversation restarted all around them. Tam flipped open the flat screen display of the handheld and addressed it quietly. "Watson, where did that call come from?"

A pause. "My systems show no record of any incoming or outgoing cellular connections, Glorianna."

Tam took a deep, calming breath and managed not to snap. "That's impossible, Watson. I just—"

Tiaret's phone rang again, a call that was, apparently, completely normal. "McBride. Baihu—is that you? You sound—Yes. Yes. I'm at lunch right—What? Say that again, using the smallest words possible. All right, I have to admit, that sounds pretty... strange. Yes. I'll be right there." She hung up. "Glorianna, I'm sorry to cut our meeting short, but I'm afraid I'll have to go."

"You're going to see Baihu." It wasn't a question, and Tam rose as well, slipping the handheld back in its case and shouldering her courier bag.

"Yes. I don't think—"

"I know you mean well, and I thank you for your concern. But I need to talk to him again, myself, and if we go together, it'll just save me from going off alone, don't you think?" Tam tried what she hoped was a charming smile, only to see it deflected off of Tiaret's complete immunity to charm. "I really need to talk to him. And I'd appreciate any help the two of you can give me. Something is obviously going on here—this is the second time since I arrived that something intruded without a trace into my companion's systems. I just want to ask a few questions, and then I'll go. Is that acceptable?"

"I can see there's not much I can do to change your mind." Tiaret collected the check and paid it without comment. "Let's go—I've only got an hour for lunch, and we need to meet Baihu over at Northwestern Memorial."

Tiaret called her office to let them know she'd be late getting back from lunch, she'd received a call from a client whom she needed to see at once, a lie but not much of one. Baihu had been one of her clients, once upon a time, she explained, as they took the elevator up to the ICU waiting room. Said former client was waiting for them in the hall outside the waiting room proper, which was full of the assorted relatives of the ward's residents, its door closed. Tam took note of the fact that he looked a little bit more frayed around the edges than he had when they'd met only a day earlier.

Tiaret apparently agreed with her. "Baihu... dare I ask what's happened?"

"Oh... a couple of things." He wet his lips, and took a deep breath. "I just spent a very unpleasant night having visions of the entire city of Chicago up and vanishing when I wasn't looking. Not the city itself, all the buildings were still here, but all the people were gone. Then, just as I finished freaking out about that, I got a phone call from the hospital telling me that my grandmother was awake." He paused, took a deep breath, and continued. "By the time I got here, she was unconscious again. But she left me a message."

Tiaret gestured for them to find a suitably quiet corner before demanding, "And was this message, perhaps, an SOS?"

"I don't know. It was her pet name for Gwyn." He fumbled in his back pocket and pulled out a piece of hospital stationery, on which was scrawled in a very messy hand two Chinese characters. "Tiaret—this is well past weird."

"I know." Tiaret replied. "Glorianna and I have just had a very strange experience of our own. Something intruded into the city phone network—not just the cellular phones but the landline phones, as well. Rang everything in the restaurant that we were at. Sounded like… well, like nothing I've ever heard before. Voices. Thousands of them, at least."

"What the hell are we going to do? Between all this and the virus, too—"

"We don't know that the virus is connected to anything, Baihu," Tiaret replied, a bit too sharply, Tam thought. "It could just be a bad season for it. Happens all the time, all over the world, and we're not immune to that."

"Wait," Tam interjected. "Wait just a minute. What's this about the virus.… The encephalitis thing that's going around? Is that what you're talking about?"

"Baihu has a theory that our annual encephalitis outbreak is being made worse—"

"And might even be caused by—"

"Yeah, that, too. Anyway, Baihu thinks that the encephalitis thing might be suffering from malicious external attention." Tiaret continued, with a glare at Baihu for interrupting her. "There's a certain amount of validity to the possibility. Grandmother Feng-huang isn't exactly the average old lady on the street. She's a skilled practitioner of the Art. Even if she'd gotten it, she should have been able to fight it off—not without effort, but she shouldn't be as sick as she is. I've asked some friends of mine about it."

Baihu smiled crookedly. "Thank you. I take it you don't think I'm crazy, then?"

"No, I still think your theory is insane. I just think you might also be right," she replied, tartly. "And I think it's quite odd that your Granny woke up just long enough to point a finger at our friend Gwyn."

"Who is this 'Gwyn'?" Tam's fingers itched for the handheld and a stylus, wanting to check that name against her list of Chicago-area contacts.

"He's been my best friend since high school. Though, if he knows anything, I'd like to think he'd just come right out and tell me," Baihu told her.

"I'd like to think that, too, but Nuad's got every reason to be tight-assed as far as security goes, and I expect that's the one thing he's managed to fully instill in Gwyn." Gretchen's tone was very, very flat. "You going to talk to him?"

"Yeah. I've tried calling him three—two times, and I keep getting his answering machine." Baihu transferred his attention to Tam. "I'm sorry I interrupted your meeting, Glorianna."

"Nothing to apologize for. In fact, I think we can be of help to each other." Tam tried to keep her tone even and level, despite the excitement suddenly bouncing around in her chest. "You see, I've been experiencing some weirdness since I came to this city, too. In fact, my artifact computer system, Watson, has been experiencing something very similar to a viral intrusion."

Baihu inclined his brows questioningly. "What do you mean…?"

"I think whatever's causing your weirdness is trying to get my attention." Tam pulled out the handheld, and let him take a look at it. "My system is something rather more than off-the-shelf from Best Buy. It would take a lot to get inside it, and even more to get back out again without leaving signs of its intrusion behind."

"Viruses, huh." Baihu held her eyes, his look frankly appraising. "Stuff that intrudes where it's not supposed to be with the intent to cause harm, often for no good reason."

"Right," Tam said, excitedly. "You see—"

"The linkage. The similarity. Yes, I do. I think we can help one another, don't you?"

"Yes. Most definitely."

Gwyn lived in one of the less desirable neighborhoods on the city's South Side, in an apartment building that might have been pleasant and well-kept sometime during Prohibition. Baihu asked her to lock her door as they rolled up outside its graffiti-tagged front steps, and Tam did so without having to be told twice. Theirs was the only car on the block that didn't look as though stealing it would bring down the immediate wrath of a drug dealer or a pimp or something equally unsavory. Tam hung close as they went up the steps, Baihu leading with way with the confidence of familiarity, stepping around places where the entry hall floor sagged, disguised by a threadbare hall rug, and over risers on the second-floor staircase that had begun to dry-rot and split. The second floor hallway was lined with garbage bags on both sides, and its walls, seepage stained and painted a color that might have been white at some time in the past, were punctuated at regular intervals by numbered doors, themselves painted an extremely unpleasant shade of green.

"Why does he live here?" Tam asked, thoroughly appalled.

"Honestly? To freak out his parents." Baihu knocked once on what she devoutly hoped was the right door. "They live up in Winnetka, north of the city. His dad's a neurosurgeon and his mom's a trained attack lawyer with one of the big firms inside the Loop."

"Well, that's mature." Tam sniffed, and immediately regretted it.

Baihu offered a smile in response. "I never said that perfect maturity was one of his cardinal virtues. He's very good at what he puts his mind to doing, though." Another knock, a bit more forcefully this time, which brought a disgruntled yell from the apartment next door.

Tam edged a little closer and turned her back to the wall, hoping that she wouldn't have to touch it. A few more minutes passed, and, finally, Baihu finished losing his patience. He knocked hard enough to rattle the door on its hinges. "Come on, Gwyn, I know you're in there—your car's parked outside! Open the freaking door!"

That got a reaction, mostly from the neighbors, whose deluge of four-letter commentary made Tam blush furiously. It also brought a response from inside, the sound of multiple locks disengaging. The door cracked open, and a hoarse, sleep-thickened voice emerged. "Christ, Bai, do you have any idea what time it is?"

"It's 2:36 in the afternoon. Let us in—we need to talk to you." Baihu looked perfectly prepared to straight-arm the door open, which Tam found immensely endearing.

"We?" the unseen speaker asked, even as he opened the door. Tam got a flash impression of intense paleness as he receded into the dimness of his apartment: hair so blond it was nearly white, skin whose natural enemy was clearly sunlight, clad in a pair of antiseptic green hospital scrubs from the waist down. He crossed the room in two steps and turned on a floor lamp. "What—oh. Who's the biscuit?"

Tam had no idea what a biscuit was supposed to be, but she was absolutely certain such a term had no business being applied to her. "Glorianna." She introduced herself icily. "And you must be—"

"Gwyn," Baihu interjected, stepping not quite between them and making introductory gestures. "Don't mind him, Glorianna, we all suspect he was socialized by New Yorkers. Gwyn, this is Glorianna—her father and Granny worked together for a little while it seems, so she's kindly offered to give me a hand with some things. So be nice. And what the hell are you on?"

Gwyn did, in fact, look as though he were suffering from severe sleep deprivation or an unhealthy relationship with some heavy recreational chemicals, and possibly both. There were dark circles underneath his gray-blue eyes, and the eyes themselves were so bloodshot there was almost more red than white to them. He moved with a sort of twitchy energy that didn't seem wholly natural as he cleared off the futon for them to sit on. "Jeez, Bai. I'm on two and a half hours of sleep. I've been working extra shifts down at the morgue—every hospital in the city's short-handed when it comes to trained personnel right now."

Baihu's posture relaxed fractionally. "Well, that explains why you haven't returned my calls."

"Yeah. Back-to-back-to-back, and then they sent me home because I couldn't stand up straight anymore." He dumped the pile of dirty clothes and random bachelor detritus into the darkest corner he could find. "Make yourselves at home for a minute. If you want me to think, I at least need a shower."

Baihu glanced at Tam, and nodded. "It'll wait that long."

"Be right back." Their host vanished through the gap between two bookcases. "And you most assuredly are a biscuit, Little Princess."

Tam spluttered, Isaac visibly stifled a laugh, and any response she might have made was drowned out by the sound of ancient plumbing groaning to life somewhere beyond the bookcases. She had to firmly resist the urge to whip out the handheld and ask Watson to find the definition of the term "biscuit," certain in the knowledge that the reply would have nothing to do with pastry. Instead, she took several deep breaths, counted to ten, and let her gaze travel across the bookcases, which were stuffed to capacity with novels, CD and DVD cases, medical texts, a profusion of notebooks in various states of disintegration, and a handful of dust-gathering knickknacks, most of which appeared to be imported from Japan. One of them caught her eye, a glossy black feather, its quill wrapped in red and white thread.

"He's a medical student?" Tam finally asked, and found herself addressing Baihu's back as he made himself busy in the kitchenette—two standing cabinets, a sink, a bachelor-sized refrigerator, and a microwave.

"Last year. Forensic pathology and… uh… whatever it is you call the field of study for a coroner. Something to drink?" He put whatever he was working on in the microwave.

"No, thank you." Tam firmly resisted the urge to remark that at least his profession didn't require a good bedside manner. Or any manners at all, really. "Moros?"

"Yep." The microwave beeped, and Baihu extracted its fragrantly steaming contents, in probably the last clean coffee mug in the whole place.

"Somehow that figures."

Their host chose that opportune moment to rejoin them, still damp from the shower but fully dressed in a black T-shirt and khaki cargo pants, his pale hair plastered to his skull. "Okay, what's this—"

Baihu handed him the mug. "Drink. Then talk."

He accepted the mug, took a swallow, choked, gagged, and, eventually, managed to get it down without drooling it all over the already-stained carpet. "You just gave me something to help me detox, didn't you? You asshole. I wasn't finished enjoying that state of toxicity yet."

"You are now." Baihu crossed his arms over his chest, drew himself up to his full, impressive height. "I need to know what you were doing with Granny."

"Dude." Gwyn made a face and finished the drink in two hard swallows. "I keep telling you, there's no such thing as a GILF. No matter how much plastic surgery she's had. Not that I think Granny had plastic surgery but, well—"

"Granny's in the hospital. She's got encephalitis."

"No fucking way." He found a horizontal surface and put the mug on it. "When was she admitted? Where was she admitted?"

"Almost two days ago. Northwestern Memorial." Baihu's eyes narrowed a dangerous fraction. Tam decided that she wouldn't necessarily want to be on the business end of one of his glares. "Answer the question."

"That's not possible." Gwyn looked legitimately shocked. "I just talked to her this morning, Bai."

The look on Baihu's face was a marvel to behold. Tam stepped in to translate. "We just came from the hospital, and I assure you that she wasn't in any condition to call anyone. She's in very critical condition and comatose." Tam paused, weighed how to phrase what she wanted to say, and continued. "She did briefly regain consciousness late this morning, and left a message for Baihu. Her name for you. When did you get the call?"

"Lemme think." He rooted through the dirty clothes for a towel. "I worked till about eight, when some morning shift relief came in, puttered around for about an hour more helping them get up to speed… traffic sucked… I got home about quarter of ten. I couldn't sleep, too wired, so I tried to read, but I couldn't concentrate, so I was laying down and… probably about 11:30ish?"

Baihu nodded. "I got the call from the hospital a little past noon, about Granny waking up. By the time I got to the hospital, she was unconscious again. What'd she say?"

"I need a drink. With alcohol in it." Their host crossed to the refrigerator, rooted around for a second, and settled for an orange.

Baihu took a breath between his teeth. "Gwyn. What did she call you about?"

"I can't tell you." He steadfastly refused to meet Baihu's glare, methodically peeling the orange. "I'm sorry, Bai. I can't."

"Why the hell not?"

Gwyn and Tam both jumped half a foot, the orange landing in the sink as it independently dove for cover. Tam was briefly gratified to see someone at least as frustrated as she was by this situation. The satisfaction was extremely short-lived, and she stepped forward quickly to lay a calming hand on Baihu's arm. Gwyn tried, half-successfully, to look as though he wasn't retreating by taking a few steps back and leaning on the sink.

"All right." He licked his lips, looked mournfully at his breakfast floating in a half-inch of neglected dishwater, and continued in a would-be soothing tone. "I'll tell you what I can. It's not much, but... a couple of months ago Granny asked me to do a bit of research for her. She didn't say it was anything particularly urgent—she just wanted me to compile some stuff from Nuad's Athenaeum, stuff that she couldn't access for herself. From the restricted section, y'know."

"If it wasn't anything serious, why can't you—" Baihu began, his glare sharpening again, only to be cut off.

"I didn't say it wasn't serious. I said it wasn't urgent. Granny was apparently operating under the assumption that she'd have some time to—" He stopped, almost literally choking on what he'd been about to say, visibly unable to continue. "She thought she wasn't operating under serious time pressure." He finished, somewhat lamely. "She might have been wrong. She specifically asked me not to discuss what I was doing with you. Then she made me swear that I wouldn't discuss it with you, no matter what. Or anyone else for that matter, until she was ready to let me."

"Are you telling me that my grandmother *oathbound* you to silence? Toward me?" Baihu sounded more than a little outraged by that, and Tam found she couldn't much blame him for it.

"Not just you—but, yes, you in specific." Gwyn replied. "When she called this morning—or whatever sounded like her called—she asked me a couple of questions about my progress. Then the line crackled and—"

"You heard what sounded like hundreds of voices speaking all at once?" Tam hopped in, and earned a startled look of her own.

"Yeah. We've got some fairly ancient wiring down around here but that seemed somewhat weird even by my standards." He paused again, and gave Tam another assessing look, a bit more respectfully this time. "Then the interference or whatever it was went away, and the last thing I heard was Granny saying my name. I fell asleep waiting for her to call back."

"That probably wasn't your grandmother who called here, Baihu." Tam looked up at him in time to see him reaching the same conclusion.

"You're right... it probably wasn't." He turned a somewhat apologetic look on his friend. "I'm sorry I yelled. I've been under a lot of stress. And I'm sorry to drag you out like this, but we need your help. Something weird, in a bad way, is going on."

"No shit."

They filled him in on the ride to the hospital, where Baihu was due to relieve his Aunt Mel. By the time they got there, they'd even managed to convince him that all of it was real and even that there might be some causative link between all of the great variety of weird occurrences.

"Look, I'm not arguing that it's impossible, okay," he informed them over the remains of their supper, hospital commissary sandwiches and oily coffee, "because God knows it is. This can't have been any ordinary bug to get Granny. But how're we going to identify whatever the fuck it was that hit her? I'm willing to bet they wouldn't smile on high ritual diagnostic work in the middle of the ICU."

"I wasn't planning on trying anything in the middle of the ICU." Baihu's withering glare wasn't as impressive as his threatening glare, but he gave it the college try. "I was thinking about the blood and tissue samples they take for testing here in the hospital."

"How would we get access to something like that, though?" Tam felt compelled to ask, trying for voice-of-reasonableness. "Those samples are biological hazards, aren't they? It can't be easy to get to them, or get them out of the hospital even if you could get to them."

"Blood and tissue samples are easier to get a hold of than the narcotics. Every hospital's different in the way it handles biological storage. Some places, they don't even lock them up." Gwyn's voice lowered slightly as a pair of nurses crossed near the door. "The handling protocols are generally all the same, but sometimes there's a central storage area and sometimes there's a storage area on each ward. We'd need to find that out before anything else."

Tam pulled out the handheld and stylus. "Watson, can you find the technical schematics and floor plans for Northwestern Memorial Hospital?"

"Just a moment, Glorianna." Fortunately, they were within sufficient range that Watson could piggyback himself into the hospital's internal network. Within seconds, the requested information was scrolling its way up the handheld's tiny screen.

Tam looked up to find both her companions staring at her. "What?"

"What the hell is that?" Gwyn asked, raising a pointed eyebrow at Watson.

"It's... radiating.... You're right. What is that? It feels *alive*." Baihu seemed to be resisting the urge to lean across the table and poke it.

"Watson. His name is Watson." Tam turned the handheld so they could see the screen, putting Watson's little-old-man icon in one corner. "He's one of my father's creations."

"It's intelligent?" Baihu and Gwyn exchanged a glance.

"He's very intelligent, yes," Tam replied, "since he found what we were looking for in fourteen seconds."

"Heh. Okay, Glory, point taken." Gwyn leaned in closer. "Scroll it slowly.... Okay. Yeah. It looks like Northwestern uses a central bio-storage area. Right there in the first sub-basement."

"What kind of security would we be looking at?" Baihu asked, and Tam queried the data Watson had collected.

"It doesn't really look like the storage area is the most highly secured part of the hospital," Tam announced. "The storage area doors are kept locked, but a physician's access card opens them all."

"That figures." Gwyn smiled. "I have an idea.... "

It turned out to be much easier than Isaac would have guessed to get access to the hospital's standard-issue staff scrubs. They just waited until the ICU ward staff room was empty, strolled in, and snatched two sets from the cabinet. This proved an easy enough endeavor for Gwyn, who was solidly average-sized, as were most of the scrubs. Isaac, on the other hand, ended up wearing something intended for an orderly sized at least six-six and built like a defensive lineman for the Bears.

"Jeez. Like this won't stand out."

"This wouldn't be a problem if you'd just eat a little pork fried rice every now and then, Bai. Here, put on the lab coat—it'll disguise it a little." Gwyn bent down to examine the combination on one of the individual lockers. "Watch the door. This might take a minute."

Isaac did as he was told. "What are you—"

Behind him, the locker combination spun and the door opened. "Staff ID badges. Well, a staff doctor ID badge for me, anyway. You can be my orderly. Grab one of the badges out of the dirty laundry bin over there.... "

"Why didn't you just do that?" Isaac asked, and was aggravated to find that Gwyn was absolutely correct, and the first scrub shirt he found had a forgotten badge pinned to it.

"Because fucking with staff psychiatrists is the greatest joy of my life. Let's go."

Gwyn, Isaac was forced to admit, had confidence enough for both of them, and walked through the halls of the hospital as though he belonged there, breezing past nurses, doctors, and family members with equal insouciance. Isaac hung close and tried not to look too much like a gangly Chinese twenty-something with no formal hospital experience wearing the poison-green scrubs of a man twice his body weight. As they entered the elevator, he touched the bead headset he was wearing and murmured, "You've got us, Glorianna?"

The headset crackled a little, but that was to be expected. "I have you on visual, tracking through the security cameras. I'll start redirecting them sequentially starting now."

"Thanks." Isaac nodded to Gwyn. "She's covering our tracks."

The elevator doors opened, revealing an empty hallway lined in doors labeled with plaques. They both paused and glanced each way. Fortunately, the door they were looking for wasn't hard to find. The bio-storage area actually took up its own corridor, separated from the rest of the sublevel. The keycard Gwyn filched worked, and, within moments, they were inside the bio-storage corridor, searching for the ICU storage room. It was the last one on the corridor, a small room filled with four refrigerated cabinets, a stack of freshly sterilized sample cases on a cart, and a line of portable refrigeration cases against the far wall. Gwyn handed Isaac a sample case, selected one for himself, and started opening doors. "This one."

"What should we be looking for?" Isaac stared blankly at rack upon rack of samples, vials of blood and other, less identifiable substances.

"Stuff like this." Gwyn held up paired vials, exposing the label. "Or, like me, you could let your fingers do the walking. Feel for it."

"Oh. Yeah. Sorry."

"You're provisionally forgiven because you have an excuse. But we'd better work fast."

Isaac could only agree, and bent to the task. Gwyn, as it turned out, was right. Running his hands over the racks slowly and extending his senses showed him more than looking for labels. His fingers would tingle and his eyes would prickle with sympathetic tears as he touched what he was looking for. These vials—samples of blood and spinal fluid—he removed and added to the carrier case he was holding. Gwyn was doing something similar, it seemed, because his case was filling just as quickly.

"I think we've got enough."

The door slammed behind them, the lock, which hadn't been turned before, engaging from the outside.

"Shit."

A moment later, the fire alarm began ringing.

"Shit some more."

Isaac and Gwyn both lunged at the door, juggling their sample cases as they did so. "Here... try the keycard."

The keycard didn't work.

"Up to our knees in shit." Gwyn asserted, kicking the door for good measure.

"What," Isaac asked, "are we doing to do?"

"Calm down. Think. What are we dressed as?" Gwyn took a deep breath. "We'll... just wait for security and..."

"Talk our way out of it? We're doomed." Isaac reached up and touched the headset. "Glorianna, did you see what happened? Nnngh. Yes. Okay. Get out of here—we'll take care of ourselves."

"So? What happened?"

Isaac took the bead out of his ear, shoved it in the pocket of his scrubs. "Later. I hear footsteps. I hope you're as charming as you think you are."

"I assure you, charm isn't going to have anything to do with it." Gwyn stepped forward to bang on the door and yell for help.

Part II

The Ninefold Lotus was quiet and dark, its inhabitants asleep or standing watch at the hospital. It was closer to dawn than midnight by the time Baihu's battered Honda hatchback pulled up in back, loaded to capacity with three passengers, two improperly procured cases of biological samples complete with their own coolers, and, in the rear storage area, an immobile vampire wrapped in a blanket that hadn't been washed in six Fourth of Julys. For a long moment after the car stopped, they just sat there, listening to the engine cool, each weary for his or her own reasons.

"Glorianna," Baihu finally said, pulling the keys out of the ignition and handing them over the back of his seat, "the rear door key's got a little blue chevron on it. Can you take the coolers and unlock it, please?"

"Sure." Tam bestirred herself as Baihu got out and pulled the seat forward for her. She handed the coolers first to him and clambered out. "Where would you like me to put them?"

"The downstairs is the shop area—the rear door opens into storage. Just put them inside for now and turn on the lights. They're on the wall right inside the door. Thanks. Oh! The car keys, I'll need them." They separated the two key rings, Tam going to the door and Baihu to the back of his car, where Gwyn waited.

"A fucking vampire." Gwyn observed, as Baihu unlocked and lifted the hatch, to reveal their enshrouded prisoner. "What the hell, Bai? This just keeps getting weirder and weirder."

"I don't know. I really don't." Baihu shook his head. "You want the feet or the head?"

"The feet." They got themselves arranged and trotted quickly to the open door, where Tam was waiting to close it behind them.

"Over there—behind those bins." They made their way through the narrow passages of the storage room and deposited their burden, covering him further in a heavy rug remnant. "There. I don't think he'll get any light." Baihu paused, considered, wondered aloud, "Does anyone know if vampires are really vulnerable to sunlight?"

He and Tam both glanced at Gwyn, who returned their looks rather irritably. "Just because I specialize in the dead doesn't mean I know anything about the undead. In any case, it's better safe than sorry in that regard, don't you think?"

"Yeah." Baihu couldn't help but agree. "Let's go upstairs… my apartment's on the third floor."

Tam had never been more tired in her life, and the walk up three flights of narrow steps finished draining what was left of her energy, even though she wasn't carrying anything. Baihu's apartment turned out to be a tidier, somewhat better appointed version of the archetypal two-room bachelor pad and, within moments of opening the door, she found herself sinking deep into the overstuffed cushions of the sofa and having a glass of iced tea pressed into her hand.

"Thanks." Tam sat up as straight as she could, and turned her attention to the two refrigerated cases sitting on the coffee table before them. "So… what now?"

"We should call Tiaret," Baihu proclaimed immediately.

"No, we should not call Tiaret—because you know what she'd do right now? She would hear the thrilling saga of how we knocked over the bio-storage locker of Northwestern Memorial Hospital for samples appropriate to use in ritual magic while contending with the interference of one of our fair city's undead residents who is, by the way, currently staked downstairs and she would freak out. And possibly call the police. Or at least advise us to turn ourselves in. Because Tiaret is all upstanding that way." Tam was mildly amazed that Gwyn got that all out in one breath. "Granted, once she started thinking clearly, she'd see things our way—"

Baihu and Tam both snorted, simultaneously.

"All right, perhaps that was just my wishful thinking but stranger things have happened *today*." He finished his tea in three gulps. "I think we should do whatever we're going to do with the samples detection-wise and get rid of the evidence. Even refrigerated, they're only going to last so long before decomposition sets in now. Then we should call Tiaret, once we've got something solid to tell her. Or, rather, you can call her, Glory, because, of the three of us, you're the one she's least likely to assassinate through the phone when she hears about this. Seeing how you're an out-of-towner and all."

"Gee, thanks." Tam put all the sarcasm she could manage into those words, which, given the circumstances, wasn't that impressive. "What sort of detection magics do you have in mind?"

"We don't have the time for anything too fancy, I don't think," Baihu admitted, slowly. "And, frankly, I think we're all a little bit too wiped to pull off any high ritual stuff even if we wanted to. Agreed?"

"Agreed."

"Yeah."

"Then let's keep it simple." Baihu pulled himself to his feet. "You two pick the samples that we want to use. Not all of them—just the ones that seem likely. Don't over-think it... just choose. I'll get the workspace ready."

Gwyn was gentleman enough to carry the cases into the kitchenette and even had a spare pair of latex surgical gloves for her to use as they went about their task. His method of selection appeared, to Tam's eye, to be extremely random until she realized he must be applying some sort of enhanced scrutiny similar to her own, though without a Watson to act as an intermediary.

"Do you do this sort of thing... often?" she asked, somewhat cautiously, as they sorted. It had been her observation that levels of formality and etiquette tended to vary dramatically. Granted, this didn't seem to be the most proper of groups, but people could be funny about things nonetheless.

"Hmm? The doing things on the fly that seem patently insane to any rational observer or the small-group magic thing?" He looked up, flashed a quick smile, and Tam could see how he could be likeable when he wasn't making himself obnoxious.

"Both. I'm afraid I don't have much experience in either." Tam hoped she didn't sound as nervous as she was beginning to feel.

"The insane things? Not that frequently. The magic? Since we graduated from high school." He took the sample she handed to him and added it to the collection in one of the carrying cases, nine in total now. "Don't worry. It's not that terrible, or that hard. Just follow our lead, and we'll all work what we can do in." He paused, looked her over again. "You don't have a cabal?"

"Not even a teeny one." Tam shook her head. "I've... my formal education has been kind of spotty. Mostly, I'm self-taught. Sort of. Watson actually has a lot of information inside him, locked away inside security protocols that I can't open yet. I've learned a great deal from what I can access, though—and I've had a mentor or two. I've been traveling a lot."

"Well, for what it's worth, the joys of communal practice can sometimes leave a lot to be desired. But a smaller group's not so bad. C'mon."

In the five or ten minutes it took them to select the samples, Baihu had almost completely rearranged the living room, producing a compact but entirely usable ritual space. Apparently, the coffee table doubled as an altar on occasion, because it was covered in an embroidered cloth, and three large, flat cushions were positioned around it. A metal plate sat in the middle, surrounded by a circle of what looked like ground salt. Gwyn put the samples they'd selected on that plate, arranging and rearranging them until he had them in a configuration that suited him.

Baihu emerged from what had to be a walk-in closet, carrying a brass censer and a small plastic grocery bag. "What do you think—do we need incense?"

"No." Tam said, immediately, before she could consider how rude that might be.

"*Fuck* no." Gwyn added, glowering. "Keep your patchouli stink away from me, hippie."

"Okay, no incense it is." Baihu gestured to the table. "Please… you first, Glorianna. Whichever place you want."

Tam settled for the nearest cushion and folded herself into it while her hosts made themselves comfortable. This involved, to her eyes, quite a lot of unnecessary squabbling and clashing of elbows—which, her tired mind realized after a moment, was part of their personal ritual. She didn't even need any of her special methods of observation to perceive that. As they settled down, their personal, wildly different energies came more fully into sync, Gwyn's bright, cool white bleeding into Baihu's warm, vibrant green, and Tam wondered, exactly, when she'd started making those particular color associations with them, or if it was something she was really seeing. Gwyn laid his necklace with all its little bone charms on the table, Baihu added a handful of little objects—a tiny eight-sided mirror, a little golden horn, a cast metal bell—and Tam pulled out her handheld, sitting it so that they formed a roughly equilateral triangle. Everything took on a faintly bluish cast in her vision as her own contribution came online. She was suddenly aware of them, at a level somewhere above or below conscious awareness but filtered through physical perception just the same. It gave her a sudden, sharp pang—these two were friends and more than friends, people who trusted one another utterly and worked together with almost seamless cohesion despite their differences in personality and Path, filling in the cracks in each others' knowledge and capabilities. It struck her that she'd never known that, ever, not with any living human being.

She wasn't sure which of them started incanting—she thought it might have been herself, reading off the data scrolling up the handheld's screen—but soon they were all doing it, and only she in something resembling English. Somehow that didn't annoy her as much as the pretentious use of pseudo-Atlantean gibberish in ritual generally did, possibly because there was no pseudo-Atlantean in action. Baihu was speaking Chinese—here and there she caught a phrase she recognized, possibly a prayer cycle or mantra—and Gwyn was drawling in one of those languages that used improbable strings of consonants with nary a vowel in sight. It hardly mattered, as the background hum of spoken tongues was just that, background, white noise, something to focus against. She pulled the stylus out of its holder and began tapping in requests for more data as various salient points scrolled by. Something was taking shape in the raw information, but she didn't know quite what...

"There... right there. Do you see it?" It was Gwyn, and Tam glanced up from the screen as her queries yielded results, a shape to what they were looking for.

"Yes," Tam admitted, glancing back down again, and then looking away, trying to blink the unpleasant after-image out of her eyes.

"Me, too." Baihu said, after a moment, looking a little pale and ill himself. "Nasty."

"Very nasty. Look at the way it feeds back on itself." Gwyn raised a hand, his fingertips tracing a pattern in the air, reminiscent of the outline on Tam's screen.

"Please don't do that. I think I'd like to hurl as it is," she blurted out. "What—how—who the hell would think of something like this? It doesn't have any purpose but... "

"But to kill stuff real good, yeah." Gwyn observed. "That's pretty much it. The way the spell's wrapped, the way it curls back in on itself and interacts with the organic properties of the real disease. Encephalitis is nasty, but it's also survivable, caught quick enough. This?"

"This will kill anything that gets it. Eventually. It's just a matter of time." Baihu sounded as sick as Tam felt. "Can either of you see how it ties together, exactly?"

"Not... exactly, no." *His grandmother has this running in her veins.* Tam felt the knowledge, and the contact-shared grief, spreading around inside her, making tears come to her eyes, blurring her vision. "I'm sorry, Baihu, I—"

"I can't see it, either, Glory, so don't blame yourself. Whoever did this didn't want anyone to unravel it too easily." Gwyn cut off her incipient attack of self-pity in mid-emotional paroxysm. "Doesn't mean we won't do it. Just means it'll take more time that we'd like."

They spent a few more minutes examining their findings with senses visual and otherwise.

"Did you just see one of the strands in the spell go out?" Baihu asked. "It looked like the filament in an old light bulb going cold.... "

A long moment of silence passed. Then, his massive reluctance obvious, Gwyn observed, "Someone connected to one of these samples just died. Probably. I'm not sure but... probably."

"How long do you think someone... would have, once they contract it?" Tam asked, her throat thickening up again.

"Not long would be my guess." Gwyn reached up and rubbed his eyes. "How long before it gets into the local biosphere and becomes more widely dispersed?"

"I don't even want to think about that." Baihu admitted. "How do we stop it?"

"Good fucking question." Gwyn lifted his hand away from his eyes. "Let's shut it down for now—looking at it's giving me a headache."

"Glorianna... is there any way to save what we just saw on that PDA of yours?" Baihu asked.

"Yes. In fact, I've been logging this whole thing. Saving it now." And she did so, isolating the file as best she could. "I've got it all. Now what do we do with it?"

"It's late," Baihu observed with the careful enunciation of the well and truly exhausted.

"It's not late, it's early," Gwyn corrected, in the tone of someone who was intimately acquainted with the differences by means of both lifestyle and inclination. "Tiaret'll be in the office in another couple of hours. And we all need to sleep. And I fully intend to call in dead."

The idea of sleep sounded enormously good to Tam, though the concept of calling a cab to take her back to her hotel held no particular charm, due in large part to all the steps she'd have to descend in order to manage that feat. "Perhaps we shouldn't separate? We're only going to get together again in a few more hours, anyway—to talk to Tiaret and to do something with our guest."

"You have a point." Baihu began the laborious process of getting to his feet. "Glorianna, you can have my futon if you want it. I've got clean sheets, and the door locks, so no one would bother you if you want to sleep. Gwyn and I can crash down the hall in the sitting room."

"That would be lovely, especially considering that I was thinking of just laying down right here." Tam accepted his hand up. "What are we going to do with the vampire?"

"I have absolutely no idea."

She sometimes wondered if they realized how pathetic they were. They probably didn't, but she wondered it nonetheless. She wondered if they ever lay awake in their beds at night, staring up at their ceilings, their white or yellow or blue painted ceilings, and realized the totality of their own worthlessness. Of how little they actually mattered, how petty and idiotic their little grievances with the world really were, how empty and hollow their lives, their relentlessly normal and boring and pedestrian lives.

Probably not.

Probably never occurred to them.

Probably never dawned on them that they had something to be grateful for, something that could be taken away from them at a moment's notice, something that could be turned into a little pile of broken bits at less than a moment's notice. Not even now, not even after all the crazy things that had happened since they were all just little kids, after all the terrorist attacks and wars and divorces and moves across the country and shit that had uprooted them in ways great and small. Not a goddamned one of them realized how good they had it, how much they had to be grateful for, how perfect it was to be pathetic and normal and happy.

Sometimes she hated them. Truthfully, most of the time she hated them now. Not all of them, and not all of the time… but mostly. More often than not.

"You're sure this is on the up and up, Gi—Nicnevin?" one of them asked. "I just… uh… don't wanna get busted. My parents would have a fit if I—"

"It's not illegal," she said, coolly, spiking him to the ground with her best witheringly regal glare. "Do you really think I'd be that stupid? You can order it online—it's just hard to get and expensive. Otherwise, I'd have had it for ritual before now."

"Okay, all right, no, I don't think you're stupid, Gi—Nicnevin." His metal-ringed face relaxed in a somewhat sheepish smile. "What is it, anyway?"

"Good stuff. From Europe. Pure botanical consciousness-expansion, completely THC-free." She smiled, making it into a real expression and not just a baring of teeth.

"My source says they used to use it all over the ancient world to help connect to higher powers, but that it was almost wiped out long ago."

This brought a murmur that traveled all the way around the gathered "coven," sprawled out across a couple of close-spaced, public picnic tables amid the remains of hot dogs and pizzas and potato chip bags, most of them still sucking on their sodas. She drew herself up, now that she had most of their attention, having read more than a few books about the primal role of High Priestess as Goddess. "It was like they did with the familiars and the books and anything that they could lay their hands on. They burned it all, and left us the ashes. But there were some places where it wasn't as bad. What I'm getting comes from Eastern Europe, one of the places where it survived in the wild, and then was cultivated when the witches there came back out of hiding."

The coven nodded, talked among themselves, generally agreed. The coven had a bedrock belief in the existence of They as a force inimical to themselves, a vast, world-spanning conspiracy dedicated to making their privileged but predictable suburban lives as miserable as possible. Their They was everything from bitchy step-parents forbidding the weekend use of the Escalade and step-siblings stealing clothes and narcing every chance they got to snotty cheerleaders in the locker room to that one stupid fuck in home room who couldn't wrap it around his head that they'd do anything he wanted just for five minutes of attention. She knew that if the coven, her friends, her followers, ever met the *real* They, it would be the end of their lives, their sanity, their world.

"We have thirteen now—the traditional circle of thirteen—we have what we need to make it all work." She stretched her arms out over her head, reaching for the sky, and all six of her boys and at least two of her girls caught their breath as she did so. "Soon it'll be time. The best drawing-down time we'll ever have. Just a few more days… and it'll all be in our hands."

Tam found it easier than she'd thought it would be to sleep in someone else's bed. Hotels were one thing—she'd been in enough of them that hotel beds no longer kept her up all night, tossing and turning, looking for some comfortable position to sleep in. On the other hand, she'd never had a steady boyfriend, or any boyfriend at all, really, in school, and, even if she had, she wouldn't have slept over in his dorm.

So it surprised her that, no matter how tired she was, she'd had her head on Baihu's pillow for approximately fifteen seconds before she fell asleep. And woke up, some time later, not feeling at all self-conscious about it, sleeping in one of his oversized T-shirts, underneath his sheets. It was very strange, half-pleasant and half-unnerving, that she'd gotten so close and so comfortable with him and his abrasive idiot friend so quickly. A by-product of the communal magic, probably, and one that she hadn't experienced before.

The Watson handheld sat on the futon next to her, encased in its padded, waterproof carrier and in hibernation. She sat up and brought him online. "Good morning, Watson. I trust everything is okay?"

"As well as can be expected, Glorianna. I have your physical location as… somewhere near South Archer Avenue, in the vicinity of Chinatown. You are not precisely plottable, at the moment… is your locale protected somehow?" His voice had a slightly more mechanical sound on the handheld's tiny speakers. Tam made a mental note to work on that at some point.

"Yes. I'm going to enter the address here now." She did so. "Add that to our listing of significant locations under the name Ninefold Lotus Healing Arts Academy. It's the place of business of Baihu's family, who were kind enough to offer me a place to crash last night."

"Done." A pause. "Will you be returning to the hotel today, Glorianna? If not, I shall instruct the concierge to permit housekeeping entry forthwith."

"I will be, but housekeeping can come in anyway." Tam chewed the end of her stylus and tapped a new query on the screen, checking the status of last night's efforts. "The file I saved last night remained completely isolated, right?"

"Entirely, Glorianna."

"Good. I want you to use the active isolation interaction protocols to open that file and examine its contents."

"As you wish, Glorianna. I shall do so immediately." The screen flickered for a moment as the requested security protocols engaged, and Watson began examining the collected raw data. "Good Lord... this is..."

"Yes, it very much is. That's what's causing the current encephalitis outbreak—or, at least, that's what we think is causing it."

"Monstrous. Absolutely monstrous. I have never seen anything like this." Watson, for the first time ever, seemed genuinely flustered. "What sort of mind would even conceive of such a thing?"

"We were wondering pretty much the same thing," Tam admitted. "More importantly, we were wondering how to stop it from entering the biosphere and how to break it. Stop it functioning in the people who already have it."

"Yes... I can see that those two goals would be high priorities." He murmured. "If I may... I would like to import a copy of this file to my primary and continue examining it more closely."

"Do you think that's a good idea? It's a magical virus, after all—if there's even the remotest chance it could affect you, I don't want you taking the risk."

"It seems somewhat unlikely that a magical virus intended to affect organic physical processes could make the leap into my systems, Glorianna." He sounded faintly amused. "But I understand and appreciate your concerns. It is magical in nature. I will keep the file inside the most stringent isolation protocols available to me during the examination. Will that be sufficient?"

"For now it will be. I'll contact you later to see what you've uncovered." Tam snapped the handheld closed and looked around for her clothes—which she found, neatly folded, exactly where she'd left them the night before. A quick shower made the idea of wearing them again somewhat more bearable, and, a few minutes later, she stepped out into the narrow hallway outside Baihu's door in search of the sitting room.

She found it without too much effort—it was right down the hall, after all—and discovered that her partners in crime were still asleep, Baihu on the couch, Gwyn on a reclining chair. And she realized, somewhat belatedly, that it was only ten o'clock, and that she'd slept barely five hours. A refreshing five hours, but five hours nonetheless, and that yesterday they'd gotten Gwyn out of bed on two hours' rest and Baihu likely hadn't slept much, either. She decided immediately that they deserved at least a little more shut eye and followed her nose in the opposite direction, from which an enticing aroma was emanating.

The Tsu family communal dining room was a pleasant place, with its many windows and its long table sufficient to serve the entire extended family. Baihu's cousin Mei was an extremely sweet woman and her baby daughter was as cute as cute could be, and Tam ended up holding her, somewhat awkwardly, as Mei fetched another pot of tea and some breakfast, over her objections. Baihu's Aunt Mel was similarly kind and pleasant despite her visible weariness, when she and her husband came in from the hospital, where they'd sat the family's night vigil. Tam, whose entire family consisted of her now-absent father, found herself being swept along quite quickly into the currents of not-quite-normal daily life at the Tsu household, eating breakfast and fielding questions in English and two dialects of Chinese.

Once things had settled down some—after Baihu's two youngest cousins had gone back upstairs—Tam brought out her handheld and made a call. "Hello, DCFS? Could I speak to Ms. McBride, please?"

"Good morning, Glorianna." Over the phone, Tiaret sounded less than pleased with the universe. "How can I help you?"

"Is that a trick that everyone has, or is it unique to you?" Tam asked, genuinely curious.

"It's not a trick. I received a call from the office of the Hierarch's chief of security this morning, suggesting to me that you and my two young friends might have been up to some hijinks last night, and strongly advising me to step on you all thoroughly before he was forced to do so." Tam resisted the urge to groan aloud. "Now... perhaps you'd like to tell me exactly what happened?"

"Well." Tam licked her lips. "It was partially our fault and partially not. We thought that, if we had some blood and tissue samples from people affected by the encephalitis outbreak to examine, we'd be able to determine if the virus had been tampered with in any way."

"Logical. So which of you decided that breaking into the storage facility at Northwestern was the best way to proceed with that little mission?" Tiaret really did have the whole "I am extremely disappointed in you, young woman" voice down pat, and Tam squirmed in her seat.

"It was sort of a group decision. Or, rather, we couldn't think of anything better at the time." Tam regathered her forces and soldiered on. "Gwyn and Baihu retrieved the samples, while I hid them from hospital security—but someone else interfered with our plan. A vampire."

A pause on the other end of the line. Then, "A vampire?"

"Yes. He found Gwyn and Baihu in the storage unit and called security. But I caught him before he could get away completely. We have him downstairs in the storage room here at the Ninefold Lotus." The silence on the other end of the line was starting to get oppressive. "Tiaret?"

"I'm all right." A sigh. "A vampire. Okay. And you have him. And you got the samples. Please tell me that you discovered something to justify this little act of grand theft bio."

"Well... yes. The virus has been magically enhanced. Someone deliberately made it deadlier—possibly easier to catch, too, but we need to do some more analysis before we can say that with any certainty." Tam belatedly wished she'd gone to some other room to have this conversation; Mei and Mel were both staring at her. "I've got my companion working on that currently. Right now, we're trying to figure out what to do with the vampire. Or we will be once the boys wake up."

"That's most certainly something, then. Very well. I'll call the Hierarch's office and let them know what's going on. Don't do anything until I contact you again." Tiaret hung up.

Tam didn't feel at all safe taking a cab back to her hotel, not with what they'd just learned about the vampire—pardon, Kindred—interest in the enhanced encephalitis virus, and their readily apparent ability to come and go without being easily noticed. Even Tiaret volunteering to drive the vampire, Loki, back to wherever it was he wanted to go didn't really relieve Tam's unease. The boys conferenced while she packed up the laptop and assiduously avoided any contact whatsoever with the restraints Gwyn had used to help keep their pallid guest bound.

It wasn't like her to be afraid for no reason, but Tam found that she couldn't stop her hands from shaking. She just wasn't accustomed to dealing with this sort of thing.

"Glory." Gwyn tapped her on the shoulder. "C'mon. I'll drive you back to your hotel."

"Okay." She hoisted her satchel to her shoulder, too disturbed to even argue.

Gwyn's car was the only thing about him that suggested he was actually a doctor-in-training, a newish Mercedes-Benz two-door that clearly hadn't come off a repo lot anywhere. Tam found just sitting in it vaguely comforting, materially real and in no way related to any of the strange turns the last couple of days had taken. He kept casting glances at her as they drove, and Tam knew that he was picking up on her discomfort. She wanted him to say something, or to say something herself, but didn't know how or where to start.

"It's okay." When he finally broke the silence, she almost jumped, shooting him a startled look. "Seriously."

"I don't know what—" She stopped, abruptly, backtracked, thought again. "What do you mean by that? Because I know what I'd like you to mean by that but—"

"You're over-thinking, Glory." He flicked her a slightly amused look. "It's okay. I know you're freaked out. You've never met a vampire before, much less thought about a whole bunch of them in one city before, right?"

"Well, yes," Tam admitted, slowly. "I guess at some level I knew that if we existed, then… other things did, too. Spirits and demons and things—I mean, I've seen documentary evidence that they do exist, even if I've never met one, so not believing in them would have been stupid. But… this is different. We're… food to them, and that's…"

"On the creepy side, yeah. I know. I wasn't completely honest with you when I said I didn't know anything about them." She shot a startled look at him, and found him wearing a crooked smile. "One of the places I hang out occasionally is run by one of them. Very personable, never gives me a hard time. She knows what I am, and I know what she is, and we've pretty much agreed to leave things like that."

"She's… never…?" Tam asked, trying not to twitch at the thought of it.

"Never. And, for what it's worth, I don't think this is going to lead to anything unpleasant for any of us, either. Seriously." He shifted smoothly, turned. "It's got too much potential to blow up in all our faces if things get too public. We all hide for a reason, after all, and we've all got good reasons to want to clean it up as quietly as possible and continue in our respective directions."

"True." Tam hadn't thought of it that way. In fact, she hadn't thought much about all the implications, which Gwyn had clearly been working on, at least to himself.

"Just avoid bleeding around him if we see him again, and we should be fine." He pulled up in front of her hotel's main entrance. "And don't take any unnecessary chances with any more dark alleys."

"I don't think I will. Thank you for driving me."

"You're welcome, Little Princess."

He just had to do something to wreck the impression that he wasn't an absolute jerk.

Tam got out and slammed the door behind her, still flustered and out of sorts but no longer as nervous as she'd been. Housekeeping had clearly been through her room to replace the complimentary toiletries and towels. She took a shower and changed her clothes and felt extremely foolish about having been upset at all.

Watson had clearly been at work in her absence, as well. A collection of analysis documents sat in the printer tray for her attention: the results of his detailed examination of the data they'd collected, a breakdown of the spell's structure and theoretical intended effects, primary and secondary, and his theory on how it was constructed. "Thank you, Watson. I'll have to tell the others about this tomorrow. We're all supposed to be meeting up again."

"You're welcome, Glorianna. It was the least I could do to help combat this abomination."

That was a bit more personality than even Watson showed, and Tam looked up, eying him closely. "Is something bothering you, Watson?"

"This... virus... represents an abuse of power, Glorianna. An abuse and a misuse that your father would never have countenanced, and neither should you. In fact, it disturbs me greatly." He rose from his chair and receded for a moment into the illusion of distance of the room he sat in, withdrawing several volumes from further back in the library's stacks. "There are certain magical practices, and forms, that are intrinsically malevolent. You have thus far been fortunate enough to avoid those practices instinctively yourself, and to have had no congress with those who pursue them. It is, however, time for you to learn something about them, the better to protect yourself against them."

"I won't argue with you about that. While you're at it, can you pull up whatever you might know about, well, vampires? Because some things happened today that make me think I should brush up on that topic, too..."

Doctor Thaddeus Jasperson Poole, known to the Consilium at large as Nuad, lived in the Prairie Avenue Historic District, by himself in one of the few cavernous Victorian houses on the block that hadn't been demolished, turned into condos for wealthy metropolitans, or converted into a museum celebrating the lily-white gentility of South Chicago's former greatness. Gwyn had a bedroom and a study there, which he rarely used, and a place to park his car where it wouldn't be stolen, which also didn't much concern him considering the security system he employed. The house's security system was hardly less impressive, for Doc Poole was a paranoid old bastard, and Gwyn possessed the keys to the front door and the various layers of defense that otherwise would have reduced him to a state of twitching catalepsy.

"Doc? Are you home?" It was patently inconceivable for Doc Poole to not be home, as he left the house at all only under the most extreme circumstances. The upstairs study light had been on as Gwyn pulled up outside, but it was generally better to announce himself from the bottom of the stairs. Just knocking, he had discovered the hard way, could have not particularly funny results if Doc was asleep in front of the study fireplace with a snifter of brandy at his elbow, as he often was these days.

"Yes." The single word floated down the steps. "Do come in, Gwyn."

The stairs creaked alarmingly on his way up them, and he made a mental note about broaching the subject of a getting a handyman in to maintenance them (again), when the situation had settled down. Normally, it was all he could do to get the old man to unbend enough to let someone in to help winterize the place in October and shovel the walk. Some arguments needed to be approached from other angles.

Doc Poole's study didn't exactly conform to the traditional stereotype of the Moros inner sanctum. He did not, for example, use skulls for bookends and there were no stuffed or mummified objects hanging from the ceiling, no pickled two-headed calves in jars of briny solution on the coffee table or even any resident ghosts that Gwyn knew of. If Doc Poole was haunted by anything, it was the past, and his study was its shrine, full of books about vanished aboriginal peoples and glassed-in cases of artifacts. As Gwyn'd suspected, the old man was in his enormous, wing-backed chair next to the fireplace, a half-full snifter of some fine brandy on the tiny table next to it, and the newest book on the Cahokia mound-builders open on his knee.

"My wayward apprentice." A little smile tugged at the corners of his mouth, deepening the creases that had been carved by a lifetime or two. "I hope you realize that you've annoyed our colleague Mimir quite thoroughly lately. Well done."

"Master," Gwyn couldn't help smiling back, "pissing off Mimir wasn't, I admit, my primary goal—but as far as unanticipated secondary effects go, it's acceptable. Tiaret called?"

"Our excitable colleague did, indeed, telephone me earlier in the day about your exploits. It seems I'm to keep a tight rein on your activities, lest our glorious Hierarch take exception to them. So whatever you're about to do, my boy, make every effort not to be caught at it, hmmm?" He retrieved another glass from the potables cart. "Brandy?"

"I'm afraid I can't right now. I haven't eaten in hours." He took a seat directly across from his mentor, in a somewhat smaller chair of similar design. "Do you remember when I asked for access to the restricted rooms a few weeks back?"

"I haven't yet lapsed into senile dementia." The doctor marked his place and laid the book aside.

"I'm sorry, that was a stupid question." Gwyn paused, and considered how to phrase what he needed to say next. "I was wondering, if you have the time, if I could ask you a few questions about some of the things I was studying. I'm beginning to suspect a connection between those things and certain events that are taking place here in the city."

Doc Poole inclined a curious eyebrow. "Really? Ask away…"

Hospitals made Baihu nervous. He hated their designed-by-interior-decorator color schemes. Their sterile and antiseptic smells annoyed him. He was unnerved by the way the memory of old illness and old pain seemed to cling to even the newest structures, unbanishable by any means that he could command. He'd gone to college with the righteous intention of studying Western medicine in addition to the traditional Chinese forms his grandmother was teaching him, and he'd even gotten pretty far—until he'd reached the hospital clinical training parts of nursing, and fallen all over a dislike he hadn't realized he had, until then. He'd gone on to get a degree in physical therapy and an LPN license on the strength of what he had managed to learn during his short-lived career as a student nurse, but he'd never successfully tamed his dislike of hospitals.

The ICUs were, of course, the worst because you would not, by definition, be in the ICU if there weren't something seriously wrong with you. It frequently took all his self-control not to just creep around the various cubicles, poking and prodding and seeing what good he could set in motion for people on ventilators, on six different kinds of monitoring equipment, on IV drips of antibiotics. Probably not a lot, without the chance to do a full-blown diagnosis of their ills, but it would have made him feel like less of a waste than sitting in the waiting room while they lay in various states of dying. It also likely would have either gotten him forcefully ejected by the ICU staff or, worse, looked at more closely by hospital security, and so he kept to his seat in the waiting room with the youngest of his aunts, his working notebook open across his knees, waiting for something to happen or for inspiration to strike.

The virus was magically enhanced, but, at the root, it was just encephalitis—something that could be treated and the damage it left behind dealt with. He sketched the general shape of the spell they had all perceived the night before, the shape that had burned itself into his eyes, his mind, something about its sheer obscene malignancy troubling him even in his sleep. They'd need to put their heads together, and probably a couple more heads besides, to fully work it out and find how to unravel it, but in the meantime, was it possible to do something to treat it?

He tried, gamely, to follow down that path, to work out some sort of treatment regimen that might counteract the most damaging effects. He tried, but his mind wasn't having any of it and his eyes kept traveling back to the drawing, the inward-curling spiral of malice. Someone who *hated* had made that, hated with an intensity he could only imagine. Sure, Baihu disliked hospitals, but what he really meant was that they made him uncomfortable and that if he didn't have to visit them he just wouldn't. That wasn't really hate. This spell, this virus, was *hate*, profound and bilious hatred for . . .

For what?

He wondered. For people, obviously, because otherwise it wouldn't have been packaged in a manner meant to kill as many people as possible. Whoever had made this thing didn't just get irritated when his neighbors played their stereos too loudly or if somebody cut him off in traffic. Whoever made this thing wanted to pump strychnine into the veins of every waitress, journalist, parent, and whatever else in Chicago . . .

That didn't work, either, he realized, as he let his eyes go unfocused, let the inward-curling spiral blur in his vision. That was giving too much credit for motivation, assuming that whoever made this thing had a reason for wanting others dead. And that might not be the case. Maybe it wasn't even that he needed the motivation of even a petty annoyance to lash out. Maybe it wasn't so much people that he hated as life itself, manifested in people....

The thought curled around inside his head, settled into place, chilled him to the bone. Maybe it wasn't vengeance for some petty slight or human stupidity that prompted this. Maybe it was just bone-deep hatred of... life. Of being alive. Of the messy sprawling nature of existence, the tastes, the smells, the sounds....

The sounds. Something about that stuck in his head, struck a cord, reminded him of something. He closed his eyes and stretched his thoughts, trying to remember what it was....

The city... the silent, empty city... full of lights and vast buildings and wide streets but nothing else, no living things... no real life at all, just the wind... and the silence....

The silence... the dead river flowing into the dead lake... the gray sky raining black feathers...

He let himself sink more deeply into the vision.

The Ninefold Lotus was quiet when Isaac, barefoot, weary to the bone, finally made his way back to it in the early, rainy hours of the morning. He was soaked to the skin and unnaturally cold—it certainly wasn't cold outside, so he figured it must be coming from inside, from the little ball of spiritual ice sitting at the core of his mind and soul, letting him think and act coolly, reasonably. He wasn't even ungrateful for it as he opened the back door and went inside, up the steps and to his apartment, past the earliest risers among his relatives in the family dining room. He waved them back as he went down the hallway to his apartment, then shut and locked the door behind them.

He didn't know how much longer the unnatural cold calm would last, but there were things he needed to do while it did. He picked up his phone and called Glorianna and Tiaret and Gwyn and Loki, told them to turn on their televisions to the local news. Once three of those four actually woke up enough to follow instructions, and then when they finished freaking out, he told them what he knew. Told them about what he saw. Told them about whom he'd met. Told them that he wanted all of them to get together to compare notes, as soon as possible, because their little problem had just gotten bigger, much bigger. No one disagreed. Even more surprisingly, no one really argued. It took and hour and a half to talk to everyone, and, by the time he was finished, the chill was beginning to wear off, the ice cracking like the ice in the heart of a glacier, flaking away in great chunks and exposing the raw, torn-up earth underneath.

Kids. They were only kids. High school aged and maybe a little younger, according to the news reports. Most of them were already dead, had been dead when he'd encountered them, though some of them probably didn't even realize it. Jimsonweed. Jimsonweed with all the possible tropane alkaloids at maximum concentration, the best possible means for causing hallucinations, delirium, tachycardia, respiratory arrest, coma, death. And something had responded to all that death, something vast and primal and offended, something enraged by poisoned blood spilled on the concrete, by children so brutally and suddenly cut down.

Something.

He shuddered, helplessly, at the memory of it. As the ice inside him continued to crack, break open, recede, expose places that hadn't been open to him in years. Decades. Most of his life. The parts of him that had seen things....

Terrible, terrible things.

A boy with blood running down his acid-scorched face, into his mouth, from a skull fractured and beaten into his brain with a hammer. A man in a business suit, reeking of gasoline and smoldering like a matchstick, his face smeared with soot, his eyes empty puddles of greasy ash. Two little girls, naked and cold and white as snow, their faces frozen in rictus smiles that bared their sharp, clear teeth....

The things he'd known since he was a child.

The things he'd known since his mother had left him alone to go to work and his father had left him alone to go to do whatever he did, and there was no one else to hear him cry, frightened, alone, hungry....

The things (*the girl with the bandages on her mouth, with her mushy voice and her eyes full of glittering hate of him, of everything*) that had crawled out of his closet, the things (*the burned thing, blackened to bare flesh and bare bone, melted shreds of clothing still clinging to what was left of its barely held-together body*) that had slipped out from under his bed, the things (*the mother, pale and bloated, dripping water in drops and puddles and splashes, rotting face sagging off its bones*) that he'd seen, that he'd heard, that he'd known about all his life....

It was all he could do to stand, all he could do to open his door and go back to his family, and comfort them and tell them that nothing was wrong.

In fact, something was wrong, very wrong. And he was beginning to fear that he knew what it was.

Part III

Poole & Updike Funeral Home was a Queen Anne monstrosity, bigger than any of the other houses in the Wicker Park neighborhood the house occupied, set back off the street behind an imposing expanse of manicured lawn. The driveway circled around back to what Gwyn referred to as the "receiving area," where lay a small parking lot for visitors and the entrance into the house's basement-level working rooms. Tam looked around curiously as Tiaret followed Gwyn's Mercedes up the drive. Off to the west was the enormous Woodlawn Cemetery, close enough that the funeral home looked like a part of it. Immediately behind the funeral home was a smaller burial ground, separated from the larger cemetery and the rest of the grounds by a low stone wall topped and gated by a wrought iron fence. To the east, the wooded lot faded into the backyards of the other houses on the block, tastefully landscaped with a selection of ornamental plants that hid the security lamps. Most of the plants, Tam couldn't help but notice, were poisonous: orange-berried nightshades, various kinds of jessamine, rhododendrons.

"Tiaret," Tam asked, "what kind of person is this guy?"

Tiaret gave her an amused look. "An old-timer. Lived here for decades, along with his cabal, until the dust-up in the '80s—he found it expedient to relocate for a while until things settled down. He moved back as soon as he could afterward."

"What about his cabal? Will we be meeting some of them, too?" Tam got out and looked around. No one else was in evidence yet, though there were lights on in the back of the house.

"Not unless you want Gwyn to let you into the private plot over there." Tiaret got out and hiked a thumb in the direction of the little walled compound. "They didn't make it. Nuad himself almost didn't make it, but he had just enough extra luck on his side when they came after him."

"Oh." Tam said, and looked across the parking lot at Gwyn, locking his own car.

"Yeah, that pretty much covers it. Nuad got driven out with the metaphorical pitchforks and fire, lost most of his oldest friends and his wife, and a good chunk of his life's work was either stolen or destroyed. To say that he's not very fond of much of our society nowadays is putting it mildly." Tiaret shook her head. "But this is his city, as much as it's anybody's, so he came back. And took on our dear Gwyn as his apprentice, which is a marriage of misanthropic worldviews such as the Consilium has rarely witnessed."

Lost in thought, Tam followed the older woman across the parking lot and up the rear steps to the porch. She'd never thought that being tied up with a cabal would be all sunshine and roses, but the idea of actually settling down and joining one was slowly starting to grow on her. Once her father was found and brought back home, of course. There was something appealing about the easy relationship between Baihu and Gwyn, the trust they had in each other, and Tam could think of a couple of dozen things worse than turning to Tiaret for advice or instruction or just plain support. She found she lacked the imagination necessary to picture herself joining a group of people who meant that much to her, only to lose them all, and have to continue on without them.

The porch wrapped all the way around the building and brought them to the front door, which was helpfully unlocked. The downstairs area had clearly been made over for the purposes of offering bereaved family members the maximum degree of comfort affordable by interior decorating, all muted earth tones and tasteful decorative touches, exquisitely dried flowers and framed Biblical verses, thoughtfully placed boxes of tissues.

A wide staircase led upstairs to the chapel and viewing rooms. Tam suspected the presence of a well-hidden elevator somewhere.

"The business office is in the back." Gwyn led the way, glancing around as he went. "Doc—we're here."

"Yes, I know. I saw you coming up the drive." The voice that floated out to meet them was deep and smooth, cultured, and Tam immediately felt more at ease about its owner. "Please come in. I would have met you, but I just received a telephone call."

The business office maintained the same earth-tone color scheme as the rest of the first floor, though a bronze plaque hung on the door, indicating that it was PRIVATE—AUTHORIZED ADMITTANCE ONLY. Next to the door, bracketed to the wall, were two more plaques: G. PATRICK UPDIKE, FUNERAL DIRECTOR and T. JASPERSON POOLE, FUNERAL DIRECTOR. Gwyn's mentor sat at the room's single, enormous marble-topped desk, his hand still on the receiver of an ancient rotary phone. Tam was struck by the warmth of his smile, which didn't seem forced for public consumption at all, and the vivid blue of his eyes, which stood out even more against his dark suit.

"Good afternoon, Tiaret, Baihu." He rose, tall and straight but not imposingly so, and came around from behind the desk, leaning heavily on a silver-headed cane. "And you must be the Little Princess, of whom I've heard so much in the last several days." He took Tam's hand and actually bestowed a kiss on it, much to her surprise. "I'm afraid that I don't have as much time to assist you as I believed I would. The coroner's office will be bringing a client in this evening, and I perforce must make myself available to them. Gwyn?"

"Yes, master?" Somehow that didn't sound weird coming off Gwyn's lips, directed at this man.

"I've already performed the majority of the basic preparations in the chapel. I shall leave the specifics to you." He made a little gesture with his hands, and they stepped aside to let him out of the office. "There are pastries in the upstairs refreshment area, as well as sufficient quantities of coffee and tea, I believe. If you'll come with me?"

The upper floor of the house had been converted into two huge viewing rooms with seating for at least a dozen, an area for refreshments, and a small chapel, complete with stained glass windows, a bier for a coffin, and real wooden pews. To Tam's surprise, it looked just about ready to use, with marble stands for flowers set up and a large picture of a youngish woman on the inside and a lectern with a sympathy book just outside the doors.

"Mr. Updike will be conducting a funeral service tomorrow, so I must request a high degree of decorum be observed," Nuad informed them, as he walked Gwyn around the perimeter. "Worldly violence should be left at the door. Voices should be kept moderate, particularly as I am not entirely certain when the coroner's ambulance will be arriving or how long they will be staying once they do arrive. Vulgar displays of power will not be tolerated by the building's innate protections and may result in unpleasant consequences for any offenders."

"The funeral home has sorcerous defenses?" Tam asked in what she thought was a whisper to Tiaret, not sure if she should be disturbed by that or not.

"Not all of the dead who lie next door went to their reward as gladly as others, Glorianna," Nuad informed her from across the chapel. "One must occasionally take extreme measures to prevent them from badgering the freshly deceased, who are often quite unsettled by their own change in state. As with the living, those dead who offer no harm to this place and those within it are free to come and go as they choose. Otherwise, I am very much of the opinion that a hostile action deserves a hostile reaction."

"Oh." For the second time in a half-hour, Tam found herself at a loss for words.

"Speaking of which, Baihu, I was grieved to hear of your grandmother's illness. If you require my aid in delivering appropriate restitution to her assailant, do not hesitate to call on me." Nuad rested a hand on Baihu's shoulder in passing. "Grandmother Feng-huang has been a good friend to me these many years, and I should think ill of myself if I did nothing for her in her hour of need."

"Thank you, Master Nuad. I'll certainly keep your offer in mind." Baihu smiled, rather strained around the edges, but genuinely.

"Very good. Tiaret, I will leave the governing of these young people in your capable hands." The elder magus swept out of the chapel. "If you require my assistance this evening, I will be downstairs in the business office until your affair is completed, at least."

Gwyn waited until the sound of his master's footsteps had vanished before letting out a low whistle. "The end is nigh. He actually stayed in a room with more than one living person in it for longer than ten minutes."

"Interesting times," Baihu replied. "Shall we?"

"By all means."

The actual warding of the chapel was accomplished quickly enough, and made use of objects already on hand: dried flower wreaths from the attic storage rooms, a handful of tiny mirrors that Baihu had brought with him. Sealing the results of their combined efforts would occur when the doors to the chapel closed, once all the guests had arrived. Tam kept herself occupied and out from underfoot by picking a seat in one of the viewing rooms, drinking a cup of tea, and making inquiries on the handheld about any magi named Nuad. The results pulled up a number of intriguing documents about a cabal called Delphi, pursuant to that group's activities in Chicago, the disposition of certain items from said cabal's Athenaeum after its "disbanding" in 1988, and her father's efforts to obtain some of those items for his own collection.

It occurred to her that, of all the people she'd talked to when she first arrived in the city, that the only call that was never returned had been made to Nuad.

"I need a smoke. And by need I mean want really badly. You coming down?" Gwyn's voice sounded close to the top of the stairs.

"I think I'll spare you my stock lecture on the evils of even herbal cigarette smoke for now." Baihu peered around the corner. "Glorianna, can I interest you in another cup of tea?"

"That would be lovely." Tam rose and went to join him in the refreshment area.

"Oh, sure. Suck up to the cute redhead." Gwyn smirked at them both on his way down the stairs. "Don't do anything I wouldn't do, Bai."

"One day you'll have to specify what you actually mean by that." Baihu accepted Tam's empty cup and refilled it with fresh-brewed, something green and crisp and vaguely citrus. "Don't mind him. Among other things, he thinks I need a girlfriend. If he got along with his family better, I'm sure he'd throw every unmarried cousin he has at me."

"Don't apologize. He reminds me of a male version of one of my friends back in Boston. She, too, labors under the delusion that no one is ever voluntarily without companionship of the opposite sex." Tam sipped, realized what she'd said, and hurriedly added, "Which isn't to say that I'd say no if you wanted to have lunch again. Or something like that. Under better circumstances. He has a lot of cousins?"

"Scads. He's related to half the North Shore." Baihu's smile pulled one out of her as well. "For what it's worth, I hope better circumstances come around sooner rather than later. This whole situation has been pretty crazy, and I appreciate you going to so much effort on our behalf." He paused. "I'll translate what I can read of my grandmother's journals for you, as soon as I possibly can. And if I can't find anything useful on my own, we'll see if you and your—familiar?—can do me one better."

Tam's heart jumped a little. "Baihu, you don't have to do that. I mean, I'm glad that you're offering, but I didn't do this to obligate you to help me that way. I mean—"

"I know. But I think the trade's a fair and amicable one, given the circumstances. Let's go have a seat. I want to give Loki another call, and the others should be getting here soon."

Downstairs, the front door opened and the sound of multiple sets of footsteps echoed up from below. The werewolves were on the wary side, and behaved not unlike, and yet not entirely like, a real wolf pack, at least according to the small compilation of document abstracts Watson had access to. Most of the complete files resided in regions of his system that her permissions did not allow her to access, a fact that frustrated Tam not a little.

Tam dug the documents she'd prepared for the meeting out of her satchel, the detailed analysis of the virus she and Watson had developed, but held onto them for the time being. The vampire was running late, and she didn't want to have to repeat herself more than necessary. Of course, once he got there, it took quite a bit of talking to get him calmed down. Tam made a note to herself to query Watson's database regarding diplomacy between vampires and werewolves. Fortunately, once they got past all the drama, things moved at a good clip.

"They're the ones trying to warn us. I mean *it* is, the Murder is. I guess it ain't so much warn as—well, it's what they are. They can't even help it."

Crows. Tam couldn't remember if she'd had any odd encounters with crows since she came to Chicago, but she didn't think so. Voices, weird intrusions into Watson's usually inviolate system, yes, but not crows. A sudden jolt went through her as an image flashed across her mind's eye: a heavily pixilated crow feather, sitting at Watson's feet. She opened her mouth to remark on that, and closed it again as the conversation moved past, to spiritual immune responses that were well outside her realm of experience.

She had decided early on that she'd best serve in this situation by keeping an accurate record of what was said, what was theorized, and what was agreed to, using the handheld's various recording functions to minimize the possibility of misunderstanding or miscommunication later. Consequently, she kept her mouth shut and her eyes open, except when she had something useful to offer. The assertion by the vampire that this situation had happened before sent her searching, and yielded a series of document abstracts related to recurrent supernatural phenomena that she bookmarked to research more thoroughly later. Nothing turned up in response to her query regarding the term 'the Murder of Crows' beyond the dictionary definition of the word 'murder' in that context.

As requested, things were kept largely civil, despite several opportunities arising to the contrary, though Tam found her considerable distaste for Loki in no way lessened by the fact of his viral infection and, in fact, enhanced by his attitude in general. All the talk about ritual sacrifices and unknowable forces aggravated every structural-rationalist fiber in her body, particularly coming out of the fanged mouth of a thing she knew damned well thought of her as prey. She found herself in total solidarity with Gwyn for the first time ever when Baihu offered to feed him, and spent the time they were out of the room, drawing blood, pacing around the confines of the chapel and comforting herself with the idea that, if he tried anything, Nuad would reduce him to an honest-to-goodness corpse before Loki could even start to weasel.

The meeting began to break up after a few hours, with all sides agreeing to obtain the freshest information they could and at least talk again in a few days' time. Tiaret, in particular, offered their services to scry for the location or identity of the mage responsible for the creation of the enhanced virus, which worried Tam just a little. She'd never scried before, much less carried out such a procedure in a group. She hoped sincerely that the learning curve on that one wouldn't be too steep. As the meeting dissolved into small talk and side conversations, she began packing up, closing the handheld and returning it to its padded, waterproof carrying case, then stashing it away in her satchel.

When she looked up, she found the youngest of the werewolves, Little Blue, watching her intently.

Tam had absolutely no idea what to do or say, and the little werewolf didn't at all appear inclined to help her out on that score, either. "Er... Can I help you with something?"

"What is that... thing?" He tossed his chin in the direction of the satchel, setting a dozen shiny thingamabobs attached to his coat jingling.

"Thing? Oh, the handheld. It's a portable remote relay to my..." What was the word Baihu had used? "To my familiar."

"Your familiar." Little Blue looked up at her with unsettling intensity, dark eyes glittering like a night sky filled with millions of stars. "Doesn't seem that way."

"What do you mean?" Tam frowned.

"I felt it, when you were waving it around a little while ago. That's no familiar, spirit, or thing." He shook his blue-streaked head. "That's something using you, not something you use. You might want to get one of your own people to look at that for you. Before it gets any worse."

And, so saying, he trotted out after his alpha, leaving Tam standing shocked and disturbed in his wake.

Tam was beginning to think she should just check out of the Hotel Monaco and ask Baihu if she could have a corner of the sitting room to set up in. She was spending more time at the Ninefold Lotus than the hotel, anyway, and it would save her a couple hundred dollars a day. She suspected he'd even be happy to have her. It was more a lack of time than a lack of inclination that kept her from asking as the impromptu cabal reconvened in Baihu's apartment the next evening, after Tiaret and Gwyn had gotten off work and Baihu had returned from standing day watch at the ICU.

Tam had spent the day preparing herself by reading up on the documents she had access to regarding common group scrying procedures and the underlying theories involved, all written in her father's clear, no-nonsense prose. It gave her a certain degree of comfort to see things spelled out so clearly and so directly, even if things wouldn't turn out that way in practice. Practically, she wasn't sure how well scrying for the identity of the virus' creator would actually work, what sort of defenses might be in place to prevent such a thing, or how they'd overcome them if such things existed. None of the documents she had access to offered much in the way of comfort on those issues, at any rate, though she made certain they were loaded for reference purposes on the handheld before she called for a cab.

Sometime during the day, Baihu had found the time to strip his living room almost to the bare walls. All the furniture, except the low coffee table altar, had been removed, even the throw rugs and the bookcases and the decorative wall-hangings. These things had been replaced by woven mats and flat pillows on the floor, arranged around the freshly polished altar, which had also been precisely reoriented to point south to north. Each wall now bore a large, framed octagonal mirror, flanked by plates of carved green stone set in frames of wood and elaborately braided cord that reminded Tam of icons. She could never remember the proper name of the things, but she knew they were symbols of good fortune and protection, representations of Buddhist deities and the like. Wind chimes hung in the windows, which had been opened to admit the unseasonably warm evening breeze, and the air still held the faintest trace of a spicy incense smell, though no censers or braziers were obvious. Small, glass-shielded oil lamps provided all the light there was, reflected and amplified by the mirrors.

A heavy, barely carved vessel sat in the middle of the altar, along with Baihu's favorite ritual tools, his cast metal bell and bowl, and the wooden sounder he used on both. Tam glanced a question at him as she approached, and he replied with a gesture. "Pick which place seems best to you, Glorianna. Have you eaten?"

"Before I left the hotel. But thank you for offering." She paced around the altar, found that no one place in particular leapt out at her, and picked the spot opposite Baihu. "When do you think the others will be here?"

"Shortly. I just got off the phone with Gwyn. He has to swing by his apartment to change, but then he'll be here. And Tiaret left her place about a half an hour ago, so she'll be here soon, too." He seated himself, tucking his legs neatly together in a position that would nonetheless let him get up quickly. "Is there anything I can help you with before we get started? I only ask because Gwyn told me that you haven't done a lot of work in a group before, and I know how intimidating it can be."

"Now that you mention it…" Tam brought out the PDA and the documents she'd downloaded earlier. "My father had plenty of theoretical information on the process of scrying in his writings, but, as you know, some things are a good bit different when you try them for the first time."

"Oh, yeah. Here, let me take a look."

They spent the hour it took Gwyn and Tiaret to arrive going over those documents and being treated to the fruits of Baihu's experience, which, while not vast, was significantly greater than her own. Not for the first time, she found herself thinking that, were the situation just a little different, she wouldn't mind staying in Chicago and getting to know these people better. Tiaret actually made it to the Lotus first and was ushered in by Baihu's uncle. She was apparently familiar with Baihu's ritual habits, because she'd come dressed to flex, in sweatpants and an oversized T-shirt rather than business casual work clothes.

"You'll be forty one day, too, and I hope to be there to see it." Tiaret waved off his attempts to help her down, and she settled herself heavily on the cushion provided for her. "Where's your malcontent partner in crime?"

"Pulling up outside." Baihu admitted.

"Good. Maybe he'll even get his ass up here before my legs fall asleep."

Gwyn came up unescorted, looking freshly laundered and fully rested for the first time ever. He took the place left open for him without argument or even a snarky comment, which surprised Tam to no end, and laid his necklace of little bone charms on the altar. "You did the setup already, Bai?"

"Yes. Raised the *chi*, made sure the flows were all okay." Baihu brought the vial of tainted blood that Loki had donated to the cause out of the case in which he'd been storing it. Tam couldn't help noticing that it was not only refrigerated but also had protective markings drawn all over it in permanent marker. Most of the blood, though not all of it, went into the vessel in the center of the table and what remained was returned to the storage case. "Just in case we need a relatively intact sample of the virus."

Tam nodded, and no one argued. She laid the handheld on the altar and punched up the graphical image of the virus, which she had already decided to use as her meditative focal point. Tiaret added her own focus to the mix, a small, round object that Tam initially mistook for a compact but, when opened, revealed a sort of compass, marked around the edge in Atlantean letters and numerals. Quietly, without ceremony, Baihu picked up his bowl and sounder. The resulting tone was clear and pure, not particularly loud but intensely resonant, felt almost as much as heard. Tam closed her eyes, which she rarely did, given her propensity for visual focus, and let her mind settle on the sound, analyzing the way it changed across the duration of its existence. The tone never seemed to actually end: it just melted smoothly into the next tone Baihu sounded and continued on as the notes flowed on.

Glorianna opened her eyes, freed for a moment at least of the need to think of herself, even in a small way, as Tamara Hollister. She reached out and picked up the handheld, sending away the image of the virus for now, and set the tiny machine to randomly scan the contents of the storage devices it had access to, somehow feeling that was the right thing to do. To her right, Tiaret gazed with a serene non-expression at the compass, patiently waiting for some response from its gold-chased pointer. To her right, Gwyn held his necklace at eye-level, gazing through the aperture of a bone charm in the shape of a waning crescent moon at the dark surface of the vampire's tainted blood....

Which was rippling slightly, though none of them had moved enough to even slightly shake the table. Simultaneously, the handheld's screen flickered, and Tiaret's compass rotated slowly counterclockwise.

"Bai," Gwyn observed in an almost too-calm tone, "I think something's happening. And I didn't really do much yet."

"Neither did I," Baihu replied.

Glorianna hesitated for a moment, her thumb hovering over the rapidly flickering handheld's power key. "Maybe we should stop...?"

"No." Tiaret's voice, sharp and underlaid by a sound not unlike thunder, startled Glorianna so badly she nearly dropped the handheld.

"Glory's got a point, Tiaret." Gwyn visibly tried to lift his gaze from the rippling surface of the blood and was just as visibly unable to do so. "I've got a bad feeling about this."

"What kind of feeling did you expect to get?" The compass was rotating more rapidly now, its pointer little more than a metallic blur.

Glorianna wrenched her gaze away from it and glanced down at the handheld in the forlorn hope of settling her stomach and regaining her fractured concentration. What she saw there did nothing at all to help that goal. Formulating out of the sharp, bright lines running up and down the handheld's screen was a face, a familiar face, which she hadn't seen in years. "Daddy!"

She laid her hand on the screen in surprise—and the shock that ran up her arm was like a serpent of electric sensation, forcing her fingers, her joints, her whole spine into spasm as it smashed into her skull, sizzled behind her eyes, slammed her down hard. The last thing she saw, before darkness swallowed her, was the bare wooden floor coming up at her face, and the last thing she heard was Baihu shouting her name.

When Tam regained consciousness, she was lying in Baihu's bed again, though this time she was in her own clothes. Someone had taken off her shoes and socks, for which she was grateful, and put the handheld where she could reach it on the bedside table. The shades were drawn to keep out the afternoon sunlight—somehow, she knew it was the afternoon, though she had no real sense of exactly how much time had passed, hours or days. It was just the quality of the light itself, a waning cool golden that reminded her of autumn in New England.

She sat up slowly. Oddly, her thoughts were totally clear. She wasn't disoriented or confused, and a careful mental inventory showed her that she didn't appear to have any suspect gaps in her recent memories. She recalled, very clearly, being shocked. She supposed that she must have fainted, which annoyed her quite a lot. She'd managed to get through a great deal over the years without having to do anything as girly as faint, so naturally she'd have to do it in front of not one but three other magi. A few quick stretches told her that she didn't appear to be suffering any physical ill effects, no lingering pain or stiffness anywhere, not even a headache. She supposed she probably had Baihu to thank for that.

Her shoes and socks were tucked under the bed, next to the bedside table she'd owned since her eleventh birthday and the antiquing trip she'd nagged her father into going on. It was an old Shaker piece and one of the first things she'd wanted enough to offer to pay for out of her own allowance. A part of her wondered how it had gotten to Chicago; a larger part was simply glad that it was there, solid and real and comforting, a link to her real home. The handheld appeared to be dead, which didn't surprise her. If it had suffered some kind of power-pack malfunction, that could account for the shock she'd taken, and that meant she'd have to replace or repair the battery before she could use it again, at any rate. She laid it aside.

The hallway outside Baihu's apartment was wider than she remembered it being, and furnished differently, too. The Ninefold Lotus never gave her the impression of being a museum, or a convenient place to store less-portable possessions, somewhere to come back to every now and then but not a place where real life happened. This was not that home, that place where Baihu and his family gathered around a giant table for communal meals or sat together to read or color or play board games. Yes, the dining room was still there and so was the table but it wasn't the same thing. The chairs all matched. That disturbed her more than the inactive handheld.

There was no one in the adjoining kitchen, no one in the sitting room at the further end of the hall. Neither was there a television, much less a video game system. No couch with mismatched cushions or an inexpertly crocheted throw-blanket, no half-broken lounge chair sitting in the corner. Now it was all tastefully upholstered and perfectly matched with pillows set just so and knitted lace antimacassars on all the arms and backs. It was so wrong she couldn't put it into words, even to herself.

"Baihu?" No answer, from anyone. The Ninefold Lotus felt empty, which it had never felt before, and she found herself climbing staircases and opening doors in the hope of finding another living person, even that annoying Gwyn, because he was significantly better than nothing. In every room, she found more things, more of her things, more of the things from her father's house, more of her house.

The last private door on the first floor had a folded paper good-luck hanging dangling from a little rubber suction cup on it. Tam flung it open with a force she usually reserved for throwing annoying books across rooms and stepped inside.

Her father sat at his desk, reading glasses perched on his nose and an enormous dossier file open before him, reading with his usual single-minded concentration. Tam came to a complete halt a few steps inside the door and didn't even notice as it drifted shut behind her, rebounding from the force she'd directed against it. Her father took no notice, either of the door bouncing off the wall or of her entrance. Tam was breathing rapidly, half in tears, frustrated and more than a little afraid. The sight of him made her catch her breath.

"Daddy?" The word fell out of her mouth before she even had a chance to think about not saying it.

She received no response. Her father's steel-gray eyes never lifted from the pages of the document he was reading.

"Daddy, please talk to me. I'm so—What's going on here?" Tam fought to keep a tremor out of her voice and in the process completely failed at not whining. "Why are you here? What is this place? How did you get here?"

Nothing. Pages turned. Then, "Daddy's busy, Princess. Run along... I'll come tuck you in later."

"Later?" Tam could not remember the last time she'd shouted in the presence of her father. In fact, she couldn't remember if she'd ever shouted in the presence of her father. "What do you mean, later? I've been looking for you for five years, I've been looking all over the world, and you want to talk to me later? You're busy?"

"Tamara Annabelle," in that tone he used when he was oh-so-very disappointed in her, disappointed in something she'd said or done or failed to say or do, without even looking up, "yes, I'm a very busy man. And I'm sure what you have to tell me is very, very important... to you. But I assure you, it can wait."

"It can't wait!" Tam grasped the edge of the dossier and yanked it away with all her strength, sending papers flying the length of the study where she'd spent so much time, so much time trying to decode her father's journals, so much time trying to piece together his movements, so much time trying to figure out what he was doing that was so important that he'd leave her alone, always alone, with no one to meet her when she came home. "It can't wait, Daddy. People are dying, and I need your help. I can't do this by myself... I can't access all of Watson's functions, I don't have all the keys. I need you to—"

"To do your thinking for you? To hold your hand and tell you everything will be all right? To carefully arrange the circumstances of your existence so you can achieve your full potential? Is there anything you can do for yourself, Tamara?" He stood, turned his back, stared out the window. "I've waited. Lord knows I've waited, Tamara. I've waited for you to grow into someone whose company I might actively desire to keep. It was pleasant enough once you learned how to talk. There was a certain charm in you, then, at least for a while. But you were just so… slow. So average. Oh, brilliant enough compared to the plodding dolts you went to school with, but for my daughter?"

"What?" She could barely force her lips to form words. "What do you…"

"What do I mean? Dear girl, I think it should be obvious. After all the effort I put into you…" He shook his head sorrowfully, and still wouldn't turn to look at her. "It took exposure to an Atlantean artifact to open your eyes to the truth of your nature. It requires the constant assistance of an Atlantean artifact to allow you to blunder your way through the world. I swear, if I didn't know better, I'd think your mother cuckolded me with the dullest pool boy in Massachusetts just to spite me."

Tam didn't know, exactly, when she started crying. "Do you… Have you ever cared about me? Just about me? Why did you leave me?"

"Cared about you? Of course I care for you, pet, my dear Little Princess." He sounded like he was talking about a cocker spaniel. "But if I were given the choice of traveling to Tibet to speak with the last living inheritors of our traditions and staying home to attend an interminable series of your birthday parties and graduation parties and God alone knows what else juvenilia that you think requires my attention…? What would you do, Princess?"

Heavy. He felt heavy, as though his body were a statue cast out of solid lead. It didn't feel like natural weariness, like the usual side effect of working long hours and sleeping badly. Even the worst double shift at the morgue wouldn't leave him spaced like this, unable to lift his own head, sit up, twitch a limb, open his eyes. By contrast, his head felt weirdly light, weightless, disconnected from his ungainly body.

Someone moved relatively nearby. He wanted to say something, but the process of formulating a coherent sentence in his head was a daunting task. His thoughts kept running into one another, past one another, tying in knots. With far more effort than it should have taken, he managed to focus enough to come up with something simple.

"Where…" His mouth and throat were intensely dry, his tongue felt like it was made of sandpaper. "…am I?"

"Jason?"

A wave of relief washed over him. He knew that voice, it was his dad. With another Herculean effort of will, Gwyn got his eyes to open a crack, enough to get a blurry impression of his surroundings before he was forced to blink. He wondered, vaguely, when Baihu had painted his apartment psychiatric hospital mauve and replaced all his stuff with vital monitors, medication drips, an ECT rig. A hand gripped his own, firm, warm, comforting.

"Dad," Gwyn asked in what he hoped was a conversational tone, his raging need for something to drink notwithstanding, "what the fuck is going on?"

A long, hesitant silence greeted that question. It wasn't the use of language, because that generally provoked a quick response, no matter what the circumstances. He forced his eyes open again and was treated to the sight of his father looking halfway to tears, face carved with undisguised emotion. Which, all things being equal, was a shitload more disturbing than feeling doped up and immobile. He'd spent most of his middle teens in various states of heavy medication, voluntarily and otherwise, and now that he knew what it was, the sensation was almost like an old, annoying friend. Waking up with his father attending tearful and distraught at his bedside, on the other hand, was a strangeness he'd never had the pleasure of experiencing before.

Somewhere out of his limited line of sight, a door opened, admitting two sets of footsteps and what sounded like a push-cart. "Dr. Hyndes?"

"Yes?" His father responded before he could, so he let Dr. Hyndes, Sr. take it. The effort required to think and talk at the same time was reaching the level of diminishing returns, his thoughts disconnecting from each other and his body under the influence of whatever psychoactive chemicals were in that IV drip.

"I'm sorry I'm late, Doctor. I just came from the lab. Your son's results are in." Gwyn shifted his head as much as he could, got a glimpse of a tall, good-looking man in dark blue scrubs under a white lab coat, with a smoking habit he should really stop right now before the carcinogenic nodules forming in his lungs got any more encouragement. "I'm afraid that his condition continues to prove extremely resistant to conventional therapies. The Risperdal has had no significant effect on his incidence of hallucinations, and he continues to be unable to communicate clearly.... "

"Risperdal? You put me on Risperdal?" Gwyn yelped, the brain fog abruptly cleared by the cold wind of outrage. "I thought we established ten fucking years ago that I'm not actually schizophrenic, Dad, so what the hell is going on here?"

All conversation in the room ceased for a moment, as both the doctor—his doctor?—and his father stopped to look at him.

"He's not incapable of perceiving and interacting with the real world—yet. But, as you see, he's rapidly losing the ability to communicate clearly. He comprehends language, but not how to formulate coherent sentences." The miserable little fuck with the psychiatric medicine degree continued smoothly. "As his condition continues to deteriorate, this can only get worse. He already has one of the most tenacious cases of disorganized schizophrenia I've ever encountered."

"Yeah, like you've been out of school for more than a year. Dad, you can't believe this idiot." Gwyn exerted all his strength and actually got his fingers to close on his father's hand. "Listen to me. I'm not sick."

To apparently no effect whatsoever. "What do you recommend, Dr. Zartarian?"

"There are two possible treatment options available at this point, beyond ongoing chemical therapies. Electroconvulsive therapy has had some positive effect in patients manifesting joint schizophrenic-depressive symptoms, such as your son has presented in the past.... "

"Electroshock. Great. Dad, you can't be taking this seriously."

"Alternatively, a more permanent solution would be a surgical intervention." A long pause. "Severing the nerve clusters in the frontal lobe of the brain, the frontal lobotomy, will effectively cure the worst and most persistent symptoms of the schizophrenic disorder. Unfortunately, it will also bring about a permanent and irreversible change in your son's personality."

"Between you and me, Dr. Zartarian, there are times when I feel my son could use a permanent and irreversible change in personality." The doctor chuckled. Gwyn felt the urge to bounce up swinging, but lacked the motor control to do so. "Would I be permitted to attend in the surgical suite?"

"Dad!"

"Dr. Hyndes, considering your credentials, you might even be able to assist."

It felt like days before she found the top of her desk. Her entire world was made up of paper: client evaluations numbering in the thousands, endless reams of assessments, recommendations, formal complaints to be signed and passed on, manila folders to file in the appropriate spot once all she could do had been done. She was hemmed in on all sides by filing cabinets painted in slightly differing shades of beige, drawers neatly labeled in alphabetical order and by year, pasted in layers of old Post-it notes.

The oldest of the filing cabinets were covered in a thick film of dust, and she hated to touch them, even to brush past them, because they left greasy gray smears all over everything. There was nothing more she could do about any of those things, anyway, and she really wished someone would remove them. The apartment was too small to contain them all, as well, and she knew there had to be more storage space somewhere. Somewhere that she didn't have to look at them, think about them, hash over things that were over and done with a decade and more ago. It wasn't her job to follow up those cases, anyway.

Tiaret finished signing off on the last case file on her desk, and heaved herself to her feet. Even as she rose, her inbox began filling again, piling up with fresh files, fresh problems, fresh lives in need of fixing. She sighed, went to the newest of the filing cabinets, the least dusty, and opened the appropriate drawer. The contents, of course, immediately tried to come pouring out, the illegally obtained firearms, the little baggies and vials of recreational pharmaceuticals, the dirty needles and broken condoms, the warrants for child endangerment and failure to pay child support. But she had the method of containing those things down to a fine science, and managed to sweep them all back up and in with the new file, and slammed the whole thing shut before anything could escape to bother her again later. Which was just as well, because the new pile had become a couple of new piles, and were teetering on the edge of collapse by the time she got back to her desk.

She took the first file down and received an unpleasant shock: it was an old file, one she'd cleared quite a while before. Years before, in fact. She hadn't looked at it since, hadn't even thought about it. It wasn't her job to concern herself with any of those cases once she'd done her part for them. A quick check showed her that all of the files were old, some from the beginning of her career with DCFS, none less than three years old. She shoved the very oldest ones aside without even bothering to glance inside. None of the "kids" in those files could rightly be called kids anymore. Most of them, in fact, were old enough to have screwed-up children of their own, and, in many cases, no doubt did. Not looking inside didn't really help. She had to glance at the names and dates and that, of course, called up faces. Associations. Recollections. Little tidbits that she'd known and deliberately chosen to forget, because holding on to those memories never helped. She wasn't omnipotent. There were limits to what she could do within the confines of the law, within the confines of the foster care system, within the confines of her clients' own human frailty.

None of the piles were getting any smaller, no matter how fast she shoveled documents aside. In desperation, she resorted to burning them, whistling the four notes that summoned her brightest, hottest flames, and dropping the rapidly disintegrating remnants into her metal trashcan. Soon the can was filled to overflowing with ashes and cinders, but she was at least making headway. One pile was almost completely finished, and she was down to the last three files.

McBride, Georgette.

McBride, Kevin.

McBride, Andrew.

Her flames guttered and died.

Baihu realized that something was wrong more or less immediately. For one thing, he was sitting in a closet, and he was fairly sure he hadn't been a few minutes before. He knew it was a closet because it was full of clothes that no one wore anymore and it smelled rather strongly of old sneakers and boots treated with way too much mink oil, even for winter in Chicago. He felt around for the doorknob, which seemed to be far too high up, and, with a bit of effort, managed to reach it and get it open.

His apartment and everything in it seemed far too large. It took him a moment to realize why. He was small. His arms and legs were short, his hands and feet tiny and chubby. He felt his face and discovered no glasses, which he hadn't needed before he turned eight. It wasn't the first time he'd gone spirit-walking in the thought-form of a child, but it was the first that it'd happened involuntarily, which he found moderately disturbing. Even more disturbing was precisely how young he seemed to be. He walked in an unsteady toddle, as though he were just learning, and his hands were so small, the fingers so tiny....

His bowl, bell, and sounder sat on the altar, where he'd left them, but the configuration of the altar itself seemed subtly wrong. The alignment was just slightly off, the flows of *chi* distorted. He knelt, as best he could on his tiny legs, and closed his eyes, letting his awareness of the house and the flow of its energies stretch out. It took all his inner strength not to recoil from what he found. The flows of *chi* were more than just distorted; they had been warped and tainted somehow, twisted in a manner that recalled the contortions of the magically altered encephalitis virus. Bent out of true, the flows no longer protected the magi working within them. Instead, the *chi* stripped their minds and spirits bare, exposed them to outside attack and influence. Even worse, he had no sense of the others, their presence and unique energies, not even Gwyn, to whom he was closer than any of the others.

"Iiiiiiiisaaaaaaaaaaaaaaaaaac.... "

His eyes flew open, his heart suddenly thundering. He knew that voice.

"Iiiiiiiisaaaaaaaaaaaaaaaaaaaac... come and play..."

He scrambled to his feet and half-ran, half-fell to the still-open closet door, which he slammed shut before the thing stirring inside it could get all the way out. He planted his back against it and held on to the knob, which kept trying to turn under his hand. The living room was bare of anything he could use to block the door from opening, even if he'd had the strength to move a chair or a table, which he didn't think he did.

"Isaac… I know you're there…." The voice sounded mushy, thick, underlaid by a slow, steady pattering. "I just want to play…"

Something warm and sticky was starting to pool around his feet. He refused to look down at it. He already knew what it was, and he didn't want to see it. The altar was too far away to reach before the closet door opened, but it was still his best chance. He let go of the doorknob and ran, leaving bloody footprints across the living room floor as he went, diving for the bell and its sounder. Behind him, the closet door flew open and bounced against the wall.

"Peekaboo… I see you…."

The weight of the bell knocked him off balance as he grabbed it, pulled it off the altar. He wasn't strong enough or coordinated enough to hold the bell and the sounder at the same time, much less to use them properly. As he rolled over, the bell still clutched in his hands, he caught a glimpse of the boy emerging from the closet, the boy dressed in old-fashioned clothes with the trail of blood spilling over his face from the split in his skull.

"It's okay, Isaac…" The boy-shaped thing crooned, blood drooling off his lips and splattering on the floor with every word. "I just want to play."

Baihu struggled back to his feet, leaning on his bell, pulling it as high as he could off the floor once he'd risen. "You're not allowed to call me that."

The bloody boy stopped its shuffling forward motion, half-crouched like a rat. Its eyes, bloody, inhuman eyes, froze and fixed on the bell.

"My name is not yours to use." The thing hissed as he brought the bell up higher, and hurled it as hard as he could at the stone vessel in the center of the altar.

The bell and the vessel made contact with the most ungodly sound that Baihu had ever heard, a noise that combined equal parts broken temple bells ringing with the clamor of the Loop at rush hour with the high-pitched tone of vital monitor machinery failing with the roar of a swift-moving fire consuming building after building. The vessel tipped and spilled; the bell continued on its way, striking the floor and adding a half-dozen more tones to the sound. The boy-shaped thing howled, the sound of its screams mingling with the distorted ringing of the bell. It wasn't the most pleasant thing Baihu ever worked with, but it was better than nothing. He scrambled away, grabbing the sounder as he went, striking it against the dangling wind chimes and the surface of the icons, adding their sounds to the cacophony.

He saved the mirrors for last, striking their frames gently, sending the sound rippling through their surfaces. As he did so, the flows of the *chi* began to change, unbending, untwisting, returning to true. He became aware, abruptly, of the others again, somewhere inside the spirit-shadow of the house, relatively close. The bloody boy hissed and skittered back, spraying bloody spittle as it went, vanishing back into the closet from which it came. Baihu felt himself changing, growing taller and stronger, the illusion of childish weakness that had been imposed on him splitting and falling away like a brittle chrysalis. The sound was slowly dying away, but before it did, he lifted his bowl and sounder, and laid them both together. The pure notes he coaxed from it sent ripples of cleansing energy through the web of wards and defenses built around the house, breaking the dark intrusion holding the others, drawing them back into contact with themselves.

Around the table, their spirit-shadows flickered into being. As Baihu began the process of waking them, rejoining their spirits to their flesh, the wind rose, ringing the chimes, coaxing from them a sound like a human voice. A voice that spoke a name not his own.

Despite the fact that Baihu disapproved in general of dispensing medicine for every little ache and pain, he was not above keeping an institutional-sized bottle of Advil in his medicine cabinet. Faced with the simultaneous demands of his cabal's senior functioning maga and his best friend, he was also not above brewing a couple of pots of the hard stuff, the blackest black tea available in Chinatown. Tam was grateful for both of these concessions, because she had a skull-pounding, post-magical reaction headache and the process of pouring globs of raw honey and whole milk into a giant mug of hot tea now constituted a ritual of comforting normalcy. That fact didn't appear to be lost on the others, either, who lingered over their cups and the honey pot and failed to engage in even the slightest bit of casual conversation.

Glorianna curled herself in a corner of the futon, drank her tea in tiny sips, and resolutely refused to close her eyes more than she had to, even to blink. Even so, afterimages kept dancing across the inside of her eyelids, blurred and indistinct but disturbing all the same. The cushion shifted slightly as Baihu sat down next to her, cup in one hand and his chin in the other, visibly exerting the effort necessary to keep them from shaking. Gwyn and Tiaret joined them a moment later, and for a long time they did nothing at all except sit and drink and try not to internally freak out too obviously. More than once, Gwyn half-opened his mouth, as though he wanted to say something, only to close it again, visibly frustrated, either incapable of finding the right words or unable to speak the words he wanted to say.

The silence, Tam thought, was getting to be plenty uncomfortable. She could not, however, bring herself to break it. Doing so would set in motion a chain of events she wasn't sure she wanted to see, much less control, but she was damned sure she didn't want to start with herself. With what she'd seen during their joint scrying session, with what those Things had said to her while part of her Awakened mind had been in contact with them. She was utterly not ready for that yet, so she kept her mouth shut, except for tiny sips of tea, and concentrated hard on not crying, despite the stupid, irrational urge to do so welling up inside her.

Just as silence was about to cross the line between uncomfortable and sheer torture, Baihu set aside his cup. "What do we do about the virus?"

Those words had a profound effect. Gwyn, who'd been sitting on the edge of his chair, all nervous tension, slumped back into his seat with a strangled sound halfway between a laugh and a groan. Tam, inexplicably, felt her teariness receding into the background. Tiaret shot Gwyn a quelling look and shook her head as it obviously bounced off, turning her full attention on Baihu. "Have you given any thought to treatments? Or how any such treatment might be delivered to the victims?"

"I've given it thought. Do I have a practical approach? No. Theoretically, the methods used to cleanse one's own body of disease and toxins, or to strengthen oneself against the same, might be able to provide some kind of relief if you could find a means of delivering it to others." He pushed his glasses back up the bridge of his nose. "The problems with that are making any such magical antiviral agent in the first place, then making it strong enough to overcome the virus in question without a lot of trial and error in terms of efficacy, and then actually getting it to the victims, provided you get past the first two issues."

"Number three's the big one, because I'm sure we could eventually put something together, even if it's only a stopgap to keep these people from dying until we ultimately break the viral spell," Gwyn added, lifting his head from its place along the back of his chair. "If a blood sample goes missing or gets contaminated or whatever, you can always draw more blood. Somebody gets a treatment in ICU that hasn't been signed off on by at least two attending physicians and then maybe dies anyway? The lawsuits will never end. Not to mention the consequences of getting caught trying to physically administer anything we cook up."

"So what you two are suggesting is that there's no point in even attempting a treatment," Tam observed, carefully, hoping that she was somehow misinterpreting.

"I wish I weren't," Baihu replied. "You have no idea how much I wish that weren't the case. My grandmother—" He stopped, wrestled his voice back under control, continued on. "I don't say it lightly. But we'd waste too much time trying to treat the symptoms when what we need to do is root out the ultimate spiritual disease."

"You're willing to potentially sacrifice the lives of everyone who already has this... infection?" Tiaret asked, her gaze cool and level. "When there might be something you could do to save them?"

"You're going out on a narrow fucking limb there, lady, and I don't think you want to," Gwyn snapped, almost instantly, making Tam jump. "And that's a big 'might,' while we're at it. I said that we could probably come up with a treatment eventually. In the meantime, people would keep getting infected and all the people who've got it now will likely be dead of it before we could produce anything workable. I don't see you laying any brilliant ideas on the table."

"That's because I don't have any." Tiaret gave him a look that shut his mouth quite thoroughly. "I'm not saying that you're wrong. I'm not saying that there's a treatment and that we should spend our time and effort looking for it to the exclusion of other approaches. And I'm not saying that we should. I do, however, think that needed to be said out loud. We can't save them all. Trying will only scatter our energies when we most need to be focused. Are we in agreement on that point?"

Tam nodded, silently, so very glad that she hadn't been the one to say that out loud.

"Yeah," Gwyn said softly. "I know it."

"Yes." Baihu took a deep breath, let it out again. "So, now that that's been established, what's our approach?"

"Logically," Tam began, trying to ignore her almost painfully dry mouth, "our objectives are actually twofold. We need to find some means of neutralizing or otherwise breaking the viral spell, and we need to find the person responsible for casting it in the first place, because doing the one without the other is fairly pointless. I would say, since the spell seems to be made up of equal parts life and death, that the task of analyzing and breaking it would belong to you two." She nodded at Gwyn and Baihu. "Tiaret and I could take on tracking down the magus. Physically, that is. After all, I've spent the last couple of years getting rather practiced at ferreting out people who might not necessarily want to be found and your line of work is at least marginally similar, right?"

"True." Tiaret acknowledged the point. "You two?"

"I think we should probably get T-shirts made with that phrase on it." Gwyn sucked down the last of his cup of tea. "I've got no argument with that division of labor. I can even talk to Nuad about letting us use one of the secure rooms in the house, if you like."

"If you wouldn't mind."

"Okay. I'll give him a call later. I'm on the midday shift at the morgue for the next couple days, so we'll need to meet after I get off. Acceptable?"

"It'll have to be." Baihu unfolded himself and began collecting empty cups.

"Similarly…" Tiaret turned to Tam, "I have to go into the office tomorrow. My case-load is particularly robust just now, and I fear that I am so far behind on my paperwork that I may not see the light of day before Christmas."

Tam nodded. "That's okay. I can do some research, and we'll meet in the evening."

"Very well. Young lady, gentlemen, I move that we take the balance of this evening to recover from tonight's exertions and start fresh tomorrow. There's nothing to be gained from going off half-cocked and exhausted."

General murmurs of agreement greeted this statement. Before they parted ways, Baihu's Aunt Mel brought them dinner and he insisted they stay to eat it. "A grounding element to reunite us in the real world," he called it, and Tam was inclined to agree, feeling much more centered and real an hour later with her stomach full of fried rice and barbecued pork dumplings and lo mein. Tiaret volunteered to drive Tam back to the hotel, an offer she accepted gratefully.

"Did you get any particular impressions from that experience that we just had?" Tiaret barely waited for her to get the door closed before the questions started.

Tam, who was still getting her thoughts in order on that particular topic, opened her mouth, closed it without answering, and was silent for a long moment as their car entered the late-evening traffic flow. "I don't know. I'm not really skilled at this sort of thing."

"All right. Let's try this another way." The older woman's hands flexed on the steering wheel as though they were grasping a human neck. "I was shown something intensely personal during our contact with whatever that was. I assume it was the same for you."

Tam nodded. "Yes."

"I'm not going to ask you what that was. I don't really want to know, and I'm sure you don't want to tell me. But I think the key lies in there." She tapped her well-manicured nails together. "I received a flash-impression, at the end, just before Baihu brought us back, of something female. Something feminine in the malice, the way it went straight for the points of emotional vulnerability."

"I thought so, too." Tam looked out the window to avoid meeting Tiaret's glance in her direction. "I thought the whole thing was sort of… It reminded me of when I was in boarding school and the girls there used to tease me about my father never coming for any of the usual events. It's stupid, I know."

"It's not stupid. Your father is a magus. I can tell you from personal experience that that's a complicating factor that most parent-child interactions could very much do with-out." Tam glanced back, and found Tiaret looking rueful. "Granny Tsu is the exception that tests the rule, in that regard."

"Do you come from," Tam tried to come up with a good way to phrase it, "a family with magical heritage, too?"

"Who, me? Oh, no. My folks were both completely ordinary." A trace element of bitterness in her voice. "They ran a corner store in our neighborhood. When I was eleven, my father was shot. After that… well, my mom didn't handle it well. I tried the best I could to help out, but there's only so much you can do when you're too young to work legally. DCFS put my two younger brothers in foster care, and my aunt raised my sister and me."

"I'm sorry." Somehow, that didn't seem entirely adequate. "I…"

"It was a long time ago. And not your problem, so you've got nothing to be sorry for." Tiaret bestowed a Look on her. "From what little you've said, it's not as though your life has been all cotillions and cruises, either."

Tam couldn't help smiling, just a little, at the mental image that painted. "No. But it hasn't been all bad, either."

"Neither has mine. What's your game plan?"

The sudden change in topic caught Tam by surprise. "I'm not sure yet. I was thinking of playing things a little by ear, seeing what I can turn up in the information we've already got. I'm thinking that there's got to be a connection between at least some of the victims of the virus. We just need to suss it out. What about Baihu and Gwyn?"

"Not a bad place to start. Give me a call at the office if there's anything you need me to do while I'm there." A pause. "What about them?"

"How did you meet them? I'm curious because I've never really had that kind of relationship before. A cabal." Tam could feel her ears turning pink, that sounded lame even to her.

"And you're curious about them, too." A little smile twitched at the corners of Tiaret's mouth. "Baihu is one of my success stories. I met him when he was in foster care, and I was randomly assigned his case. He was about seven, had been in the system for about two years, and was already fully Awake. His grandmother was trying to obtain permanent legal custody while his parents went through the last stages of what can charitably be described as a bloody vicious divorce. According to Granny, his dad never did want custody, being the feckless and irresponsible sort. His mom convinced herself it'd be much easier to get remarried to a nice Jewish boy if she didn't have a kid. Despite all that, he managed to come out the other side better adjusted than he has any right to be."

Tam blinked. "He was Awake at seven?"

"It's not unusual for practitioners of his particular Path. They tend to wake up early and then last longer than most, if Granny is any indication. She made Baihu's transition to his true nature pretty smooth." They were almost to the hotel. "Gwyn didn't have it quite so easy. His parents are, to put it delicately, not the sort who are inclined to believe that their son was having genuine supernatural experiences. Or even to believe in supernatural experiences, period. He was diagnosed with pubescent-onset schizophrenia with depressive complications at about thirteen. He was really Sleepwalking, not hallucinating, but he spent the majority of his middle teen years on antipsychotics and antidepressants, to which he added an unhealthy recreational chemical habit, to help kill the pain." Tiaret pulled up smoothly in the hotel's drop-off lane. "He and Baihu were going to the same school by then, and were in one of those little after-school support groups for kids from troubled backgrounds together."

"So they've been friends for a long time." Which made sense, considering how well they worked together despite their differences in Path.

"Yes. Gwyn credits Baihu with saving both his life and his sanity, which isn't far from the truth. They've been working together since Gwyn finished waking up." Tiaret hit the door locks. "One day, you'll have to tell me all about your dramatic entrance into our world."

Tam rolled her eyes heavenward. "One day, when I figure out how it all happened, I will."

Tam dawdled as long as she could, writing list after list of search strings on the hotel stationery, before she finally turned to Watson. It wasn't that she was afraid of him, she told herself more than once. It wasn't. But it was patently obvious that his defenses, his multiple and interlocking means of preventing intrusions into his system, were not at all proof against the things they were facing now. This thing that Heartsblood and Baihu insisted on calling the Murder of Crows. The magus who'd remade the virus or whatever was helping her. Something had attacked her at least once through him, and could likely do so again, if she weren't careful.

She realized she'd passed from preparatory dawdling into outright dithering over whether or not to use her own computer for research purposes. She supposed she could go to the public library and make use of the machines there, but that would also mean compensating for parental control filters and search engines of distinctly inferior nature. With a sigh, she tore the used pages off the notepad and opened the laptop's hood. The screen flickered, coming out of hibernation mode. Watson sat in his chair, as completely composed as ever. The floor of the room was covered to the depth of his ankles in crow feathers, a fact to which he seemed serenely oblivious. He didn't speak. He didn't move. He just looked up at her with strangely bright, glittering eyes.

Tam suddenly wished she had Baihu here for backup. "Watson?"

His head moved, a short, jerky motion that was neither a nod nor a shake.

Tam wet her lips and tried again. "What... who are you?"

A sound like dozens of crows cawing all at once emerged from the speakers, rising and falling in a manner like human laughter. Clenching her hands on the arms of her chair, Tam fought the urge to flee from the source of that sound. After a moment, the sound stopped, the speakers popped with static, and the screen flickered again. Watson, alone, the floor the same wine-colored carpet it always was.

"Who are you?" Tam asked again.

"Glorianna, are you feeling quite all right? You don't seem yourself." The voice was Watson's, the same as always, lightly accented and so very proper. For the first time, Tam couldn't feel any comfort from that, and she knew if she asked him he'd find no traces of an intrusion.

"I'm fine. I just have some work to do that I need your help with." She deployed the system browser and search engine. "We think we know what's going on, but we need to find who's doing it..."

It didn't take anywhere near as long as she thought it would, with Watson's superior search and compilation abilities to assist her. The vast majority of the enhanced virus' victims were young—teenagers, early twenty-somethings—with a smattering of older people like Baihu's grandmother randomly scattered among them. Tam started looking for the possible connections between them, the single random element that they all had in common. There had to be something or, in this case, several somethings. A dance club called the Skullery, a hangout for morose types and the vampires who preyed on them, covered a good number of the victims of twenty-something range. Tam wondered if the CDC or the city public health authorities had put the pieces of that together, yet, or if they were still operating under the unusually bad but normal outbreak theory. It didn't matter, ultimately, because talking to the CDC about the undead viral vector was a non-starter, but it'd be interesting if they noticed. A private high school on the North Side—well, okay, several different high schools on the North Side, but it was the private one, the Rosedale Academy, that scored the most connections. Not only did a sizeable portion of the virus victims come from that school, but five of the thirteen victims of the poisoned Kool-Aid ritual that Baihu and Heartsblood stumbled into attended that school, as well.

Thirteen confirmed victims of their magus. Two hours later, Tam was looking at thirteen individual background profiles and searching for how kids so different from one another were connected. The Rosedale Academy was one link, and the school's website had a message up on the main page, indicating its condolences to the parents and explaining where others wishing to extend their condolences could do so. Three of those five kids were active in school academic associations, particularly the Comparative Religions Club. So were six of the other victims, in the equivalent associations at their schools. Tam started looking up individual home pages, which the vast majority of them possessed, and ended up wading through an awful lot of amateurish art and woe-is-me poetry before she finally hit paydirt, hidden on someone's links page.

The Nightshade Network, a tiny banner at the bottom of the page, done in shades of purple and a font that wasn't meant to catch anyone's eye. Tam clicked the link and found herself redirected to a login page for a bulletin board, which demanded registration to even view the various forums. It seemed to be devoted to "alternative spiritualities" and service to the "pagan communities in the greater Chicago area." Tam rolled her eyes, rolled them some more when she was informed that her first and second choices were already taken, and finally got in with a random selection of letters that looked vaguely Welsh. It was, however, worth it. The board was alive with self-styled teen pagans freaking out over what had happened, trying to get in touch with one another and determine what had happened, who was affected. All thirteen of the victims were identified by real name and Craft name, which she noted down for future reference.

So was a fourteenth, whom no one seemed able to find. Gina—no last name, but who was known to attend Rosedale Academy, who was identified as the group's priestess, and was also known by the name Nicnevin. Tam searched the boards for posts by anyone operating under that user name and found nothing. Either she used another online ID or else she'd deleted all of her prior posts.

Tam snapped open her cell and hit the speed dial.

"Gretchen McBride, Department of Child and Family Services." The voice on the other end of the phone sounded weary and stressed.

"Tiaret? It's Glorianna. I think I have something." Tam didn't particularly relish adding any more bad to Tiaret's day, but some things were unavoidable.

Dr. Jason Hyndes took ruthless advantage of his status as senior intern and peon at the morgue to claim a desk position and the small mountain of backed-up paperwork sitting thereon. He wasn't in a temper that leant itself gladly to weighing disembodied organs. He wasn't, for that matter, in the mood for reading about anybody's disembodied organs, but found the process of paperwork review to be somewhat preferable to being up to his elbows in waterlogged viscera. They were still pulling cars and bodies out of the river, and their office was getting that overflow, in addition to all the standard operational DOAs.

It also didn't help his temper to be reminded that he'd seen the bridge disaster coming but, as usual, hadn't been able to do anything about it. He sorted the files according to source of aggravation, bridge first, then encephalitis victims, then all the normal stuff, and buried himself in shootings, overdoses, car accidents, and deaths of unknown providence for a good five hours. The first encephalitis case he came to looked normal enough. Seventy years old, female, with a long history of health problems, depressed immunity that would make her easy pickings for an opportunistic encephalitis infection. A very opportunistic infection, given that the total duration of her illness, from diagnosis to time of death, was a little over a week. Possibly one of the victims of the enhanced form, though not necessarily.

He tried to put it out of his mind, because wallowing in guilt about things that he couldn't do anything about was a waste of time and energy. That fact didn't really help. He'd kept Granny Tsu off his mind by virtue of being righteously pissed at her and her ingrained Mysterium bullshit, burdening him with secrets he didn't want to know and forcing his silence when what he knew might help, or at least might make a few things clearer. His conscience gnawed at him with dozens of tiny, sharp, poisonous teeth for thinking ill of her, for not going to the hospital to see her, for not even making the time to sit with Baihu in the ICU waiting room. The *geas* she'd laid on him sat in the back of his throat all the time, sometimes an annoyance like a tickle that refused to evolve into a full-blown cough, sometimes a garrote that kept him from blurting out everything he knew, even under pressure. The *geas* was always at its strongest in the presence of his best friend, ready to choke him if his will to secrecy wavered, which was more or less constantly when it came to Baihu. Sometimes just thinking about him caused it to trigger with a viciousness that left him breathless and reeling.

It had been there so long, so ever-present in its malignant watchfulness for any sign of weakness, that it actually took him a while to realize that it was gone. It dissolved without sensation, without warning, but the comprehension of what that meant dawned quickly. Getting through to the Northwestern Memorial's ICU proved to be impossible; the switchboard operator kept bouncing him around from department to department. No one was home at the Ninefold Lotus or, if there was, they weren't picking up the phone. Baihu's cell phone was turned off, and dialing that number repeatedly just kept dumping him into its voicemail box.

The last three hours at work were the longest Jason had ever spent doing anything. He didn't even wait to conduct the normal shift-switch briefing, just ran for his car as soon as the clock hit time, and beat his own land speed record getting to the Ninefold Lotus. He knew something was wrong the minute he pulled up outside. The lights were on downstairs, in the first floor storefront, but the upstairs was completely dark, which was thoroughly unnatural for the time of day. Most of the family was clustered in the shop, all of them various shades of pale, strained, and tearful. Baihu was nowhere in evidence.

"Gwyn." Aunt Mel came out of the storage room as he entered, her eyes red and puffy, clearly having just spent some time composing herself. "Grandmother—"

"I know." Jason abruptly found himself holding a couple of armfuls of tearful woman, which wasn't the last thing he expected but close to it. "I'm sorry, Mel. Truly I am." He fished a reasonably clean bunch of tissues out of his jacket pocket. "Here. It'll be... All right, it won't be okay. But at least she's not suffering anymore."

"Your bedside manner really does suck." Mel offered him a watery smile, and blew her nose on a napkin. "I tried calling your house... Baihu..."

"I was at work," Jason replied, quietly. "Where is he?"

"Upstairs." Her voice sank. "He's... not himself, Gwyn. I've never seen him like this."

"Probably nobody ever has." He glanced around the room, took in Mei and her baby, the kids, Grandpa Tsu sitting in the corner, his head in his hands. "Listen. Get everybody out of here. Don't go to a neighbor's house—go to a hotel or something. You need money?" The look she gave him could have peeled flesh. "I was just asking. Of course you have money. Just... go someplace safe."

"Someplace safe? What could be safer than our own home?"

"Trust me. Just this once. You don't want to be here right now. Okay?"

It took fifteen minutes of vigorous conversation over in the corner, in two dialects of Chinese and several of whiny American teenager, but Mel ultimately saw his point. They hustled out without so much as an overnight tote; the only piece of luggage they carried was the baby's diaper bag. The look that Mel gave him in passing promised serious Tsu-woman style retribution should the situation not merit such extreme measures. For a change, Jason hoped to deserve such vengeance.

A cold draft wended its way down the second-floor staircase, thick with the smell of lightning strikes and wet city pavement. Jason took the stairs slowly, mentally formulating what he wanted to say. It wasn't easy. There were some conversations that no friendship should ever have to bear, and he was dead sure this was going to be one of them. Provided that anything as civilized as conversation actually went on. Baihu didn't lose his temper often, but when he did, the results tended to be painful for somebody. God knew, he had excellent reason to be pissed off now.

The second floor hall was dark. It took him a second to realize why. All the light fixtures were hanging from the walls in masses of half-melted wiring, light bulbs and frosted glass fittings shattered and blackened.

"Bai?"

The cold breeze was coming in through the windows at either end of the hall. He couldn't tell for sure, but he thought they might be broken.

"Baihu?"

The door to his apartment was closed. As Jason approached, it flew open, opposite the direction it was supposed to, half ripped off its hinges by a hard, cold blast of wind that carried a flurry of detritus out into the hall with it. He waited until the worst of it had passed, then came to the door, and peered cautiously inside. "Baihu, are you...?"

"Did you know?"

Jason had to force himself not to jump and flatten himself against the nearest wall. Baihu's voice seemed to come from the air itself, curled up close next to him, directly in his ear, and at the same time from somewhere further away. It also seemed far too calm.

"Bai, come on…. Where are you?" He glanced down the hall, into the apartment, which seemed to be in a significant state of wrecked. He extended his perceptions, slowly, carefully, and yanked them back as quick as he could.

Absolutely *incandescent* rage. He had never felt Baihu so angry, and still so cold. Up on the roof. He was up on the roof where, despite his inability to keep anything with chlorophyll in its veins alive, he kept a small garden of potted plants. The roof garden was accessible only from the fire escape that snaked up the side of the building past Baihu's apartment windows. Jason crossed the room carefully, wincing every time the pieces of something crunched underfoot, not wanting to imagine what he was stepping on. The wind caught him as he crawled out onto the fire escape, trying to yank him in at least two directions, both of which ultimately led to the ground. He flattened himself down as close to the wrought-iron steps as he could and climbed slowly, face and hands windburnt and frozen before he was halfway to the top.

The last of the daylight was fading off the western horizon as he pulled himself over the lip of the roof. Baihu stood in the middle of a scattered mass of wreckage that had been three shoulder-high wooden trellises, a series of low potting benches, and a number of heavy terracotta planters. The wind rotated around him, curling around from at least three directions to lift bits of wreckage off the roof's surface and send them soaring away. As Jason watched, the wind picked up a piece of planter and flung it past his head hard enough to bounce off the wall of the building opposite and shatter into even more pieces.

"You didn't answer my question." Baihu's voice was empty of emotion, expression, entirely too calm. Jason felt all the hair on his body trying to rise as the air around him crackled with fury looking for an outlet.

He closed his eyes. A vision flickered across them, one he'd seen before, one of him and too much blood and not enough pain, his head cradled in someone's lap. It could be tonight. There were worse ways to die.

"Yes, I knew." He took a deep breath and expelled it in a burst of frost as the local air temperature dropped even further. "She—"

"YOU KNEW!"

No normal language, those words. They echoed in the sky and off the walls and lanced through his skull like a stroke of lightning. He felt the grief and rage and betrayal in them in his blood and bones. A howling sledgehammer wind hit him from behind, lifting him completely and heaving him across the roof to land in a heap practically at Baihu's feet. None too gently, either, and his head swam from the impact.

"Bai." It was all he could do to get the words out against the rush of wind clawing furiously at his face, "Bai, listen to me! She didn't—"

"SHE HAD NO RIGHT!"

The wind grabbed him again, heaved him up—straight up, and he got a good, long, stomach-churning look at the patterns the street lights and the security lights made on the alley pavement as he tumbled, buoyed by absolutely nothing, more feet than he wanted to think about overhead. He was almost glad when he hit the roof again, instead of falling all the way.

"She had no right," Baihu whispered feverishly. "She had no right to keep this from me. She had no right to meddle with my mind, with my soul, make me forget so much about myself. How could she do this to me?"

Jason was certain at least a couple of his ribs were cracked, from the pain shooting through his chest every time he breathed. He held perfectly still for a moment, watching as Baihu spun away, his shoulders shaking with a sob of equal parts rage and grief. Carefully, slowly, Jason worked his way back to his feet, half-crouched to provide the lowest profile he could to the wind.

"Baihu." Jason breathed out, hoping for soothing. "Please... stop this. Don't do this. It's not—"

"It's not what? It's not me? It's not who I am? How am I supposed to know who I am? She took my memories from me. She hid part of my own soul from me. She made me believe—" His voice cracked. "She violated me. My own grandmother. Just like those things did..."

"It wasn't like that, Bai! She didn't—she was trying to protect you! My God, you were six. You'd been hurt, wounded in spirit, she didn't want you to suffer that much, that young." Jason blinked tears that had nothing to do with physical pain off his lashes. "She only meant it to be temporary—a patch until you were old enough to handle it on your own—"

"But it didn't work that way, did it? Things like that never do. You can't carve out a piece of someone's soul and expect them to heal completely around it. It doesn't work that way." He half-turned, and Jason retreated a step back from the look on Baihu's face, the icy, insane fury in his eyes. "And you. You knew about this, and you kept it from me. I trusted you more than anyone else in this world and you deceived me. You betrayed me. *You helped her do this to me!*"

"No! Isaac, I—" The wind rose around him, a shrieking, clawing thing, half-alive with the rage that animated it. It was like trying to breathe broken glass, stand up against a Force Ten gale on the lakeshore, and it drove him to his knees, gasping, eyes tearing, unable to see or speak or hear anything over the voiceless roar. He threw out a hand to balance himself, and something caught his wrist. He felt the bones stand up to the pressure exerted against them for a fraction of a second before they snapped, grinding against one another. Whatever had him took him the rest of the way down, driving all the air out of his lungs with the force of the impact and setting off a spectacular fireworks display inside his head. Hands. There were hands closed around his throat, shaking him like a terrier shaking a rat, thumbs exerting bone-crushing pressure on his windpipe. He absolutely could not breathe.

His last totally coherent thought, before the red-tinged darkness of pain and shock and oxygen deprivation dragged him down, was, *Can't lie if you can't talk. Good thinking, Bai.*

Wind rushed by all around him, but it was a different category of wind than the one that had carried him here. This wind already had his life contained within it, and so wasn't interested in taking any more from him. It curled around him, sweet and cool, like the first breath of autumn after a long, hot summer. Refreshing.

He opened his eyes. Darkness all around, except for the place he was standing, which shone with his own silver-gray stormlight. Something fluttered past him, and he reflexively reached out to catch it: a crow's feather, lightning-stroke white, as bright as he in the darkness. He stroked it, absently, wondering about its significance, if it had any, or if this was just another obtuse spirit-game meant to annoy the living fuck out of him until he finished dying.

He heard her before he saw her. The *taptaptap* of her cane sounded real enough, as though it were falling on stone and not the Grim Path, the road that led only one place. It wasn't Granny Tsu—Grandmother Feng-huang, with her feathers of pheasant and peacock, though the shape was similar. She walked with a cane. In her hand, she held a fan of black crow feathers, and wore a rippling crimson robe adorned with the same. He found he couldn't be afraid of her, though the eyes that glittered in her wizened face held not even the slightest trace of humanity. She wasn't the threat, after all. She wasn't the real problem.

The Murder of Crows smiled serenely up at him. Beckoned him close. Whispered in his ear.

From somewhere far away, he heard someone calling his name.

"Gwyn… oh, God, Jason…"

Something warm and wet was falling on his face. Falling all over him, to be more exact. Raining. It was raining, a warm, spring rain, completely out of place for the season. He took a deep breath and coughed, convulsively, as it burned in his throat and chest. He opened his eyes, and a face swam woozily into view.

"Bai." He sounded like he'd scrubbed the inside of his throat with steel wool, and felt like it, too. "S'okay. M'all right."

"No, you're not." Warmth blossomed inside his chest, radiating outward, thankfully killing the pain first. "I'm so sorry, Gwyn. I—"

"Temporary batshit insanity. Forgiven. You owe me a fuckton of massages. On demand." Gwyn pushed himself up on his good elbow. "Stop crying. Right now."

"I can't." Baihu's voice caught in his throat. And the tears running down his face really wouldn't stop. "She's dead, Gwyn. She died, and there was nothing I could do to save her. And I… I almost… I remembered everything all at once, and I was so… angry. I wasn't even sorry that she was gone. I could have killed you. I—"

"No, you couldn't have." Gwyn replied, softly. "It's not my time yet. But it was Granny's. And it's time I told you what I know about the Voices in the Dark."

"Is that what they're called?" Baihu took his broken wrist in hand and started kneading it gently, working the bones back into alignment, and Gwyn was very glad for whatever was keeping the pain at bay.

"In what I've managed to find, yeah." Snap, crackle, and he could flex his fingers again. "There hasn't been much confirmable. Stuff like this never really is. But, yeah, the Voices in the Dark, first called that in Aristede's journals, near as I can tell. Doc doesn't have them all. And a couple of other documents dating from about the time of the Fire."

"They didn't come into being at that time. They…" Baihu hesitated, took his glasses off, rubbed his eyes with the heel of one hand. "They feel older than that. Much older."

"They probably are. Aristede and one of his colleagues, some hot shit spirit magus from out East, theorized that the Voices have always been here. The Murder of Crows, too. Primal forces, worrying at each other constantly." He caught Bai's hand as it came back down. "They just show different faces to their victims when they appear."

Baihu shuddered, a whole-body thing that left him half-slumped and let Gwyn get an arm all the way around him. "The bloody boy. The boy that Heartsblood saw, that he kept trying to tell me about. It was him, the one who always came to me...."

"Bobby Franks."

"What?"

"You aren't the only one who's seen it in that form. He looks like Bobby Franks, the kid that Leopold and Loeb killed. Blood, acid burns, the whole nine yards. They steal the faces of the dead." Gwyn coughed hard as the broken bones in his chest healed with one last twinge. "They steal the faces of the dead and use them to spread fear, horror, break down the wills of their victims. What happened to you isn't your fault, Bai. You were vulnerable to them, and there was nothing you could do to protect yourself from them."

"I know." His head dipped lower.

"You know it, but do you believe it?" Gwyn caught his chin, pulled it up. "You were a child, Bai. Granny told me that when she finally got them to give her custody of you, you were so drawn inside yourself from the pain that she almost couldn't reach you anymore. So she did what she thought was best, she made you forget all of it, and hoped that you'd grow up strong enough to face it, to deal with it on your own. And then this happened."

"I believe it. I even believe that she was trying to do the best she could." He closed his eyes. "That doesn't make it any less wrong."

Baihu wasn't, initially, inclined to sleep. He insisted on cleaning up, and calling his family back, which was accomplished in due course. Before Gwyn left, he forced Baihu to lie down on the sitting room couch and close his eyes, engage in a brief meditation sequence, and, before he'd finished his first "ohm," he was out like a light.

Satisfied, Gwyn left and, rather than heading to his own apartment, went to the morgue, far too wired to sleep himself. There was, after all, plenty to do at work, and the graveyard shift was always happy for the help. Around four AM, as he stood with his hands wrist-deep in the chest cavity of somebody with a two-packs-a-day-for-twenty-years habit, his cell phone rang.

"There's no reason to wait anymore. In fact, there's every reason to move as quickly as possible. Loki is running out of time—he'll need to feed again soon, and we can't be sure he'll be able to get to us before that happens. The clock's ticking on everyone infected, too." Baihu offered the same level look to everyone gathered around the table: Tiaret, Nuad, Glorianna, Gwyn. "If Regina Howe has come home any time in the last few days, she knows we're on to her. She may have already known, and just didn't care. Whatever she's doing... it's getting close to peaking. We need to do something before that happens."

A general murmur of assent ran around the table, even from Tiaret, which he found quite gratifying.

"Gretchen." His use of her name brought her attention fully to him. "I know this is hard for you. And I'm glad you came to help us despite it."

Tiaret nodded, slowly, her glasses catching the candlelight as she moved, flashing like the lightning glistening in the back of her eyes. "There was never any possibility that I wouldn't, Baihu."

"Good to know." Baihu smiled tightly. "Nuad?"

The elder magus stepped forward, unfolding the pale cloth in the center of the table. It was marked in exceedingly fine, pale golden lines with the traditional pentagonal form, oriented so that they each stood at the terminus of one point.

"Place your focal points." Nuad's tone was cool and businesslike.

Nuad laid his cane on the table, at the very tip of the pentacle, and the others placed theirs as well: bone charms, compass, bowl, the handheld. From his pocket, Nuad brought forth a tiny soapstone bowl, small enough to fit in the palm of his hand, and Baihu produced the last of their tainted vampire blood to place in it.

"Speak these words: we come together in this sacred place, outside the bounds of space and time, to unmake that which has been made, to unbind that which has been bound."

It came out in five different registers, but in rough synchrony. "We come together in this sacred place, outside the bounds of space and time, to unmake that which has been made, to unbind that which has been bound."

"One of our own has acted against the compact between life and death, defiling the ways of both. One of our own has birthed an abomination and unleashed it against those for whom there is no defense." It was a ritual condemnation, not a responsory. The rest of the cabal was silent as Nuad spoke. "One of our own, named Regina Howe, called among us Nicnevin, has trespassed and will face judgment for her acts. This we so swear."

"This we so swear." A bit more uneasily, but together nonetheless.

"Before us is the product of malice, of the unnatural mingling of the ways of life and death. The harm it has done cannot be undone." Nuad's voice softened, gentled. "We can but act to save those who have not been harmed."

From somewhere within his jacket, Nuad brought forth a small knife, its blade the length of his longest finger, its hilt horn wrapped in age-darkened leather. He wrapped his hand loosely around the blade and drew it across his palm, parting skin and drawing blood. He passed the knife to Gwyn, who repeated the process, holding the blood drawn in his cupped palm and handing the knife along. Soon they were all so wounded, some more deeply than others, and the blade set aside.

"Above the vessel, the hand with which you guide your power."

They laid their hands together above the tiny pool of dark blood, fingers touching, sharing warmth and power. A pulse of energy ran through their joined hands, which they all experienced differently. To Glorianna, it felt like the faint static charge from a freshly started computer screen; to Baihu, like the warmth of spring sunlight lying on his skin. Tiaret felt tiny bolts of lightning crawling across her fingers and Gwyn the cool caress of autumn wind.

"Now, the blood."

Nuad spilled his blood over their joined hands. It trickled through the gaps between their fingers and fell into the soapstone vessel with a sound like falling rain. In sequence, each added his or her blood, as well. The sensation of gathering energy grew stronger, radiating upward from the vessel to press against the palms of their hands with almost palpable force.

"To know a thing is to have power over it." Nuad's voice rolled out again. "This thing is an abomination of the ways of life and death, partaking of both, honoring the nature of neither. This we know."

"This we know," the cabal chorused. Beneath their hands, the dark liquid in the vessel began to glisten, lit from within.

"Within this abomination, the forces of life and death are twisted to feed upon one another in self-perpetuating harm. Within our blood, the forces of life and death lie balanced, each in its own season, each in its own time." The contents of the bowl were glowing visibly now, a deep carmine radiance that cast bloody shadows all over the room. "We call upon the forces of life and death that lie within our veins, within our hearts, within our souls. We call upon the forces of life and death within the veins, within the hearts, within the souls of all who suffer the depredations of this abomination. We call upon the forces of life and death to unmake this thing! We call upon the forces of life and death to cast it out!"

For a moment, nothing overt happened. The baleful radiance continued to pour out of the vessel. Then, abruptly, the surface of the blood began to bubble. Within seconds, it had reached a hard simmer, and, a few seconds after that, a boil. It bubbled over the edges of the soapstone vessel in a bloody foam. Then, with a sound like a teakettle reaching boiling, the liquid shot upward against the resistance of gravity in a single writhing, frothing column to surge against the bottoms of their hands.

"Do not let it pass!" Nuad's voice cut through the chorus of disgusted exclamations that greeted this development. "Do not part your hands."

They clung to each other as best they could, hands slick with blood, against the force exerted on their grip by the magic animating the blood, the virus itself. Twice it fell back into the vessel and twice surged back out again, perceptibly weakening each time. The third try was the weakest, but also the worst. Instead of exerting brute force in an effort to break their hold, it tried a different tack, surging up amid their fingers, looking for cuts, scrapes, torn cuticles, anything to allow it access to their bodies, their lives. Repelling that attempt took a bit more from each of them, a sharing of strength, a surge of healing energies and raw celestial force that drove the blood back into its bowl. From their joined hands, a column of braided life and light, electric force and easeful death, speared into the quivering, frothing mass of the virus' malice, rending it, unraveling from its fleshly link.

It dwindled rapidly after that. The blood in the bowl coagulated first into a dense gelatinous mass and then desiccated into a fine red powder. The blood on their hands did likewise, drying and flaking away, dissolving before it could touch the altar cloth.

"Well done," Nuad said quietly. "Hands be parted—the task is done."

It took them a moment to do so. The energies still resonated between them and inside them like the echoes of a song only they knew the words for. They were all reluctant to end that, the intensity of the mystic communion, to become just individuals again. No one seemed to let go first; they all parted together, and the sensation remained even though they were no longer in physical contact.

"That... could have gone a lot worse," Tiaret opined, reaching up to remove her glasses and clean them on the corner of her shirt.

"It did," Baihu replied hollowly. "Just not for us."

"Bai, you know as well as I do that anyone weak enough to be killed by the counter-spell was going to die anyway. The neurological damage would have been too advanced for any normal doctor to fix it." Gwyn gave his mentor a grateful look. "Thank you for helping us, master."

"You are, as always, quite welcome." Nuad took up his cane, and the others gathered up their instruments as well.

Glorianna flipped open the handheld screen. "Yes. It worked!"

"Glory?"

She grinned and held the little machine out, screen facing them. On it was what looked like a graphical GPS display marked by a single pulsating green dot. "That's her. I set the handheld to gather data from our working, tracing the routes the spell took, filtering out any address that was a hospital or a private home, then filtering any hit where the spell terminated successfully. This is the only one that didn't terminate. It has to be her."

"Or, at the very least, something worth investigating." Baihu straightened up. "I'll call Heartsblood and Loki."

As it turned out, it took awhile to get a hold of everyone. Baihu called Loki more than once and didn't get an answer on any attempt, which didn't exactly break Tam's heart. She was just as happy to leave the bloodsucking freak out of it, since she couldn't see what he'd bring to the effort besides sarcasm, and they had Gwyn for that and more besides. The werewolves seemed to have made the trip on foot and still were much more prompt, which saved them from the trauma of trying to sandwich everybody into Baihu's hatchback and Tiaret's sedan.

"That's right along the lake, in one of the parks, I think." Gwyn shot a look at the back of Baihu's head.

Glorianna, riding shotgun, minimized the GPS screen and started rooting around for map links. "I think you're right. I saved a whole lot of current and archival maps when I first got here and—yeah, here it is. Not only is it a part of the park system, it's got archaeological significant ruins in it. Native American earthworks, or what's left of them."

"If Aristede's theory about all this is correct, if the Murder of Crows and the Voices have always been here, that might be significant." Tiaret, sitting behind Glorianna, struggled forward to look over the back of the seat.

"Yeah. The cyclical nature of the whole thing—it's happened more than once, who knows how long it's been happening? The Powatomis, that's who, but they're not here to ask. Or the Cahokia, for that matter." Gwyn poked Baihu in the shoulder. "You'll wanna turn up ahead, Bai."

"Gwyn, I've lived in this city my whole life, too." Baihu reminded him from between clenched teeth. "What are we going to do if it is her? The counterspell we worked on the virus didn't kill her—if Glory's little thingamabob is correct, it might not have even burned the virus out of her system."

"Let the werewolves—"

"Uratha."

"What the fuck ever. Let them mess her shit up and while they're at it, we stop whatever she's doing. Then we administer the bitchslap to end them all."

"Gwyn," Tiaret snapped.

"Tiaret, I would like to remind you, again, that whatever else this girl is, she's been randomly dispensing death and destruction to just about everybody she's met for at least the last month. You'll forgive me if my heart doesn't bleed for her." Gwyn snapped back.

"You two? I asked for brilliant ideas, not arguments. If no brilliance is forthcoming, put a sock in it." Silence reigned. "I'll take that as a lack of ideas. Glory?"

"Letting the werewolves take on whatever spirit-things she might call up to protect her isn't a bad idea," Glorianna admitted. "They're optimized to deal with things like that, and, except for you, we pretty much aren't."

"True. I'll run that past Heartsblood when we get where we're going and see what he thinks. The rest of us should... just prep what we have, I think. Be prepared for anything, as much as possible."

The park was one of the dozens of smaller plots of land along the Chicago lakefront, not exactly densely wooded but not totally devoid of trees and bushes, either. Tam couldn't see all the way across the park from the road to the lake, at any rate, even with the help of the security lamps set up along the walking paths that wended through it. The park wasn't even fenced or gated, and the grounds blended into the back lawns of the apartment complexes that sprang up just beyond its outermost edge.

"The reading's stable. She's not moving." Tam, for some reason, felt the urge to whisper as they huddled up in the space between the parked cars to share information and ideas. "It looks like she's closer to the lake than the road."

"Yep, she is," Heartsblood confirmed, without even looking at the readout. "Not too far away, either."

The alpha wolf and his entire pack were tense, covering each others' backs already, scenting the air. Even to Tam, who didn't have the advantage of a supernaturally enhanced nose, the wind coming off the lake seemed thick. Dense with something more than just moisture, coating everything it came into contact with. She abruptly felt grimy, as though she hadn't bathed in a week, or had just waded through sewage up to her chest.

"God. She's doing something out there. You can practically taste it." Gwyn sounded vaguely disgusted. "Bai?"

"Yes, I feel it, too." He sounded weirdly serene, calm in a way that was almost more disturbing than the feeling riding the air. "Dredging the dark waters for something she can use to finish this thing. Heartsblood."

"Yeah?"

"She'll have spirits to protect her while she's working. Nasty ones. Can your people handle them while we handle her?"

"That's what we're here for."

"Good. Let's hurry, before she gets too far along."

Despite the circles of light cast along the well-lit paths, which they avoided, there were still plenty of hazards to navigate of a perfectly mundane nature. The ground wasn't entirely even, and there were more than a few abandoned pieces of play equipment scattered around. Under the trees, picnic tables and trashcans loomed out of the darkness and roots grew up underfoot. As they got closer to the lake, the wind perceptibly picked up, growing stronger and fouler.

The girl stood at a point overlooking the lake itself, seated on a breakwater railing, her legs demurely crossed, weight on her hands. All tarted up in her clubbing gear, she was barely visible against the dark water and the dark sky, her silver jewelry catching the light of the nearby security lamp. She was crooning softly into the rising wind, a wordless song that sent a ripple of growls through the Uratha when they heard it and took all the color out of Baihu's face. Tam thought she heard them as they came out of the copse of trees from which they'd been observing her. The set of her shoulders changed slightly, and she hopped down from her perch. The pitch and tone of her song changed, too, from cajolery to an outright demand.

The wind shifted directions, from north-northwest to true west, bringing with it a stinging, slashing hail of—something. Glorianna's first impression was of some incredibly cold and thick snow squall or hail or something similarly solid. It wasn't rain. Something lodged in her wildly blowing hair and when she pulled it free, she found herself holding a handful of crow feathers, small ones.

"That's enough, Regina." Tiaret's voice was quiet, but held the promise of a storm in it, just audible above the wind. Glorianna hung close to one side and Baihu the other, with Gwyn bringing up the rear.

The girl turned to face them. Her eyes were the color of the lakewater, the feathers, jet black. When she blinked, inky streams of liquid trailed down her face and dripped off her chin.

"It's coming. You should run for your lives now," she crooned, her voice a sick-sweet parody of real concern.

"That's not possible anymore, is it? You've made sure of that. We know what you're doing, Regina. This is your last chance. We can force you to stop—maybe that's what you want, it's probably what you've needed —but I warn you, at this point there's only one way for us to do that. Think. Even now there might still be another way, we could help you try to find it, but not after this. There's nothing after this."

The wind rose again, buffeting nearly hard enough to knock Glorianna off her feet. She found herself clinging to Tiaret's arm just to keep her balance. One of the monitoring programs on the handheld chose that moment to go off, a high-pitched tone drilling into her ear from the bead headset, the tiny screen flashing a warning in an alphabet she only half-recognized.

"Nothing. Yes, nothing. Now you understand. I can finish it. No one else could, so I did it myself. And that's what it needs, too. Look at it. Look at its pain. Carrion-flock!" she called. "Meet our eyes. Do you see the peace beyond the fear? Yes, even you can end. We've made it possible. Come."

"Tiaret!" Glorianna shouted as best she could over the screaming wind. "Something big is—"

She was about to say "coming." The word never made it out of her mouth, because all hell broke loose first. Everything shifted. The sky, the ground, the horizon between the two, as all of Glorianna's perceptions were wrenched sidewise a couple hundred degrees, out of anything resembling physical reality. She staggered and nearly fell, but Tiaret held her up, forcing her to stand against a dark rush of power that suddenly had physical presence, genuine weight. It took an effort to breathe, to think around the oppressive force of it, the accumulated psychic anguish of the Murder of Crows and the malice of the things feeding that pain.

"Glorianna!" Tiaret shouted in her ear. "The east point. Take. The. East. Point! We need to isolate her!"

Glorianna wanted to ask how to do that but didn't think that question would be entirely well received just then. Instead, she put her head down and let the wind help move her. A diagram from one of the documents she'd looked at recently flashed into her head, a diamond-shaped ritual form for an under-strength cabal, and she did her best to anchor herself at the point Tiaret indicated. Opposite Gwyn, to the west. Baihu to the north. Tiaret to the south.

"You must focus yourself on containing her, Glorianna, and countering her workings." Watson's voice, in her ear. "But for now, containment is the primary objective."

Glorianna ground her teeth and refused to respond. She put the handheld on the ground between her feet and began breathing deeply as she could, drawing her strength up around her. The wind slacked slightly, and she pushed that force out of her, beyond her skin, out into a defined, perfect circle around her. The wind all but died, at least where she was standing, and she saw the others doing likewise, building defenses around themselves, and reaching out for each other. She felt Baihu and Tiaret both reaching for her, and she returned the gesture, stretching out with her hands, physical and otherwise, to receive what they offered and give of herself in return.

Glorianna felt the urge to move. She stooped to pick up the handheld and went with the impulse, moving counterclockwise against the force of the storm, which was a good bit easier than she thought it would be. Their counter-working was having an effect, though how much of one she couldn't really tell.

Something flickered out of the corner of her eye, something that wasn't a mass of feathers whipping past at hurricane speed. Shapes were taking form in the spaces between the feathers. The werewolves were already among them, fighting as though they shared a single mind. Glorianna reached the northern point previously occupied by Baihu, anchored herself, put the handheld back between her feet, looked around for a better perspective on things.

"Excellent, Glorianna, you've done—" Watson's voice died in a screech of static so high-pitched it drove through Glorianna's head like an ice pick. She clawed the bead out of her ear and threw it, eyes watering from the pain. Something was happening on the handheld screen, but what she was seeing didn't make any sense. The screen was bulging out as though something was pushing at it from the other side.

"Tiaret!" she shouted, hoping to catch the older woman's attention, but she was grimly focused on the girl Regina, Nicnevin.

To her right, Baihu had turned his attention from the center of the diamond outward. A boy, or something wearing the shape of a boy, stood a few strides away from him, unmoved by the storm, its scored and burnt face washed in blood trailing down from a narrow wound in its skull.

"Baihu!" She wasn't the only one to shout it. Gwyn did, too, though neither of them moved.

Baihu, on the other hand, did. He glanced over his shoulder, past Glorianna, and then turned back, stepping out of their diamond and into the storm beyond it. His eyes, like Regina's, had the blackened, polluted look about them, which shocked Glorianna to the core.

Something grabbed her ankle, something bitter cold and sharp enough to sever tendons, or what felt like it, at least. Her knee buckled, and she came down hard on it, sending a jolt of pain up to her hip. A wild look told her everything she needed to know. Something was crawling out of the surface of the handheld, something clear and cold and covered in spines, sharp flanges, gears. Glorianna fell back on her rear and kicked her leg out, hoping to break the thing's grip. It flew clear but left deep gouges on her ankle, trailing blood over her instep. The handheld landed at the edge of Glorianna's personal zone of protection, and the *thing* continued to drag itself free, writhing almost like a tentacle.

It was all she could do to bring herself to touch it. The thing immediately tried to grab her, lashing across her chest and arm as she did so. She flung it away, as hard as she could, past the circle of her will's protection and out into the black feather rain. The last she saw of it was a flicker of sparks, dying away rapidly, and she turned her attention to more urgent matters.

Such as saving Baihu, who, damn him, seemed single-mindedly dedicated to not letting that happen. Neither she nor Gwyn could get his attention. He was absolutely focused on the boy, the bloody-faced boy that Gwyn had told her about, the creature that had tormented him during most of his childhood. She had no idea why he'd even want to be that close to the thing, ever again.

She forged her way toward him, and as she did, she heard his voice.

You don't need to do this. Oblivion is not the only release from pain. Take my hand. Take my hand and be healed.

Tiaret and Gwyn were having a screaming argument behind her. She wanted to shout at them, get their attention where it really needed to be, but she was too late. Even as she watched, Baihu's form flickered, faded, blinked out of existence. The bloody boy went with him.

And something shifted, something fundamental. In that instant, the balance of mystic forces changed. Glorianna felt it resonate through her like a struck harp string. At that same moment, Regina screamed—a wail of anguish, of perfect and total despair. A hand caught her own, Gwyn's hand, hot after the bitter and unnatural cold that had enveloped them.

"Do it now!"

She didn't know what "it" was. Or, rather, she didn't want to think about it. She closed her eyes, and turned her face away, and let him take what he and Tiaret needed of her to finish the job. She felt something break, and her perceptions skewed again, flinging her mind sideways and knocking her physically flat. Glorianna slammed hard into the pavement, scraping her chin and cheek on the concrete as she hit the ground. Somewhere nearby, she heard at least two other bodies hitting the ground, too, one heavily and one lightly. Tiaret swore.

Glorianna opened her eyes and found the world to be gratifyingly stable. No black feather rain, no crazy perceptual distortions, no half-visible things lunging out of the corners of her eyes. She sat up, slowly, feeling vaguely sick to her stomach. Tiaret lay nearby, flat on her back and gasping for air. Gwyn was on his feet, barely, leaning hard on his own knees and trying not to fall over. Between them, the girl, Regina, lay perfectly still, unmoving, unbreathing, the foulest odor Glorianna had ever smelled rising off her.

Nearby, Baihu also lay perfectly still, unmoving, unbreathing. The little red wolf that Heartsblood turned into sat next to him, whining softly, nosing one of Baihu's hands.

Epilogue

Tam spoke to the Hierarch and the officials of the local Consilium the next day, as did Tiaret and Gwyn, representing himself and his mentor, who politely but firmly declined the invitation issued to him. While it had been possible, through the malignant efforts of Regina Howe and the caprice of the Murder of Crows, for every magus within the city limits beside themselves to be blinded to the phenomena of the Murder's rising, no one managed to miss the aftershocks that rippled out from its propitiation. Sorcerers as far west as Colorado and as far east as Pennsylvania had felt the spiritual shockwaves, according to the repulsive head of Consilium security, who seemed to think that was their fault entirely, and not the direct consequences of averting a supernatural cataclysm of unimaginable severity.

Tam had to restrain herself, forcefully, from telling him exactly what she thought of him. Gwyn didn't bother exercising that restraint, since they mostly knew what he thought of them anyway, and stalked out of the Walsh Industries boardroom in which the meeting was held shortly thereafter. Tiaret made a perfunctory but entirely correct excuse for him—his best friend wasn't even twenty-four hours dead, and he didn't possess the best temperament for dealing with authority figures even under less trying circumstances. That, coupled with the collected information they were able to provide, saved any of them from serious censure, at least for the time being. Tam was, however, firmly but politely invited to leave, as she'd overstayed her own estimate several days before and the Hierarch evidently felt the need to send someone packing over the whole affair.

She made her travel arrangements that evening, the old-fashioned way, by phone, and began packing up. She washed clothes in the courtesy machines provided by the hotel, because she was just about out of anything decent to wear, and because it delayed the moment when she'd have to deal with Watson. The handheld was completely gone. She didn't know, exactly, what happened to it. She supposed, when she threw it away, that it could have gone over the breakwater and into the lake. If so, she had no particular desire to go diving for its remains. She could always build another, using the technical specifications in her father's journals and the materials left over from the original construction in his workroom.

Watson himself was another story entirely. She'd returned to the hotel that night to find his screen dark, cracked across in a spider-webbed pattern, glass fragments lying on the keyboard as though it had been broken from the inside out. When she'd opened the casings, a ghost of the foul odor that had clung to Regina Howe's corpse had wafted out, along with the equally unpleasant stink of vaporized plastic and melted wire. The casing was scorched almost to the point of structural failure in several places. The etched crystalline elements that made up the processors, the internal and external communication relays, the invaluable storage media, were all burned black and cracked by the heat that had destroyed them. She hadn't been the one to create those elements. She had no idea how they were produced or when or where or how to go about procuring repairs for them. Even if she could get replacement parts for such an advanced machine, for a thing that was half made out of magic and half the forgotten technology of a superior culture, she wasn't sure she'd know how to effect even basic repairs. She certainly didn't know how to cause an entity like Watson to come into existence, even if she could provide such an entity with an appropriate physical housing. The components went back into their padded traveling cases to be shipped back to Boston.

Tam concentrated on the practicalities, because thinking about the deeper losses hurt too much. Portions of her father's life that she'd never known about, never touched, had been hidden in Watson's archives. That was gone now, traded for her own life in the heat of the moment, when that decision had seemed the only right one to make. She almost regretted it.

She regretted Baihu more, but felt almost as though that regret wasn't really hers to have. They'd met by chance, been dragged together by circumstances, and had worked well together when they had to. She liked him, even though they were basically strangers, and his death hurt with a bewildering intensity, given how little time they'd had together. It made no sense.

Before Tam left, she purchased a condolence card from a stationery shop, and sent it to Baihu's family. Tucked inside was a gift that Tiaret had assured her was appropriate, a check containing a startlingly large number of zeroes that in no way salved her conscience. It was all that she could do.

Tam boarded her plane late in the evening the second day after, and did her best not to look back. After five years of fruitless searching, she very much wanted to go home, even if her father wasn't there. At least his absence could almost be considered normal.

The Tsu family did not let grass grow under its feet when it came to the just and proper funeral rites for its members, and they were also fairly traditional in most of their requirements. It was cremation, of course, for both Granny Tsu and Baihu, though of the two, Granny had more of her personal affairs in order when it came to such issues. Her tombstone had been carved years before and kept in storage at Updike & Poole against the day of her departure from the fleshly coil, her urn selected and set aside for her use. Bai didn't have a stone yet, but he would soon, and, in the meantime, his ashes sat in state in the chapel in an elaborately enameled yet tasteful urn, to allow those members of the local community who knew him to pay their respects.

Quite a few did, which Jason Hyndes found gratifying if not particularly comforting. Quite a few also knew what to bring, and the bier was covered in painted and folded paper *dzi dzat* offerings to his spirit, flowers, fruit, incense. His proper funeral, in a few days' time, promised to be as well-attended as Granny's had been, which was saying something. More people had crammed into the little private cemetery behind the funeral home than he'd ever seen there before and he hoped to never see that many again.

Jason considered it a triumph of hard-won quasi-maturity that he wasn't dealing with this situation by medicating himself with every recreational substance he could find. He'd refrained from killing Mimir without the aid of anything to balm his nerves, a fact of which he was proud. He'd attended Granny's funeral and answered questions for people who'd been too embarrassed, or graced with tact, to ask them of her grieving family. He'd told himself he wasn't going to have more than one crying jag a day, and had mostly made the resolution stick by way of merciless self-abuse, working every minute he wasn't asleep. He'd spent every night in the chapel, waiting to see if Bai, even the slightest trace of him, was lingering or if he'd gone straight to whatever waited for him beyond the death of his body.

Thus far, nothing had shown itself, not even a flicker of lower soul. Mostly, Jason ended up sleeping on a pew.

It was past midnight, and he was just starting to drift in the direction of sleep again, when the floor behind him deliberately creaked. He half-turned and found Daniel Aaron Vickery standing in the door of the chapel, looking about the way he felt: guilty for being alive and not sure what to do next.

"I thought I'd come to pay my respects," Daniel said, softly, and approached a few steps when he wasn't immediately blasted off his feet.

"You're welcome to it, Heartsblood. I know Bai liked you—and I don't think he'd mind the hour." Jason pulled himself out of his slouch by sheer force of will. "As you can see…"

"Cremated. I'm afraid I won't be here for the burying. I'll be leaving early in the morning, going back home." The werewolf reached into his jacket pocket and pulled out a small object, a folded paper crane. "For what it's worth, I liked him, too. And I wish that this didn't have to happen, at all, but mostly not to him."

"You and me both." He rose, wavered a little on his feet as he realized how tired and worn he was.

Heartsblood caught his elbow and held him up until he was steady enough to stand on his own. "You doin' all right?" His nostrils flared slightly, and Jason wondered, idly, if bone-tired and grieving had their own smells. "You need to rest. How many hours have you been awake?"

"Too many. Not enough. I still see it every time I sleep."

"You ain't the only one." Heartsblood's grip on his elbow didn't slack any, and Jason found himself being steered slowly down the aisle. "But my People, we've got a way of dealing with such things that I think y'all lack."

"Really?"

"Truly."

Howling with Heartsblood turned out to be far more therapeutic than Jason ever thought it would be. The sun was rising on them by the time they were finished, and Jason had passed tired, into wired, and come back around to tired again. Tired enough, in fact, to give Heartsblood the keys to his car and let the werewolf drive him home. He dozed most of the way and woke up completely only once they pulled up in front of his building.

"That was… good of you. To help me out that way." Jason told him, as Heartsblood turned off the engine and handed him keys. "I…"

"I know. Thank you, too." Heartsblood smiled, a weary and faintly tremulous smile of his own. "Make them remember, and maybe next time it won't come to this."

"I'll try."

"That's all I ask."

Heartsblood walked away, in the direction of the South Loop, and Jason went inside, still too tired for anything resembling deliberate thought. Reflex more than anything else made him check his mailbox, hanging on the entrance hall wall. Inside was a small package, wrapped in plain brown paper and marked with just his name, which revealed a black-velvet-covered jeweler's case. Aristede's watch rested in a nest of velvet inside it, its hands frozen, its mechanisms unmoving. He looked at it, really looked, and realized the thing wasn't broken, wasn't just wound down. Its main spring was paused, waiting for something to set it in motion again. Somehow, Jason—Gwyn—failed to find that totally comforting.

YOU CAN CONTINUE TO EXPLORE THE WINDY CITY IN THE WORLD OF DARKNESS™

Vampire: The Requiem Trilogy by Greg Stolze

Vampire #1: A Hunger Like Fire™

(WW11235; ISBN 1-58846-862-3); $6.99

Persephone Moore has it all—looks, brains, ambition, and an unquenchable hunger for the blood of the living. In this first novel enter into the danse macabre of the undead of Chicago. Persephone sees the city as a moveable feast, and as an opportunity, but with every night she feels herself grow little colder, a little more monstrous. How long before her hunger consumes her whole?

Vampire #2: Blood In, Blood Out™

(WW11237; ISBN 1-58846-866-6) $6.99

Ever since his Embrace, Duce Carter has been a firebrand among the Kindred of Chicago, fanning the flames of revolution against the city's Prince and its hidebound elders. But when Chicago's Carthians turn on Duce in the wake of a brutal assassination attempt, the only person he can go to for help is none other than Persephone Moore, the Prince's only childe. Is Persephone the friend she claims to be, or is she an agent of the shadowy forces who are out to destroy Duce?

WHITE WOLF PUBLISHING

Vampire #3: The Marriage of Virtue and Viciousness™

(WW11238; ISBN1-58846-872-0) $6.99

Word has spread among Chicago's Kindred that Prince Maxwell is to grant an indulgence, a one-night lift on the ban imposed on destroying fellow vampires. The Damned scurry for position and ready their long-delayed revenge. But no vampire's rage is more consuming than that of Solomon Birch, the fallen zealot of the undead church known as the Lancea Sanctum. Birch's enemies know that if they don't strike first, he surely will.

ALL THREE BOOKS AVAILABLE NOW